D0016771

THE DARK
FLOOD RISES

Also by Margaret Drabble

FICTION
A Summer Bird-Cage
The Garrick Year
The Millstone
Jerusalem the Golden
The Waterfall
The Needle's Eye
London Consequences (group novel)
The Realms of Gold
The Ice Age
The Middle Ground
The Radiant Way
A Natural Curiosity
The Gates of Ivory
The Witch of Exmoor
The Peppered Moth
The Seven Sisters
The Red Queen
The Sea Lady
The Pure Gold Baby

SHORT STORIES
A Day in the Life of a Smiling Woman: The Collected Stories

NON-FICTION
Wordsworth (Literature in Perspective series)
Arnold Bennett: A Biography
For Queen and Country
A Writer's Britain
The Oxford Companion to English Literature (editor)
Angus Wilson: A Biography
The Pattern in the Carpet

THE DARK
FLOOD RISES

MARGARET
DRABBLE

CANONGATE

Published in Great Britain in 2016 by Canongate Books Ltd,
14 High Street, Edinburgh EH1 1TE

www.canongate.co.uk

3

'Going On' from *An Almost Dancer, Poems 2005–2011*, by Robert Nye,
published by Greenwich Exchange, London 2012

British Library Cataloguing-in-Publication Data
A catalogue record for this book is available on
request from the British Library

ISBN 978 1 78211 830 5
Export ISBN 978 1 78211 831 2

Typeset in Sabon MT by Palimpsest Book Production Ltd,
Falkirk, Stirlingshire

Printed and bound in Great Britain by Clays Ltd, St Ives plc

To Bernardine
1939–2013

Piecemeal the body dies, and the timid soul
has her footing washed away, as the dark flood rises.

D. H. Lawrence, 'The Ship of Death'

THROUGH winter-time we call on spring,
And through the spring on summer call,
And when abounding hedges ring
Declare that winter's best of all;
And after that there's nothing good
Because the spring-time has not come –
Nor know that what disturbs our blood
Is but its longing for the tomb.

W. B. Yeats, 'The Wheel'

She has often suspected that her last words to herself and in this world will prove to be 'You bloody old fool' or, perhaps, depending on the mood of the day or the time of the night, 'you fucking idiot'. As the speeding car hits the tree, or the unserviced boiler explodes, or the smoke and flames fill the hallway, or the grip on the high guttering gives way, those will be her last words. She isn't to know for sure that it will be so, but she suspects it. In her latter years, she's become deeply interested in the phrase 'Call no man happy until he is dead'. Or no woman, come to that. '*Call no woman happy until she is dead.*' Fair enough, and the ancient world had known women as well as men who had met unfortunate ends: Clytemnestra, Dido, Hecuba, Antigone. Though of course Antigone, one must remember, had rejoiced to die young, and in a good (if to us pointless) cause, thereby avoiding all the inconveniences of old age.

Fran herself is already too old to die young, and too old to avoid bunions and arthritis, moles and blebs, weakening wrists, incipient but not yet treatable cataracts, and encroaching weariness. She can see that in time (and perhaps in not a very long time) all these annoyances will become so annoying that she will be willing to embark on one of those acts of reckless folly that will bring the whole thing to a rapid, perhaps a sensational ending. But would the rapid ending cancel out and negate the intermittent happiness of the earlier years, the long struggle towards some kind of maturity, the modest successes, the hard work? What would the balance sheet look like, at the last reckoning?

It was the obituaries of Stella Hartleap that set her thoughts in this actuarial direction, as she drove along the M1 towards Birmingham, at only three or four miles above the speed limit.

The print obituaries had been annoying, piously annoying, in a sexist, ageist, hypocritical, mealy-mouthed manner, reeking of *Schadenfreude*. And just now, yet another mention of Stella on the car radio, in that regular Radio 4 obituary slot, has revived her irritations. She hadn't known Stella very well, having met her late in the day in Highgate through Hamish, but she'd known her long enough to recognise the claptrap and the bullshit. So, Stella had died of smoke inhalation, having set her bedclothes on fire while smoking in bed in her remote farmstead in the Black Mountains, and having just polished off a tumbler of Famous Grouse. So what? A better exit than dying in a hospital corridor in a wheelchair while waiting for another dose of poisonous chemotherapy, which had recently been her good friend Birgit's dismal fate. At least Stella had nobody to blame but herself, and although the last minutes couldn't have been pleasant, neither had Birgit's. Not at all pleasant, by all accounts, and without any complementary frisson of autonomy.

Birgit wouldn't have approved of Stella Hartleap's end. She might even have been censorious about it. She had been a judgmental woman. But that was neither here nor there. We don't have to agree with anyone, ever.

Her new-old friend Teresa, who is grievously ill, wouldn't be censorious, as she is never censorious about anyone.

I am the captain of my fate, I am the master of my soul. A Roman, by a Roman, valiantly vanquished.

There is a truck, too close behind her, she can see its great dead smeared glass underwater eyes looming at her in her driving mirror. In the old days, Hamish used to slam on his brakes in situations like this, as a warning. She'd always thought that was dangerous, but he'd never come to any harm. He hadn't died at the wheel. He'd died of something more insidious, less violent, more cruelly protracted.

She chooses the accelerator. It's safer than the brake. Her first husband Claude had believed in the use of the accelerator, and she was with him on that.

Francesca Stubbs is on her way to a conference on sheltered housing for the elderly, a subject pertinent to her train of thought, but not in itself heroic. Fran is something of an expert in the field, and is employed by a charitable trust which devotes generous research funds to examining and improving the living arrangements of the ageing. She's always been interested in all forms of social housing, and this new job suits her well. She's intrigued by the way more and more people in England opt to live alone, in the early twenty-first century. Students don't seem to mind cohabitation, even like it, and cohabitation is forced upon the ill and the elderly, but more and more of the able-bodied in their mid-life choose to live alone. This is making demands on the housing stock which successive governments are unable and possibly unwilling even to try to satisfy.

Fran is in favour of a land tax. That would shake things up a bit. But the English are extraordinarily tenacious of land. They hate to relinquish even a yard of it. The word 'freehold' has a powerful resonance.

No, there is nothing heroic about the housing stock and planning policy, subjects which currently occupy her working life, but old age itself is a theme for heroism. It calls upon courage.

Fran had from an unsuitably early age been attracted by the heroic death, the famous last words, the tragic farewell. Her parents had on their shelves a copy of Brewer's *Dictionary of Phrase and Fable*, a book which, as a teenager, she would morbidly browse for hours. One of her favourite sections was 'Dying Sayings', with its fine mix of the pious, the complacent, the apocryphal, the bathetic and the defiant. Artists had fared well: Beethoven was alleged to have said 'I shall hear in heaven'; the erotic painter Etty had declared 'Wonderful! Wonderful this death!'; and Keats had died bravely, generously comforting his poor friend Severn.

Those about to be executed had clearly had time to prepare a fine last thought, and of these she favoured the romantic Walter Raleigh's, 'It matters little how the head lies, so the heart be right'. Harriet Martineau, who had suffered much as a child from religion, as Fran had later discovered, had stoically remarked, 'I see no reason why the existence of Harriet Martineau should be perpetuated', an admirably composed sentiment which had caught the child Fran's attention long before she knew who Harriet Martineau was. But most of all she had liked the parting words of Siward the Dane who had commanded his men: 'Lift me up that I may die standing, not lying down like a cow'. She didn't know why this appealed to her so strongly, as she was herself very unlikely to die on a battlefield. Maybe it meant she had Danish blood? Well, she probably had, of course, as many, perhaps most of us in England have. Or maybe she had liked the mention of the cow, which she heard as strangely affectionate, not as contemptuous.

She was much more likely to die on a motorway than on a battlefield.

The Vikings hadn't approved of dying quietly and comfortably in bed. Unlike her first husband Claude, who was currently making himself as comfortable as he could.

She has pulled away from the truck, and is now overtaking a dirty maroon family saloon with an annoying sticker about its 'Baby on Board'. There is an anonymous dirty white van just behind her now. It isn't raining, but it's dirty weather, and there's grimy February splatter and spray on her windscreen. There's worse weather on the way, the forecast warns, but it hasn't reached her yet. It's been a grim winter so far.

Why the hell is she driving, anyway? Why hadn't she taken the train? Because, like all those people who insist on living alone when they don't have to, she *likes* being on her own, in her own little space, not cooped up with invasively dressed strangers eating crisps and sandwiches and clutching polystyrene coffee and obesely overflowing their seat space and chattering on their mobiles. She is hurtling happily along to the car park of a Premier Inn on the outskirts of Birmingham, guided by her satnav, and looking forward to her evening meal. Some of the other delegates will be staying at the Premier Inn, and she is looking forward to seeing them. She'll be able to get away from them if she wants to and take herself off to her anonymous bedroom to watch some regional TV.

Fran loves regional TV. You find out a lot of odd things, watching regional TV up and down the land. She's glad she's still got the energy and the will to drive around England, looking at housing developments and care homes. She's a lucky woman, lucky in her work. Sometimes, in her more elevated moments, she thinks she is in love with England, with the length and breadth of England. England is now her last love. She wants to see it all before she dies. She won't be able to do that, but she'll do her best.

The charity that employs her doesn't cover Scotland and Wales.

She wouldn't mind dying on the road, driving around the country, though she wouldn't want to take any innocent people with her.

The dirty white van is far too close. The bad name of white van drivers is well deserved, in Fran's opinion.

There'd been another section in Brewer's, called 'Death from Strange Causes'. It wasn't as good as 'Dying Sayings', but it had its charms. Memorable recorded deaths, most of them occurring in antiquity, had involved the swallowing of goat-hairs, grape stones, guineas and toothpicks. According to Pliny, Aeschylus had been killed by a falling tortoise. Many have been killed by pigs. Some choke to death with laughter. Nobody, as far as she knows, has yet thought to keep the white van tally, which must be high.

She is looking forward to seeing her colleague Paul Scobey again. As she checks in at the Premier Inn reception desk, having parked in the allotted space in the subterranean metal car cage, there he is, sitting on an orange and purple couch in the foyer, nursing half a pint and watching a super-coloured soccer match on a giant overhead TV. He waves when she spots him, and she goes over to say hello, begging him not to interrupt his viewing. Paul is her friend and ally. He is far too young to share her first-hand empathetic familiarity with some of the needs of the elderly, but he has a pleasantly sardonic manner, a detachment that she finds enabling. He doesn't expect people to want what they ought to want. So many in the geriatric business can't understand the perversity of human beings, their attachments to or impatience with irrational aspects of their old homes and neighbourhoods, their sudden detestations of members of their family with whom they had rubbed along without protest for years, their refusal to admit that they were old and would soon be incapable. Paul seems unusually accepting of the changing vagaries of human need. He's in favour of community living and co-operative schemes, but he understands those who refuse to downsize and need at the end to die alone in a five-storey building, fixing the threat of a mansion tax with a cold eye.

Carrots and sticks, says Paul. If you want to get them out, you have to tempt them out.

Fran doesn't like that phrase, 'carrots and sticks'. Old people aren't donkeys. But he's got the right ideas.

He has a mother living stubbornly alone in the house where he had been born, in the low-rise Hagwood 1950s estate on the western edge of Smethwick. He speaks of her sometimes, but not very often. He talks more about the merits and failings of corporation and council housing than he speaks of his mother, but Fran knows that thoughts of his mother inform his thinking. And he also has an elderly and long-demented aunt, his mother's older sister Dorothy, living very near to where they are now. A visit to see her is on his two-day agenda, and Fran has agreed to accompany him, to see the small care home where she has lived for years. This was his neck of the woods, not Fran's, although he himself now lives down south in Colchester.

Paul pats the couch by him, suggests she sit, and she sits. The leathery fireproof hollow-fill foam of the couch sinks deeply under her modest weight. She'll have to struggle to get up.

Paul is a gingery fellow, sandy-haired and lashed, lightly freckled, strikingly pale-skinned, pleasantly featured in a snub-nosed boyish way, in his mid forties she supposes, a little younger than her son Christopher. Hazel eyes, not Viking blue. He had wanted to be an architect but the qualifications took too long, he'd needed to start earning, and he had settled for planning and housing. His views on aesthetics (not often requested) are surprising. He has a nostalgic private weakness for Modernism, but recognises that most old people in England detest Modernism (not that they get asked much about their preferences) and prefer a post-modern pseudo-cottage, bungalowesque, mini-Tesco mix. You can get all those features into a housing estate quite easily, as he knows from the avenues and crescents of Hagwood.

His expertise lies in adaptation. He really knows, or thinks he knows, how features of a dwelling space ought to be adapted to the ageing and disabled, to the increasingly ageing and increasingly disabled. He relies on Fran, who is well ahead of him on the road of ageing (though as yet far from disabled) to advise him and offer him her insights. He had been fascinated by her account of the woman who had died because she hadn't been able to open the bathroom door. There was nothing much wrong with her, apart from her loss of grip. She'd been unable to turn the doorknob, couldn't get out to the phone to dial 999 after a very minor stroke, and had passed away on her cold bathroom floor.

If she'd had a lever-type doorknob instead of an old-fashioned screw doorknob, she'd have been alive today. If she hadn't shut the door after herself (and what on earth was the point in doing that, as she lived alone?), she'd have been alive today.

Killed by a doorknob.

For the lack of a nail the battle was lost.

You have to be careful, when you're old.

And all for the want of a horseshoe nail.

Fran declines a beer. I'll see you down here at seven, she says. And up she goes to her room, to kick off her boots and lie on her bed and gaze at the rich daily life of the Black Country and the West Midlands. It's on the chilly side in her bedroom, there must be a thermostat somewhere, but she can't find it. Never mind, you can't die of hypothermia in a Premier Inn.

She likes her bedroom. She likes the whiteness of the pillows, and the rich loud purple of the Inn's informative boasts about its reliable facilities and its notable breakfasts. It's very purple, the Premier Inn branding.

~

There are several items of soothingly mild interest on the regional news – a promotional chat by some staunchly upbeat florist's about a Valentine's Day event, an interview with a volunteer at a food bank, a report of a non-fatal knifing at a bus stop in Bilston, and, most unexpectedly, an item about a small earthquake which had hit Dudley and its neighbourhood at dawn that day. It had caused little consternation and most people had not even noticed it, although one or two said their breakfast crockery had rattled or a standard lamp had fallen over. Cats and dogs and budgerigars hadn't liked it, and had wisely seen it coming, or so their owners said. This was routine stuff, but Fran's attention is caught by a lively account by an unlikely young woman who claims that she had been rocked on her moored narrow boat by a not-so-small and inexplicable wave. 'It wasn't a *tsunami*,' says this spirited red-cheeked person, posing picturesquely and entirely unselfconsciously in a purple woolly hat, a padded red jacket and cowboy boots on the wharf just along the canal from the Open Air Museum, 'but it was definitely a *wave*, and *I* thought it was coming out of the limestone caverns, I thought the quarry sides had given way, or the mining tunnels had collapsed, or maybe a great river beast was making its way out of there, been there for millennia waiting just for me!'

Fran likes this person very much, she admires her relish and her imagination and her Wolverhampton accent, and she admires the interviewer and the cameraman for realising how eccentrically photogenic she is. 'To tell you the truth,' says this robust young person, 'I'm always hoping something really really terrible is about to happen, like the end of the world, you know what I mean? And that I'll be right there? You know what I mean?' And she smiles, gaily, and then pronounces, 'But it was only a very small earthquake, they say it was very low on the Richter scale, so it's not the end of Dudley after all! I'm not saying I *wanted* a bigger one, but it would have been interesting. You know what I mean?'

Fran does know exactly what she means. She too has often thought it would be fun to be in at the end, and no blame attached. One wouldn't want to be *responsible* for the end, but one might like to be there and know it was all over, the whole bang stupid pointless unnecessarily painful experiment. An asteroid could do it, or an earthquake, or any other impartial inhuman violent act of the earth or the universe. She can't understand the human race's desire to perpetuate itself, to go on living at all costs. She has never been able to understand it. Her incomprehension isn't just a sour-grapes side effect of ageing. She is pleased to see that this healthy and happy young person shares some of her metaphysical defiance. It is an exoneration.

One wouldn't mind dying of a cataclysm, but one doesn't want to die young by mistake, or possibly by human error, as her son's latest partner had recently done. Untimely death is intermittently on Fran's mind, alongside housing for the refusing-to-die elderly and her more-or-less-bedridden ex-husband's dinners. Christopher's glamorous new love Sara had died aged thirty-eight of a rare medical event and Christopher believes that the doctors had done her in. Fran is not to know if this is true or not, as she has never heard of the rare condition that had killed Sara, but she feels that Christopher's current mindset of blame is doing him no good. Maybe he needs it to get by. It is not much comfort to reflect that, like Antigone, Sara has escaped getting old by dying young, and she has not offered this palliative reflection to Christopher. It does not seem appropriate. She had not disliked Sara, but could not disguise from herself the knowledge that it is Christopher she grieves for, not Sara.

So it is, with degrees of kinship and of mourning. If her son

Christopher, bone of her bone and flesh of her flesh, had died, that would have been another matter.

She had not been confident that Christopher and Sara had a long future together, but had not expected it to be quite so brief. Their mutual past had also been brief. They hadn't been together for long.

Fran doesn't meddle with her children's lives, but she'd liked what she'd seen of Sara. Though she suspects that in Christopher's life Sara had embodied something of what we now call a mid-life crisis. Mid-life crises, in Fran's ageing view, are a luxury compared with what she has seen of end-of-life crises. But Sara hadn't even had time for a mid-life crisis.

Sara had been taken ill very suddenly in a very large bed in a large luxury hotel on the Costa Teguise on the island of Lanzarote. Christopher had been in bed with her and had witnessed the crisis and been landed with the consequences. She had been rushed to hospital in Arrecife, then flown back to a private hospital in South Kensington, where she had died twenty-four hours later, having been given, according to Christopher, the wrong medication. If she had stayed in Lanzarote, where he was told the medical services were first class, he believed she would not have died. The wrong decision had been made in repatriating her. He had not trusted the good advice offered by the islanders.

Sara and Christopher had not been on holiday in the Canaries, as most visitors to those tourist islands are. They had been working, but who would believe that? Well, all those who knew the serious-minded and ambitious Sara would have known it, but it was true that Christopher had been there on a semi-freebie, as a freeloading partner, while Sara was engaged with her team in research for a documentary film about illegal immigration from North Africa. And, more or less fortuitously and it had at the time seemed fortunately, she had hoped to record an interview about the political goals of a woman from the Western Sahara who happened to be on hunger strike on the polished tiles of the departure lounge of Arrecife airport when they arrived. She was a surprising sight, holding court in the departure lounge, and was a gift to a film-maker. Or so Christopher had told his mother.

Christopher had been keeping Sara company, being himself temporarily unemployed, and his presence in that bed that night during her attack had been for her a blessing, in its way. It would have been worse for her had she been alone. But on paper his role could not look heroic.

Fran knows that Christopher is shortly to return to the Canaries, to find out what has happened to the Western Saharan contingent, to tie up loose ends, to sort out questions of medical insurance, to see some of the ex-pats who, he said, had gone out of their way to help in the crisis. She gathers that there was one elderly couple who, in the emergency, had been more than kind. Theirs was the advice he should have followed and did not.

Fran had not at first been able to follow the politics of Christopher's confusing account of the Sahrawi woman's airport protest, which she was holding against the allegedly brutal Moroccan domination of a largely unrecognised North African state which called itself the Sahrawi Arab Democratic Republic. Fran had never heard of this state, and finds it hard to retain its name, but it does indeed exist. She has looked it up. It is a cause of little interest to the British or, initially, to Fran, but after Sara's death, out of respect to Sara and Christopher, Fran has tried to get to grips with its unrecognised existence. It is a story of nationalism and political activism, and the heroine of it is a Sahrawi woman called Ghalia Namarome who is fighting for the independence of her homeland. Christopher's film-maker partner Sara, who specialised in human rights documentaries for an independent company called Falling Water, had been taken by the manner in which Namarome had materialised at the airport before her very eyes.

Fran's son Christopher, when he is in work, is, more frivolously, a television arts presenter, known for his colourful clothing and his idiosyncratic manner, which had, of late, gone a bit too far.

How Namarome had landed up in Lanzarote airport was a convoluted tale, involving the confiscation of her passport and her deportation from the airport of her home town of Laayoune. On arriving at Laayoune on her return from the US, where she had been presented with some kind of peace prize, she had refused to tick the citizenship box that said 'Morocco'. She identified herself as Sahrawi and Western Saharan and would not acknowledge the Moroccan label. So she sat there in limbo, in the Spanish Canary Islands, in a modern holiday airport in no man's land, this stylish protesting woman in her large dark glasses, with her shimmering headscarves and robes of turquoise and pink and gold, amidst the red-faced sunburnt British and German and Scandinavian tourists in khaki shorts and cotton dresses, queuing as they waited to check in for their flights home. She sat there, on a mosaic of patterned oriental carpets, of less than magic carpets, refusing to budge and accepting no sustenance but sweetened water.

Namarome was the same age as Sara. Sara, although British-born, was of émigré Egyptian descent and spoke Arabic. Sara had been struck by the would-be martyr and her passive resistance. They had, Christopher told his mother, conversed, and Sara had managed to film a brief interview. They had spoken of the Oasis of Memory, the Wall of Shame. Apparently, Fran had learnt from Christopher, there is a great dividing wall of sand and berm and brick built across North Africa, rather like the barrier wall that separates Israel from the West Bank but much much longer. Few in the West know or care about it.

It is ironic that Sara, who had seemed to be in such good health, was now dead of a rare tumour of the nervous system, whereas Namarome was courting a public death by hunger strike. No, 'ironic' is too light a word for the contrast.

Fran is not at all sure how Christopher's relationship with Sara had been faring before this abrupt end. He'd been with her, on and off, and a little tempestuously, for a couple of years: his first lengthy and publicly admitted affair since he and his long-term wife Ella had split up. But something in his most recent communications, both before and now after her death, had suggested they were already drifting apart.

Christopher doesn't talk to Fran all that much about his emotional life, but he drops hints, makes black jokes. She'd sensed he wasn't very happy before Sara's death, but he must surely be even more unhappy now.

The melodrama of the present situation is unpleasing, distressing. Sudden death and a hunger strike. Fran is more at home with the real low-key daily world of sheltered housing, and yet she cannot deny that she had also been morbidly attracted by the aspect of public martyrdom attached to the Western Sahara case. Was Namarome preparing, had she perhaps already uttered her last words to the press? Would they rival those of Walter Raleigh, of Danton?

She's worried about Christopher, she's upset about Christopher, but she's not sure how deep her sorrow goes. She keeps forgetting about it. She can't tell whether that's good or bad, natural or unnatural.

Some believe that our emotions thin out as we grow old, that we are pared back to the thin dry horn, the cuttlebone of self-ishness. That is one well-recognised theory of ageing. Fran often wonders if this will happen to her, if it is already happening without her marking it. It seems to have happened to Christopher's father Claude, Claude, her first husband, but that for him is excusable, in his present slowly deteriorating physical condition. Claude has retreated into comfort and laziness and selfishness. Into the search for comfort, which he cannot always find, though he does better than most of his age. He's lucky not to be in pain. He knows he's lucky.

Claude does not seem to have fully grasped what has happened to Christopher, and he never really took in the colourful but distanced existence of Sara.

Cuttlebone isn't a good metaphor for Claude as he is now quite plump, but that's partly the steroids.

Occasionally Fran exercises herself by trying to recall the passionate and ridiculous emotions of her youth and her middle age, the expense of spirit in a waste of shame. Or in a waste of embarrassment, or of envy, or of anxiety, or of wounded vanity. The attempt to cheat in the sack race, the red bloodstain on the back of the skirt, the fart on the podium, the misunderstanding about the ten-pound note, the arriving too early at the airport, the mistake over the visa, the table where there was no place name for her, the overheard remark about the inappropriate cardigan, the unforgivable forgetting of a significant name. She doesn't worry about some of the things she used to worry about (she doesn't need to worry about bloodstains on the skirt, though she worries now about the soup stains on her cardigan, the egg yolk on the dressing-gown lapel), but she certainly hasn't achieved anything resembling peace of mind. New torments beset her. Her relentless broodings on ageing, death and the last things are not at all peaceful. Lines of Macbeth, from *Macbeth*, repeat themselves to her monotonously, even though they are not particularly applicable to her lowly estate:

And that which should accompany old age,
As honour, love, obedience, troops of friends,
I must not look to have.

I must not look to have.

What comfort would they be to her: honour, love, obedience and troops of friends: as night fell?

La notte e vicina per me.

Those were the words that an elderly Italian woman, an old crone who swept the stairs, had uttered to Fran when she was working as an au pair girl in Florence, a hundred years ago.

La notte e vicina per me.

But old age has its comforts, its recognitions.

Fran's Freedom Pass is a comfort, but they are threatening to take that away from her. She values it disproportionately. It is a validation of work, of worth, of survival, of taxes gladly paid over a lifetime. It is her Golden Bough, her passport from the world of work to the uselessness of old age.

Venerable old age. *Valued* old age.

My God, the bullshit and the claptrap.

Honour, love, obedience, troops of friends.

I must not look to have.

La notte e vicina per me.

The egg yolk on the dressing-gown lapel.

~

The dining area of the Premier Inn is geared to dispel elderly apprehensions, not to reinforce them. It is noisy and colourful and full of large busy middle-era middle England middle-aged people talking loudly and cheerfully and eating highly coloured meals, most of them from the hot red end of the spectrum. The flagship paperwork of the Inn is purple, but its food, at least on this month's menu, is red. Red-orange battered fish, scarlet spaghetti, tomato-red pizza, prawns and peppers and paprika, chilli and chorizo and cajun. Pale Paul, after some joshing with waitress Leila, has ordered a brave black bottle of dark red Merlot, which Leila pours with a generous flourish into vast globular glasses for the four of them assembled at the table. They will be needing another bottle in no time. Fran settles into her chair and inspects the menu with anticipation. She'll go with the flow. She orders scampi and chips and a propitiatory side salad, which, when it arrives, features jolly surgical sections of not-quite-deseeded red pepper.

Sipping her Merlot, Fran feels a transfusion as of the redness of young blood begin to course through her hardening veins and arteries, pumping life and youth back into her, flushing her cheeks and warming her stiff fingers and her cold, gnarled and bunioned feet. A transfusion of ketchup and wine, of colour and vigour. It is good to be with the younger people, and in a dining area full of mid-life folk tucking unashamedly into large plates of fodder. Paul himself, although full of a restless energy and powered by a sharp brain, is in person rather a pallid, bloodless, colourless man, a celery and endive man, but Graham and Julia give out a warmer physical glow. Graham, a heavy-weight fifty-something avant-garde architect from Sheffield, is almost gross, in a handsome kind of way – his hair is swept back in dark untidy old-fashioned waves, his thick neck bulges within his open-necked red shirt (he is more than a bit of a leftie, an heir to the Socialist Republic of South Yorkshire) and a purple spotted handkerchief pokes its familiar and suggestive way out of his jacket pocket. Barbecued ribs had been his main order. Forty-year-old Julia is red of lip, with cheeks heightened by blusher as well as by wine: her thick glossy bell of dark hair has a henna sheen to it and her dimples are engaging. She is in the process of trying to wipe some startlingly orange curry sauce from her shiny white silk blouse, where it has spattered her bulky but shapely left breast. This mishap has hardly interrupted her animated gesticulatory discourse on the estate she'd visited the week before, an ageing high rise which boasted (as do so many) the highest proportion of trapped and isolated old folk in Europe – the usual story, non-functioning lifts, unlit stairwells, disabilities, gangrene, graffiti: children, grandchildren and great grandchildren all in jail: gangs in the shopping precinct, carers who didn't care and didn't show or wouldn't stay more than five minutes.

Asking for demolition, asking for a blow-down, the Heights, some of the old folk had said, but others had been loyal to them, didn't want to budge, were fond of the view over the new shopping centre and the graveyard of the foundry where their men had worked. In the good old days when men *had* work. Most of those left stranded up there are women, the men died off early.

Women live too long, says Fran, spearing a scampi tail and dabbing it into the tartare sauce. We need a plan to get rid of us. A magic lozenge.

Fran, somewhat perversely, lives in a high rise herself these days. She knows about high rise.

We *all* live too long, says Paul politely, diplomatically, nibbling at his buffalo wings.

A magic lozenge, a suicide booth, a one-way ticket to Switzerland, agrees Julia lightly, to whom old age and death are as yet unimaginable, although she knows so much theory about geriatric care.

But care is for other people, it would never be for her.

What do you think they put in it to make it this colour, Julia asks, staring in admiration at the napkin-resistant splatter on her chest. Agent Orange, Sunset Yellow, Allura Red, Carmoisine?

Are those real words, asks Fran, and Julia says yes, they are, they are the names of food colourings, apart from Agent Orange, of course, and had any of them ever sampled the Bilston Chip? There's a fish and chip shop in Bilston with the most brightly coloured orange chips you've ever seen. Lurid. Technicolor. Delicious. Best fish and chips in the Black Country. We ought to give them a whirl.

Do you think preservatives make you live longer, or do they kill you off, asks Fran. She has often wondered about this. The environmentally correct answer is that they are really really bad for you, but maybe, in their own way, they are contributing to our disastrous longevity. E-agent manufacturers must be doing research on this, but they haven't yet dared to start boasting about their findings.

She tries to avoid cooking with preservatives, and takes care to provide wholesome meals for Claude.

Fran, well turned seventy, has to her own surprise become a carer of sorts and a provider of sorts for her husband Claude, whom she had divorced in a fit of self-righteous rage nearly half a century ago. She spends a lot of time running across London to his flat with plated meals. Now, as she tucks into her scampi and chips, he will be enjoying a deliciously pure portion of fish pie on a bed of wilted organic spinach, topped with parsley sauce. He'll probably be listening to Maria Callas, because that's what he does.

~

That night, in the comfortable Premier Inn bed that rashly guarantees a sound night's sleep to all sojourners, Fran has a curious and interesting dream about Tampax. It is decades since she's had to remember to supply herself with tampons, and these days she never gives them a conscious thought, but in her dream she was struggling to arrest with an inadequate bung a constant thin pale and surprisingly watery flow of menstrual blood: the blood flowed through the tampon and through her fingers and onto her bare legs. This sensation, this dream experience, was strangely undistressing in its mood and flavour and texture, indeed pleasant rather than unpleasant, and when she wakes and tries to question it, she wonders whether it has sprung from the redness of the meal of the night before, or from her motorway thoughts about Macbeth, or from some new and about-to-be-apprehended aspect of time and the ageing experience.

For ageing is, says Fran to herself gamely as she presses the lift button to go down for her breakfast, a fascinating journey into the unknown. Or that's one rather good way of looking at it. The thin flow was the blood of life, not of death, reminding her that she is still the same woman, she who had once been the bleeding girl.

~

Over breakfast, her good mood continues, indeed intensifies. She has had to dodge the rain and pop out over the road to buy her newspaper, as the hotel doesn't seem to cater for that kind of extra, but she likes the Asian mini-store and the bearded young chap behind the counter and his fine display of fizzy drinks and spicy snacks and sweeties. His friendly greeting is in itself a little adventure. And when she gets back and settles at her table by the window, she finds herself to be almost entirely happy. Fresh newsprint, good coffee, assorted texts, some messages on her BlackBerry, what more could the modern world offer? She has selfishly forgotten, for the moment, Christopher's distress. As we age, yes it is true, it is true, we become more and more selfish. We live for our appetites. Or that's one way of looking at ageing. Old people are very selfish, very greedy.

One of the personal messages is from her old and onetime friend Teresa, who has re-entered her life after decades of separation and forgetfulness, and with whom she is enjoying a curious last fling of intimacy. Teresa is dying, but she is dying with such style and commitment that Fran is deeply impressed and encouraged by this last passage. The message is to confirm a meeting in a week's time. Fran looks forward to it, and replies to say so. Yes, she is on for lunch as agreed, and will bring sandwiches.

Teresa is uplifting. She isn't greedy, like Claude, she is too ill to be greedy, but she does still enjoy a smoked salmon sandwich, and, if Fran gets round to it, she would take well to a little home-made chicken soup.

There is something robust and cheering about the sight of the Premier Inn Full English Breakfast and those who are devouring it. It is even better than the bright red dinner. Fran doesn't go for the Full English herself, but requests a soft-boiled egg with toast. She would quite like to go over to the side table to make her own toast, but the not-so-young young woman labelled Cynthia, Cynthia with her chalk-white face and her raven-black hair, is so helpful and eager to please that Fran surrenders and allows herself to be waited on. All around Fran, younger people in their thirties and forties and fifties tuck into fried eggs and bacon and beans and hash browns and mushrooms and fried tomatoes and fried bread, all wielding their cutlery with an air of gusto. Condiments flow, the red and the brown and the mustard-coloured, and loud piped music resounds. Both Claude and Hamish would have hated the piped music, but Fran doesn't mind it at all.

Her egg, when it arrives, is perfection. The yolk is soft, the white is firm. How is it, how is your egg, my angel, tenderly asks the kindly not-so-young woman.

Perfect, says Fran, with emphasis. Perfect, she repeats.

Yes, perfection. She reads the headlines and the lead story, moves to the continuation of the story on page two. She feels a powerful surge of happiness, a sense that all is well with the world, that she is in the right place at the right time, for this moment in time. She has had a good night, comfortable, pain-free, in a big white wide premier bed. And now she is at one with these munching people, she enjoys their enjoyment, as she spoons her chaste and perfect egg. And she is at one, through her almost-reliable friend of a newspaper, with the miscellaneous events of the turning world.

The conference is not quite as jolly as the Premier Inn, but it has its highlights. The paper on the long-continuing fallout from the Thatcher 'Right to Buy' in the 1980s and the affordability of social housing and the chequered history of Housing Choice and the motivation of registered social landlords is routine, and routinely depressing, but the paper on the new technologies is fun, and is meant to be fun. It is light relief, the comic slot. It ignores finance, decay, demolition and death, and goes for the future. The lecturer is young and sparky and fast-talking and mid-Atlantic of accent, although his CV claimed he'd been born in Walsall. He'd studied in the States and in South Korea, and he is an enthusiast for the robot. Robots would save the elderly from the woes of the ageing flesh. He runs through some of the more familiar low-tech gadgets with which the elderly can already defend themselves from starving amid plenty or perishing on the cold tiles of the bathroom floor. Screw tops and tins and jam jars, bath taps and door knobs, socks lost under the bed, telephones and remote controls could all be attacked by humble devices available to all. But, Ken says, the Brave New World offers electronic and digital wonders that could achieve much, much more.

On Ken Walker's screen, darling little green articulated, not-quite-anthropoid monkey climbers with agile prehensile sensitive fingers mount walls and retrieve objects from high shelves, or bustle beneath chairs, beds and sofas to recover possessions dropped or mislaid (mobile phones, medication, peppermints, e-readers? Cigarettes, death lozenges of Nembutal from Brazil, marked for Veterinary Use only? Half bottles of whisky?). The delegates are shown an old-fashioned pack of playing cards being eased and pincered out from beneath a bookcase, a scenario that gives out a perplexing cultural message: surely nobody plays with a canvas deck these days? A discreet little scarlet ground-level scooting saucer, a flying saucer of the floor, launches itself from a dock under a comfy automated reclining armchair and bustles around the skirting boards and fitted carpet, ingesting crumbs and fluff. A more sophisticated bright lime-green highly laminated robot cleaner with a smiley face is seen vacuuming dust from every orifice of a superbly high-tech upmarket elderly person's apartment, as the elderly person lies serenely in bed doing a jigsaw of Windsor Castle on a tray. Is there an allusion here to the extraordinary longevity of the royal family? And we do know that our poor Queen likes doing jigsaws.

There is a robot to feed your cat or groom your dog. We are all aware, says young Ken, that having a pet adds years to your life. They are studying the neuroscience on this even as I speak, says keen Ken.

~

Fran, at this point in the presentation, has a very clear picture of her ex, Claude Stubbs, settled plumply on his day bed, with his handsome tabby cat Cyrus upon his knee. Cyrus is good for Claude, but Fran has taken on some responsibility for both man and cat, and they are a worry to her. Fran likes Cyrus, indeed she often says to Claude that she prefers Cyrus to Claude, and she would have liked to have a loyal cat of her own, but on balance she prefers driving restlessly around England, from conference to conference, from housing estate to housing estate, from sheltered home to sheltered home, from gadget to gadget, from Premier Inn to Premier Inn, from soft-boiled egg to soft-boiled egg. She is not ready to settle yet, with a cat upon her knee.

She's not very good at concentrating on one subject at a time. She never has been. Her mind wanders, in an endless stream of consciousness. Perhaps everybody's does, but she suspects not. Some people have an ability to concentrate, to focus. She lacks this. Her mind wanders now, back to Claude, back to her early married life, and onwards to a never-ending succession of plated meals.

Her mind never or hardly ever wanders now to sex, as it once did, though the fact that she is able to make this inner observation means that she has not forgotten about sex altogether. The menstrual dream had been a reminder, a link to the past of sex and the tampon.

She has read in newspapers, indeed in an article in her favoured upmarket newspaper, that 'surveys' show that some men, many men, think about sex every three or four minutes of their waking lives, whatever they may be doing. At work, at play, in transit, writing reports, giving public lectures, studying in libraries, waiting at tables, unblocking drains, mowing lawns, shouting in the stock exchange, fitting new tyres to old cars, changing in the locker room, climbing mountains, at the checkout in the supermarket, they think about sex. Not about love, or a loved one, but about sex, sex in the abstract, sex as an act, sex as sensation.

She doesn't think that even at her most libidinous she had

thought about sex per se that often. Women are different from men, although we must not say so.

She now finds herself thinking far too often about food. She blames Claude for this, perhaps unjustly.

~

Fran frequently finds herself newly and repeatedly astonished to have become, so late in the day, Claude's minder and carer. She can hardly believe that she has slipped into this stereotypical womanly role. She had been married to Claude so briefly and for most of their marriage so acrimoniously, and they had both lived so many other variant lives since their four embattled procreative years together. And yet she finds herself imprinted, enslaved, *imprisoned*, and in more ways than one. The habits of her body and mind had been marked forever by those four short early years.

No, she says to herself sharply, as she doodles snowdrops and daffodils in the border of Ken's robot notes, *imprisoned* she is not, no, far from it, but this restless wandering, this inexplicable wandering she surely owes something of that to those four years. Imprinted yes, *imprisoned* no.

Claude has no rights in her at all, no claim on her at all.

It's the cooking and catering that have done her in. Claude, who is indeed physically somewhat imprisoned, thinks about food most of the time, although he wouldn't admit it openly. And as a consequence Fran thinks about it too. She has been infected by his greedy dependence. She is thinking about food even now, even while watching Ken's robots and listening to statistics about mobility problems in the over-nineties. She is infuriated by the way food, shopping for food, and cooking the stuff she's bought have re-infiltrated and taken over her consciousness. It's not that she doesn't enjoy eating, she'd quite enjoyed her scampi and had been in love with her soft-boiled egg, it's just that she doesn't want food to be on her mind so much. How has this happened to her? Is it guilt, greed, reparation, preparation for her own death, an attempt to salvage the past?

Prepare your ship of death for you will need it. Prepare it, O prepare it. Stock it up with viands and with wines.

Chicken soup, if she has time, and a smoked salmon sandwich for Teresa.

Here in the Black Country they call good food 'bostin' fittle'. Fittle means vittles. Good vittles, bostin' fittle. They have their own language here. It hasn't been knocked out of them yet.

The orange Bilston chip, the fluorescent nasturtium-coloured deep-fried potato chip. The pure and perfect egg.

She wonders briefly about Namarome's hunger strike, and what is happening to her now. Had Namarome thought with longing about food, as she sat there defiantly on the polished tiles of Lanzarote airport, watching the queues of holiday-makers from northern Europe, many of them very large, some of them obese, with their plastic bags full of crisps and snacks and duty-free? Had visions of deliciously spiced North African meals, of couscous and lamb, of chermoula and harissa, of coriander and cumin and pickled lemon, floated deliriously past her as she sat there starving, or had her mind been on higher things?

Fran sometimes thinks of trying some Moroccan cookery, but she's not sure if Claude would like it.

She thinks Namarome has by now been deported to the Spanish mainland. Christopher had tried to explain that Namarome had no quarrel with Spain. Her quarrel and her country's quarrel were with Morocco, not Spain or the Canary Islands.

Fran's thoughts flit very quickly and briefly to the last meals of those on Death Row, a subject too recent and perhaps too indecent to be catalogued by Brewer, though she supposes it may feature in the *Guinness Book of Records*. As far as she can recall, cheeseburgers and pizzas feature high on the list. You really wouldn't want your last meal on earth to be a cheeseburger, surely?

Last time Fran had visited Claude, she'd left him six plated cling-filmed meals in the freezer, to be eaten in the correct order, marked with big red numbers on white freezer labels. 1 Chicken Tarragon, 2 Potato Anchovy Bake, 3 Kedgeree, 4 Lamb Casserole, 5 She Forgets, 6 Chick Peas with Bacon. She's not always so organised. Claude can't quite rely on her good will and her bounty, and it's better that way.

Call no man happy until he is dead. Claude can't be very happy these days, cooped up as he is, although she has at times suspected that something in him gets a bit of a kick from being able to bully his ex-wife. But that had been an ignoble thought, and when she had aired it to her friend Josephine, one of the few survivors to have known her in the early days, Josephine had ticked her off, telling her that, on the contrary, she, Fran, was getting a kick out of being able to bully the old boy in bed, from playing Lady Bountiful to a chap who could hardly move for steroids and other medications. And maybe this was true.

Josephine's role as long-standing friend has involved some putting-down of Fran, and Fran, most of the time, has for many years appreciated and accepted this.

Teresa is both older and newer in Fran's life. But Josephine has been more consistent.

Josephine had known Fran and Claude when Claude had been a junior house doctor and had been working the strange long late hours that had been so trying to Fran's sleep patterns, career plans, social life, sex life and digestion. Fran had resented the demands of his profession with what now seems to her to be disproportionate rage, as the hours had not been of his choosing and had laid the foundations for a distinguished and lucrative career, but she can still remember that she had been driven nearly out of her mind with solitude, claustrophobia and baby-minding, stuck in the flat in Romley with two babies and no friendly human being in reach except Josephine, who was similarly isolated with her own two little ones. Romley was the back of beyond and neither of them had regular access to a car. Fran loved her babies, as most (but not all) mothers do, but although they were hard work they didn't fill the time, and the evenings were very long and very lonely. You weren't allowed to say so, but they were. The intensity of those years had scarred her for life, and seeing more of Claude in these his latter days brings it back to her, the anger, the sense of splitting, the giddy loss of identity, the waves of terror and inadequacy, the clinging to little splinters of her past more youthful more hopeful self. It hadn't been post-natal depression, no, nothing as medical or nameable as that, it had been a kind of existential anguish, a terror in the face of adult life. Now, in the very different panics of old age, she comforts herself occasionally by reminding herself that she was even unhappier, more intensely unhappy, when she was young.

It's cold comfort, but it is a comfort. She wouldn't want to go back there, into those swirling storms, that cosmic turbulence. She must be further on than that, in the long journey of existence. She must have moved on from there. She *has* moved on from there.

The Tibetan Book of the Dead. There's a thought. A strong thought. The Way of the Bardo. The journey after death. She has a DVD somewhere, with commentary by Leonard Cohen, which she's been meaning to watch for a long time, but she's a bit apprehensive about it.

She cannot help but see a lifespan as a journey, indeed as a pilgrimage. This isn't fashionable these days, but it's her way of seeing. A life has a destination, an ending, a last saying. She is perplexed and exercised by the way that now, in the twenty-first century, we seem to be inventing innumerable ways of postponing the sense of arrival, the sense of arriving at a proper ending. Her inspections of evolving models of residential care and care homes for the elderly have made her aware of the infinitely clever and complex and inhumane delays and devices we create to avoid and deny death, to avoid fulfilling our destiny and arriving at our destination. And the result, in so many cases, has been that we arrive there not in good spirits, as we say our last farewells and greet the afterlife, but senseless, incontinent, demented, medicated into amnesia, aphasia, indignity. Old fools, who didn't have the courage to have that last whisky and set their bedding on fire with a last cigarette.

Julia and Paul and Graham, in their middle age, are they happy, confident? They look it. She hopes they are. Paul is a bit of a worrier about small things – train times, punctuality, vouchers, that kind of thing – but he knows what he's doing.

Ken with his robots? Ken is a bit manic, she considers.

Perhaps you need to be manic, to imagine his kind of future.

Claude is walled up in the red-brick Kensington flat he's lived in for some years, first with his second wife and now, ultimately, alone with Cyrus. Well heeled, well padded, well attended, well pensioned and retired from stress: bored, with the unalleviated boredom of inert old age, but comfortable. Or that's how she sees him, she, forever on the move. A self-made man, a re-made man. If you met Claude these days, if you'd met him a few years ago in his prime, you'd never have guessed the lower-middle-class world that he'd come from. He'd been a striver, he'd made himself into a successful West Londoner, and as a Kensingtonian he would die. In red-brick Kensington, in a second-floor mansion block apartment with polished floors and brass fittings, where the lifts always worked. There would be hell to pay if they didn't. With maintenance fees like those that Claude paid, of course the lifts worked. There was a concierge to see to that kind of thing.

Fran's only Romley friend Josephine, bizarrely but perhaps boldly, has recently moved to what Fran considers an extraordinarily quaint development in Cambridge, where, she says defiantly, she is very happy and very busy. It is a pretentious and expensive retirement home, built to give its residents the illusion that they are living in a Cambridge college. Its architecture is inauthentically but allusively Gothic, with pointed leaded windows and arches. The brick is a sober yellowish grey, the paintwork a crisp and holy white, and a church-like tower rises up over a recreation complex which houses exercise machines and an indoor swimming pool. The gardens are landscaped as though they were college courts or quads, with tidy lawns and weeping willows and little box hedges edging not very imaginatively planted parterres, and in the centre of the main quadrangle there is a stone-imitation plaster fountain with a boy holding a dolphin which spouts water. It looks as though it ought to be a copy of a Renaissance original, but it isn't, Josephine says, it's modern.

Jo's attitude to her new residence is an interesting mixture of haughty deprecation and proud affection. Fran believes and trusts that Jo may well be happy there, in a way that she herself could never be. She has visited Athene Grange a few times, from her hideout in Tarrant Towers in Cantor Hill, and been introduced to some of the more congenial neighbours, with whom Jo occasionally takes a morning coffee or an evening drink (though never, Jo says emphatically, a *meal*), and she has seen the games room where Jo not very often plays bridge.

Josephine and her late husband had spent ten of their middle years in Middle America, in academe in Missouri, and Jo claims to have been impressed by the manner in which Americans are so much readier than the British to accept the concept of Twilight and Sunset Homes. They are far less attached to property and privacy than we are, she had asserted. They move house and home more readily, are much more realistic about their needs. They don't stand on their rank and dignity, they go for what's comfortable, for whatever works well.

I'm much more comfortable here than I was in that big house in Norwich, says Jo. I didn't like Norwich, I didn't like the university, I never had any real friends there. I know more people in Cambridge than I ever did in Norwich. I've always had friends in Cambridge, and I used to have family here. We used to have Christmas here. I've known Cambridge since I was a child. Anyway, I couldn't afford to go on living there on my own, the house was too big. I downsized, and now I'm living as I like. I've got selfish in my old age. I live as I like.

Some retired dons in Cambridge still live in comfort and dignity in college properties, Fran knows. And she knows that Jo knows that Athene Grange is mimicking that comfort and dignity. But if it mimics them to her comfort and satisfaction, so what?

Fran is fond of her flat in Tarrant Towers, although it is a bad address, a bad postcode, and the lifts often break down. But the view is glorious, the great view over London. She likes to watch the cloudscapes assemble from afar, the great galleons of cumulus sailing her way on the approaching storm; she likes the red-streaked clouds of evening, the pierced and the torn caverns beyond the beyond of the everlasting blue, the rents and the gashes and the intimations. She endures the lowering blanketed greys of winter, the monotonous dull skies of February, and waits for the opening drama of the spring. Elevate, sublimate, transcend, that's what the view tells Fran. And climbing up the concrete stairwell once or twice a week is good for the heart.

She likes Tarrant Towers. She likes its insalubrious garage space. She couldn't do without a garage. She needs her car, she needs to keep moving.

~

Imagine Claude Stubbs. Imagine him released from Fran's controlling vision of him, if we can. Yes, he is there, he is occupying his own space. Cyrus the stout tabby is settled on the end of Claude's day bed, his softly rounded white-tipped front paws curved comfortably inwards towards one another in a slightly camp submissive gesture that Claude finds deeply endearing. The claws are sheathed and amply padded. Cyrus is not a young cat and he enjoys the circumstances of Claude's confinement, he is pleased that Claude is not well. Claude hardly ever goes out now, except on forays to the hospital, so Claude is almost always there to be with Cyrus. Cyrus approves of this regime. The radio is playing, the television is on although the sound is mute, and Claude's mind moves towards the next plated meal, which he thinks is potato, egg and anchovy bake, a dish he believes to have been invented by Fran, though in fact it is a debased version of a recipe she once read in a Jane Grigson book in the 1970s, in the far-off days when she used to hope that one day she would learn how to cook.

Claude has little notion of Fran's increasingly vexed relationship with food. He has never had to cook anything, ever, except toast and an egg. He likes the anchovy bake, so he won't have it for lunch, he will save it up for supper. Something to look forward to. His minder, who is called Persephone, has already been in to see to him and has left him a plastic box containing chicken and avocado sandwiches on brown and an M&S tropical fruit salad. Claude is supposed to like mangoes, and most of the time he does, though perhaps not quite as often as they appear on his menu. Persephone is a tall good-looking black girl with expensively smooth dark gold hair. She says she's from Zimbabwe, and she's forty years younger than Fran. She makes him think about sex, but thinking about it is all that he can do. She told him this morning some rigmarole about the flowers that one of her beaux had sent her for Valentine's Day. Orange lilies, and a huge golden metal heart sticking up out of them. A bit dangerous, a bit menacing, for *flowers*, said Persephone. More like a weapon than a love offering.

Persephone is no fool.

It's bloody freezing out there, said Persephone, you're better off here in bed.

People often say thoughtless things like that to Claude. He doesn't mind as much as he used to. He's got used to it. He wouldn't like Persephone's life, no, not at all.

Persephone likes Cyrus, or pretends to, and never complains about changing the cat litter. But she is well paid to do that kind of thing. At least she doesn't have to change Claude's litter or empty his bedpan. Not yet.

He's mobile enough to get to the kitchen, with the aid of his Chelsea and Westminster NHS crutches. He's not on the NHS, or not wholly on the NHS, just as when in practice he wasn't wholly on the NHS nor wholly private. He's always been an opportunist. He acquired the crutches as an outpatient in an earlier and less terminal state of affairs, and although he was supposed to have returned them long ago, he hasn't. They've been standing in the cupboard in the spare room for years. They've come in handy now.

With the crutches, he can still get, very slowly, to the lav, as they used to call it in Romley. He doesn't always get there in time, as he sometimes misjudges the urgency and the difficulties of the journey, but he gets there.

Imagine Claude, imagining his first wife Francesca. Fran is

at a conference up north somewhere. She's always buzzing around the country, despatched by that Quakerly quango on geriatric housing that employs her. Quango, charity, NGO, he's never been quite sure what it is, but it's something to do with the elderly, and it does pay her a salary. She's a busybody, a typical social-worker middle-class busybody type. And however public-spirited she may think she is, she is as utterly selfish as anyone he has ever known. She's just as selfish as all his colleagues rolled together – the surgeons, the oncologists, the anaesthetists, the consultants, the chief medical officers, the professors, the heads of all the royal colleges. Everybody is selfish, and Fran is as selfish as the rest of them. She doesn't work for the public interest, but because she likes doing it, because it keeps her busy, because it makes her feel important and on top of the game.

What game? At her age? It's tragic, it's pathetic.

He visualises the potato, egg and anchovy bake. He likes salt, and maybe his salt intake has contributed to his present lamentable condition. There's probably double cream in there too. Too late to start worrying about all of that now.

Maybe Fran is trying to kill him off. She had threatened to murder him several times, half a century ago, but there wouldn't be much in it for her if he died now. She'd be let off the plated meals, but it's Claude's convenient view that, in her masochistic womanly way, she enjoys making them.

She doesn't know what's in his will, and would never ask. She doesn't even ask what provision he's made for their two children and his grandchildren. But she knows Persephone is pricey, and his life expectancy is actuarially uncertain. Who knows how long he and a succession of Persephones could survive before he ran out of money?

He knows, but she doesn't.

He will have half a bottle, perhaps a bottle, of the very good

Chablis with the bake. He has resolved to drink expensive wine until he dies. Neither of his wives could tell one bottle from another, let alone one year from another, although both of them could knock it back. He has decided to enjoy what he can, while he can.

Fran now lives alone in a high-rise council flat on a dismal North London estate, having recently moved from a much nicer ground-floor garden flat in Highgate where she lived with that man Hamish. He has never seen the council flat, but she has described it to him, briefly and provocatively. He has accused her of slumming, but she has denied this. She has used lofty words for her lofty eyrie. Atonement, absolution, amnesty. No, none of those words is quite right, his memory for words is going, but he's sure one of those that she used to justify her choice of residence begins with an A. And she had mentioned the view, what she called the overview.

Odd how one can remember bits of words, but not always the words themselves. Maybe it's a word that he applied to it, not her. Anyway, it began with an A. Proper nouns go first, then abstract nouns, then nouns, then verbs. So he's been told.

It's a damn sight nicer in Tarrant Towers than in Romley and Chingwell and Chingford, she had told him.

He hadn't attempted to defend Romley. Romley had been hard on her, he recognises that, though he wouldn't admit it to her then or now. The Romley hospital had been a hard apprenticeship. It's been demolished. It escaped the recent round of NHS scandals by getting itself pulled down and relocated further out in almost rural Essex.

On telly, there is some kind of auction going on, a downmarket daytime version of the *Antiques Roadshow*. It is dumbly and silently failing to compete with Classic FM, a channel much loved by Claude. He discovered classical music as a teenager, and this daily programme is aimed at his level. He knows it can annoy seriously musical people but he is not seriously musical. Culturally, he has always enjoyed striking an unsettling pose between the philistine and the mandarin, and somehow Classic FM fails to annoy him at all. He used to enjoy it while driving, but now he likes to feel part of the stay-at-home family of the housebound, the housewives, the retired, the unemployed, the home-workers, the put-your-feet-up-you've-earned-a-rest brigade. The presenters speak to him pleasantly, with exactly the right degree of polite but friendly intimacy, cheerful and respectful but with a touch of irony, much less annoying than the feigned chumminess and barely disguised condescension and contempt of some of the Radio 3 clever chappies and well-spoken ladies, who don't seem to be able to get it right these days. They're culturally adrift on Radio 3, they don't know who they are. The BBC as a whole has lost its way, that's Claude's view, and he thinks the licence fee should be abolished. It's made some astounding mistakes, it's dug its own grave.

Claude even enjoys the Classic FM commercials, as they attempt to sell him car insurance and medical products and barbecues and tickets to concerts and homely holidays in dullish English counties. The travel news, with its accidents and lane closures and roadworks, is a comfort to him, for now he is no longer driving or being driven, he is safe in his day bed, not stuck in the stationary fast lane or stranded on the hard shoulder. All over Britain, people are having a bad time at the wheel. Classic FM makes him feel part of the human race, without having to pay a high price for his inclusion.

He will never drive again. He's got over feeling that that is such a bad thing. He will never operate again, and that is a relief.

Claude isn't nearly as bored as Fran thinks he must be. He's bored, but he has his resources. And one of them is Classic FM. It is all so surprising, its ever-present availability. Brahms,

Rimsky-Korsakov, Mahler, Chopin, Berlioz, Gounod, Bernstein. The presenters are full of genuine and well-informed enthusiasm for their products. He loves Alan Titchmarsh and John Suchet. He hears Barenboim, Menuhin, Nigel Kennedy, Maria Callas. Greatness pours through the air and floods his apartment.

Claude Stubbs is an impassioned admirer of Maria Callas. He has had an intense fantasy relationship with her for many years.

He has half an hour of Callas on CD most evenings. He usually times it to coincide with the Pill. He has to take a lot of routine medication to stay alive, but the semi-legal Magic Pill which he prescribes for himself is something else. Others might think of it as an anti-depressant, but to Claude it brings psilocybin euphoria. It elevates him, briefly but unfailingly, to a sublime state. It's better than all the drugs he took when he was a young physician. It's the business, it does the trick.

~

The conference is over and Fran has spoken, competently but in her view rather boringly, reporting on the Ashley Combe Trust's continuing support of research into models of integrated housing developments for the elderly. Raised flower beds, patent window catches, isolation valves for gas appliances, key lockers for visiting carers – a medley of suggestions and possibilities, some of which she has inspected and tested in practice, some of which exist as yet only in theory, but most of them far less futuristic than Ken's dapper range of robots.

She is staying one more night in the refuge of the inn, at her own expense, as she doesn't want to drive all the way back to London in the dark and face the possibility of a non-functioning lift on arrival. She can face the stairwell in the mornings, but not so well in the evenings. (Once, exhausted, she had slept in the garage, in her car.) And Paul has asked her to accompany him on his visit to his aunt in Chestnut Court in Sandford Road. For moral support, he said. He'd like to know what she makes of Chestnut Court and his aunt. Two people visiting makes it easier than one, he said. A platitude, he said, but she well knows it to be true.

Fran doesn't mind platitudes. A few platitudes, every now and then, are restful. They draw one back from the brink of the flames.

Fran was pleased to be asked by young Paul, flattered that he valued her opinion and her company. They have become good professional friends, despite the age gap. Yes, of course, she had said, she'd be happy to give him a lift.

She thinks, briefly, as she negotiates with the satnav's help the tricky one-way system of Sandwell, of Christopher and Sara and the volcanic craters, and of unexpected death. No platitudes there.

A small earthquake had shaken Dudley.

The Canaries had been formed and transformed by volcanic activity on a massive scale.

Sandford Road turns out to be one of those long curving streets that lack all architectural cohesion. It was cut off from the old dying shopping parade by a 1970s stretch of dual carriageway, over which arched a steeply sloping narrow flimsy pedestrian walkway. Sandford Road had found itself on the wrong side of the tracks. It had wandered and struggled through many decades of build and rebuild, juxtaposing cheap modern maisonettes with little 'carriage houses' with stretches of turn-of-the-century terrace with once-desirable 1930s semi-detached dwellings. Nothing grand, but many variants on the theme of decent inexpensive housing for decent folk, with the older build-ings now in slow decline. Some of the houses are set back behind small front gardens, others front the street. One or two mature and as yet leafless trees from an earlier epoch rear defiantly upwards to the light, from painfully carbuncled and root-buckled pavements.

Fran finds a space to park outside a run of four late Edwardian three-storey red-brick terraced villas that had been done up in startling style, with bizarre ornamental stained-glass panels let in to some of the front windows and doors, and modern iron gates with ornate designs picked out in gilt and turquoise and scarlet. These houses must, she surmises, belong to an extended family group or to a cluster of an ethnic minority with pronounced and eccentric views on decor, or indeed, most probably, to a combination of the two. One of the front windows has an image of a not very English running deer surrounded by white blossoms engraved upon it or set into it. She can't begin to think what it is doing there. She points it out to Paul, who doesn't seem as surprised by it as she is. He's seen it all before.

Asian? Eastern European? Bizarre.

She loves it. She loves how it all is.

And there is Chestnut Court, the modest care home that says it specialises in schizophrenia. Unlike Josephine's Athene Grange, it obviously isn't purpose-built. It is a rather shabby spreading asymmetrical 1930s terrace house, on two floors with two wide bay front rooms, and above one of the front rooms a wide bay-windowed bedroom, the master bedroom, the room with a view. It doesn't have a local authority look about it, even though it is largely funded by the local authority. It is quiet, it is calm, a backwater amidst the changing waves of demolition and renovation. And there Aunt Dorothy from Brasshouse Lane has lived becalmed for many years.

Each room its own TV, home-cooked food with the menu changing weekly, access to local church and local shops, medical attendance, visiting chiropodist. All for £358–£420 a week. It is very reasonable. Compared with Claude's outgoings, this is very reasonable.

Dorothy is petite. She is small and perfect. She is very old but she is perfect. Her skin is clear, unblemished and almost without wrinkles, her eyes are a lucent blue, her lips are pink with a perfect shade of carefully applied pale girlish lipstick, her silver hair is thin but arranged to perfection in gentle but neatly controlled curls and waves around her perfect brow and her heart-shaped face. Once a fortnight she is taken in a taxi to the hairdresser for a shampoo and set. She had been a beauty. She is still a beauty. She is fragile. She is delicate, a porcelain figurine. She is beautifully preserved and presented, in the over-heated upholstered lounge of the very homely home. Grey skirt, a prettily embroidered cream blouse, a pale blue cardigan, silver earrings and a pearl necklace. Rings on her fingers, proper rings, not mail order trinkets, and a silver bracelet.

She has been beautifully presented to reassure her nephew Paul, Fran assumes, but she cannot detect any hint of hidden or underlying neglect. This is a very small outfit, a domestic operation, a 'home from home'. There are only five other residents, two of whom are up in their rooms, while the other three are somewhat slumped and dozy in recliners at the other end of the lounge, watching a muted TV. Paul, Fran and Dorothy sit upright in the little bay window with their tea and shortbread biscuits, while Dorothy tells Fran the story of her life. Fran is a new audience, and she listens politely and attentively.

She cannot understand much of Dorothy's tale. She is familiar with various forms of dementia and confusion, and knows people who cannot carry a conversation or remember a thought sequence for more than two or three minutes at a time. Dorothy is not like that at all.

Dorothy wanders from past to present seamlessly, in a stream of consciousness that loops and circles and turns in on itself.

Albion Road, the war, the air raids, the gas light with a mantel, West Bromwich Albion, bread and dripping, my father, he was always so angry, Junior Mixed and Infants, the old Board School, her bouts of pneumonia, her TB, her colostomy (she pats the bag, affectionately, softly swelling under her grey skirt). The church, the vicar, that time she spoke at her friend's funeral, her son who came to see her when he could, her husband, she married him when she was seventeen. Her father was angry. God was so good to her. Her plans for her funeral, her favourite hymns, the first time she'd been put in hospital, Suzette the manageress, Claire the stylist at the salon, the new shopping mall, the darkies have taken over everywhere. The day thou gavest Lord is ended. Darkies are everywhere. Look, this is the ring he gave me, my Charlie, it's sapphires and diamonds. Hopscotch in the street and dancing to the gramophone. Her father was angry when she did handstands, he didn't like her showing her knickers, he gave her the strap if she showed her knickers, he bought a coat for £2 at the pawn shop but he didn't live to wear it, but her mother lived to be ninety-four.

I hope I don't last that long but God disposes, they help me to change the bag, there's always a helper on duty here.

He didn't like me showing my knickers. I was always the pretty one, my little sister Emmie she was the clever one.

As she mentions her sister Emmie, she looks in a puzzled way at Emmie's son Paul, as though wondering who he is and what his connection with this narrative.

The pumping station, it's all bricked up now. My dad worked, he worked for the water board. Yes, God is very good, they wheel me to church every Sunday. Our church is one hundred years old. I like to read, I like stories, we get these magazines.

It's a very vocal form of dementia, if dementia it is. The three residents at the other end of the room speak not at all. They must have heard Dorothy's stories innumerable times. She is the talker, she speaks for them all, she is the muddled memory of their generation.

Fran tries to follow, picks out the recurrent motif of the angry father, wonders if he was the explanation of why his daughter is here, year after year, unageing, unchanging, living it out to the end.

Dead at forty-eight, he was, it was his lungs.

Paul's grandfather, that would have been.

After an hour, manageress Suzette joins them to break it up, for they had dutifully done their stint. Dorothy recognises the nature of the intervention at once, and makes no attempt to detain her visitors. She is well-mannered, docile. She presents them each with a parting gift, a card from a children's play pack, which she has coloured in with bright acrylics. One shows a butterfly, the other a country cottage. She has worked them carefully, not going over any of the edges, none of the colours overlapping one another.

She seems to have taken to Fran, and urges her to visit again when next she finds herself nearby. Just pop in, says Dorothy, you'll always find me here.

'She loves colouring in,' says Suzette gaily as she ushers them out into the hallway. Dorothy remains sitting at the table, gazing not after her guests but out at the street, her frail mauve beringed hands neatly folded in her lap.

Suzette is a stoutly confident tawny-blonde sixty-year-old with a short sharp defiantly razored hairstyle, all points and tips and highlights. No shampoo and set and hot curlers under the hood of the dryer for her. She is dressed in a bold tight fuchsia and black geometric print stretchy fabric dress with a scooped neckline. She is brisk and breezy, supplying the movement and energy in the house that her charges lack. Her parting handshake is powerful. She is a strong woman.

Who owns the premises? Who is making money out of this?

Who employs Suzette? Is anyone making money out of it? It looks more like a break-even one-off situation to Fran. Not a chain, not part of a lucrative exploitative string of Chestnut Care Homes, just this one homely house hanging on in Sandford Road. Too low-profile for a scandal. Just surviving, as best it could.

There had been a scandal recently, in another much larger Sandwell care home. Several residents had fallen ill with food poisoning and a twenty-three-year-old care worker had been arrested and detained in a secure mental health unit. She was suspected of having deliberately contaminated their food.

Leave the mad to feed the mad, let the dead bury the dead.

Fran drives Paul back to the Premier Inn, where he says he'll ring for a cab to get to Birmingham New Street. He has to get back to Colchester. She doesn't even offer to drive him to the station. She is far too tired.

And Paul is subdued.

'She must have been a beauty,' offers Fran.

'I don't think she's unhappy,' says Paul, unhappily.

He had volunteered, earlier in the day, that his mother hadn't seen her sister in thirty years. They had quarrelled, terminally. Emily in Hagwood and Dorothy in Chestnut Court. Both their husbands were dead. Dorothy has a son, the son she had mentioned, he isn't a fantasy son as Fran might have supposed. But he had emigrated to Australia, a fact which she doesn't seem to have wholly grasped. He wasn't much use, her son Ralph, on the home front.

Fran is thinking of the bouts of childhood pneumonia, of the TB, of the bowel operation, of that occasionally vocal colostomy bag, of all the skilled surgery and intensive care and nursing and expense that have gone into keeping this confused old woman alive and smiling and putting on her jewellery and being wheeled to church and colouring in and looking at fashion pictures in magazines and wandering softly in her wits. She realises she's been thinking of Dorothy as belonging to the ultimate generation, to the phalanx of the truly old, but Dorothy's wartime memories had marked her as being only a very few years older than Fran herself. Fran can just about remember the war. Dorothy is in her seventies, not even in her eighties. She could live another twenty years.

Sometimes Fran thinks she can understand the impulse that makes a twenty-three-year-old want to kill off a lot of useless old people.

We can all expect to live longer, but it's recently been claimed that the majority of us can expect to spend the last six years of our prolonged lives suffering from a serious illness, in some form of pain and ill health.

Fran found this statistic, true or false, infuriating. Longevity has fucked up our pensions, our work–life balance, our health services, our housing, our happiness. It's fucked up old age itself.

Fran can no longer wholly control her thought processes. As she lies on her guaranteed-good-night's-sleep bed, watching the evening news and eating a packet of some novel kind of Gujarati mix (satisfyingly spicy but rather too many peanuts), washed down with a bottle of not-quite-cold-enough screw-top 13 per cent Spanish white purchased from the friendly bearded Muslim newsagent over the road, she finds herself planning Claude's next week of meals. She doesn't want to be doing this, but she can't help it.

He'll be running out of plates and plastic boxes, he'll be expecting her to turn up soon with some more.

What about soup? She could make a thick vegetable soup,

no, a vegetable soup with bits of bacon, no, a lentil soup with chicken pieces. Claude used to say he didn't like soup, half a century ago, but he's not in a position not to like it now, is he? He has to take what he's given, now.

She could get a good chicken, make enough soup for both Claude and Teresa.

Lardons. That's the word she's looking for. Bits of bacon, ready chopped. Good in soup. Soup freezes well. There's yet another word for lardon but she can't quite get it.

He used to get back from the hospital after the night shift, and she'd have made the healthy thrifty chunky soup and all he had to do was warm it up. But that wasn't good enough. He wanted HER to be there to WARM IT UP FOR HIM. And she in bed and worn out with the children sleeping or not sleeping or waking or not waking and the sense of unutterable inadequacy, the sense of rejection, the fear, the panic, the sexual rejection identified with food rejection, the sense of *not being* that women have, you'd think she'd have grown out of it by now, by her age, at seventy-plus, but no, it intensifies, it gets worse and worse.

So he'd say he didn't like soup. Root vegetables, carrots, potatoes, no parsnips, he couldn't tolerate parsnips, what other root vegetables are there? Onions. Celery.

Bacon bits. Pancetta. Got it, that's the other word, pancetta. Lardons. Pancetta. Foreign words for bits of bacon.

The treadmill of the food mind, like a hamster in its cage. Sometimes she thinks she is going mad, really mad, she will end up in a home like Dorothy, mindlessly colouring in. She used to enjoy colouring in, she remembers a book of flowers and birds and butterflies she had when she was a child, a treat just after the war shortages, and how she'd cried when the water colours ran together into a muddy brown. The failures, the failures. The tough beef, the stew with frilled yellowy gristle,

45

the bloody undercooked lamb, the disintegrating fish overcooked in the oven. He wouldn't eat the fish, the guests wouldn't eat it, they'd pretended they were allergic to fish rather than try to eat her fish, she hadn't forgotten that, she hadn't forgotten anything, and it had been good fish too, from the fish shop, in those days when there was a fish shop.

She'd better snap out of this, she's going downhill fast, down to that place that it was so hard to clamber out of.

Lardons. They were the solution, the solution to everything. We didn't used to call them that. God knows what we did call them. We didn't call them that other word either, pancetta, we'd never heard of pancetta.

Bread and dripping, Dorothy had mentioned. You couldn't offer that to man or boy now, not because they wouldn't eat it, although they wouldn't, but because meat doesn't produce dripping any more. The meat isn't real meat any more. Even when it looks like meat, it's something else.

Fran takes another swig of the oaky Spanish, mutes the news, looks for her mobile, panics when she can't find it. She's just an old woman endlessly groping in the bottom of her bag, checking her keys and her mobile every ten minutes to see if they are still there, but there it is, in the wrong zip bit. Why can't she remember always to put it in the same compartment? It doesn't bode well, Christ, it doesn't bode well.

Claude answers within three rings. Hello, Francesca, how's it going?

Relief, hearing his voice so not unfriendly, so not at all hostile. He is pleased to hear from her.

Fine, says Fran, good day, just checking you are OK, everything OK?

Everything fine, says Claude, I've just finished the potato and anchovy bake, it was delicious. Persephone brought me a bit of green salad this morning so I've had my greens too.

Oh good, potato and anchovy isn't really your five a day, is it?

To hell with five a day, it's very nice. You do look after me, Fran, I don't deserve it.

No, you don't, but we all need more than we deserve, don't we? *Oh reason not the need.*

How was your day, how was the conference?

Good. It was fine.

Good.

I'm going home in the morning, I'll come over and see you in a couple of days when I've sorted myself out, bring you some more supplies.

Thanks, have *you* had *your* supper yet?

No, I was just wondering whether to go down to the restaurant or to pop out for a pizza. The food here's not great but the breakfasts are good.

You were never a breakfast girl, were you?

No, but here they do you a perfect soft-boiled egg, it's a treat.

How's Cyrus?

Cyrus is fine, aren't you, big puss?

Paranoia dissolves, retreats, thins out, but one day it won't, will it? One day it will entrap her in its dark nets and fogs and she will sink under it. It would be a pity to die dismally, in that darkness.

She wants to die in the light. Enlightened, in the light. Let there be light, oh God let there be light.

Endgame. She and Josephine are planning to go to see *Endgame*, God knows why. Or is it *Happy Days*? She can't remember which. Jo is in charge of booking the tickets, it's Jo who has suddenly decided they ought to get to grips with Samuel Beckett.

Some fear the approach of dementia. Fran is acquainted with many people with dementia, she has very recently inspected blueprints for dementia-proof housing designed by a team at the University of Watermouth, she has read books about dementia, she has helped out (but only once, she can't boast about it) at a social event for dementia patients and their carers. But Fran doesn't think she is on the road to dementia. Her parents had never shown any sign of mental deterioration, they had been conscious (although not always peacefully and happily) to the end. Her brain functions well, her connections are quick, her memory is serviceable and subject only to a well-within-the-normal-range of lapses about names and products and titles of books and misplaced objects. No, what she fears is paranoia and subjection and rejection, and a return to that sense of worthlessness that had gripped her when she was newly married to Claude and spent so much time worrying about *ruining the food*. Maybe these sensations are returning to her because she has re-engaged with Claude, or maybe she has re-engaged with Claude because she needs to return to them. Maybe this is a necessary stage.

Food is a metaphor. But for what? She worries away at this. There is a deep entangled mystery. Sometimes she thinks she should go/have gone to an expert, to an analyst, to have this explained to her, but most of the time she thinks that she can work it out for herself in the end.

The end is nigh, but she'll keep on trying.

It's not too late.

And she would be too ashamed to talk about food to an analyst. It is too trivial, too obsessively trivial.

Food disorders are for the young. And this isn't really a food disorder, it's more like a cooking disorder.

Fran hates media chefs. They proliferate, they spread fear and panic.

She has somewhat half-heartedly developed her strategies for confronting and averting late-onset ailments. Walking, working, swimming. Climbing the tenement stairs, up and down, down and up, as though climbing up and down an Escher construction site. Networks, tasks, the occasional crossword puzzle. The discipline of plated meals for Claude, the new fortnightly vigils with Teresa. The renewals and transfusions of energy from Paul and Julia and Graham and other younger professional acquaintances up and down the land. The driving about, looking at projects, and the feeling of an occasional wave of oneness with the ordinary plight of the ordinary human race. The keeping-in-touch without-being-too-annoying with her son Christopher and her daughter Poppet and her ex-daughter-in-law Ella and her grandchildren.

The 'wider interests' that are meant to keep us from falling down the funnel.

Lying there on her wide white plump bed in the Premier Inn, she realises that she has knocked back too much of the Spanish wine and is feeling hungry, but is too drunk to go out for a meal. They don't seem to do room service, and anyway room service sometimes takes hours and hours. She could go out and buy herself a slice of pizza. But she is too tired to go out to buy herself a slice of pizza. She has left it too late to go out to buy herself a slice of pizza.

She could go downstairs and order a plate. A hot plate. Scampi and chips with loud Muzak. A glass of red. She is sick of this Spanish white.

Valentine's Day. Shrove Tuesday. Good Friday. Easter Sunday. We measure it out.

See the water and the blood from his riven side that flowed.

Poor Hamish. He had died at Easter, on Easter Saturday. A sombre day to die. A disproportionate number of people die in hospitals at weekends, for obvious reasons. He had been a statistic. But at least he had died on a serious day.

Claude had enjoyed cutting people up, and he'd been exceptionally good at it.

W. B. Yeats, her friend Jo's favourite poet, was good on old age and our insatiable dissatisfaction, as Jo keeps telling her. She doesn't really need telling, she read Yeats for herself, in the days when she read poetry. 'I can't get no satisfaction', that had been one of the great songs of her youth. She used to play it to herself loud loud loud, it was the only song she really liked, though the Beatles she could tolerate.

Sex, food, satisfaction.

I can't get no satisfaction.

She'd meant to text Christopher a routine good will message, HOW R U LOVE FX, but why bother, her fingers are too stiff and clumsy at this time of night, and she is redundant both to Christopher's life and to Sara's death.

She heaves herself up and forces herself to go downstairs for a Red Meal. She thinks with longing of the potato and anchovy bake, and of the chicken and tarragon, with their paler shades and more subtle flavours. She does make them for herself, sometimes. But sometimes she just can't be bothered. She often thinks she should always cook double quantities of everything, and freeze half for Claude, half for herself, but there is something wrong with that as a concept. She can't work out what it is, but maybe one day she will. She's cooked double occasionally, but she's never made a habit of it. She thinks of Paul, Julia, Graham, Ken of the robots, and the strong-armed sixty-year-old Suzette, who could have tossed the frail little body of Aunt Dorothy, colostomy bag and all, over her shoulder and carried her up the stairs without missing a step. Suzette had seemed to be a kindly woman, but who knows what motivates her? Maybe one day she too will lose the plot and poison all her brood.

There just aren't enough strong younger people around these days to infuse the energy into the elderly. The feeble, as never before in society, in history, are outweighing the hale. The balance is wrong. The shape of the bell curve is a disaster. It's a dystopian science fiction scenario, a disaster movie.

The hunter gatherers wouldn't have let themselves get into this kind of predicament. They abandoned the elderly, or drowned them, or clubbed them to death, or exposed them on snowy mountainsides. They kept on the move.

Fran is on the move too.

~

Nor know that what disturbs our blood
Is but its longing for the tomb . . .

~

Ivor Walters sits on the little low balcony of the familiar bar overlooking the promenade that runs along the curving bay. He sips his warming beer. He is filling in time before meeting Christopher Stubbs at the airport. A pastel-pretty pink and beige and pale blue collared dove perches on the back of the little white bistro chair at the table on the next balcony, looking at him from time to time. It puts its head on one side, and looks at him. The sun, predictably, is setting. It is a very reliable sun. Sunset and sunrise do not vary much in these climes. He watches the slow march of the people on their daily pilgrimage. They are walking back from the beach to shop for their supper in one of the many small and almost identical supermarkets, or to eat fish or burgers or pizza in one of the many small and almost identical restaurants, or to spend an evening watching football in one of the many English pubs, where they will get drunk on beer or on Canarian or Spanish wine or (in the case of the ladies) on recklessly dispensed tumblers full of sweet holiday liqueurs.

You cannot really call their slow march a *passeggiata*, a *camino*, a *paseo*, for these pilgrims are too humble and lacking in style for such words. He observes them as they plod and trudge: the fit, the fat, the brown, the red, the weathered, the wizened. Cleavages, thighs, shorts, sandals, walking sticks. Wheelchairs, mobility scooters, buggies. Half term is over and most of the larger children have flown away and gone back to school, but the little ones in their pushchairs are always with us, accompanied by a few truant siblings. A sunset procession, a slow pedestrian parade. Occasionally a jogger varies the rhythm of the procession, but there are not many joggers. The pace is slow.

The surface of the path is hard and trim and newly laid and neatly bordered. He knows the island well and he has seen its improvements and its upgradings. Much public money has been spent on footpaths and roadways and viewpoints. He knew this path when it was rock and sand and mud and grit and spume, when it was raw and painful to the sandalled foot. He is slowly ageing with the island, he has watched it adapt itself to the ease and the pleasure-seeking of the perpetual procession. This is a good country for babies in buggies, and a good country for old men. Ivor is not yet old, as others are old, but he has lived here long enough. If Bennett dies soon, which he may, Ivor can go back to England. But if Bennett survives into his late eighties and nineties, which in this mild climate of mummified and everlasting life he equally well may, it will be too late for Ivor to go home. It is a common story.

Bennett is here for his health and Ivor is here because Bennett needs him to be here. Bennett is slowly drying out like a Guanche mummy of the caves and dunes. Ivor needs Bennett because Bennett holds the purse strings. It is too depressing, and yet not ignoble. They are bound together by the needs which succeed love, by the needs which succeed sex and affection. Ivor does not like thinking in these terms, but it is hard to avoid them. They sit by him, these considerations, looking at him from time to time, as does the pretty collared dove with its pale and pearly plumage.

Ivor tries to keep Bennett entertained, he is loyal to him. Ivor is a good man, at the very least he tries to be a good man. Most would call him a good man, but, by his own high standards, he might fail.

It is better not to look too closely at Ivor these days, in Ivor's view. He is, or was, a strikingly handsome man, and he still attracts flirtatious attention from men and women alike. Blond, bronzed, with the bluest of forget-me-not blue eyes, and the most even of features. A pin-up boy, a collector's item. Bennett had collected him long ago, when Ivor was only seventeen and knew no better. Ivor worries now about his wrinkles. He is proud that he still has a full head of hair, white now rather than golden, but you can tell that it once was golden for it has that light silvery radiance, the white-gold thistledown brightness of the birthright blond. He keeps it just very slightly on the long side. Dashingly, but not effeminately long.

Bennett and Ivor have engaged with the life of the island. They know some of the local celebrities and intellectuals, most of them also elderly, some of them ancient, many of them also here for reasons of health (and at least one of them in retreat from scandal). A few are indigenous, but a very few. Bennett is himself now something of a local celebrity, and he speaks good Spanish, so he can participate more fully in the cultural and social life of the island than Ivor. Ivor is not a linguist, although he is good at small talk, at seeing to drinks, at opening bottles, at pulling up chairs for older guests in his own and other people's houses. He is an asset. People cheer up when they see Ivor is of the party.

Bennett knows a good deal about Spanish and Canarian

history, for he has written about the Spanish Civil War and Lorca and Franco and Guernica and Picasso, and about the now-forgotten but once-celebrated philosopher Miguel de Unamuno, whose ambivalent political affiliations have for many years intrigued him. He has written a famous essay about Unamuno's brief Canarian exile to Fuerteventura, under the dictatorship of Primo de Rivera. That distinguished Spanish academic had unwisely made a public protest about the preferential treatment of one of the dictator's courtesans, La Caoba, 'the Mahogany Girl', and Unamuno had ended up on a boat from the mainland to what was then the dullest and scruffiest and least visited of the islands. Ivor and Bennett have been several times to pay homage to him in his humble dusty museum-house in Puerto del Rosario, a port formerly known as Goat Harbour, and they have seen his carved wooden desk and his carved wooden bed with its white lace coverlet.

Unamuno's white, massive and strangely Fascist statue rises up on the lower slopes of the great and stately Montaña Quemada. That too they have seen, from the vertiginous road, many times.

Unamuno's sojourn had been brief, to merit such memorials. A matter of months. But Fuerteventura had lacked celebrities, and it makes the most of him.

Ivor has never been able to follow the ups and downs of Unamuno's posthumous reputation. He remains an ambiguous figure. He knows that Unamuno symbolised for Bennett something about the caprice of fortune, the humiliation of academics, the dangers of political vacillation, the neglect of posterity, but Ivor has never known precisely what, or why.

Ivor knows less than Bennett about the Canaries, but he is learning, perforce. And he knows some aspects of the Canaries that Bennett does not know.

He has learned a lot over the years by typing up Bennett's

for that cottage and that solitary gardener of the sinking sun, but he had never found them. They had been a mirage, a trick of the light. But the vision of the old man had encouraged him to agree to settle here. And the house, when they found it, was special. It was exceptional, it was beautiful.

A man could die even here.

The house was inland and a little upland, but with a view down towards the sea. On the small island, nowhere is far from the sea. It stood on the outskirts of an undistinguished village, near a roundabout marked by one of the playful moving sculptures created by the island's dead gay magus, the artist César Manrique, and it was built on one storey, spreading over a series of volcanic bubbles and caverns. The irregularity of the black pitted lava and the whitewashed walls enchanted Bennett. The shapes of the house were organic, fanciful, natural, devised by the natural surrealism of the eighteenth-century volcanic eruptions. It was the perfect house for a man who struggled for breath climbing stairs. It had been designed and built to a high standard in the good years, and was complete with pool, sun terrace, palm trees, a well-planted euphorbia garden of many colours, a fish pool, a tennis court. It had a gaiety and a lightness of spirit, and it seduced them both. Water from the desalination plant on the east coast of the island poured ceaselessly, merrily, from fountains and taps and shower heads. The sea was before them, and behind them the volcanoes, and their gardens were full of the music of running water. At night the sky was bright with the stars that had guided Columbus from La Gomera towards the unknown west.

A man could die even here.

Bennett had said this line when he first saw the house and he was fond of repeating it. Ivor knew it must be a quote, but had never worked out where it came from. He kept forgetting to try to find out. He didn't really want to know.

The house was called La Suerte, Good Fortune, and they kept the name.

Bennett liked to say that you couldn't say the house and its grounds were in bad taste, or vulgar. Anywhere else on earth they would have been monstrously so, but here they weren't even camp. They were part of the fantasy of the landscape. They were ahistoric. They weren't in any kind of taste at all. They were elemental.

Bennett and Ivor were happy there, or for some years they were happy. Bennett was finishing what he said would be his last big book, a merging of cultural history and his later and enjoyably acquired scholarship of art history, and he was well enough to fly back once or twice to see his editor and his publishers and to check references and illustrations and copyright and to give diplomatic and convivial lunches to a colleague or two. The airport was hell, but the flight itself was not too taxing, and the island was in the same time zone as London, so there was no problem with jet lag. And there was Ivor, to make the bookings, to see to the bags, to cajole the women at check-in and to chat up the air stewards about extra leg room for Sir Bennett.

The island, away from the ceaselessly busy airport and the false golden sand of the tourist beaches, had a curious emptiness that was in itself soothing. The silence of noon in the unfrequented colonnaded piazzas of the small inland towns was profound. The green and blue shutters of the houses were perpetually closed, the expensive and extensive new sports grounds eerily deserted, the avenues of palms in stasis. No children played in the immaculate playgrounds. Where had all the children gone? Unnaturally long and hard shadows fell towards the evening, as in a painting by de Chirico.

After Bennett's first slight stroke, travel was not so easy, and Ivor began to feel more apprehensive about the future. But by then they had made friends on the island, Spanish friends as well as ex-pats, and Ivor had a few younger drinking companions whom he would meet in the bars in town. Bennett did not enquire about these relationships. He was well past his jealous years. The shouting matches of the past were over.

They gave parties at the house, good parties. A Nobel Prize-winner, a distinguished and outrageous elderly actor, a few historians and other assorted academics, a notorious bridge player who had once partnered Omar Sharif, a man of the theatre who owned a de Chirico, a handful of Sunday painters – it was a very painterly landscape, though not many had done it justice – and a chorus of locals who specialised in being amusing. Convivial friends, most of them ageing but nevertheless convivial, and a few younger spirits who stuck by Ivor and looked out for him.

People liked Ivor.

When the book was published, to respectful if somewhat subdued acclaim, Ivor began to wonder how Bennett would keep himself busy for the remainder of his life. Ivor was busy looking after Bennett, but Bennett needed occupation. He was accustomed to hard work. He started to talk about possible projects in a way that made Ivor slightly uneasy. For years he had talked about writing a life of General Lyautey. He'd had the idea long ago on their first holiday visit to Morocco, but Ivor had never taken it very seriously, he'd thought of it as an after-dinner *jeu d'esprit*. A provocative notion: a gay biography of a right-wing gay orientalising French general written by a gay left-of-centre English Hispanist historian-turned-art-historian – surely not? But now Bennett had returned to the concept and started to talk about it again. He'd talked about it for a year or two and asked Ivor to order him up some books, but it wasn't easy to get hold of the source material in the Canaries, and Ivor watched his old friend becoming gradually disheartened by his own incompetence, by his lack of grasp and intellectual vigour and attack. It wasn't that his mind was going, but he'd lost his perseverance. ('I've lost my alacrity', he would sometimes say, mournfully, when down in the dumps.)

He would never get to grips with the gay general. The subject was beyond him, too big for him, and too distant. He would never be able to give a proper account of his own attraction-revulsion relationship with the swashbuckling sabre-rattling French and Spanish in Morocco, and their aesthetic cults of violence and beheadings. The Foreign Legion and *Beau Geste* were beyond his narrative reach. (Bennett had loved *Beau Geste* when he was a schoolboy, but Ivor had never read it.) He'd never be well enough to go to Morocco again. Morocco wasn't very far away, just a short hop over the ocean, as the Berbers and the Mauritanians had found it, but it was a short hop too far for Bennett. They could go by boat, perhaps, Ivor wondered? There were passenger ferries, there were cruises. That's what old people do these days, they go on cruises. Ivor tried to work out the possibilities, but he wasn't happy about the Lyautey dream. Neither, he could tell, was Bennett.

Lyautey was famous, or infamous, for his passions for the handsome young soldiers under his command. Had Bennett wanted to whitewash him, to justify him? Ivor didn't even know, as the project hadn't got that far.

They'd been to look at his tomb in the Invalides in Paris: a pompous manly erection, where his ashes had been reinterred in 1961. De Gaulle had given a speech on the occasion. Bennett was interested in military and military-style monuments. Unamuno, Lyautey, the tomb of Franco in the extraordinary Valle de los Caídos.

They don't erect statues to historians. Or not very often.

Ivor didn't like to watch Bennett becoming a disappointed

old man, fearing oblivion. He deserved better than that, and Ivor deserved better than that.

Bennett, Ivor knew, had felt professionally discomfited by developments in Spanish historiography, by archaeological revelations on the Spanish mainland. The recent laws on Historical Memory, on the right to excavate the mass graves and the cemeteries and the battlefields of the past, had provided an excess of new material which he would never be able to assimilate. He had gallantly welcomed the new openness, but it had made him feel lamentably out of date. A whole new generation of historians, writing both in Spanish and English, had taken over the much-disputed and still embittered field. His work wasn't rejected or derided, it was still cited, but it was being steadily supplanted.

Somebody was even writing a book about why, allegedly, the Spanish Civil War had attracted the attention and indeed participation of so many English homosexuals. An exploration of the A. E. Housman syndrome, of the beauty of doomed youth. Bennett had refused to be interviewed for it, and Stephen Spender had (just) pre-empted an interrogation by death. He'd lived to a good age, had Stephen. (Bennett could do some wicked parodies of Housman; his party piece was Hugh Kingsmill's 'What, still alive at twenty-two, A clean, upstanding chap like you?')

The next project Bennett dreamed up, after the waning of the Lyautey dream, was more manageable, more within his reach, and Ivor encouraged it, with a sense that it would fill the time pleasantly, even though the book would never be written. It would give their excursions an illusion of purpose, and Bennett loved to have a purpose.

Bennett had decided to write a short, scholarly but popular history of the Canaries. There was surprisingly little in English or even in Spanish about this volcanic group of small islands sitting in the Atlantic, not far off the North African shore: a mirror image of the Galapagos, which they had visited in the days before it was considered an ecological crime to go there. The Canaries, the Isles of the Blessed. The history of the islands was short and at the same time mysterious. Bennett believed, or pretended to believe, that the millions (yes, literally millions) of English-speaking visitors who poured in and out each year would welcome some reading matter more stimulating than the tedious selection of magazines and mass-market English and German paperbacks available in the mini-markets. There were some guidebooks on sale, but they were very basic. There were one or two little books on Canarian food and on Canarian flora and on the history of the indigenous and intriguing Guanches of Tenerife, but they consisted more of captioned pictures than of text. The best guides written in English were by an intrepid British walker, who advised on climbing volcanoes, crossing dunes and *barrancos* and lava pans, finding *casitas* and goat tracks and avoiding dogs, but even he didn't offer much historical information. Bennett thought he could fill a gap.

The Canaries were now a peaceful backwater. Their peoples weren't obsessed, as so many on the mainland still were, by tales of revenge and violent death, by family vendettas, by the executions and defenestrations of yesteryear. They weren't even very interested in independence, although you could occasionally spot graffiti demanding 'Españoles Fuera' or 'Viva Canarias Libre' or 'Canarias no es España'. There had been betrayals and dispossessions, but they had been small in scale. The Canaries did not swim with spilt blood. Their dried mummies were very ancient and very dry.

Bennett has accumulated a pile of cuttings and jottings, but he hasn't yet got much further than typing out a beautiful epigraph from his fellow historian Gibbon, who had never visited the islands, though he had written feelingly about them in an essay entitled 'On the Position of the Meridional Line':

A remote and hospitable land has often been praised above its merits by the gratitude of storm-beaten mariners. But the real scene of the Canaries affords, like the rest of the world, a mixture of good and evil, nay even of indigenous ills and foreign improvements. Yet, in sober truth, the small islands of the Atlantic and Pacific oceans may be esteemed as some of the most agreeable spots on the globe. The sky is serene, the air is pure and salubrious: the meridian heat of the sun is tempered by the sea-breeze: the groves and vallies, at least in the Canaries, are enlivened by the melody of their *native* birds, and a new climate may be found, at every step, from the shore to the summit, of a mountainous ascent.

Gibbon made the islands sound very agreeable, as indeed they are, but Ivor suspected that very few tourists would be at all interested in purchasing a history of them. They were not great readers, the visitors. They preferred sunbathing and football on pub TV. They would not care about Plato and Plutarch and Atlantis and King Juba II and Juba's physician Euphorbius, after whom the ubiquitous and various Canarian plant was named. (King Juba had married, according to Bennett, the daughter of Antony and Cleopatra, which to Ivor seemed surprising and unlikely: what kind of woman could she have been, this Roman-Egyptian queen, which parent did she favour, what kind of colour was she?) The surfboarders from Norway and Uruguay would not wish to learn about the Roman general Sertorius, ally of Marius and Cinna and adversary of the bloody Sulla, who had attempted to set up a Utopian colony on Tenerife. They would be even less interested in William

Wordsworth, who had once planned to write an epic poem about Sertorius and the small, peaceful, dwindling band of his followers who had hung on in the islands until the Norman invasion. They would not want to read about the disputed ethnic origins of the doomed (but genetically surviving) Guanches, or to speculate about how they had got there in the first place. They would not share Bennett's curious fixation with the fact that by the Middle Ages the inhabitants of the seven islands had lost the art of navigation.

They must have had ships once, or they couldn't have got there, could they?

(Unless, suggested Ivor, they had been dumped: and it turned out that this was indeed one more than plausible historical hypothesis. Ivor wasn't very well educated but he was good at lateral thinking.)

Ivor could see that it was rather odd that when the Portuguese and the Normans and the Genoese rediscovered the Canaries in the fourteenth century, they encountered separate populations on each of the seven islands, all speaking different languages, and with no means of getting from one island to another, even though some of them could see their neighbours and wave to them, if they felt like it, over the water. As in the Galapagos, evolution had taken its own course.

The seven islands: El Hierro, La Gomera, Gran Canaria, La Palma, Tenerife, Lanzarote, Fuerteventura – separated both by water and by language.

Bennett seemed gripped by what Ivor considered a childish or perhaps senile fascination with this aspect of island history. It was his King Charles's Head. It had replaced the gay Lyautey as an obsession. It was, Ivor thought, connected with his pleasurable memories of swimming. Bennett had, until very recently, been a keen swimmer, ever eager to leap into any tempting stretch of water. Ivor, who was not so keen on the indignities and discomforts of getting wet, had watched his friend practising his slow and stately breaststroke in the Mediterranean and the Caribbean and the Pacific, in the Red Sea and the Black Sea and the North Sea, in the Danube and the Rhine and the Rhône, in the Thames and the Barle and the Windrush. He had seen him ploughing up and down the homoerotic blue lengths of hotel swimming pools in Los Angeles and Toronto and Melbourne and Rio de Janeiro. He had seen him jump into green and murky shallow ponds in the English counties and into unlikely and deeply anti-erotic algae-covered waterholes in the Midwest. Bennett still enjoyed their well-maintained turquoise pool at La Suerte, although he was less eager these days to attempt even the milder island bays of the Atlantic. He'd lost his footing and been knocked down by a wave on the curving beach at the little fishing port of Arrieta late one morning and that had put him off swimming in the sea.

But Bennett remained fascinated by the fact that the indigenous Canarians, in the Middle Ages, didn't build boats and didn't swim and didn't trade from island to island and didn't speak a common language. In Ivor's view, he was excessively fascinated by this. Ivor didn't think of himself as an intellectual, but he did wonder in a Freudian kind of way *why* Bennett found this *so* interesting.

It *was* interesting, of course, and the handsome lads from Senegal who propositioned tourist ladies to buy handbags these days, were, physically, very attractive.

God knows how they got here, but they did.

The survival of the fittest.

These days, would-be immigrants from the mainland of Africa were frequently wrecked off the eastern shores of the islands. Young men, young women, children. The chancers. Some drowned; some made it to the detention centres; some survived to sell excellent fake handbags, until they were moved on or deported. One of them, one fortunate one plucked from the thousands, had been taken under the wing of a friend of theirs, the friend with the de Chirico, the friend with a chequered past and an eye for art, and he lived with him in comparative splendour in his rocky sardine fortress on the neighbouring island of Fuerteventura.

Most of the twentieth- and twenty-first-century immigrants could not swim. They trusted themselves to the leaking vessels, but had never learned to swim. Bennett was unduly fascinated by this.

Ivor was finding it hard to work out whether or not Bennett was, to put it bluntly, losing his wits.

Bennett's reaction to the news of Sara Sidiqi's sudden and at first inexplicable death had been very odd. He hadn't seemed to take it in at all, or not in any way that we would now call 'appropriate'. He didn't want to know about it. The subject of her death was not at first admitted as part of his conversational range. Yet, earlier, he'd appeared to follow in detail the whole complicated story about the Western Saharan protest at the airport, had spoken to the press about it, had signed the letter to *El País*, had seemed quite chuffed to be summoned to appear on one of the local TV stations with their Nobel Prize friend to talk about the hunger strike and Sahrawi nationalism. He'd been more than happy to give his views on Namarome to Sara, and to invoke the name of his late acquaintance, the novelist and useful public intellectual José Saramago. Saramago would certainly have stood up for independence of the Western Sahara.

And Bennett had really taken to Christopher Stubbs.

Ivor had been taken with Christopher too. He had seen some kind of gleam of hope, of escape, of unexpected support, or at least of temporary relief, in Christopher Stubbs, and that was why he was sitting on the balcony of the bar waiting, on his way to drive to greet him on his return.

They'd met, the four of them, only once or twice, in Sara and Christopher's short and dramatically curtailed stay on the island: Christopher had been given Bennett's name as a useful contact by a college friend he knew in the Foreign Office, and when Christopher rang La Suerte, it was of course Ivor who picked up the phone. (Bennett wasn't deaf, but he liked to pretend he was, and, although garrulous in person, he hated the phone.) Hospitable drinks at the magical black-and-white volcanic house had followed, and some briefing of Sara on local politics by Bennett, on local facilities and personalities by Ivor. They had all got on well: Ivor and Bennett were pleased with the influx of new young blood. They were cheered by the apparition of two handsome and healthy young people still in mid-career, still working, not yet tottering on the verge of retirement. They were impressed by Sara's even younger research team and her Libyan cameraman. They were all staying in comfort at the big César Manrique-styled hotel in Costa Teguise.

The foursome had spent Sara's last evening together, the evening before she was taken ill. They'd had dinner, at Bennett's recommendation, in the last old-fashioned fish restaurant right down by the almost abandoned rusting old port, a far cry from the developed strand and promenade of the new resort. Las Caletas still preserved an unfashionable dark Spanish wooden gloom, with plastic-sealed wooden-framed salt-stained casement windows jutting out and overlooking the waves. It had a history. It had seen the boats sail out.

It served, amongst other marine delicacies, limpets. They were plucked, living, straight from the public rocks of the cove below. Sara had never eaten limpets. They were horrible, warned Ivor, tough and leathery like whelks, *worse* than whelks, but she had wanted to order them, for fun: they looked so like little volcanoes, she pointed out, little ridged volcanoes, they echoed the strange conical shapes of the landscape, she had to try them.

She'd never seen them on a menu before, she'd never have another chance.

Ivor was to wish that he hadn't remembered that she had said that.

Sara was a confident quick-witted young woman, in the prime of life, full of vitality, with a handsomely curved strong fleshly nose and a wide clear brown brow and well-defined, well-arched eyebrows and long lashes and richly springing black hair tied back with a yellow scarf. She wore a décolleté heart-scooped white T-shirt.

She had been much amused by the louchely infantile hand-painted ceramic gender signs on the wooden slatted doors of the restaurant's primitive Servicios: a cherubic little boy standing and pissing into a chamber pot decorated with dolphins, the handsome back and bare bum of a woman with her skirts hoisted over a floral bucket. She'd photographed the signs, discreetly, on her mobile.

Christopher, after a bottle of wine, had talked a little (but not too much) about his own career. He had made a name for himself as a presenter and co-producer of an arts programme, but had fallen out with his company and his employers and was looking for another niche. He said he was in the process of setting up his own production company. Ivor claimed to have seen him on screen, but Christopher thought Ivor was being polite.

Ivor wasn't sure whether he was being polite or not. Christopher did look and sound familiar, with his boldly balding bronzed head, his heavily framed tinted glasses (which he kept on throughout the darkened meal), his expensively coarse-fibred red-and-yellow striped-and-blocked shirt, his confident yes-it's-me manner and his cultivated East London (or possibly Essex?) proletarian accent. He looked like somebody one might well recognise. But so did so many people.

Bennett took to Christopher, regardless of whether Christopher would be of any use to them or not. He found him amusing. He egged him on to talk about television rivalries and programmes about Francis Bacon and David Hockney and William Tillyer and Joe Tilson (it seemed Christopher as a programmer and presenter had favoured the visual arts), and volunteered, though without any attempt to expand vaingloriously on the detail, that he had known some of these people. 'Your shirt's a bit Joe Tilson', he interjected at one point, a remark which delighted Christopher. Christopher in turn was more than willing to cede to Sir Bennett's authority and seniority, to demonstrate that he knew his work and had even read some of it. He made gracious enquiring allusions to Goya and Lorca and Unamuno and Picasso and Tàpies, while confessing a little disingenuously that Spain was not his thing.

Ivor was pleased by these interchanges. It always pleased him when Bennett received fitting and ego-calming recognition. And he was relieved that Bennett seemed to be responding 'appropriately' (that odd word again, so often these days in his thoughts) to Christopher's anecdotes.

Old age veers towards the inappropriate.

Bennett, on form as he was that night, was very amusing. He was a good mimic (his Hockney was excellent, though Hockney was a soft target) and he made them all laugh.

And to Sara, Bennett also responded well. He liked her style, Ivor could see. He was on the ball and gallant and eager to be helpful. He suggested locations, he spoke (but not too much) about his little project for an islands history. He recommended the monumental Museo del Emigrante, which told the other side of the emigration-immigration story, and he found she already knew about that, though she hadn't yet had time to go there. She should try to get to Tenerife and La Laguna, she should see the mysterious pyramids praised by Thor Heyerdahl, and she must certainly go across to Fuerteventura – less than half an hour on the ferry, amazing to think that the indigenous peoples over so many centuries had never built a boat. She ought to see the cemetery at Gran Tarajal on Fuerteventura, described by its mayor as the graveyard of Africa. Not on the tourist route, obviously, but well worth a visit from your point of view, said Bennett.

A memorable location, and on television its silent dead would speak.

Ivor was sometimes surprised by what Bennett remembered. He was sure he would have forgotten their visit to the dull and quiet little town of Gran Tarajal, with its walled cemetery on the hillside and the plain marble plaques recording the nameless dead. It was some years ago now, and Bennett still remembers.

DEP Immigrante 12.12.2001
DEP Immigrante 11.7.2002
DEP Immigrante 6.7.2002

Ivor wonders how many more deaths will by now have been recorded and added to the roll call that they saw.

Descanse en Paz.
Rest in Peace

Ivor found that phrase deeply touching. Sometimes he longed to rest in peace, and reflected, not without bitterness, that he wouldn't have merited much more than these nameless ones by way of an inscription of his exploits.

He saw all the nameless dead as handsome young Senegalese and Mauritanians.

Who, he wondered, would deck Ivor's monument with little vases of weatherproof, unnatural artificial dark orange and purple roses? Who would push Uncle Ivor's wheelchair when the time came? Who would write his obituary?

Christopher and Ivor and Bennett had discovered, as they gossiped in Las Caletas, that they had an acquaintance in common, a friend less bland and more surprising than the man in the Foreign Office who had originally suggested Bennett as a contact. The name of Simon Aguilera had once been notorious and was still newsworthy, although he had long ago taken refuge in peaceful unadventurous Fuerteventura, in flight from the publicity and hostility that had pursued him ever since the scandal that had undone him, and in search, like Bennett, of a calm dry climate.

In search of redemption and eternal peace.

Son of a once-admired Spanish Republican émigré intellectual, the precocious and many-gifted Aguilera had made his name very young in the avant-garde theatre in Paris in the 1960s, an *enfant terrible*, and had seemed set for every kind of success. But he had been undermined by the creeping revisionism that had slowly destroyed his father's reputation (what exactly had happened, and to whom, and at whose prompting, in 1936 in Alicante?) and then had undone himself utterly by killing his wife. It had been an international cause célèbre. He'd got off lightly because the French are soft on *crimes passionnels*, or so the British press had been pleased to comment.

But he had killed her, for all that. With an axe.

Knowing a murderer was a bond, more of a bond than being acquainted with a middle-ranking diplomat from a minor public school.

Christopher had met Simon Aguilera in London at a show of Contemporary Italian Art at Christie's, where they had fallen into conversation before a de Chirico that Simon was intending to buy. Simon had recognised Christopher from his TV show (always flattering) and they had adjourned to a nearby fish restaurant for one of those lunches that prolong themselves, over the second bottle, into the afternoon. They had told each other much, and forgotten most of what they had told. Only the flavour of the conversation remained, along with the flavour of the oysters and the turbot poached in Pernod. This had been before the days of Sara, and they had not kept closely in touch since then, although they had exchanged an occasional message about auction prices and false attributions in sales rooms.

Christopher had not mentioned him to Sara before this visit. He had felt uneasy about the murdered wife.

But the three of them had spoken well of Simon Aguilera and his exploits, at Las Caletas, over the bite-resistant rubbery garlic-reinforced limpets. ('Quite like snails,' Sara had commented, 'but not as nice.') Sara had listened with interest, without an air of judgment. Simon had recently adopted a Senegalese immigrant, Sara should go and speak to him, he's very photogenic, said Bennett with his louche old-world chuckle.

But Sara hadn't had time to go across the narrow strait to Fuerteventura. She'd intended to go there, she'd had a contact in the Red Cross at Puerto del Rosario, who was eager to speak to her about the protection of immigrant minors. She'd done her research. It's a pity it will all have been wasted.

~

Ivor Walters sits on the balcony in the evening sun, waiting for Christopher, who is flying back from London to Arrecife even now. He will be here in an hour or so. The chartered planes are in a perpetual peaceful descending and ascending convoy, bringing hither and taking hence. In one of these Christopher would soon be listening to the landing instructions. In five minutes, Ivor will rejoin his car and drive to the airport to meet him, to collect him and take him back to La Suerte and Bennett and an evening meal.

Distances are small and manageable on the island. It's easy to time journeys to the airport.

When Christopher disembarks, he will no longer see the woman from the Western Sahara sitting on her carpet in the departure lounge, for she has been transferred to a hospital on the Spanish mainland, and is recuperating, to fight again another day. Her vigil, at least for now, is over. They will be pumping liquids into her, reviving her.

Ivor wonders what will happen to Sara's prestige project. It will probably never be made. It will die with Sara. The Libyan cameraman had managed to record Sara briefly interviewing Namarome, but would that sequence ever reach mainstream television? Now Sara was gone, nobody in the English-speaking world apart from a few Arabists and human rights professionals would be interested in it or try to push it through. There was one Labour MP in an outer London constituency who bangs on about it, but nobody takes him very seriously. It will be stored, as everything these days is stored, in case history changes its mind, but it won't reach out. Even if Namarome dies, it won't reach out. It would take more than one death in the Western Sahara to interest the Western media, when so much of the rest of North Africa, further to the east, is brewing up a different and worse kind of turmoil. The Western Sahara is a dull and empty quarter, when you compare it with Libya, Syria, Iraq, Iran or Egypt, which are in the process of fomenting greater and greater cataclysms and atrocities and migrations on a scale that will make the Canarian voyages seem tame and domestic. These new waves of migration will obsess the media and ruin and rescue lives for years, perhaps decades, perhaps a century to come. Images of flight and desperation comparable to and perhaps in time exceeding those of the Second World

War will fill our screens, but Sara is dead and will never see them, although perhaps Ivor and Christopher sense the dark flood that approaches.

Immigrants arriving by boat to the Canaries from Africa will remain a story, with a tourist perspective, but the British are very wary of it. They will be more concerned with the siege of Calais, with the Syrians at the gate, with babies drowned on the shores of the isles of Greece.

But for now, in the present, Ivor is looking forward, perhaps too much and unwisely, to seeing Christopher Stubbs again and to renewing their acquaintance. Christopher is going to stay with them at La Suerte, while he sorts out the health insurance difficulties and winds up one or two other matters to do with car rentals and local suppliers left unresolved on their sudden departure. Ivor and Bennett have offered hospitality and succour and Christopher had been surprisingly keen to accept them. Ivor had wondered if the island would hold too bad a memory for him, but he seemed to have had a very different reaction to the prospect of his return. He wanted to revisit, to expunge or exorcise.

Maybe Christopher's relationship with Sara had not been all that it seemed. Ivor had caught a glance or two, even in the surreptitiously smoky murk of Las Caletas. Maybe Sara had been a bit too much of a challenge.

Christopher has an ex-wife somewhere, and children. His relationship with Sara had not been unencumbered.

It is true, as Ivor had encouragingly and truthfully pointed out to Christopher in various friendly emails, that life on Lanzarote was, in most ways, astonishingly stress-free. Good weather, good roads, reasonable food, as yet reasonably stable euros, great calm. No politics, no beggars, nothing of extremity. Nothing much going on at all, really. It was a good place to recuperate from emotional shock.

A man could die even here.

Sara had nearly died here, but she had gone home to die.

Ivor wonders whether he also will go home to die. Who will push Uncle Ivor's wheelchair?

Christopher, Ivor fancied or fantasised, had responded to Ivor's friendliness in a friendly way.

Ivor can tell that Bennett too is pleased at the prospect of having someone new and so much younger to talk to for a few days. He had been speaking with some excitement about the things he was going to show Christopher, the people he'd like him to meet, as though unaware that their guest might not be in sightseeing or party mood.

Bennett is bored with Ivor's unfailingly reliable, dutiful and high-minded devotion, and with the geriatric round of occasionally peevish neighbours that composes most of their social life. Sometimes he breaks out in an ominous burst of anger against Ivor, shouting that he hadn't meant to spend his whole life stuck with him, that he didn't want to die at the mercy of someone who'd been battening on him for fifty years.

Feeble, volcanic old man's eruptions, followed by the great cool spent peace of the wide evening sky.

Ivor sometimes thinks he feels the spirit of the Lord watching over him on this island. It's probably a trick of the light, or of the landscape. He has started, secretly, to visit the plain silent unfrequented little white chapel on the hillside, where he kneels down and prays. His prayers don't have any words. No one is ever there, but the chapel is never locked.

Bennett, the old-style rationalist-atheist-humanist intellectual, wouldn't approve of that at all. Ivor doesn't really know why he's doing it, but it is a solace. It takes him into another dimension of living and dying, it uplifts him. It may be a false solace, but there's more truth in it than in the endless discussions about doctors, diets, symptoms and medications, about dwindling royalties and bad reviews by old enemies, about the menace of e-books and the demise of booksellers and the new historiography.

Ivor had once tried to read Unamuno's most famous work, *The Tragic Sense of Life*, attracted to it by its title, but had found it to be incomprehensible gibberish. He's not clever enough to know whether this is because it is incomprehensible gibberish or whether it's because he, Ivor Walters, is too ill-educated and too stupid to understand it. There had been a time, there had been a solid stretch of some years of time, when he would have been able to cross-question Bennett in some depth about these distinctions, and have enjoyed discussing them, but that time has now passed. Ivor has resigned himself to the once inadmissible knowledge that living most of his life with a man so much cleverer, so much better educated than himself has not been easy, and may not have been good for his character and his immortal soul.

It must have been pretty annoying for Bennett, too, at times.

The elderly Unamuno had survived his short exile in Fuerteventura, and had returned to Spain. But a decade or so later he had come to a sad end. Although something of a Nationalist fellow traveller, according to Bennett, he had been compelled to speak out against Franco and was driven out of his own University of Salamanca at gunpoint by a Fascist general shouting, 'Death to intelligence! And long live Death! Viva la Muerte¡'

Franco's wife had given the old man her arm, as he left the Ceremonial Hall, but whether in support or derision is still disputed. Some issues are never settled, in Spain.

When Unamuno went to his club that evening, his friends turned on him and called him a traitor. He had a heart attack, and died a week or so later.

Bennett had sometimes fancied he had been getting a bit of

the cold shoulder at his London club, but nothing on this scale. Nobody had ever shouted at him, or pointed a gun at him. But he had thought he could hear them laughing at him.

Ivor waits for Christopher.

~

Christopher, when the plane lands, switches on his mobile while waiting for the seat belt sign to be turned off, in case there is a message or an update on arrangements from Ivor. Ivor had seemed to him from their brief acquaintance to be very dependable, if something of a worrier, maybe very dependable because something of a worrier, and Christopher is certain he will be there at Arrivals, waiting.

There isn't anything from Ivor, but there is a text from his mother Fran. HOPE ALL WELL AM ON WAY HOME FROM WEST BROM FX. Like most of Fran's messages, this seems superfluous and irrelevant, and yet he does find it comforting, as he is no doubt meant to do. It's nice that she thinks about him. He assumes that she thinks about him more than he thinks about her, because that is the way of things. He is fond of his mother, though increasingly puzzled by her. She hasn't been a very *useful* mother of late. When he and his sister were little, she was there because she had to be, but she'd been fairly hopeless and absent and inattentive as a granny, and hadn't really got on with his wife Ella, because she'd never tried hard enough to get to know her. And although she had seemed proud enough of his TV career, she wasn't very interested in it. Once, she even admitted, not wholly as a joke, that she hated arts and culture programmes. Arts and Culture, she had said, what words, what words! And now she seemed unable to settle down to being elderly, she was forever on the move, as though in perpetual flight, in a restless panic. She'd sold the lease of the nice 1920s flat in leafy Highgate where she'd lived comfortably with that nice Hamish, and moved to a tower block. Why on earth had she done that? At her age?

It was none of his business, she could look after herself, and if she killed herself on the motorway, that was her choice.

He hopes she doesn't kill anyone else, or find herself convicted of drunken driving. That would be embarrassing. She is a drinker, but he thinks she doesn't drink at the wheel. She didn't when they were children, although of course she didn't drive much then as Claude monopolised the car, but she did drink on the premises when they were in bed. She used to shout and scream too, all by herself downstairs there in Romley. It had been frightening, but not very frightening. He wonders if she still screams to herself, or whether she's got over all of that. She used to yell *I want I want I want*, or *Can nobody help me, can nobody help me*, but he and his little sister Poppet had never let on that they could hear her. They stayed upstairs, out of harm's way.

Fran's Cantor Hill tower block with its dank and stalling lifts and its dangerous basement garage was a stupid idea, but Bennett and Ivor had seemed, in contrast, to have found the perfect retirement home. On the level slopes, in the warmth of the day and in the shade of the evening. He thinks of it with a curious kind of longing, as though it offers even to him, to a bereft stranger, some kind of peace. An image of peace.

His father Claude was also a drinker, although he has to take it a bit easy now. Claude is surprisingly keen to stay alive, and is a surprisingly good patient, stuck up there in his Kensington apartment with his fat cat Cyrus, attended upon intermittently by his energetic first wife and daily by the glamorous Persephone. After a self-destructive trajectory, he seemed to have discovered a secret source of resilience, a late-flowering will to live.

Christopher is a drinker himself, a committed and semi-secret drinker. He's got a large brutally oblong plastic bottle of airport vodka concealed in his baggage, as he doesn't trust his hosts to supply enough or indeed any hard liquor. They are wine drinkers, he suspects, not serious drinkers.

~

So, a couple of hours later, previously primed in the privacy of his spacious terracotta-tiled white-walled emerald-green-shuttered bedroom, Christopher sits on the terrace with Bennett and Ivor overlooking the many paved levels of the cactus and euphorbia garden of La Suerte. He can sip slowly and calmly and moderately at his cool Spanish wine. He doesn't need to gulp. As Bennett sets himself out to be entertaining, Ivor, watchful, proffers from time to time soft little denture-friendly smoked salmon and cream cheese squares, ready to intervene if Bennett seems to be straying into unsuitable territory. Fortunately, Bennett does now seem to be aware that Christopher is here for a solemn purpose, and he does not make irrelevant jokes or irreverent allusions. He chatters pleasantly on, about Omar Sharif and José Saramago and the King of Spain's daughter, about Chatto and Windus and Thames and Hudson, about the hot craters of Timanfaya and the salt pans of Janubio, about the local skills in viniculture, about Columbus and the Von Humboldt brothers, about Iris Murdoch and César Manrique, about the reclusive but seductive Simon Aguilera.

The night sky seems, to the slightly drunken Christopher, to be unusually bright and star-studded and vast. There is no wind, but the palm trees of the garden's eastern slope seem to be managing a very slight sway and rattle.

Otherwise the flat peace of the still air is terminal. But pleasantly, soothingly so.

It is better here than at that clinic in Switzerland.

Sara had struggled horribly, until knocked out by morphine. On the plane home, stuck full of unsightly and alarming tubes, she had slipped into a coma from which she had never fully emerged. That was another way of ending. It had the merit of being short. It had seemed long, to Christopher, but he knew it had been short. The flight had been a nightmare beyond all imaginings of death. That had been the worst, and the worst was over.

Indoors, an hour later, over seafood risotto and tomato salad, Ivor feels safe enough to enquire about the likely fate of Sara's project. As he had suspected, Christopher thinks it will almost certainly be shelved by the parent company. She had been the driving force behind it, and without her energy and charm there is nobody to push it through. Money has been lost, and nobody wants to throw good money after bad. You can only run so far with an international human rights story, a black immigrant story. And Namarome has given up her hunger strike, she isn't going to provide the media with a martyr.

Ivor can tell that Christopher's professional eyes and ears are turning towards the possibilities of different lines of Lanzarotean drama, set in this temptingly warm, scenic and sculptured land. He has been seduced, as his hosts had been some years ago, by this blessed abandoned dwelling place. A keen, an almost professional observer of other people's behaviour, Ivor guesses that his new friend, even in the throes of alleged grief, cannot prevent himself from dreaming up new ideas to pitch at commissioning committees. What is he planning? A documentary about the strange life and ironically tragic death-on-the-roundabout of artist César Manrique, about whom he has asked several questions? A satirical portrait of the island as a sunset refuge for the émigré elderly? Perhaps he could be persuaded to make a biopic about Sir Bennett Carpenter, the white-haired Grand Old Man of Anglo-Spanish letters? Bennett would love that, and could probably cope adequately with the attention. They could rope in the more picturesque of their neighbours to dress the set.

Or perhaps a film about civil partnership? A film about the surviving younger partners of ageing or deceased homosexuals? A film about this ludicrous new concept of gay marriage?

We are a dying breed, reflects Ivor. The very thought of us is old-fashioned.

It's a pity Christopher probably won't stay long enough to see this year's Mardi Gras carnival, with its bizarre and extreme gaieties. Drag queens tottering on lofty platform shoes with eighteen-inch heels, wearing tinsel headdresses three feet high, and jewelled brassieres, and ostrich feathers. Fuchsia, lilac, orange, turquoise, silver, emerald-green. As a sixteen-year-old, pre-Bennett, Ivor in closet secrecy had liked to apply a little very pale pink lipstick, a seaside summer lipstick, to his handsomely curved Adonis-Antinous lips. But he hadn't developed that aspect of his personality. Bennett had saved him, captured him, imprisoned him.

Over the last few years he and Bennett had enjoyed watching the gala in its extensive live coverage on the many island channels of local TV. It was too tiring these days to go in person, the roads were too crowded with spectators, one might slip and fall. The shows were amazingly bold and amateur. One of the young men at the big event in Gran Canaria had fallen off his platform shoes and off the platform itself, into the crowd, all captured live on camera, to the drunken amusement of the spectators. Bennett had been a wee bit worried. He hoped the poor boy hadn't injured himself. 'His *poor* mother, I do hope she wasn't watching!' he had said. This had been one of his catchphrases, over the years, dating from a moment of high drama at a 1970s party in Notting Hill Gate.

Ivor refills Christopher's glass, attentively but not over-attentively. Christopher has started to drink faster and faster as the meal progresses, and worldly-wise Ivor can see, as through an airport scanner, the shape of the plastic vodka bottle lying in wait for him, concealed in his suitcase. He knows Christopher will be wanting to get back to it soon.

Ivor and Bennett have never been heavy drinkers, but they have known some in their time. Bennett is old enough to remember Francis Bacon and Denis Wirth-Miller, the Wild Man of Wivenhoe.

Denis Wirth-Miller, to Bennett's astonishment, had married his lifelong lover Dicky Chopping in a civil partnership when they were both in their nineties. Bennett had found this unseemly and grotesque. The old scarecrows, the old death's heads, the old skeletons, he had loudly protested.

Tomorrow, Ivor and Bennett will take Christopher out to dinner in the restaurant at Nazaret. The food's not up to much, but the building is theatrical. Bennett and Ivor like its many corridors and catacombs and its lamp-lit caverns cut deep into an old quarry in the hillside, although Bennett is too nervous and wobbly these days to explore its steep hinterland.

They'd better not go back to Las Caletas, where Sara ate her first and last limpets. That wouldn't be a good idea.

And, as we have said, it is not a good idea to look too closely at Ivor. He wouldn't like it, and we do not have the right to get too close to him. We have no permitted access to the inwardness of him. We know a lot about him, and we can describe his public behaviour, which is polite, circumspect, considerate. We can describe his public and even some of his more private actions, such as his new found church-going, and the lipstick he tried on as a boy. But we can't get too close. He wouldn't want us to see the dark shadowy violet-grey blotch on the right of his hardly wrinkled forehead, a blotch sitting above his eyebrow. It may or may not be spreading month by month. It is a handsome shadow, it decorates his handsome palely tanned visage, as an artificial beauty patch used to highlight the features of a Regency buck.

We don't want to be privy to Ivor's thoughts about this omen.

Fran Stubbs doesn't mind our looking into her head, indeed she insists that we do so. She's keen on the confessional mode, not necessarily with other people, but with herself. Ivor is not.

~

Josephine Drummond, settled in Athene Grange, prides herself on having made herself comfortable. She has domesticated fear. Like her friend Fran, she observes the varied ways we find of dealing with old age. Like Fran, she takes both a detached and a personal interest in these matters. Their views on what is best differ. They exchange notes on their progress, and on the progress of their friends and neighbours. Josephine supplies Fran with literary allusions and case histories from her residency, and Fran supplies Josephine with sociological anecdotes from the Ashley Combe files and with notes on and from her colleagues.

Josephine, although in excellent health, has met Old Age halfway by moving to Athene Grange, and is determined to make friends with her. *La Vieillesse*, that is what she sometimes calls Old Age, after the title of a terrifying book on the subject by Simone de Beauvoir.

She thinks Fran is crazy to have moved to Tarrant Towers. A Gothic adventure, and surely unwise. It will come to a bad ending, predicts Jo. In her view it was a decision taken in haste, after Hamish's death. She does not voice this view to Fran. She has been to Tarrant Towers a couple of times, and has not liked them much. They are the other extreme. When she thinks of them, those lines on death by one of the Graveyard Poets, she forgets which, come unbidden to her mind:

> In that dread moment, how the frantic soul
> Raves round the walls of her clay tenement.

She doesn't impart these lines to Fran.

Fran, she reflects, as she takes a pause from the small print to drink the last dregs of her cold tea, has bravado. She dresses with bravado. Whereas Jo believes in erring in the direction of discretion and safety. One of the phrases that has upset her since girlhood is 'mutton dressed as lamb', and she avoids this accusation, without much effort, by wearing easily available sombre colours – greys, fawns, ochres, dark blues and many shades of black. Her steel-grey hair is luxuriant and long and she secures it with an enamelled clasp or a bone pin, in an amateur kind of bun. Fran, in contrast, has her short and thinning hair cut regularly and dyed in subtly gradated layers of grey, white, bronze and gold. Jo admires the time and money and effort she puts into this, for she could not be bothered to go so often to a hairdresser, and she does not fancy the rather institutional person that comes fortnightly to Athene Grange. She washes her hair once or twice a week, in the bath, enjoying the feeling of it floating free like weeds in the water. She likes to lie on her back, almost submerged, and run her hands through it as it floats around her, and to tug gently at its roots, taking satisfaction in its continuing abundance. She massages her scalp, vigorously, under the water, and thinks of forests of kelp and of sea anemones.

She lets it dry by itself as she wanders around her apartment. She has got a hairdryer, but she doesn't often bother to use it. 'By itself', that's a curious grammatical construction, she sometimes reflects, as she gives words, as she sometimes does, to the process of drying her hair. The phrase gives her hair a fine independent agency.

Fran Stubbs has taken to wearing garments with many-coloured stripes – T-shirts, jerseys, cardigans, jackets. Jo thinks the stripes daring and wonders if maybe stripes are in fashion.

Fran would be surprised to hear that her stripes are daring. She buys what she likes, and there seem to have been many striped garments on offer over the last year or so. She bought what she saw in the shops. That's her take on fashion.

Josephine may fancy that she looks like a regular grey-haired old lady, but in fact she doesn't, she looks striking and eccentric. She isn't humble enough to look regular. She doesn't look apologetic, although her clothing is sombre. She looks too confident, too indifferent.

This dark late afternoon in February, in her cosy stress-free apartment, Josephine is struggling with the paperwork of her Personal Pension Plan, having temporarily despaired of understanding how to operate her new DVD recorder. Many things are taken care of in her new life, but some problems remain stubbornly her own, and stubbornly resistant to reason. The DVD recorder, for example, offers far too many options and it takes a very long time to do anything at all. It is infuriatingly slow. You switch it on, and for a long time it makes no response, apart from saying HELLO. Is this progress? The not-so-young man who delivered it had given her a quick demonstration, but she had received the impression that he didn't understand it either and was eager to get away before his incompetence was revealed. He had pointed to the Return symbol and the Escape symbol, and told her she'd be needing those two, and then he'd run away. She'd been trying a bit of everything, jabbing at button after button, and had once or twice managed, as it were by chance, to record a programme – an episode of a Scandinavian thriller, a half-hour of *Gardeners' World* – but she could never remember what sequence had produced which result, or indeed any result, and could never confidently repeat an occasional success. And she didn't know how to delete. There must be some way of deleting, but she hadn't yet found it.

She's had an email conversation with her son Nat about its uncontrollable behaviour, but it hadn't got them anywhere. He says he'll come and have a look at it, when he gets back from India or Australia or Sri Lanka or wherever he's got to.

Her Personal Pension Plan offers a different kind of challenge, of a more serious nature, but she can't make head or tail of the wording of it. She has a very small regular academic pension, based on her many years of teaching English Literature, mostly in Adult Education, and she has her state pension, and she also has this private thing, into which she paid some of her savings long ago on the advice of a very boring man called Brian Fuller. Brian Fuller had set up her husband's much larger pension, and had at the same time talked her into taking out a policy of her own. She had a sense that it was losing money, and couldn't understand why she had to go on paying out a percentage of her savings to this man who had in other respects disappeared from her life when her husband died. Once a year he sent her something called a portfolio, but it seemed to go down and down, and anyway, her friends told her, it would only display a notional valuation – it didn't mean what it said, it wasn't worth what it said it was worth, it probably wasn't worth the paper it was written on.

And was it taxed, this hypothetical money, did it count as income, or was tax on it pre-paid or deducted at a distant source by the invisible Brian Fuller? She had no idea.

To be fair to Brian Fuller, he did occasionally express a written willingness to meet her for a consultation, but she could not think of anything she wanted less than to see Brian Fuller again. So she ignored these letters. She did not even file them, she ripped them up and threw them in the bin. She would have paid a great deal of money never to have to see him again.

And, no doubt, was, indeed, over the years, doing just that.

It was no good, she couldn't get to grips with it. She began to shove the papers back into their ancient bulging brown canvas concertina file and heaved a loud and histrionic sigh at the empty room.

Would she be sent to jail for tax evasion? She has a good friend who was sent to jail for assisting a suicide, and is always boasting about it. But tax evasion, or tax stupidity – they can't be thought of as a noble cause.

~

She switches on the television, and waits patiently for it to decide to do something. It should be the six o'clock news, if the TV set graciously allows her to watch it. She is slightly uneasy about falling into the category of women-hopeless-with-money, women-hopeless-with-technology, but only slightly. What the fuck, as Fran might put it, does it matter? She is in several dishonourable categories already, being elderly being the worst of them, and one or two more won't make much difference.

The phone goes, but she can't be bothered to answer it. Her new phone, like her new DVD recorder, is a bloody nuisance. She used to feel neglected when people didn't ring her, but now she is relieved. Silence is preferable to confronting its options. She knows how to ring out on it, and that's good enough.

At six thirty, because it is Thursday, she is going round for a stiff drink with her fellow inmate. It is her week to go to him. Next week he will come to her. They meet at this time of the day on every Thursday except when prevented, as they some-times are, by more compelling invitations. They both consider this a 'civilised' arrangement. They vie with one another to provide yet more and more interesting beverages, a competition that requires little effort and no culinary input. Both are fond of Scotch, and in the last eighteen months they have sampled one or two fine brands, as well as testing themselves on less palatable but equally fortified snifters of bourbon and rye. (The word 'snifter' is occasionally deployed by Owen, because he knows it annoys and amuses Josephine.) Vodka they consider boring, though they occasionally attempt a dry martini. Pernod makes a change, and some of the Italian *aperitivos* are fun. And even vodka can be livened up with tomato juice or consommé and a heavy hand with the condiments. Brandy isn't good at six thirty, although Owen sometimes talks affectionately about a Brandy Alexander, whatever that may be. Last week Josephine, having acquired a bottle of Martini Rosso, had proposed mixing a Manhattan, and that had gone down well. They had discussed, inconclusively, the purchase of some maraschino cherries, in case they ever made another attempt at this retro cocktail.

Owen had also been in the English Literature industry, though on a higher and better paid plane than she, and they like to talk about what they are reading, or about the books they had taught in the past. Josephine also likes to talk about her self-appointed research project, and Owen tolerates her discourse about her very small but (to her) intriguing discoveries. There is an element of forgivable because too-transparent condescension in his attention: he has published several volumes; she, so far over her whole career, only a couple of papers. He once pointed out to her, kindly and not unjustly, that many women have late-flowering careers and pursuits, so it's all right for her to indulge herself comfortably with Victorian and Edwardian literature now, in her old age. He views her research as a hobby, not unlike tapestry.

Josephine also does tapestry.

Owen had been a Cambridge, Downing-bred Leavisite when young, and was still engaged in an arcane self-perpetuating and now inevitably one-sided dispute with the Master about Joseph Conrad and Thomas Hardy, T. F. Powys and John Cowper Powys. (Owen champions Hardy and John Cowper, against Leavis's Conrad and T. F.) Josephine was a graduate of one of the first post-war plate-glass universities, which had exposed her to Marxist interpretations and early dawning glimmers of feminist readings. She is now working on deceased-wife's-sister fiction, a sensational genre and peculiarly fascinating, she assures people, once you get into it. It's much more fun than the fortnightly reading group at Athene Grange, which is too middle-brow for her tastes and favours novels by Elizabeth Taylor and Barbara Pym. She admires *Mrs Palfrey at the Claremont*, but she doesn't need to discuss it, there is nothing in it that she anymore needs to discuss.

She once taught a Taylor novel to her WEA class, in the early 1960s, when nobody else would have thought of teaching Taylor's work. That, in those days, had been a revolutionary act. It wouldn't be now.

Elizabeth Taylor was a member of the Communist Party, but she suspects the members of the Athene Grange reading group don't want to know that. Some of Josephine's family, in the 1930s, had been card-carrying Communists.

Now she explores books with titles like *The Inheritance of Evil* and *The Fatal Kinship* and *Hannah* and *With Feet of Clay*. Sometimes they come to her in the university library with uncut pages and she has to take them back to the desk and ask for them to be cut. The novel she is now reading, she purchased, uncut, very cheaply, in one of Cambridge's few surviving second-hand bookshops.

Josephine had married the older brother of her first and

not-very-serious boyfriend, which she thinks may, perhaps, some fifty years after the event, have led her back to this topic. There had been a bit of sibling skirmishing between the boys when they were students. Josephine had switched her allegiance to Alec from Terry, and Terry had been in her view disproportionately annoyed, the annoyance having been more to do with Alec than with her. She had been a pawn in their game.

She and Terry hadn't been all that bonded, they'd never got beyond the light petting stage, and Terry hadn't become deceased until much later, when he was in his fifties. So the parallels with the deceased-wife's-sister cluster of stories were far from close.

But it's an interesting subject anyway, at least to her, and Jo is happily exploring the reasons why marrying one's Deceased Wife's Sister had been made illegal (having once been, in some interpretations, mandatory) and why it had become such a contentious issue in the mid to late nineteenth century. Whereas marrying one's deceased husband's brother had never seemed much of a problem to anybody. Was there a connection with nineteenth-century attitudes to male and female sexuality and homosexuality? Or was it all to do with money, rather than consanguinity? Or stepchildren and housekeeping and unpaid domestic labour? What did Freud have to say about it, if anything, and had it been an issue in Paris and Vienna? In Edwardian Australia, it had been OK to marry your DWS, but your marriage wouldn't be recognised if you came back to England. Tricky, but handy in a plot, as the lady novelists had found.

In the Bible, as she understands it, a man is obliged, not forbidden, to marry his Deceased Wife's Sister.

She recognises that her field of enquiry is limited and of meagre academic appeal, but it's as good as *The Times* or *The Guardian* crossword. It's an indulgence.

At her age, she thinks she has earned a few indulgences. She agrees with the school of thought of American Professor of Ethics Michael Slote, who argues that in old age we are allowed to adjust our goals and watch daytime TV and play shuffleboard. (Actually, that's not what he argues, but that's how Josephine Drummond chooses to read him, and it's not wholly a travesty of the direction of his more finely nuanced reasoning.)

She's not sure what shuffleboard is, but it conjures up memories of reading Jeremy Bentham on pushpin and poetry. She'd never really know what pushpin was, either.

Occasionally it occurs to her that the nature of her study of DWS fiction retrospectively devalues the whole high literary enterprise, her life's work in pursuit of truth and meaning.

For what had her adult education classes been but a form of knitting for the lonely, an escape for the housebound, a time-filler for the bored? George Eliot, Matthew Arnold, D. H. Lawrence, Joseph Conrad, Samuel Beckett, V. S. Naipaul, Doris Lessing . . . the post-colonial novel, the feminist novel. They kill time. That's what they are good for. And what did Samuel Beckett write about? Killing time. That was his tragic theme.

She and Fran had both hated Beckett when young. They are now approaching him, in old age, warily. They have booked tickets to see a forthcoming production of *Happy Days,* with Maroussia Darling playing Winnie. But, as Fran said to her the other day, I'm bloody glad I got this far without having to know what he was on about. I'm glad I didn't go for it when I was young.

It's a question of actuarial computation, as Slote might have said. Three years of fearing death and seventy years of hardly ever thinking about it is a better deal than Beckett had, who seems to have thought about it all the time.

The timing is all. The readiness is all.

Why did Beckett age so prematurely, why did he spend his

writing life in the contemplation of death? There's time for that later, plenty of time, as Josephine and Fran have found out. You really don't need to do it when you're in your twenties or thirties or forties, as he did.

Something to do with his mother, Fran thinks. Jo thinks it was his low-grade persistent ill health and poor eyesight. He lacked animal spirits. Also, he had a hammer toe, a very inconvenient malformation. Jo has one of those too. It's not much of a bond with the playwright, but it generates a little posthumous fellow feeling.

The TV news comes to a dull dying fall about troubles on the M11 (Josephine does not share her friend's interest in regional news) and she gathers her soft rose-pink and sage-green and old-gold tapestry wools together into her little wicker basket and sets off along the corridor and across the cold dark quad to Owen's.

Sometimes she does Modernist tapestries, but she is now trying to finish a wreath of roses that one of her grandchildren had given her for Christmas. She is doing it out of pious loyalty to twelve-year-old Sasha.

Elizabeth Taylor had written a good novel called *A Wreath of Roses*. She will perhaps re-read it one day. That too had been about ageing, although Jo hadn't recognised that when she read it in her thirties.

~

Owen, this evening, is hoping to astonish her with a bottle of absinthe, and he succeeds.

'Good God,' she exclaims, eyeing the stylish dark-green bottle with admiration, 'wherever did you get that?'

Owen smiles, proudly and modestly, his charming lopsided wary judicious cunning little smile.

'An old student brought it,' he tells her, as he unscrews its top and sniffs at it. 'It's been made legal now, he tells me, but he assures me it's still got a very high alcohol content.'

He pours their generous, but well-judged doses into their twin tumblers, and adds water to the historic potion, drop by drop. Drops of Cambridge tap water fall from a cut-glass decanter. They watch the absinthe vein and cloud and pursue its own mysterious convection currents. The chalky green, the promising deadly foreign odour of aniseed and verveine. The water and the power.

Baudelaire, Rimbaud, Degas and Ernest Hemingway walk into the room and join the *hommage*.

Owen is a small man, a slight small thoughtful active man. A very private person, he prefers talking about books to talking about people. All his relationships seem to have been mediated through literature, which is not uncommon in a university town. The solitary cloistered life of Athene Grange suits him well. His bachelor career – Cambridge, Australia, Canada, Keele, Kent – had been too itinerant to earn him a college sinecure, and such sinecures are more and more rare in the modern world. Those days are over, the days when Lewis Carroll or E. M. Forster or Dadie Rylands or Anne Barton could live in comfort in rooms in their well-endowed colleges, attended by all that should accompany old age: as honour, love, obedience, troops of friends. As wines from the cellar and servants to clean the grate and lay the fire and change the sheets. Athene Grange is a serviceable, affordable, not undignified substitute. And Owen appreciates his well-defined and regulated friendship with this handsome widow, Josephine Drummond, who is no fool, no, not at all a fool.

He watches her, as she revolves the absinthe in her glass, then sips.

'Delicious,' she acknowledges. 'Delicious.'

The strong bittersweet and powerfully adult, yet at the same time childishly liquorice liquor slips rapidly down the gullet, kicks quickly up into the brain. She lets it fire and settle and fire again, like smouldering flame encroaching on paper, a flame that is wondering when to ignite and burst into its flaring colours.

'And how fares Alice Studdert Meade?' he enquires, when enough respect has been paid to the novelty and the hit of the absinthe. 'How are the uncut pages?'

Alice Studdert Meade is her new discovery, a late, possibly the last example of the DWS genre, and she has already shared with Owen her pleasure in reading a volume that nobody has ever leafed through before. He knows about the sensual satisfaction and permitted desecration of tugging the old blunt-edged silver-plated knife through the old thick rough-edged pages, and now she can divulge to him a little more of the plot – not much more, because listening to the recital of the plots of books that other people are reading, as to the stories of films that they have seen, is well known to be very boring. And, when old, one must take care not to bore.

('*An old woman should not give offence*' was an aphorism Fran had discovered, she can't remember where, and had quoted to Josephine over the phone. Josephine rather wished she hadn't. Fran thinks it was from the Italian, but she can't track it back to its source.)

But a sentence or two about Alice Studdert Meade's *The Fatal Kinship* could entertain Owen, and does.

'Vesey has discovered that Olive may be illegitimate. It all hangs on that. One way, disgrace and disinheritance, but the possibility of marriage, if she is illegitimate. The other way, honour and sacrifice and separation – and lots of money for Olive. I can't tell which way it's going to go. I really can't tell whether it's a tragedy or a romance. She's created a real genre confusion. It's clever.'

'One can usually tell which it will turn out to be. Particularly with commercial fiction.'

'Yes, one can. It's an interesting balance. Maybe something extreme will happen. I can't envisage the denouement.'

'So she's clever? She keeps you guessing?'

'Yes, she's clever.'

'And you still haven't found out much more about her?'

'No, she's a virgin field. She must have been born in the 1870s or 1880s. But there aren't any biographical notes, or not in any of the obvious places. Not even in the feminist bibliographies.'

'Wonderful that such a virgin field could still be.'

Owen dwells in and wanders through better trodden fields, but discovers in them clues, scents, fresh spoor, an occasional view downwards through the roots of a hedge bottom or upwards through a spinney.

'Yes, wonderful,' agrees Josephine.

They both fall silent, and sip.

'They do *love* one another, Olive and Vesey,' adds Josephine, and then, quickly, realising she is overstepping her special-interest time limit, she continues, 'And the cloudscape, how goes the cloudscape?'

Owen is studying cloudscapes in Gerard Manley Hopkins and Thomas Hardy and John Cowper Powys. He is writing a paper entitled 'A cloud that's dragonish'. He is in love with this phrase from *Antony and Cleopatra*. And why not, thinks Josephine. He has been waiting to use it all his life. Its time has come.

(And so, perhaps, has Alice Studdert Meade's.)

Owen is Welsh, which is why the word 'dragonish' appeals to him so much, Josephine had once suggested. He hadn't thought of that but concedes it could be so.

Sometimes we see a cloud that's dragonish;
A vapour sometime like a bear or lion,
A towered citadel, or a pendant rock . . .

Owen's reflections are all on a higher plane than the fictions of Alice Studdert Meade.

But the Alice Studdert Meade is a teaser, just the same, and Josephine is as eager to find out what happens next as were the readers of 1907. And that's a tribute to an old text.

Owen doesn't seem very interested in watching clouds in real life, but he pursues them diligently in literature. The February skies of Cambridgeshire are not, perhaps, inspiring. They are low and grey and weigh down on the flat horizon. Josephine's friend Fran sometimes speaks of the large skies she sees from her London tower. She sees dragons, citadels and pendant rocks. She sees apocalyptic sunsets and fiery cities in the sky.

'Ah,' says Owen, in answer to her prompt about his cloud project, 'I found yesterday the most intriguing phrase in Yves Bonnefoy.'

Josephine is not over-familiar with the name of Yves Bonnefoy. He comes after the period she knows and loves best. She hasn't kept up. She knows he is a French poet and essayist, possibly still alive, but that's about all she knows of him. And that's a lot more than most people know.

This doesn't matter, for Owen will tell her, but not at excessive length. He describes to her the book by Bonnefoy that he is now reading, it's called *The Arrière-pays*, it's about horizons and hinterlands and ruins and lost languages. About the never-captured, the half-glimpsed. The view of valleys and mountains from the train through the Alps, the view of the sands from the desert caravan, the view of the mysterious island from the boat's deck. The Isles of the Blessed, surfacing briefly from the waves, and like Atlantis vanishing. The floating island of San Borondon.

'Bonnefoy translated several Shakespeare plays, you know,' says Owen.

The absinthe has pleasantly coloured their communion. Their minds jump and meet on a more intimate level. Owen can see his clouds clearly, and communicates his vision, wordlessly, to Josephine.

At what might seem to be another tangent, but is not, Owen says, 'When I went to see Bennett and Ivor in Lanzarote in December, they took me to see the ruins of a castle, the ruins of the castle of Zonzamas. We don't know who or what Zonzamas was. An old Guanche chieftain, perhaps? There wasn't much to see, just great blocks of stone. Without lime or mortar. Just blocks. It was very suggestive. It could have been medieval, or it could have been a megalithic Stone Age settlement. *'Grands blocs de pierres brutes'* – that's how Berthelot described them. There's a beautiful sketch of them. With goats and a goatherd.'

Sabin Berthelot, Owen very briefly explains, was a French naturalist and amateur ethnographer, resident for many years on the Canaries. Bennett Carpenter had become very interested in his works.

Owen is a library romantic, a dried-up little locust stick of a romantic, but he sometimes ventures out of doors, and his old friend Bennett had lured him all the way to the Canaries to see the ruins and the goats and the sun. Josephine doesn't know Bennett and Ivor, though her husband had been acquainted with Bennett, but she's heard quite a lot (but of course not too much) about them. Sir Bennett Carpenter is one of Owen's more distinguished acquaintances. They had been at the same college, when Owen was an undergraduate and learning to be a Leavisite, and Bennett was a junior lecturer in Modern History, embarking on his ground-breaking studies of the Spanish Civil War. They had been good friends in their Cambridge days, and subsequently their paths had crossed in other parts of the world, in far-flung universities. They had kept in touch. They had a history together, and a continuation.

Josephine has been intending to read Bennett's first and most famous book, *The Reaper and the Wheat*, having been encouraged to borrow a copy from Owen, and hopes Owen won't this evening ask her how she's getting on with it, because she has hardly even opened it. Owen hadn't thrust the copy upon her, but he had talked about Bennett and Ivor a lot in an unusually excited way on his return from the Canaries, and she had listened with interest, intrigued by his descriptions of the couple's ex-pat warm-climate way of solving old age and the care-home problem. She had even got round to worrying by proxy about what the young but not-so-young Ivor's eventual fate would be when Bennett died. She had conjured up a vivid picture of their dramatic black tufa and whitewash volcanic home of caves and bubbles, of the scarlet and pink and olive grey and lime green and acid yellow spears of their euphorbia garden. Owen isn't of the generation that photographs everything it sees, but he had given her a good verbal description of La Suerte.

The earth hath bubbles, as the water has . . .

Words, words, she lives in words. And so does Owen.

She wonders now if Owen is going to feel prompted to mention Bennett's book (an enigmatically inscribed first edition, '*For Owen England from Bennett Carpenter, with higher hopes*'), but he doesn't. It's a long time since Owen looked at Bennett's masterwork and he has largely forgotten what was in it. His mind is now wandering around the incomprehensible ruins in the company of Bennett and Ivor and Sabine Berthelot and the ageing French poet. Yes, pursues Owen, 'Yves Bonnefoy would have liked those stones. He'd like that phrase. *Grands blocs de pierres brutes*. He's very fond of old guidebooks. And old photographs. And old postcards. And landscape phrases from the past. He's still alive, but he must be in his nineties now. He's a great man.'

'*La malinconica distesa delle colline crestace*,' Owen intones, as it were to himself. 'The melancholic stretch of chalky hills . . .'

Owen gets to his feet, for the hour of their separation is approaching, and he wants to show her his copy of Bonnefoy's *Arrière-pays*, whether she wants to see it or not. It is a strange, small, squat, surprisingly heavy little book, expensively produced by a small specialist publisher. She weighs it thoughtfully in her hand.

Owen wishes to point out to her one of the illustrations, of Mondrian's *The Red Cloud*. It is a painting Josephine had never seen before, and it is from a period of Mondrian's work with which she is unfamiliar. She knows his late and most well-known style, and long ago in faraway Missouri had stitched a tapestry (sketched for her onto the canvas by the younger of her sons) reproducing one of his red, black and yellow rectangles. But this strange free floating patch of unearthly yet earthy red, hanging over Van Gogh furrows, is, as Owen says, striking.

'Fauve?' murmurs Jo, tentatively. 'Did he go through a Fauve phase?'

Owen is not listening. He has taken the book back into his slightly arthritic lean yellow-knuckled brown-spotted hands and is turning the pages, gazing at the smudged but profoundly suggestive images of Italian paintings, churches, angels, huts, deserts and mountain slopes. He is searching, searching. A lost landscape, a haven, a mirage, an air that kills, yet flutters back to life again. A coal, smouldering.

When Jo has gone, he will have his first cigarette. He smokes two a day, always in solitude.

'Time to go,' says Josephine, rearranging her wools in her work basket. She had done a couple of moss green stitches since her arrival. It's slow work, but there is no hurry to complete.

Work box. Work basket. Needlework. Women's work. Work. Work ethic.

Both Josephine and Owen, being heavy readers, are very much attached to their early model Kindles, but it occurs to Josephine, as she rises smoothly to her feet, that Owen's quaint picture-book and the dark-blue-bound gilt-lettered 1907 copy of Alice Studdert Meade through which she is slowly knifing and slicing her way offer satisfactions not to be gained from an e-reader or a tablet. She thinks of articulating this aperçu, but can't find the words. She'll think about it, and perhaps return to it on their next week's agenda, when Owen comes to her side of the quad for a glass of Laphroaig – yes, she thinks it should be Laphroaig.

~

The libraries mean as much to Josephine as explorations of England mean to her restless friend Fran. They confirm status, confer identity. When Josephine Drummond goes into the libraries that she uses most frequently, she is received with some degree of recognition. Sometimes her books are handed over without her having to request them by name. This doesn't happen in the British Library in London, though even there she occasionally gets a friendly nod, but in Cambridge she is a familiar. Unlike some old women, she is easily recognisable, even memorable. Tall and pronounced of features, she will never dwindle into a little old lady, with all the conveniences and inconveniences which that status brings. Josephine may think she looks low-key, but she cannot help but look noticeable. She doesn't look eccentric (or this is her friend Fran's considered view) but she doesn't look negligible. Her career hasn't been distinguished, but it has been a career, of a sort, and it's not quite over yet.

Fran is still earning her living and paying her taxes. Josephine is living on pensions and occupying herself with tapestry, absinthe and Deceased Wife's Sisters. She also teaches a weekly morning course on poetry (currently *On Old Age and the Concept of Late Style*, with reference to Yeats, Hardy, Dylan Thomas, Peter Redgrove, Robert Nye and others), but the fee for that would hardly keep her in tapestry needles, and certainly not in tapestry wool, which has become very expensive. Her teaching is an indulgence. But it is a way of keeping in touch with the best.

Deceased wives' sisters are interestingly unknown, but they are not the best.

Josephine crosses the cold quad, she hears the drizzling of the feeble fountain.

When, at ten, she climbs into her bed for her half-hour of bedtime reading, she picks up *The Fatal Kinship* and reads a page or two, but decides she will delay its denouement until the morning, when she will be more alert and will enjoy it more. She doesn't want to miss any carefully planned surprises. She turns instead to Owen's friend Bennett's book about the Spanish Civil War, *The Reaper and the Wheat*, which she has for so many weeks been intending but failing to tackle. It's supposed to be a classic and has been several times reprinted and updated. She stares again at the enigmatic dedication, handwritten in faded blue ink some forty years ago, and wonders what young Bennett Carpenter had meant by 'with higher hopes'?

Maybe Owen and Bennett had been lovers, all those years ago. Owen's private life, if he has one, has been very private and is largely unknown to her. As she didn't meet him until they were both in their early seventies, this isn't surprising.

She has a feeling that Fran's son Christopher is now in the Canaries. She's known Christopher all his life. He used to play football with her sons Nat and Andrew in the Romley Marshes when they were little, and she thinks they now occasionally Facebook one another, whatever that may mean. He was a very attractive and friendly little boy, young Christopher.

She is too tired to embark on reading about General Franco and North Africa and POUM and the NKVD and George Orwell and Tom Wintringham and Esmond Romilly at this time of night, but she leafs through the illustrations, which include a poor reproduction of *Guernica*, some maps of battle locations and a portrait of Miguel de Unamuno. There are also photographs of Stephen Spender, Julian Bell, John Cornford, Jessica Mitford and other now well-known British figures associated with the period, some of whom she recognises. Amongst them is an arresting and accomplished pencil drawing of an unfamiliar and handsome young man, in an open-necked shirt, wearing an unassuming air of nonchalant gallantry. She glances at the caption, and finds that his name is Valentine Studdert Meade, an unusual name which in itself has no resonance but which nevertheless strikes her with a jolt of recognition. There can't be all that many Studdert Meades, so he must be connected with her Deceased Wife's Sister novelist. (The drawing is by Augustus John, but she doesn't bother to note that yet, nor does she register that it had been commissioned by the Artists International Association in aid of Republican Spain.)

Here must be a clue to Alice Studdert Meade, in this fairly unlikely place, discovered more or less randomly.

This, she says to herself, sadly but with some satisfaction, is Scholarship, in all its triviality. She turns to the index, to discover more about Valentine, and notes that there are several scattered early references and one little mid-volume cluster that presumably marks his death. There is also, helpfully, a biographical index: thank you, Bennett, she says aloud to the old man in the cactus garden in the Canaries, thank you. She has always approved of biographical indexes and depends on them increasingly as her memory becomes, as she puts it, less retentive.

Studdert Meade, Valentine (1911–1937), diarist and artist, born in Cambridge, younger son of the classicist Hubert Studdert Meade and minor novelist Alice Studdert Meade. Educated at Saffron Walden and King's College, Cambridge. Studied at the Slade and worked as an ambulance driver for Spanish Medical Aid in the Spanish Civil War. Killed in uncertain circumstances in February 1937 in the battle of Jarama, just east of Madrid.

Here, so unexpectedly, are clues. There's a lot to work on here.

Work box. Women's work. Needlework.

Sir Bennett wouldn't have got away with that phrase 'minor novelist' these days. And 'the classicist' Hubert, as far as she knows, is by now well forgotten. Classicists don't count for much these days. They are even less favoured than minor Edwardian female novelists. They have had their day.

She guesses that Valentine was from a Quaker family. Alice may have been a Quaker too. She hadn't even known that. She has discovered very little about her so far, not even the date of her death. There is much still to find out.

Bennett Carpenter must have used Valentine's diaries. But they haven't entered the mainstream; they haven't made him as famous as John Cornford and Julian Bell and Esmond Romilly.

One would never describe oneself as a diarist, would one? It is a posthumous label.

She has never bothered to keep a diary.

Josephine does not know if or for how long Alice had survived the tragically early death of her son Valentine. Maybe she had tried to persuade him not to go, as Julian Bell's family had tried to dissuade him. She hadn't written much in her later years. Most of her fiction belonged to the Edwardian and Georgian period. Had she written for money, or for pleasure? Jo doesn't even know that.

Josephine runs her fingers through her coarse and heavy hair and lays the books together on her bedside table. Mother and son. Reunited, they can whisper to one another through the hard covers, through the newly cut pages.

The afterlife of letters.

Too much reading has addled her wits.

~

Francesca Stubbs stubbornly climbs the many flights of her concrete tower, marking the new graffiti as she goes. She clenches her teeth tight with fortitude, heaves her bag wearily from shoulder to shoulder, and counts her way up. Like a child, she encourages herself onwards and upwards with counting and climbing rhymes. 'The Grand Old Duke of York', 'One Two Buckle my Shoe', 'Ten Green Bottles', 'The Lilywhite Boys'. She used to sing 'Ten Green Bottles' to Christopher and Poppet when they were babies, as she rocked them in the rocking chair. Hour after hour, hour after hour.

On the other side of London, Claude Stubbs has lured Persephone into his bed. It is unprofessional, but she has succumbed to his charm and his authority and to the warmth and comfort of the bed on this cold day. He has not lured her very far into it, for she is lying next to him fully clothed under a mohair blanket, but on top of the duvet. They are Beauty and the Beast. Claude says, plaintively, in his grand old man, baby-boy style, that all he wants is a cuddle. She responds, firmly but flirtatiously, that this is all he's going to get.

They are eating some small but expensive 'handmade' almond biscuits from a kitsch decorative gift tin and sipping Madeira, and watching a game show involving a giant neon alphabet and some basic spelling guesswork. Persephone cries out pre-emptively from time to time. Claude doesn't bother to join in, but he squeezes her in a congratulatory way when she gets it right.

The biscuits and the Madeira are gifts from a grateful ex-patient. He gets quite a lot of those.

Some of his patients are more grateful than he deserves. He didn't take enough out of the Shadow Home Secretary. He should have been bolder with the shadow on his lung. He'd have been alive now if Claude had dug deeper.

Persephone likes Claude. He is her favourite client, she tells him. He flatters her and makes her laugh. He's generous, he's funny, he's no kind of a threat, and he's not afraid of being ill or of dying suddenly whenever she leaves the room. He's just an old-style lecher.

She doesn't like the fearful ones.

When the show ends, she's going to stick one of Claude's ex wife's plated meals into the mike, and give it to him before she goes. He's a lucky old sod, she tells him, from time to time.

She has never met Francesca Stubbs, but she has seen plenty of evidence of her traditional middle-class slightly old-fashioned wholesome home cooking.

Claude eyes the large-breasted game-show hostess and her strange protruding upper lip and her peculiarly toothy smile. Too much tooth, too much bright pink gum. *Jolie laide*, or is that the new look? He thinks of Fran.

Fran, with her perfect twenty-one-year-old body and her taut firm small breasts. You don't see those bodies these days. Girls now are either too thin or too fat, but Fran had been perfect.

She's withered and skinny and relentless now, but then she had been flawless. But for all that they'd been hopeless in bed together, hopeless. They'd never really got it together, the two of them, never got the timing right, and yet she'd got pregnant far too easily, far too early, twice in three years, and that hadn't been good for either of them. He used to blame her for this, but now he's past it all he feels big enough to realise it may have been partly his fault.

A perfect body, and a perfectly adequate brain. But restless, dissatisfied.

She could never relax, that woman, she was always wanting more, wanting other, wanting something else. She had too much physical and mental energy and had never discovered what to do with it. But the children had turned out OK, sort of OK, very OK when you look at what has happened to other people's children. When you look at a generation of drug addicts, disgraced bankers, disgraced or incompetent politicians. Of breast-implant con men, cosmetic surgeons with bad track records. Of stand-up comics, would-be media moguls, property thieves.

Christopher Stubbs. Poppet Stubbs. His son and his daughter. They've survived.

He wondered if Hamish had managed to appease the living body of Fran, if he had managed to calm her down. Meanly, he rather hopes not. But either way, Hamish is dead now and Fran has to keep going on her own.

Christopher has made a career out of showing off. That's his father's caustic view. Good-looking, easy of manner, he's a television natural. Poppet is another kettle of fish. Earnest, in his view humourless, and probably cleverer than her brother, she is obsessed by the imminent death of the planet. She works for an environmental agency, processing statistics. She tells him she's a neo-Malthusian, whatever that may be. She has no children.

Christopher has two, and an ex-wife whose name Claude has forgotten. Effie? Ellie? Something like that. Claude likes and even, grudgingly, admires Christopher and, though he doesn't admit it even to himself, he wishes he'd come to see his old father more often.

Their mother, his ex-wife Francesca, is preoccupied by what will one day prove to be the transitory problem of the ageing process of the human body, and by whether in the very short term the inconveniences of it can be from day to day ameliorated. She thinks this is worthwhile. She thinks the project of making old people more comfortable, less pained, less panicked, is worth pursuing. It's inconsistent of her, because she doesn't make herself all that comfortable, in his view. She drives herself. Too hard, too fast. She'll be lucky if she doesn't end up in a pile-up on the motorway.

Claude doesn't give a fuck about what happens to the planet when he's gone. And the afterlife can look after itself. Poppet thinks we should all worry for future generations, and about the afterlife of the planet. Although, because, she has no children. She views the planet as a conscious creature with a life and rights of its own. This is clearly ridiculous. The planet is just matter. As are we.

Claude's arm is comfortable around the back of the warm and pliant and indifferent and supremely healthy Persephone. His hand lies in a friendly way upon the slope of her firm thirty-five-year-old breast. She is an armful. Her breasts are bigger than Fran's had been, more mature.

But Fran's had been perfect. He doesn't know why he is thinking of them now.

Claude is certain that he is going to die with ease. He will die here in bed, comfortably, relinquishing consciousness easily, when the time comes. He will die in his sleep, like his father, from one of those painless, sudden extinctions, a nice sudden arrhythmia death. He won't have a heart attack climbing up a dank urine-soaked plastic-bag-and-condom-littered stairwell, or crash into the back of a lorry on the M1, or linger on in a hospital bed moaning and muttering and baring his teeth and thrashing, pumped full of oxycodone and midazolam.

You won't find him starving himself to death on an airport or drowned on a distant beach.

It's strange that he has this confidence. In his professional life, he has seen more than most of pain, and of fear of pain, and of death. He has seen patients in agonising pain, with no prospect of a good outcome, clinging on to an unendurable existence, hoping to delay the end by any means, surgical or medical. Some are prepared to submit to anything rather than to surrender, and so, on their behalf, are their appalled and often appalling relatives. He knows that most surgeons operate too much, because they can, because they are expected to, because that is what they do. They chop and pare back and reduce until there's not much of a person left to appreciate all the effort. Just a torso, like a ruined emperor. He's done it himself, in his time. But he knows it won't happen to him. He won't be needing or requesting the too-clever interventions, the radical pruning. He's filled in all the forms. He's got his Magic Pill.

He has seen so much of death that it doesn't frighten him. He's lucky there. It could have gone the other way. He's seen it go the other way. Some of his colleagues are cowards.

He's come to the conclusion that it's a matter of luck, not of character or virtue.

Some people fear death throughout their lives. Others don't think about it very much, except when they have to.

Death has been his Bread and Butter.

~

Why, he that cuts off twenty years of life
Cuts off so many years of fearing death.

~

Christopher Stubbs gazes down from the high viewpoint by the restaurant in Nazaret, where they have paused to admire the evening panorama before going in for their dinner. They lean on the low warm white wall and hear the raucously lively and incessant croaking of frogs from a pond somewhere along the darkening pathway. They can see the slopes of spent volcanoes, the lights of small resorts spreading below them, the level horizon of the Atlantic, the expanding and exploding stars of the sky above.

It's cold and wet in England, but here in Lanzarote the air is mild.

Ivor points out the only high-rise building in Lanzarote, visible to their right, rising up from the skirts of the island on the bay of the port of Arrecife. César Manrique had managed to put a stop to high rise here, having witnessed the multiplying tourist horrors of Tenerife. This not very high tower block was built as public housing, says Ivor, but it didn't work, it was abandoned and vandalised and eventually rescued and converted into a hotel.

Ivor thinks of mentioning to Christopher that he suffers from vertigo, but he doesn't.

The theatrical restaurant is tunnelled into, scooped out of the hollows of the high hillside. It is like a larger, higher, more vertical version of Bennett and Ivor's home. It is, as promised, spectacularly scenic. It has alcoves, little lakes, walkways, stairways, lantern-lit caverns. Omar Sharif is said to have won and lost it at a game of bridge.

Bennett never met Omar Sharif, but he knows, more

importantly, the Astronomer Royal, and has been shown by him around the observatory on the island of La Palma. Over his minimalist portion of filleted sea bass, Bennett holds forth on the possibility that the still very active volcano of Cumbre Vieja on the western coast of La Palma could erupt and propel a huge chunk of Canarian land mass into the Atlantic, thus causing a westward sweeping tidal wave seventy feet high, 'as high as Nelson's column', moving at the speed of 'a jet aircraft'. A falling slab of rock 'twice the size of the Isle of Man' would create a tsunami that would first annihilate Tenerife, then wipe out two thirds of the population of Casablanca and Rabat, then inundate Southern England and, before subsiding, engulf New York and most of the Eastern seaboard, says Bennett with relish. It won't rest until it reaches landfall, and landfall is death.

It will be worse than the Lisbon earthquake, says Bennett, happily.

After this animated little oration, Bennett lapses into a sudden silence. He is trying to locate a floating memory of a highbrow catastrophe novel he's read or heard of recently, which he knows would be pertinent to this topic, but he can't quite get hold of either the author or the title. He can't get a handle on it. It's annoying, he forgets too much these days, but maybe it will come back to him. The book is a drifting shadow, detached and loose in the back of his mind. He munches, abstracted, for a while, as his thoughts begin to drift back towards his childhood, as they so often do these days. As a schoolboy he'd been a fan of Jules Verne. *Journey to the Centre of the Earth*. *The Mysterious Island*. He'd hidden away in the boiler room for many safe and happy hours, avoiding sports, devouring these thrilling volumes.

Ivor doesn't like the way Bennett has retreated and drifted off, but he conceals his ever watchful anxiety.

Christopher, who has never heard of this particular Cumbre

Vieja catastrophe scenario, is intrigued by it. It is a satisfyingly extreme prospect, and a disaster that could not be blamed on human agency. The volcanic ridge is unstable, and that's just the way it is. It's not been made rocky by refrigerators or hairsprays or TNT or car exhausts or AIDS or over-population of the planet. It is as it is. The island has never been densely populated, and humans have had little impact upon it.

Even Christopher's sister Poppet, who blames human agency for most of the ills of the world, would find it hard to blame a volcanic eruption. A volcano is innocent and pure.

Christopher dimly remembers from his college days that the Lisbon earthquake (he knows it was in the eighteenth century but can't date it more precisely) was the cause of much anguished philosophical questioning at the time, from Christians, deists and unbelievers alike, seeking to justify the ways of God to man.

Maybe we are all seeking for a neutral agency to wipe us out. An asteroid, a tsunami, a tidal wave.

Our longing for the tomb.

Preferably not a superior civilisation from the outer universes. We don't want superiority to destroy us. Do we?

Christopher's thought sequence here, as he eats his salty little side dish of wrinkled *papas arrugadas*, illustrates how much he is his mother's son. This is how Fran thinks, and although Christopher isn't aware that he is thinking about Fran, or thinking in Fran mode, he is, on one sedimentary ancient archaeological layer of his mind, laid down long ago, doing just that.

Fran, like Bennett, has always been interested in earthquakes.

Poppet (how can this sobriquet have stuck to his fierce sister?) has different views, but she is also interested in the apocalyptic. Poppet (her brother knocks back the dregs of El Grifo as he recalls this, and hopes Ivor will order another bottle) is full of some kind of unresolved anger, which she transfers to national and global issues. She has very long and inhuman perspectives. Ah, Poppet, little sister.

The local El Grifo wine (and watchful Ivor has by now ordered another bottle) has a little griffin on its wine label, but Bennett tells him that El Grifo has nothing to do with griffins or dragons; it really means 'the tap'. The name is a pun. El Grifo, the tap.

Fran used to sing them to sleep.

Yes, here comes another green bottle of white wine.

Ten green bottles, hanging on the wall.

Christopher sometimes goes through these verses to himself as he lies awake in a hotel in some unfamiliar land in some unknown time zone. He doesn't know that his mother walks herself up her punitive stairwell with them too.

I summon to the winding ancient stair . . .

Bennett emerges from his reverie, which had failed to make a connection with the submerged memory of the lost novel the title of which he has been trying to remember, and tells them instead about the great volcanic eruptions in the 1730s on Lanzarote that had created the beautiful arid icing-sugar-encrusted landscapes of Timanfaya. An edict had been issued by Philip V of Spain, invoking the death penalty on anyone who tried to flee the lava and leave the island of Lanzarote for Gran Canaria or Tenerife. Christopher wants to ask if the eruptions on Lanzarote were a predictor of the Lisbon earthquake (which must, surely, have been a little later?), but before he gets round to it Bennett has moved on to reminiscences of his boyhood longing to see a tidal wave. He knows the phrase 'tidal wave' is no longer much used, but Bennett prefers it to the new-fangled Japanese word 'tsunami' now in vogue. He describes how, on family holidays, he used to sit on the vast Norfolk beach where he first learned to swim, bored and restless with pre-pubertal angst, gazing at the flat far horizon of the North Sea, and imagining with longing a great swelling surge rearing up and sweeping inexorably towards his family encampment of deckchairs and wind-breaks and sandcastles and towels and cricket bats. It wasn't a very likely prospect, in that flat non-volcanic terrain, but little Bennett hadn't known that, at the time.

'I used to like whale watching too,' says Bennett, a little wistfully. 'Off Vancouver Island. Do you remember those whales, Ivor? I keep hoping we'll see dolphins here, but we don't. You have to go to La Palma these days, to see dolphins. I don't think I'll ever get to La Palma again. It's not very far, but those little Binter aeroplanes are very bumpy.'

Ivor feels that Bennett is getting too close to his King Charles's Head – why the Canarian islanders had forgotten how to navigate. He risks drawing the conversation back towards Christopher's last visit, suggesting that maybe tomorrow Christopher would like to go over with them to Fuerteventura on the short safe trip on the Fred Olsen ferry. They could pay a visit to their mutual friend Simon Aguilera. He too, says Bennett, lives in a remarkable house, worth the visit – perhaps they'd mentioned it when describing him to Sara as a potential source of local information? He's got some great paintings, as Christopher probably knows. And in his retreat Aguilera has become much involved with the tragedy of the *immigrantes*, and has commissioned some artwork to be displayed in one of the ancient famine towers. Maybe Christopher would like to see the famine tower? It's one of the oldest buildings on the island. It stored grain, long ago, during the emergencies.

Simon Aguilera had signed the Namarome petition and spoken about her on Spanish television, but she hadn't wanted to receive him on her airport carpet, as she disapproved of his having killed his wife.

Bennett takes to the idea of a trip to Fuerteventura. He always enjoys an outing to the other island, and Simon is always pleased to see them.

Yes, that's what they will do.

Simon's Pilar will give them a small late lunch.

Driving back to La Suerte, Ivor recognises that he is dispro-portionately, almost sinisterly relieved by the accident of Christopher's cheeringly complaisant company, and wonders if he can detain him any longer on this enchanted isle, or perhaps entice him back another day.

Bennett has spoken many times to Ivor of Plutarch's theory that Calypso's island of Ogygia, where she held the enchanted Odysseus spellbound for seven years, was really one of the Canaries. Ivor has no views on this piece of mythological topog-raphy, but he can't see why not.

He'd like to keep Christopher, for company, for a while longer. Not seven years, but a few more days.

It is good to have a visitor who is nearer his own age than Bennett's. Most of their friends on the island are in their seven-ties, some in their eighties, and most of those who loyally or sycophantically fly over to see them are of the same generation. Ivor's life, apart from more than a few errant but discreet episodes, has been subsumed into Bennett's. On the whole, he enjoys entertaining Bennett's friends and showing them around: he got on well with their recent December guest, Owen England, a polite and pedantic old boy who was always very appreciative and a good sightseer and a good listener, easy to entertain. But Christopher Stubbs is a bit more dangerous than Owen, a bit more sparky, a bit more fun.

And new. New blood. Young blood.

The lights of the only high-rise building in Lanzarote are visible below them. He eyes them as he drives homewards. They are a beacon, but he's not sure what they are beckoning him towards. It's a very Spanish-speaking hotel, not many English-speaking foreigners patronise it. Ivor has tried it out, he's had a drink there, he's been up to look at the view from the top floor, but it's not very interesting, it's a bit featureless, and neither the sky-high bar nor the pavement bar provides promising terrain for Ivor. Ivor remembers it in its derelict epoch, its blackened graffiti-covered tower-block bomb-site epoch. Once, in those long-ago days, when he'd been sitting in a café on the palm tree promenade in Arrecife, waiting for the attorney's office to open after its long siesta, he'd seen an elderly man trudging up the exposed stairwell in the heat of the afternoon, carrying several loaded plastic bags. He must have been camping out up there. Ivor was near enough to see his tired and broad-featured and weather-beaten face, to track his stooped and halting progress from floor to floor. Up and up he went, the old down-and-out, zigzagging his way up the cement flights.

An old Guanche, a throwback, one of the dispossessed. A figure from the past.

An indigenous figure, not an *immigrante*. Ivor doesn't know how he knew this, but he did. The stoop, the stance, the broad shoulders, the undefeated air of possession and persistence.

Why was the old man climbing upwards? What home had he stubbornly made for himself up there amidst the ruins of the vandals? And why? Ivor never saw him again, although he looked out for him many times, and then the building was taken over, sold on, refurbished, in the days when the tourist industry was still expanding.

In their well-remunerated academic quarter, attached to the Committee on Social Thought in Chicago, in the late 1990s, Bennett and Ivor had stayed in a spacious apartment by the lake shore on the twentieth floor of a luxurious twin-towered block that had originally been built as public housing. Like the Lanzarote building, it had deteriorated. It had been bought up by a property company, and made over and turned into far from inexpensive rentals. The University of Chicago, four miles away, placed many of its short- and long-term lecturers and guests there. Saul Bellow had visited it many times, and Ivor now knows that Barack Obama used to swim in its palm-fringed basement pool, and wonders if he had ever unknowingly glimpsed that handsome man. The view of the ever-changing lake from their apartment was superb, the water blending and sometimes frisking from yellow to green to blue to pewter to cement to turquoise, but Ivor's vertigo prevented him from fully appreciating this feature. When he was indoors, he could never sit facing the windows, though Bennett liked to place himself solidly in his vulgarly comfortable purple professorial armchair and stare out over the waters. He had earned that repose. He had worked hard, and sometimes against the grain, all his life.

Chicago had not been a friendly city for Ivor. It was too extreme, too tall, too sheer.

Twin towers. Twin towers, inviting, soliciting attack.

Ivor had paced the lakeside on the safe shore level many times, lonely and under-occupied, while Bennett brilliantly displayed himself like a cockatoo in his history seminars. Ivor had looked back from his promenades at the twin towers of the residential block. They rose so high that their brutal summits were sometimes obscured and wreathed in Olympian cloud. Between the towers, on the fifth floor, hung a garden, a hanging garden, not as magnificent as the little hanging garden of the Palazzo Ducale at Mantua which they had memorably visited one autumn during the festival. But charming in its way, with its dwarf poplars and its small lake and its ducks.

Such strange places they had inhabited, in their lives as vagrant scholars, and now here he was, driving Bennett and Christopher Stubbs home to what he hopes will be Bennett's final dwelling place, to the safety of La Suerte.

Simon Aguilera's house isn't in itself vertiginous, but it does have an exposed spiral rocky look-out tower which Ivor will never more ascend. Once was enough.

He hopes Christopher will like the house. He'd texted Simon from the restaurant, and booked them all in for lunch. Simon said he was looking forward to seeing Christopher again. Ivor can well believe that.

Pilar is a brick. She likes visitors. She loves Bennett, who can make her laugh in Spanish.

Ivor and Simon have something of a conspiratorial relationship, based on a common interest in keeping Bennett calm and happy. Pilar supports them in this project.

Ivor loves Pilar's name. Pilar. Pillar. To be called after a pillar. It's too wonderful, to Ivor. She is a pillar of strength.

Christopher nods off in the back of the Peugeot, worn out with sea air, sea food, novelty, Canarian wine, grief, relief.

El Grifo.

As he sinks under, he thinks, briefly, of his mother Fran. She had texted him about something or other. His father? Sara? Poppet? Whatever? He can't remember. Had she said she was going to Blackpool? She longs to set up Old Folks Help to Buy Communal Housing in Blackpool. Or was it in Morecombe? Or maybe the West Country? He can't keep up with his mother's ceaseless peregrinations.

His mother likes horrible places, and she has gone to live in one. It is most unsuitable. He's been over there once, and once was enough, although he agrees the view is good. But why should a *view* mean so much to her? She's a stubborn old woman. What is she trying to prove? Hamish and Highgate had been civilised and pleasant.

So, Hamish has died, and his dad Claude is still alive, and receiving plated meals from his ex-wife. He's certainly worked out how to make himself comfortable.

Christopher had disliked his stepmother Jean, a very irritating old Sloane: he's glad she's out of the picture, and he suspects Claude is too.

Why couldn't Fran live somewhere sensible, like Auntie Josephine? You wouldn't have to worry about your mother if she lived in Athene Grange.

He doesn't really call Josephine Drummond 'auntie', and never did, but these days he sometimes refers to her in this manner, by way of a generational joke. 'And how's Auntie Josephine?' he will sometimes ask his mother. He has known Jo all his life, and she has known him from before he was born. He likes her, and when he was fourteen and she was thirty-five he used to fancy her. In the old days in Romley, when he used to play football on the marshes with Nat and Andrew.

Nat's done all right for himself: he's a sports commentator, he writes and broadcasts about cricket and travels to some nice places with the team. Nice work if you can get it. Andrew went more seriously into the civil service, but Christopher has no idea in which department.

Athene Grange is perfectly agreeable, in its own dull way. Jo had invited him and Poppet to her seventieth birthday party, though Poppet hadn't accepted. There'd been some impressive cocktails. White Ladies, with a kick to them. Somebody there knew how to mix a drink. He'd caught up with Andrew and Nat, heard their updates, reminisced.

Ah Maman, you old fool, he thinks, not without affection, as he fades out on the back seat.

~

Josephine gazes at her ageing Tuesday morning class and wonders yet again if she was wise to take on such an ageing theme. In the nature of things, such classes are full of older people, so in choosing her subject she had, as they now say, 'gone with the flow'. But it threatens to be lowering, this emphasis on age. She had thought it might be ennobling or comforting or bracing (and had deliberately attempted to exclude Larkin who is none of these), but she is not sure that she has the energy to keep all sixteen of her group suspended, up there on a higher plane. *'Dans l'âme ayons un haut dessein'*, as Verlaine had said somewhere or other, and she has tried to live up to this aspiration, but she can't always maintain it. The class has discussed, through close attention to individual poems and poets, the subject of creativity in old age, the emblematic early deaths of several lyric poets, and the question of whether or not we can identify a phenomenon sometimes known as Late Style.

Perhaps it's bound to be depressing. The last act is bloody, however charming the comedy that comes before, as some other French chap remarked, she thinks she recalls, of the art of biography.

Not that the French are very good at biography, are they? It's an English language speciality.

Because some of her group are highly educated in other disciplines and over-qualified for the class, the discussions have ranged widely and into matters not covered by her prescribed course topics: they have wandered into Shakespeare's late romances and the reasons for his retirement to Stratford-upon-Avon, Rembrandt's self-portraits and his portraits of his mother, Edward Said and Theodor W. Adorno on the anger and lament of Beethoven's late work. Josephine encourages such meanderings, as they are part of what such classes are intended to inspire, but she has to rein in one or two of the more combative and exhibitionist of her students, in consideration for those who are here for simpler reasons. This morning they are supposed to be examining a 2011 poem by Robert Nye (b. 1939) called 'Going On', taken from what he says will be his last volume. She had believed it would appeal to all of them, and it does. They each have their sheet of paper with the poem upon it, and here it is:

One afternoon near Notre Dame
I watched a man negotiate
The crowded pavement, carrying
A pot of coffee in one hand
And in his other hand a cake.

I saw him passing through the throng
Like one protected, on his lips
A smile which said he made his way
Towards some little private room
Where he'd take his repast alone.

Now when I think I can't go on
What I remember is that man
With some small comforts in his hands
Passing along a crowded street
Towards a room all of his own.

The good nature and deep calm of this poem do not, however, prevent Sally Lyttelton from embarking on a lengthy and slightly aggressive digression about one of Nye's historical novels that nobody else has read. They all listen patiently, while Josephine tries to plan a diversion that will lead them back to the work in hand, and on, as she had planned, to late Yeats and the tensions between the need for comfort and the spur of rage.

Sally Lyttelton is a formidable woman, who ought to know better than to be so domineering and time-consuming. She doesn't need to domineer. Unlike some of the class, she has a perfectly satisfactory private life, and receives a good deal of attention from a wider public in her roles as a Professor Emeritus of Renaissance Studies, as a frequent broadcaster, as the wife of a former Vice Chancellor, and as the owner of one of the grander houses in the county. But these signifiers of status do not seem to have made her relaxed or easy-going. She has a sharp, staccato old-fashioned upper-class voice, with which she insists on acquiring an audience. She also has a strong contrarian spirit and, if you meekly try to agree with her, she will start contradicting both you and herself. Josephine can't understand why she comes to this not-very-advanced class. Is it to show off? Is it to enjoy a sense of her own superiority to less intellectual and worse dressed elderly students like Ellen Musgrave, retired infant school teacher, and Mr Pennington, retired supermarket manager? Is it because she admires Josephine, which, oddly, she seems to do? (They had met at a lecture on brothels and the authorship of *Pericles, Prince of Tyre* in the University Library and struck up a lively and lasting, if shallow, acquaintance at the drinks reception that followed.) Or is it because she is genuinely interested in the subject of writing about age and in the ageing process?

She is a handsome woman, in a beaky kind of way, with a thin fine prominent nose and smart short layered silver-blonde hair, and today she is wearing what Josephine takes to be a very expensive suit (could the word Chanel perhaps apply to that neat sharp collarless effect?) in a fetching yellow and charcoal grey-checked tweed, and her shoes are a dark mustardy yellow. It's quite an outfit. Maybe she is going on to a luncheon. Anyway, reflects Josephine, she's the kind of woman who won't take kindly to the insignificance of old age; she won't want to lose what's left of her good looks. Maybe she really does need to find some texts, some mantras, to see her through and up (or through and down) to the next level.

The class, although it finds Sally Lyttelton irritating, is also proud to have her as a member. She raises the tone. Josephine finds herself wondering whether Sally will write the required 1,000-word assignment, or whether she will assume that those requirements don't apply to her.

Last year Betty Figueroa had written an excellent and original little essay on Conrad's narrative technique. Betty, in her late eighties, a brave and now presumably lonely old leftie of the old school, had worked for many years as a nurse with the P&O line, and was full of interesting stories (always offered tentatively, in her hesitant and light and surprisingly youthful voice) about life at sea, from the long-ago days of the long voyage to the Antipodes to the more recent age of the luxury cruise, and she was old enough to remember an age before the fax and the phone, when communications to land and other vessels were slow and sometimes misleading.(As, she pointed out, they were in the novels of Conrad.) She was a good reader, although/because she had had no formal literary training. She was something of a mystery, with her unexpected range of allusions and her loyal trade union politics, and Josephine imagined for her a romantic past, but could not give any shape to what this past might have been.

Betty's old age shines with the aura of a lived life. A tragic love affair, a long intercontinental romance, a secret adventure, a double life? Maybe she had been a spy? Like Conrad, she knew the Far East, she knew Australia, she had travelled the wide world, and now lives alone in a ground-floor flat in Cherry Hinton. Unlike Sally Lyttelton, she is self-contained, un-demanding, fortifying. She is valuable to Josephine, and is valued.

There they all are, with their poem print-outs. (She does urge them to buy Mr Nye's poems, or at least to take them out of the library, but it's more practical to photocopy them.) Some of them keep them tidily in folders, others crumple them up in their handbags or shopping bags. Ellen Musgrave has a ring folder which she keeps in a wholesome hessian bag with an apple design on it; Mr Pennington always brings his battered briefcase; and young Irene Lipmann (who looks after a much older husband with Alzheimer's) can never find anything and often has to borrow poems and pencils from fellow students.

Josephine knows them and does not know them, as they know and do not know her: Maureen, Deborah, Mavis, Sheila, Peter, Tanisha, Gordon, Kasha, Mr Pennington, Celine . . . She has tried to learn their names, as she does with every class, but resorts to reminding them to write their names in felt tip on folded stand-up stiff card labels and to place the labels in front of them every Tuesday morning, because there are always one or two that elude her, often in a transparently discriminatory way – the quiet one who will not speak, the indistinguishably generic everyday old person, the woman who will never meet her eye. You couldn't mistake or forget a Sally or a Betty, but some of them blur and merge. Yet each brings to the room a hinterland, a history, a long sequence of events and decisions that have brought them here, together. Jo continues to be moved by the mystery of this communion.

What does it mean to them, this Tuesday morning? Is it just a way of passing time in company? Or do some of them feel, as she does, the surviving force and power of the poems and the plays and the novels they read, a force and a power and a solace that they *in the fact and in the act of reading* release and disimprison, forces that utterly transcend this institutional room and the plastic cups and the water machine and the coffee dispenser that so often goes wrong? She is sometimes tempted to judge harshly the narrow word-bound horizons of her friend Owen, but she is just the same as him, she too lives in and for words, for the words of others. *Other men's flowers*. 'These are other men's flowers, only the string that binds them is my own.' That's overly modest Montaigne. She used to have more faith in the absolute value of words, of literature, and it is only now, towards the end of life, that she questions, that she senses a diminishing. And yet here she still is, still packaging words for others, providing the string, the ring folders, the photocopies. On Tuesday mornings.

As a child, she had dreamed she might be a writer. She had written poems and stories, as children do, publishing in the school magazine, surreptitiously entering competitions, submitting to and being rejected by Sunday newspapers and literary periodicals. She never really thought she'd be able to make it, so aware was she of the gulf that separated her juvenile attempts from the grandeur of the writers she most admired, so she was not cast down by failure. Her progressive plate-glass university simultaneously knocked her literary ambitions out of her by sharpening her critical faculties and by weakening her respect for the commercial world of 'publishing': she became a reader rather than a writer, a teacher rather than a creator and, when her husband's academic migrations permitted, she committed herself to the luxury of little essays into arcane interpretation. She never wanted to write about the great ones: she wanted to read them, sometimes with others. To share them, as the jargon goes. She was, is, good at that. She likes to read in company.

Towards the end of the class, Sheila Rookwood says she would like to read out one of her own poems, a poem inspired by the theme of their discussions. She asks if she may. In principle Josephine discourages this kind of departure, because that is not what her course is for; if people want to read their poetry aloud to other students, they should go to a creative writing class. (Josephine is sceptical of the value of such classes, although she has been persuaded to see that they have an important social role.) But in practice she allows it. Nobody in this group is likely to abuse a time slot, apart from Sally Lyttelton, who is a special case. She has had groups with one or two crazy and noisy participants, with no sense of the limits of other people's interest or tolerance, but those gathered here this morning are all polite people, mutually supportive. They will listen to Sheila's poem, which she promises is short.

Sheila herself is short: petite, diminutive. She's quite young, in her early sixties, and full of a bright and engaging energy. She works part-time at Addenbrooke's Hospital, and spends most of the rest of her time looking after a mother with dementia. Her Tuesday mornings, she has told Josephine, are her respite, her refuge, her care home. She is elf-like, with a pointed chin and thin arched eyebrows and huge, grey, slightly protuberant eyes, which she enhances with mascara and eye-liner and eye-shadow of novel shades. The damage around her eyes is grave, but she does not cease boldly to accentuate them. She usually wears coloured leggings and over them tunic or smock-like garments, sometimes with elaborately and jokily uneven hemlines. Peter Pan, not Wendy. Everybody likes Sheila Rookwood.

Her poem is about dementia.

> Midway up the stair, she stops.
> She has forgotten why she is here.
> Is she going up, or is she going down?
> She has forgotten.
>
> I summon to this ancient winding stair
>
> She cannot move.
> She calls for her daughter.
> She calls for her daughter.
>
> Mamma, mamma, she cries.
> For her daughter.
>
> And crazy Jane
> Crazy Sheila
> Crazy Mamma
> Crazy daughter
> Weeping, arm in arm descend the stair.

It's not a very good poem, as a poem, but it's affecting and the group listens respectfully. Josephine, who had never been very close to her own mother, has always been disturbed by reports of the very old calling for their long-dead mothers on their deathbeds, partly because she knows that however demented she may become, she won't be doing that, and she hopes that her children, in their turn, won't be calling for her. She hopes and believes that Nat and Andrew have grown up and cut free.

Sheila has told the class stories about her mother's erratic behaviour, making light of it, making fun of it – the stubbornness over items of clothing, the obsession with putting her cosmetics in the refrigerator as though they were perishable snacks, the mislaid brassiere discovered in the depths of her handbag, the puzzled attempts to eat soup with a knife and fork, the inappropriate responses to items of news on the television. But there is nothing funny about standing on a staircase, lost in your own home.

Yeats's 'Dialogue of Self and Soul' is one of the greatest poems in the English language, and Josephine is glad she included it and its winding ancient stair in the reading list. And why should Sheila not pay homage to it? Yeats's aristocratic vision might not have encompassed this small ageing hardworking middle-class English woman, bravely battling on and fighting a fight which all shall lose, amidst the accoutrements, not of ancient scabbards and faded ensigns and flowering, silken, old embroidery, but of incontinence pads, medication packs, liquidised vegetables and alarm buttons. But here Sheila is, speaking to Yeats, encompassing Yeats. Yeats has comforted Sheila more than the carer's guide to dementia that she bought, in desperation, a book which referred to the care object as a 'piglet' – an acronym for the 'Person I Give Love and Endless Therapy To'. Sheila has confided to Josephine that she cannot think of her mother in those terms. The tips in the book are useful, but the language is undignified. Her mother is still a human being, an old woman, albeit demented, not a piglet, not a nursery rhyme toy.

As she unlocks her bike from the alley railings and sets off to the University Library and the diaries of Valentine Studdert Meade, Josephine receives a clear image of her friend Fran climbing the punitive concrete stairwell with her briefcase and her shopping bags, a visitation followed swiftly by an image of Fran's husband Claude Stubbs, Claude the Knife. She hasn't seen Claude much over the years but she'd seen a lot of him when she was living in Romley, when her husband Alec was in his first teaching post at Romley Polytechnic, a post which, against the odds, had proved a springboard to a good career. Claude too had moved on from Romley to better things. Claude had made several passes at her in the old days, as children were ferried backwards and forwards across the couple of miles between their homes, from tea parties, from excursions to the boring overfed old ducks in the park, from mutual child-minding sessions, but she had never had time to succumb. Just as well, probably, but he had been attractive, in a saturnine and incipiently fleshly way. He wasn't a bad man, Claude, but Fran was certainly better off without him.

Not that she was without him. She was still cooking him plated meals. Fran must get something out of this arrangement, but Josephine was not sure what it might be.

~

Claude Stubbs, reclining on his comfortable bed of pain, and comfortably high on his plumped pillows, has just been watching, for the second time, a clip of a newly acquired biopic about his beloved, with quotes from various interviews conducted over her lifetime. He has Callas on many a CD and DVD, in many roles, but he also has some sequences of her as herself. Here she is speaking about the death of the great love of her life, Ari Onassis, and she declaims, he interprets it, tragically, 'Da allora un giorno in più era, per fortuna, un giorno in meno.'

This sentence deeply intrigues him. His opera Italian is not good, but passable, and he recognises and in isolation under-stands every single word of this utterance, but what can it *mean*? At the age of fifty-three the diva died young, by today's stand-ards, but of what? A heart attack? A broken heart? Boredom? Suicide? Dermatomyositis? Precipitate weight loss? Of the sadness of not being able to sing anymore? We do not know. She was full of cortisone and immunosuppressants, as Claude himself is full of steroids and Chablis and psilocybin. She was a tragic heroine in her own drama, but it was a drama of slow (though not so very slow) decline, not a drama of sudden death. Thus died Brünnhilde, Norma, Medea, Tosca, Violetta, Elisabetta, Euridice . . .

Ari Onassis had died, probably unnecessarily, of a botched gallbladder operation.

Claude thinks that what she was saying was that 'from then on, one day more was, fortunately, one day less'. She was saying that she rejoiced at the death of each day for she no longer wished to live. She saw the rest of her life without Onassis and without her singing voice as a fixed sentence to be endured. She could cross the days off the calendar, as she approached the goal of death from the jail of life.

There had not been so many of them, for she did not long survive Onassis. But long enough to know despair. Claude has counted them. He has counted out her days.

The thought of her prowling angrily and desperately, lonely and bored and abandoned to grief, month after month, around her Paris apartment (for so he knows it must have been) fills him with an emotion that is not unlike pleasure. In those last two years of her life, in those dragging months and weeks and days, counting out the terrible hours, she had belonged to nobody, she had wanted nobody, she had had everything, she had lost everything, she had nothing left to desire on earth, and therefore she belonged to Claude Stubbs as much as to anyone, she was his for the imagining, his for the taking, for she was nobody's. She had entered the dark antechamber of the void amidst the crimson drapes and fluted columns, behind the iron grille and the curtained window. Every day a day the less.

Claude does not think about his own approaching death in this dramatic manner. He is stoic and calm and philosophical and has made himself as comfortable as possible. But he is glad that Callas was able to project all this terminal passion and grief for him, in her last bitterness as well as in her triumphant prime. She had acted out the glory. She was the very body of the glory. He doesn't have to go through all that. That's what opera is for, that's what theatre is for, that's what art is for. It spares us the effort. It shows forth what we don't have to go through.

Claude recognises that many find it hard to step back, to retire, to give up. His first wife Fran seems unable to stop running around, and he concedes that some of what she does may even be useful, and serve purposes other than merely keeping her busy. He was himself relieved when he completed his last operation and laid down his shining sterile silver tools forever. He had taken retirement at the proper age, but he had already had enough. He didn't yearn to go on and on chopping people up, as some of his colleagues appear to do. He didn't like the new keyhole and laser technology; he didn't want to have to go on retraining and retraining, at his age. He'd made a few mistakes in his time, as was only normal, and although he'd never been reproached for them, even by the relatives of the victims, he knew towards the end that he'd had enough. He didn't want to make a bosh of things, to go out with a bad legacy. He'd like respectful obituaries in the right places, please.

I'm dying a good death, thinks Claude complacently, as he switches off Callas and returns to Classic FM.

After a cheerful burst of Vivaldi, there's a newsflash about yet another ageing showbiz paedophile appearing in court. Fascinating, this new pandemic of child abuse.

He's been intrigued by all these late-life arrests, by all these revelations of what they now call 'historic' abuse, by the sniffing and grubbing after offences committed thirty years ago. While he's always proudly considered himself a bit of a lecher, he had luckily never fancied underage kiddies, and has never had to resort to underhand means. He's been very up-front, very overt, in his overtly carnal way. (Persephone would, he was sure, testify that he has never been underhand or oblique in his approaches.) He's intrigued, as is Fran, by the idea that you should call no man happy until he is dead, and is wondering now, as she has wondered, whether it makes any difference to your lifetime happiness if your reputation is about to be posthumously destroyed, as was entertainer Jimmy Savile's. It can't, logically, because when you're dead you're dead, and, as you don't believe in an afterlife, you won't know anything about it. But it may cast a backward shadow before you die? A proleptic tremor? You may worry in old age that the bad stuff will come out later and upset your family.

People do care, on their deathbeds, deeply, about their reputations, their fame, their legacy, their obituaries, about what happens next. He's seen a lot of that. Vanity and doubt, doubt and vanity. He's been close to those last shameful worldly torments.

He had a dubious celebrity patient once, a surgical success story at the time, although dead now of other causes. Claude had had his suspicions about this character. Although not a censorious man, he had thought this chap flash and fishy. He was a singer, of sorts, and an entertainer, of sorts: not the kind of music Claude had ever cared for, but teenagers had gone wild for it. Christopher and Poppet had known about Jax, and were impressed when the time came that their father was about to carve him up. The public image of Jax Conan had been ubiquitous and inescapable, and the private hospital in which Claude had cut out some of his larynx had been thrilled to have him there. He was an international star. Fans had mobbed the ugly forecourt, security guards had patrolled the side streets, police had been summoned to keep the peace. The private hospital loved that kind of publicity. Photographers from the pavement had aimed their zooms at the windows of what they hoped was his private suite.

Jax had been a strangely glittering figure, dressed (though not in the consulting room) in silver spangles and flounces, in purples and in reds, his ink-black shoulder-length hair cut off at a fierce Red Indian angle and his false empurpled lashes encrusted and bejewelled. But to Claude he wasn't very convincing. He was neither camp nor kitsch. He wasn't gay and he wasn't straight. He was a creep, and now of course, retrospectively, although well dead, revealed as a specimen of a classic 1970s showbiz paedophile. At the time, Claude hadn't known that that was what he was, because the category, as a category, didn't yet exist. And he still hasn't been outed by the press, because what would be the point? He's dead, and it's not easy to get money out of a dead estate.

Claude had recognised that Jax was sexually ambiguous, yes, but not in any identifiable way. All was now clear, in the retrospective spotlight. Jimmy Savile had taken a lot of dead idols down with him into the Hades of eternal disgrace, as well as some sad old men still living.

In the consulting room, Jax Conan had been humble and anxious to please. His showbiz ego had been almost touchingly subdued, as he groped to understand what Claude had to tell him. Jax was originally from Chingford, a neighbourhood Claude had known well, and for both of them the Romley accent was a default. Jax had found it hard to find a manner that was sufficiently everyday for the receiving of bad news. He looked down at his boots, he played with the rings on his fingers, he stared intently at the back of Claude's folder of notes and X-rays, he slumped, then straightened himself, and then slumped again. He asked hardly any questions. His agent, who was sitting in with him in lieu of next-of-kin, asked all the questions, about dates, prognosis, bookings, cancellations. Jax just sat there, looking confused. At one point he plucked up courage to ask what the word 'prognosis' meant, but had been unable to attend to the answer.

Poppet had been quite a fan of Jax. She'd been a very odd little girl. Lying there now, listening to an unearthly, inhuman, divine snatch from a Brahms serenade, Claude found himself wondering about Poppet. By the time he'd operated on the pop star, Poppet had long grown out of Jax and attached herself to different objects of worship, but she'd remained single and impenetrable. Maybe she'd fancied Jax because she was as odd as he was? Maybe a lot of the little girls who were attracted to and then abused by showbiz paedophiles had been a bit odd in the first place? You weren't allowed to think like that, because a new orthodoxy has prevailed. You have to think that every child is a victim. But some children *are* very odd. Jax had probably been odd himself, when he was an infant at St Jude's Primary.

Christopher's not odd. He's a normal heterosexual, somewhat disillusioned but still highly ambitious middle-aged showman. Or that's what his father thinks.

Maria Callas, by dying at the age of fifty-three, hadn't had to cope for too long with the humiliations of ageing. You can only escape old age by dying young.

Christopher's latest woman Sara had achieved this spectacularly well.

Claude had felt a thrill of power at seeing Jax Conan, as it were, at his mercy. The operation had, in the event, gone very well, as well as it possibly could have done, and Jax and his agent Rafe had been immensely grateful and had showered Claude with hot tickets to hot events, with bottles of not-very-carefully selected but very expensive bubbly, with a de luxe hamper for Christmas. Claude doesn't really like bubbly, and he can still remember the disappointment of the hamper. It had looked so promising, but its wicker and red satin treasure chest had been loaded with small tins and jars of pâté and confiture, with relish and bonbons, with small hard smoked cheeses and biscuits, and rather a lot of fake synthetic straw.

~

Simon Aguilera's house on the sandy island of Fuerteventura is as spectacular as Bennett and Ivor had promised and, as they had also promised, he seems to be very pleased to see them. Christopher Stubbs has been feeling slightly guilty about enjoying himself, but the friendly little port of departure at Playa Blanca, the heavenly weather, the blue Atlantic, the dotted islands, the gently abraded volcanic skyline, the friendly little port of arrival at Corralejo, all combine to give him a sense of physical well-being which is the very opposite of sudden death. One cannot but rejoice, on such a day, in such a light warm salt breeze, to be alive. Ivor drives them expertly down the ramp of the Fred Olsen ferry and onto the quay and through the little town and along the shoreline, past unfinished building projects and wind-carved white and yellow sand dunes and on towards a more rocky coast, then along a dirt track by the sea with a view of clear white-fringed turquoise and oddly tinted dark-red lagoons swaying with dense underwater vegetation, strange wine-dark lagoons, and on towards Simon's house which stands high and alone on a level headland, looking out over the waters. It had been, said Ivor, a fishing warehouse, and from the ruined tower, once a grain store, (the tower which Ivor refuses to ascend), the fishermen had looked out for the approaching shoals, for the ruffling shades of blue and green and darker blue that indicated changes in weather, for the boats returning before the storm.

Now Simon looks out through his binoculars of an evening for the *immigrantes*, the hungry and the thirsty and the dying, as they strain for the shore.

Bennett's house on Lanzarote is modernist and low, an organic architectural fantasy hollowed and expanded into garden and cellar, a mushroom of the earth, but Simon's dwelling on Fuerteventura rises ancient, uncompromising, expensively restored, expansive and austere. It is built of great industrial historic slabs of raw eighteenth-century stone, with huge windows, lofty ceilings, grand views.

The tower is said to be older. It is agelessly old.

Simon shows Christopher around while Ivor settles Bennett into a well-cushioned wicker chair on the terrace, where he accepts from Pilar a glass of light Spanish wine, places it carefully on a little glass table, and nods off into a light pre-luncheon doze. Ivor sits by him and also shuts his eyes but he does not snooze or accept a glass of wine. He is the driver. He glances through the European edition of the *Daily Mail*, which he had purchased at Playa Blanca, looking for news about people back home that they know.

The *Mail* is often critical, sometimes in Ivor's view libellously critical, of the people that they know, but he misses the gossip and he likes to keep up. Although not a linguist, he does know the meaning of the useful word *Schadenfreude*, and it often sneaks uneasily into his mind.

Simon Aguilera wants Christopher to see his gallery, his collection. The walls of the long room are high, white-washed, uneven. Christopher had expected the artworks to be theatrical, even loud, in keeping with a murderer whose plays and life had featured gore, a man whose mother, uncles and wife had all died violently, but they are not loud, although some of them do evoke the stage. Simon has some good North African Paul Klee, and some early and surprising Mondrian. There is a sequence of Gordon Craig designs, with actor-dwarfing pillars and staircases. Empty places, empty spaces, with an echo of the grand inland Canarian style. Awaiting animation, awaiting a caste of players that never arrives. And there is the de Chirico, in front of which, in Christie's in London, Simon and Christopher had first met. The painting portrays a pale golden sandy beach with two horses, rose and gold and grey and muscular horses, arrested in movement, their nostrils flared, their thick curled carved heroic manes as solid as stone. Behind them, the orderly white ruins of a classical temple and at their feet a broken fluted column and a solid giant starfish of a tender fleshly white-dotted orange-pink. They rear up, the horses, with a sense of eternal suspension and apprehension, strong, menacing, motionless, on the mythic shore with its curled waves and frozen foam.

Christopher stares at the horses with respect. De Chirico is out of fashion, his oils go relatively cheaply at auction, for a mere few hundred thousand pounds, yet he is so obviously a master that he gives one pause.

'You remember them?' asks Simon.

'Of course,' says Christopher.

The two men stand and stare for a short while at the horses, temporarily transfixed and frozen by their trumpet nostrils and their Medusa manes.

The only work by a Canarian-born artist, in Simon's view the only collectable Canarian-born artist, is a medium-sized mixed media exhibit by Manolo Millares, a collage made of burlap and sackcloth and twine and tar, with stains as of rust or old blood. It is a good example, says Simon, of his work from the 1960s, it's one of what he called his *arpilleras*, his cloths of memory.

'He was influenced by the mummies of Tenerife,' says Simon.

It is a sombre, human piece, with rents and with stitching. Christopher thinks his mother would like it, and wonders if he will remember to tell her about it.

He asks Simon if he may photograph it on his iPad, and Simon says of course, of course, but don't reproduce it without permission. Wouldn't dream of it, says Christopher, as he carefully frames his shot for future reference and possible future use.

Simon says that he has mixed feelings about Spanish art, about the artists who survived under Franco. He doesn't collect them, although he admires Tàpies. He bought the Millares because he thought the Canaries ought to be represented here, in his little gallery, on the island. During their association, Millares worked in burlap and sackcloth, Tàpies in cardboard. The Tàpies, he says, are much more expensive. He prefers his Millares.

On the end wall, in complete contrast, Christopher is shown two paintings that in his professional assessment are Old Masters from Italy: they are from well before his period, but his eye suggests to him they are the real thing. They are both images of women, but of women very unlike the flamboyant theatrical wife whom Simon had lost. The smaller of the two is a Virgin, a small pale tremulous quattrocento virgin in a gown of the palest eggshell blue, her golden hair beneath its slender halo swathed in a veil of the thinnest and airiest diaphanous gauze. The gauze is cream and beige and brown and slightly freckled like a speckled egg. And in her thin tapering hands she holds a moss-lined nest displaying a tender clutch of tiny eggs. She is, says Simon, the Virgin of the Nest: *La Madonna del Nido*. An unusual, possibly unique bit of iconography. She is Tuscan or Umbrian, officially 'Anon.', but attributed to various hands, including, though very unreliably, those of Piero della Francesca himself.

The other woman is of a slightly later period, and she is older, heavier, more serious. She is tall, sandalled, robed in dark red and green, a pilgrim carrying a tall grey wooden cross. Her hair is grey and her feet are ugly and worn, but her pose is majestic, for she is St Helena, the mother of Constantine. She it was who travelled to the Holy Land and discovered the True Cross, fragments of which have over the centuries been discovered scattered throughout the Ancient World. She is imposing, and not heavily idealised. Her buckled feet look as though they have walked many miles through many realms. She reminds Christopher very strongly of somebody, and as they move through to the little chamber, through a door off the main gallery, he works out that she recalls to him his mother's oldest friend, Josephine Drummond.

Auntie Josephine, with her dignified air.

Simon says the windowless low-ceilinged little chamber which they now enter is Ivor's favourite room, and Christopher wonders if it will contain erotica or homo-erotica, but it doesn't, although it does house some good pencil drawings of young men, including an elegant but rustic 1930s nobly throated open-shirted fellow by Augustus John, with a suggestion of a military vehicle or perhaps of a field ambulance in the background. And there is a short sequence of intimate Delacroix pastels of the turbaned head of a Moor or Nubian model: sketches, Simon says, for larger and more violent works of massacre and warfare.

Bennett is very fond of the Delacroix, says Simon.

'Very fine,' murmurs Christopher, politely. He is puzzled by Simon Aguilera and his strange collection, but not uncomfortably so.

Simon Aguilera's three uncles had been shot in a Nationalist prison in Alicante. Or so the official story went. Their younger brother, his father, had survived the Civil War but had been forced to work as a labourer, with many other political prisoners, on the vast monuments of Franco's war memorial. He had escaped with his wife and baby son to Paris, where Simon had been dandled on the knee of Ernest Hemingway. Or so the story went.

When they rejoin Bennett and Ivor on the terrace, Bennett has woken up and he and Ivor are vying for the attention of a fine-looking young black man in a battered straw hat who is leaning on a wooden rake in a graceful and somewhat bantering posture. Teasing and laughter have been taking place. A handshake seems to be appropriate, and Christopher offers his hand to the young man, who is introduced as Ishmael from Senegal. Ishmael smiles, in a familiar way, as one who is much at home here, as one whose gardening implements pertain more to iconography than to hard labour.

Christopher has heard the outline of his story from Ivor and Bennett, and he gazes at him with respect, as at one snatched from the jaws of death. He would like to hear more. It is a pity Sara is not here to meet Ishmael. He would have made a superb witness on camera.

Simon expands on the story over lunch on the terrace. Ishmael had not joined them at table, though Christopher had thought he might (and hoped he would). He had drifted off, with his rake, to pose, perhaps, in another biblical courtyard. Christopher is much taken with the apparition of Ishmael, and wonders if Ishmael can possibly be his real name, or whether it has been bestowed upon him by his protector.

Ishmael's mother, says Simon, had loaned him a thousand dollars to make his way to Europe. He speaks good French and English, but his first language is Wolof. (*What?* 'Wolof,' repeats Simon firmly, as though he is himself familiar with this strange-sounding tongue and assumes that everybody else will be.) He had been washed up at Gran Tarajal on the shores of Fuerteventura from a sinking vessel from Mauritania, having survived the long sea voyage from Nouadhibou. Nouadhibou, once called Port-Étienne, is now known as the largest graveyard of shipping in the world.

Sara, Christopher remembers, had longed to film in Nouadhibou. She'd seen some extraordinary amateur footage of a departing patera, laden with the doomed. She'd been very taken with the idea of getting a crew over there, but visas were tricky and it would have been way beyond her budget. There are no cheap tourist flights to Nouadhibou.

Some of Ishmael's fellow voyagers on the overcrowded and unseaworthy ship of death had perished, but Ishmael was young and strong and could swim, and he had made his way to the beach, where the rescue teams had clothed him in gold foil, like an angel, and carried him to the emergency clinic, and revived him. A few years ago they used to wrap people in silver foil, like joints of roast meat, says Simon, but now they have promoted the *immigrantes* to gold. The gold foil has better protective properties. Ishmael had survived the open seas and the waves and hypothermia, and now he was comfortably ensconced with Pilar and his patron, Simon Aguilera. He does a bit of gardening and also makes himself useful to the Red Cross in Puerto del Rosario, as an interpreter for those arrivals from Senegal and Mauritania who speak mainly Wolof. And he's studying IT online, with an American university programme. He's ambitious, says Simon, and he's smart. He'll go far.

'I'm trying to adopt him,' says Simon. 'Legally. It's tricky, under Spanish law, but I'm trying. I guess it would be tricky anywhere. It's good to have young blood around you, at my age.'

Bennett and Ivor exchange glances. Bennett had once, long ago, suggested that he should adopt Ivor, for inheritance purposes, but the intention had drained away into baffled and frustrating legal correspondence. Under English law they could have a civil partnership now, like the old fools Wirth-Miller and Chopping, or even a gay marriage, but they don't fancy it, it would seem parodic, ridiculous.

Ivor hasn't read Bennett's will. He's seen it, he knows exactly where it is; it's in the left-hand top drawer of Bennett's roll-top mahogany English writing desk in his spacious sunlit study at La Suerte. But he is too honourable to read it. Ivor's notions of honour are not of this age. They may be the death of him, but he would prefer to die with honour than to live on disgraced in his own mind.

The roll-top desk looks out of place in Lanzarote, but Bennett is very attached to it. He had written most of *The Reaper and the Wheat* on it, in his Cambridge study, in long ago longhand.

'Yes, young blood,' says Simon with relish, sticking his fork into the deliciously tender and thoughtfully home-minced burger that Pilar has provided for their repast. It is so rare that it could almost be described as steak tartare. Pilar knows that *ilustrísimo* Sir Bennett likes red meat.

Simon Aguilera has aged well. He must be in his seventies, but the rugged dark-brown Mediterranean look becomes him. He is trim, athletic, takes much outdoor exercise, plays tennis, works out, swims in the raging waves and rides the rolling swell of the cerulean surf. His iron-grey hair is crisp and curled and erect. But his long lean face is deeply carved and folded. He looks like, and is, an old roué. The lord of the sardine factory, the assassin in his retreat, seeking absolution.

Ivor thinks Simon is seeking absolution, but Bennett is not so sure.

~

Poppet Stubbs is in her forties but she is not very young. Her blood is not young. She takes after her mother, in a certain wiriness of energy, in a physique combining thin shoulders and strong legs, and she also has her mother's doggedness of purpose. Her brother Christopher has his father's more fleshly nonchalance, and like his father is something of a bon viveur. But Poppet is austere, and it is considered that she wishes to impose austerity on others. Within the family, she can influence her mother, who, as a woman, is accessible to guilt. Also, born under wartime rationing, Fran is keen on small savings. But Claude and Christopher do not care about thrift.

All of them drink too much, she thinks. Poppet drinks very little. She has witnessed too much drinking. She is of the view that alcohol is criminally cheap. Fran agrees, as a citizen, and as a person who can afford to get drunk in a Premier Inn or at home in her tower whenever she wants, but she always sees the other side of the argument. She sees from the perspective of poverty and would not wish to deprive the deprived. Poppet is ideologically austere and gives no quarter.

Poppet has bad memories of her mother screeching and tramping around the house of an evening in Romley. Christopher thinks she exaggerates these memories, has made most of them up, but maybe she has her own reasons for doing that.

Poppet does not care much for the present, but she cares about the future of the planet and its inhabitants. She has transferred her allegiance to a vanishingly distant point. She has what some of her friends and acquaintances consider an almost mystic capacity to personalise the planet and dehumanise her own concerns. Maybe, they think, she *has* no concerns? She does not seem very concerned about any of her friends, and it is hard for them to stay close to her, although some, loyally and on the whole thanklessly, continue to insist on maintaining a relationship with her. Cold though she is, she is also compelling. She is worth one's while.

Poppet is physically strong, in a muscular sense, but she is also neurologically hypersensitive to pollution, plastic bags, bad air, bad noise levels, overflying aircraft, the humming of air conditioning, muzak, artificial flavourings. She is sensitive to Agent Orange, Sunset Yellow, Allura Red and Carmoisine.

She has not dulled or heightened her senses with alcohol or nicotine or aspirin or red meat or glue, and she lives, unprotected, in a state of perpetual exposure to the jarring forces of daily life. London had been too much for her. It had attacked her too violently. She has tried to live and work in the capital and had failed. Now she is based near a village near a small county town in the West Country, and works from her computer. (She spends most of her time trawling data and processing it: her boosted broadband is speedy, her computer sophisticated. Stats are her pulse, her lifeblood.) But even in the country, on the calm Levels, she feels at times raw and besieged. Her skin is too thin for normal intercourse. She has reduced her way of life to what she considers an elegant minimalist routine: bicycling along the tow path to the village shop two miles away, growing her own vegetables, walking, talking to her cat, watching the birds, listening to her radio. She has a television, for work purposes, because she needs to see what is going on in the world, but she rarely watches it for pleasure. She watches conferences on climate change, logs into debates on the melting ice cap and coal emissions in China and log-burning in Malaysia and earth tremors on the mid-Atlantic ridge. The jazzy high-lights of her viewing are Greenpeace and other ecological protests, which sometimes hit the international news bulletins. She knows people who are out there, on the front line. She is the eye that watches them.

Sometimes she watches *The Antiques Roadshow*, but that's for different reasons.

She is fond of her little house, and of the surrounding water meadows and eel-rich waterways. Her little house is low and modest. She likes the washed pink and white-ochre of the pitted brickwork, the pink roof tiles, the faded painted peeling pale blue of the woodwork. She feels close to nature, in her solitary little dwelling by the canal, with the sky and the water, and the sky reflected in the water. Much of her furniture is made of local willow. She loves the willow too. She has a friend living not far away who built and planted herself a willow cabin on a hillside, after a Stone Age pattern. Its curved walls sprouted in the spring and came into overarching leaf.

Poppet's house is much less eccentric than that. It is a standard nineteenth-century farm labourer's brick and board cottage, inhabited in earlier years by crowding families, but now her own domain, where she lives alone, old-maidish, spinsterly, secure.

Her mother Fran has often commented on the inadequate housing stock and the growing numbers of people choosing to live alone, and once remarked, provocatively, that Poppet's way of life was not as ecologically sustainable as it might look: she is sole occupant of a space that in the past would have been inhabited by many, and if she took sustainability more seriously she should in theory be living in a commune and taking up (said with emphasis) *a lot less room*. This line of reproach didn't quite reach Poppet, who was adroit at explaining why her damp and lonely canalside cottage in a flood plain would be deeply undesirable to any local families.

She is a casuist. Most statisticians are.

She sits by her log fire, with her super-powered laptop on her knee, and her little black cat at her feet, and an old chipped patterned china soup plate of leek salad vinaigrette and chopped hard-boiled egg and chives on the little wooden table by her side. The fire sings and whistles and spits flashes of green and purple salty colours at her, little sparks of marine wood. She is trawling through the weather of the world, making bookmarks, making footnotes. Strange new areas of light pollution have been recorded in Mongolia. She has already noted that, more locally, yet more torrential rain is on its way to the Levels, in the next day or two, and has wondered if she should collect more sandbags from the Lamb and Flag. She could wheel them along the towpath in the barrow, or Jim would drop them by. He is always willing to help, but she doesn't much like being helped.

Her brother Christopher is in the Canaries. There are websites that say that the predicted grand event will happen soon in La Palma, that a new eruption is on its way. But these are apocalyptic websites, longing for the end and for the submersion of Manhattan, and they are not to be trusted.

Poppet is fond of Christopher. She thinks he likes her too, despite everything.

Poppet's life is in the past. This is why she seems so old, for she is living a lengthy and extended afterlife. The most important events of her life happened before she was twenty-three and she lives in their wake. She has endeavoured to make that wake a placid level pathway. The brimming of the still canal mirrors it.

We don't know what happened to Poppet in that most important and most disastrous relationship. Maybe one day she will tell us. Maybe one day she will tell her mother, or her brother Christopher, or someone else who knew her long ago. But maybe she will keep it to herself until she dies. It is unlikely that she will tell her father Claude, as she disapproves of him, but who knows, life and narrative have many tricks and surprises. Maybe Claude and his dusky paramour Persephone will be the first to hear an account of her disastrous, scarifying and destructive passion.

No, we don't think so. But don't rule anything out. Poppet is still young.

Poppet doesn't drink much, but she sometimes has a half-pint at the Lamb and Flag, to keep in touch with the neighbourhood and with Jim. She quite likes the building's unredeemed rusticity, and its basic vegetable bake. She can't believe that her mother Fran actually likes an aggressively cheap urban chain called Weatherspoons. She can't, she must be faking it, nobody could like a pub belonging to Weatherspoons.

The chain is really called Wetherspoons, but Poppet doesn't know that. She spells it Weatherspoons, in her head.

Fran's been to visit Poppet a couple of times, she's even been to the Lamb and Flag and met Jim. But she never feels she's very welcome, by the flat canal.

~

Fran is on her way to visit Teresa, with a plastic box of homemade chicken soup and a readymade smoked salmon and soft cheese sandwich in her handy hessian bag. She sits on the Tube, on a seat which she had managed to claim from a slower but younger rival who had been keeping a competitive eye on it as their crowded compartment approached the busy junction of King's Cross. Fran had read the eye and body movements of the previous occupant correctly, and had moved forward smartly as soon as he arose. She sat down with relief. She didn't mind standing, but it is pleasanter, at her age, to sit.

She had become familiar with this Tube journey, since her recent reunion with Teresa Quinn. It is a good few stops, and it always gives her time to reflect on the strange ways of old acquaintance, and the patterns of renewal that seem to be so arbitrary, although they surely cannot be entirely so.

Fran and Teresa had been for a while neighbours and school friends, long, long ago, in the years of austerity just after the war. Their families lived in adjoining houses, in the two halves of a semi-detached building in an industrial Midlands city that had been heavily bombed. The genteel dull residential Edwardian neighbourhood had been spared, and the two families, after a period of evacuation in the safer countryside, had returned at much the same time from their different billets (one in Cheshire, one in North Yorkshire) to resume their pre-war lives and occupations. For the four parents, it had been a homecoming to a place of reclaimed safety, but to Fran Robinson and Teresa Quinn and their four siblings it was a disruption, an upheaval, an enforced new beginning in an unfamiliar, dangerous, blackened domain.

Fran, of late, with Teresa's assistance, has been trying to reconstruct those post-war years in Maybrook Park, and of one thing both are certain: the Robinsons and the Quinns really really did not like each other.

'I wouldn't say they *loathed* each other,' Teresa had asserted, with her ever-youthful ready laughter, clutching her mug of green tea, 'but they sure as hell *despised* each other.'

Joined by party walls, their deep back gardens separated by a high privet hedge, the Robinsons and the Quinns had fought a discreet, well-mannered and largely silent war of disapproval. There were many points of dissension and causes for contempt, connected with washing lines, garden maintenance, choice of newspaper, expenditure patterns, child-rearing, and attitudes to the potato man who came round once a week with his nose-bagged pony. But the chief division was of religion. The Robinsons were C of E, the Quinns were Catholic. They weren't very Catholic, but Catholic they were, and moreover with Irish blood in their ancestry. Illogically, the Robinsons managed to despise the Quinns for not sending all of their children to an RC school: they'd tried it with their eldest, David, found it wanting, and had sent the other two to the C of E primary school, which they thought was better.

Or, anyway, said the cynical Robinsons, *nearer*.

Both Fran and Teresa were middle children. This had seemed special to them. The other four siblings, all male, didn't have much to do with one another, sticking most of the time to their own side of the family divide, but Fran and Teresa, the daughters in the middle, found one another quite quite fascinating.

'I *adored* you,' said Fran in her seventies, to her long-lost old comrade, who replied 'And I adored you too!'

'You didn't show it,' complained Fran. 'I was always tagging along behind. You ran the show, you made all the decisions, I was just a – a *follower*.'

'That's rubbish,' said Teresa, patently flattered, smiling beneficently. 'You were always ahead, you could run a lot faster than me, and remember how good you were at rounders, I could never even see the ball, but you were in with the fast set. Do you remember Jenny Morpeth? She was a demon.'

'It wasn't smart, being in with the fast set,' retorted Fran, 'and Jenny Morpeth was a dimwit.'

'We were two on our own,' sighed Teresa, with nostalgia. 'We were *sui generis*, we two. Or should that be some other grammatical construction, do you think? *Nostri generis*? No, that can't be right. We never got to do Latin together, did we? I left before we got to Latin.'

'I thought we both did a year with Miss Wilberforce?'

'I don't remember a Miss Wilberforce. What did she look like, Miss Wilberforce?'

And back they would go again, reconstructing a chronology, over the dates and the years and the names of their teachers, over their schoolmates and the numbers of the bus and tram routes, over their changing hairstyles, over their retrospective astonishment that their parents had allowed them to wander freely on public transport around the city, at the age of nine, at the age of ten, at the age of eleven.

They hadn't been at all surprised at the time. Everybody did it. Children were more grown up then.

Plaits, bobs, bunches. Hair ribbons, rubber bands with dangling cherries, a treasured green plastic hair slide shaped like a mermaid won at a garden fete.

Teresa had been twelve when the Quinns left.

The seam of memory is richly loaded, and they explore it, in meeting after meeting, in the time that is left. Fran knows that it is good for both of them that they have found one another, and that Teresa has gained a new lease, not of life, but of a pre-life, of an extending and flourishing retrospect.

Over their conversations looms the structure of the dour tall semi-detached three-storeyed Edwardian stone building that had housed them all. The avenue was built on an incline, and their front gardens sloped upwards to their adjacent front doors and their adjacent porches, identically adorned with stained-glass fanlights of stylised art nouveau tulips and lilies. There was a side entry, into the kitchen and scullery, so the paths to the front doors were not often used, except, stubbornly, and with professional dignity, by the postman. The back gardens were on the level, with high end walls adjoining another identical row of gardens and houses, a row which the Robinsons and the Quinns united in considering subtly inferior to their own, though in no clearly identifiable way.

The building had been intensely occupied by adult frustrations and ambitions and worries and pettinesses and hopes and resignations, by adolescent fantasies and misdemeanours and triumphs, by pre-pubertal childish games and fears and delusions and frightening stories. By struggles with ration books and home helps, by making and mending, by the reassuring but often disappointing cycle of birthdays and Easter and seaside holidays and Christmases, by swotting for exams and the maintenance of bicycles. A thick, swarming, divided life had filled the stonework as honey fills the cells of a hive. It had permeated the crumbling mortar between the bricks and informed the plaster and the whitewashed walls of the conjoined cellars. Like the twin valves of a heart, they were, those cellars, beating side by side.

Fran and Teresa had discovered the cellars and made them their own. They had discovered a communication between them, a secret gap through the friendly coal dust and the spider webs. A removable brick, a pathway between Number 24 and Number 26, through which they could pass messages, through which they could reach out to touch one another's hands.

The cellars were originally designed for coal, with a coalhole in front of the porch through which the dusky coalman would in the olden days drop his load, but both the Robinsons and the Quinns despised coal fires, and had moved on to the cleanliness of modern central heating, so the cellars went unused. There was no lack of storage space in those big houses, and in those days people had much less to store.

Fran and Teresa, drinking their soup and eating their date and walnut cake in the twenty-first century, speculate: have those spaces now been excavated, converted into basement bedrooms, into dens, into TV rooms? Do the houses still stand? They can find out, they can probably look at them online if they try hard enough, but they are not sure if they wish to do so. It's all too easy, now, to look at images of the street where you used to live and check the shocking property prices. It's cheating.

Both agree about the indescribable thrill of their subterranean cellar life. They would descend, each with a stubby white candle, and whisper girlish secrets.

How old were we? Eleven? Did our parents know what we were doing? Was it *sexual*? Was it *bad*?

We were like the Montagues and the Capulets in our living tomb, says Teresa, happily, adding an erotic colouring.

We were like twins, says Fran.

There is too much to talk about. On their first meeting, they had talked about Teresa's sudden and to them arbitrary disappearance from Fran's life, whisked away by her father's relocation to an engineering project in Canada. The children had been shocked but helpless, had sworn to keep in touch forever, as children do, had written pen pal letters for a while ('I was always so disappointed by yours, I thought you would be able to say something important, but you never did'), a correspondence that had dwindled to birthday cards and Christmas cards, and then into years of silence, broken only by wedding alerts, dutifully acknowledged, which had been followed, on both sides, by the silence, as it were, of the grave. Fran had imagined the life of Teresa with her American husband from over the border in Vermont, Liam O'Neill, and Teresa had imagined the life of Fran with her English husband, Dr Claude Stubbs. And then they had begun to forget.

'But to be honest, I didn't think about you *much*,' they both agreed.

They had not exchanged notifications of their divorces. Things had moved on, they had entered new adult lives.

But neither of them, it emerges, had forgotten their solemn schoolgirl oath to meet on the eve of the new millennium. They had arranged an assignation in Piccadilly Circus, at the stroke of midnight, under the statue of Eros. They admit that, over the decades, the innocent folly of this dream had retained a certain charm, as a reminder of the hopeful children they had been, of their faith in lasting mutual friendship, of those meetings with old wax candles, of the lure of the great city which at that time they did not know except through books. Each, they now discovered, had thought of the pledge, perhaps once a year or every other year on New Year's Eve, and more vividly on the Millennial Eve, which each had spent in London, Fran in Highgate with Hamish and friends and Christopher and Ella and their little children and fireworks, Teresa in London a few miles away, with her son Luke and his wife Monica and her loyal staff and her many little charges, for whom she had laid on a spectacular celebration, also involving fireworks.

They discovered that they had lived a few miles from one another for decades, unknowingly, in adjacent postcodes.

The story had unfolded, slowly, and to both of them thrillingly, over several meetings.

Teresa, after her divorce and her marriage's annulment, had returned to England with her son and reverted to her maiden name. Having qualified as an infants' teacher in Canada, she had retrained, taken a post in a school for children with special needs, some of them with life-limiting conditions, and had risen through its hierarchy to become its principal. She had become, as Fran was to be somewhat embarrassed to discover, a well-known and respected name in her field. An authority, often cited by others.

On retirement, she had been almost immediately diagnosed with cancer, which had been lying in wait for her to lower her guard, and, after submitting to the familiar routines of surgery, chemotherapy and radiotherapy, she had received a dismal prognosis. In effect, a death sentence.

It was at this terminal stage that Teresa Quinn had spotted Fran's name in a report on sheltered housing published by the Ashley Combe Trust. She had been browsing through it on the internet, because that was the kind of thing she did. Francesca Robinson Stubbs, a name from the past, appended to a paper on mobility and public transport. Teresa had, for her own reasons, been professionally interested in these matters. And Teresa had Googled Fran, and although Fran didn't belong to any social networks or have an academic website that gave out any personal details, it was easy to contact her through the Trust. Teresa knew several people on the board of the Trust. Those were the kind of people that she knew. One of them promised to forward a letter. And did so, promptly. Teresa had taken the liberty of pointing out to Professor Halligan that there wasn't any time to waste. 'Mark it Urgent, Samuel,' she had gaily insisted, in her covering note.

So here they now were, Teresa carefully and delicately extended on her day bed, with her bones in their best positions, lucky Fran curled up any old how on a heap of tapestry cushions in the old armchair, eating their Pret A Manger smoked salmon sandwiches and remembering past times. Fran had updated Teresa with news of Christopher in the Canaries, Claude in his day bed in Kensington, Poppet in her flood plain, and her own stimulating visit to West Brom and Birmingham. Teresa had been very interested in the description of Aunt Dorothy and her residential care home at Chestnut Court. Fran's concerns for the elderly complemented her own interest in care homes for the young.

Teresa (who led a very busy professional and social life in her retirement) had in turn recounted details of visits from old friends and colleagues and from her local priest. Teresa has many visitors, eager to book themselves in for a session of chat and uplift. She is rarely left unattended. She lives alone, but with a succession of district nurses, friends and cousins in constant attendance. There is always somebody ready to sleep over, though Fran has not been and will not be expected to do this. The situation is, as of now, in February, manageable. It will soon become less so, but for now all is under control.

She has a promise of a visit from her son Luke and her grandson Xavier, who are in Mozambique. They have said they will come soon.

The priest is a bit of a worry to Teresa, Fran suspects. But she may be wrong: she herself would so dislike a visit from a priest that perhaps she is over-reacting on her new-old friend's behalf. On the other hand, there had been the tiniest hint of exasperation, perhaps, in Teresa's description of his inability to dispose tidily of his umbrella.

The February weather has turned nasty, they agree. Torrential rain and high winds. Hence the concern for Poppet on the marshes.

Teresa, of course, has never met Poppet and, barring some unexpected turn of events in the very near future, never will. But she takes an interest in all Fran's doings, past and present, as Fran take an interest, an intense interest, in Teresa's lifework.

They agree that it is not surprising that both found themselves working in the caring professions, because that's what women do, and had they not both, in their cellar days, had visions of themselves as cup-bearers, as martyrs, as messianic saviours? Oh, how lofty some of their infant notions had been, as they crouched together, sometimes in Number 24 on the Quinn side, sometimes in Number 26 on the Robinson side, their arms around their scabbed knees, their hair full of coal dust, with their treat packet of unrationed glucose tablets, which disintegrated and melted so sweetly and deliciously upon the tongue!

Precociously they had discussed the plight of the sorry world and resolved to make it a better place. They had been morbidly fascinated by misfortune, and by the more extreme manifestations of the human condition – paraplegia, leprosy, blindness. They had discussed God, and whether or not he existed. Teresa, in those days, had been a believer, but even then a challenging believer. Fran had been more cautious in her speculations. Or that's how Fran now remembered it.

Fran had already been interested in last sayings. She doesn't think Teresa is now rehearsing hers, she is too busy recalling the trivia of the late 1940s and early 50s, and too discursive and too chatty to come up with an epigram.

Teresa had more than fulfilled her spiritual ambitions. Her special school had been a home and a haven and sometimes a hospice for some of the most disadvantaged children on earth, or at least, to make a more modest claim on her behalf, a claim which she would never have made for herself, for some of the most disadvantaged children in the Greater London area (but there were, of course, plenty of those, and far more than Teresa's school could accommodate).

Fran's childish veneration of Teresa has returned one hundred-fold, fortified by the manner in which Teresa, now, *in extremis*, is willing and eager to discuss pain, families, public transport (Oh, how I miss it! cries Teresa plaintively, I never would have known how much!), rude young people, multicultural London, grandchildren, climate change, the ways of God to Man, and death. Their conversation flows, uninhibited by social niceties.

Fran is curious about Teresa's ex-husband Liam and their son Luke and his Angolan wife Monica and their grandson Xavier, and interested though not surprised to learn that Luke has also entered the caring professions. He is an anaesthetist, and he is currently working in Africa. Teresa does not spell out any connection between his career and her own, but there must be one. She is also interested in Teresa's brothers, and is astonished to learn that David Quinn has made himself into the world expert on the works of Jacopo da Pontormo.

How can this be? How can an internationally renowned art historian have formed himself within the philistine and soulless bricks and mortar of Number 24 in the undistinguished suburb of Maybrook Park? There had been no art in Broughborough, or none that the Quinns and the Robinsons had ever seen. And David Quinn hadn't been a latent aesthete or an intellectual; he'd been in love with his gleaming chrome and wine-red Raleigh bicycle, on the crossbar of which he'd once or twice, when in a condescending mood, taken Fran for a scary ride. She'd pretended not to be scared, as she was honoured to be asked, but she'd been glad when, her crotch aching from the pressure of the metal and the scratching and rubbing of her knickers, she'd been able to get off.

Jacopo da Pontormo! Fran is not very good at art history, although some of her son Christopher's easy media expertise has rubbed off on her, but she has heard of him and is more than happy to browse through the glossy, large and expensively produced volume of text and reproductions that bears his name, twinned with the name of David Quinn. Teresa pointed to it, in its place high on the top shelf of the crowded living room – she is too weak to get up there herself these days – and Fran had climbed onto the library steps and hefted it down (even to her it seems dangerously heavy) and had sat there for a while, turning the pages and gazing at otherworldly images of virgins and depositions and annunciations, at swirling drapery in the most heavenly yet worldly of shades. Pink, mauve, orange, apricot, saffron and the palest of greens, wonderful colours in the grey winter of North-east London, inspiring colours to carry in her memory back to Tarrant Towers. The subject matter is deeply religious, as it would be, and the manner is mannered, or, as the jacket cover informs her, Mannerist. This, she thinks, is Catholic art at its most devout.

Is David Quinn still a believer? Was he ever a believer, that lanky boy with his acne and his side parting and his big bony hands and his bike? How on earth had he come across Pontormo?

Fran hadn't liked to ask about David Quinn's faith. She thought that might be a step too far. It's all right asking Teresa about hers, but David Quinn has a life of his own into which she ought not to intrude.

He now lives in Italy, in Orvieto, Teresa says. With his partner.

The thought of all that intensity, building up grey and grub-like and unobserved in an Edwardian semi-detached dwelling, smelling of boy and bicycle and football, waiting to hatch and swirl and shimmer and fly and float so weightlessly in all those glorious polychrome Florentine colours, makes Fran feel, inter-mittently, quite faint. How odd it is, how strange, how improbable!

Fran has told Teresa about her long friendship with Josephine Drummond. It's very satisfactory, she said to Teresa, Jo and I go right back to Romley days, we stayed friends even when she was in the States, our children sort of grew up together, and now thanks to you I can fill in the earlier years. What a bonus. I can colour in a bit more of my past.

Fran thinks, rightly, that Teresa loves to think she is of use.

Glucose tablets, pixie hoods.

They both remember pixie hoods, knitted with the wrinkled speckled scratchy wool salvaged from unravelled wartime jumpers. What hideous little creatures we were, they joyfully agree.

Peaky, wheezy, skinny, bronchitic, chicken-chested! Hideous!

Teresa is even interested in the dull, everyday and slightly lowering subject of Aunt Dorothy's colouring-in books, duly reported to her on this most recent meeting. They discuss the strange satisfaction of colouring in, remembered from long ago. Do you remember how we used to be made to pencil in a blue fringe around the islands on maps, and how we had to do the pencil strokes horizontally, all the way around, not vertically, or sticking out like a hedgehog, and how cross Miss Clay got if we did it wrong? It was called Geography! Scribble scribble scribble, neatly, all the way around the outline of the British Isles. What a waste of time, how utterly pointless, but what, in its way, what fun.

Some of my children, sighs Teresa, used to enjoy colouring in. Some of them made a terrible mess, but some were obsessively neat. It depended.

Lakeland pencils, Caran D'ache crayons, pastels. The gracious forgivingness of charcoal.

Come again soon, says Teresa, as Fran washes out and reclaims her useful plastic soup container, and bossily weeds out a few past-their-best crumpled-paper narcissi from the bunch in the jug on the mantelpiece.

It is strange, she feels so at home in Teresa's house, she feels quite settled there. Quite uncharacteristically unrestless she feels, during her hours with Teresa.

Yes, of course, says Fran. I'll text you when I've heard from Ashley Combe about the Westmore Marsh dates. It's a bit weather-dependent, this outing.

Teresa reaches out her thin white arms, and they embrace, carefully, tenderly.

Unlike Claude, Teresa has to contend with a great deal of pain, some days worse than others.

~

Teresa misses public transport, and envies Fran her uncomfortable and tiring journeys around the capital on her Freedom

Pass. Like Fran, she'd enjoyed eavesdropping. Too much surrounded during her working day by people well known to her and deeply dependent upon her, she had relished the solitude and company of ordinary strangers on bus journeys, even on the less agreeable Tube.

She also misses her gardening. She'd been pleased to see Fran sort out the narcissi, but she'd like to have been able to get out into the garden and see the snowdrops and the aconites and plan for the spring. There is a fine city view from her sloping terraced London garden, and she misses that too. Her house-plants are still doing well, she keeps an eye on them. Tender-hearted, she doesn't like to give up on any of them, even when they look past their best, and she diligently waters unpromising greenery and unresponsive shoots and nodules that have been dormant for years. Who knows, they may recover, they may have a second coming. And, often, they do.

Teresa is dying of mesothelioma. At first she told Fran she was dying of lung cancer, an allied affliction, and, as we all now know, commonly caused by smoking. Mesothelioma, in contrast, is a cancer of the lung and chest walls, and almost always caused by exposure to asbestos. Exposure often dating back many decades. Teresa had not wanted her newly found old friend to scroll back through time, as Teresa herself has been doing, in search of causation. She has been re-reading the past, trying to identify the source of the asbestos which has been at first slowly and secretly, but now not so slowly and very visibly and surely, destroying her. The school buildings, the semi-detached suburban houses, the cellars of coal dust, the Public Library, or the Woolworths in the town centre, where (they have agreed) tragic but invisibly unidentifiable old men would try to stick their fingers up their backsides? The council estate to which her family had been evacuated during the war? The school in Canada, the house in Vermont? Or latterly, the demolition of the outbuildings on the site where her new school was built? Who can say? She is not an industrial casualty, as were so many miners and shipbuilders. But she is a casualty. Of something.

Not of smoking. She had smoked cigarettes, for a few years in her youth, when married, euphorically, to Liam. But she had not smoked seriously. She has been through this, on email, with Liam in Montreal, who is deeply concerned about her and who seems to be tormenting himself as to whether he would be welcome, if he were to offer to come to see her now. (She hasn't given him much of a lead on this.) Liam hasn't smoked for years, he tells her, as though, somehow, in some way, that might reassure her.

Teresa had, after three or four meetings, decided that Fran was not a hypochondriac, and that she was also extremely fit, although, like most old people, she had a heightened conscious-ness of mortal peril. She could face the facts of mesothelioma. So Teresa had described the diagnosis and the prognosis, which had also released her to discuss with Fran the extraordinarily arbitrary nature of this particular affliction. It can be caused, apparently, by the inhalation, many years ago, of a single fibre, as well as by years at the coal face. A school teacher, pushing a drawing pin into a classroom partition, can release particles that, if inhaled, can kill. A single one of them can kill. Cause and effect seem to have no moral connection, no possible mean-ingful relationship.

Had God ordained, when Teresa was born, an innocent Broughborough babe, that she should inhale this particular fibre? Had the unknown and unknowing agents who had installed the asbestos in the wall been directly or indirectly or morally responsible for the now imminent consequence of her death? How would it affect her lot, and her acceptance of that lot, were it to be known that the builders had taken a known risk? It is an interesting conundrum. Teresa has always been attracted to such conundrums, and the casuistry with which priests and philosophers seek to explain them. Catholic though she be, after her fashion, she is also attracted to the more contemporary ethical notion of moral luck: it was bad luck that made her stick that drawing pin into the partition of the garden room, in order to display the list of supervised outings proposed for the summer vacation.

Teresa is fascinated by the example of the drawing pin. A pin is so small, so innocent. How many angels dance upon the head of a pin? How many invisible fibres did the pin release?

And would those hypothetical builders have felt guilty, or even sorry, if they knew that they had killed Teresa Quinn with a drawing pin?

And all for the want of a horseshoe nail.

Teresa feels sorry for those unwitting killer builders and classroom fitters and wishes to exonerate them from any suspicion of blame. She is non-judgmental, and she doesn't go for blame. She has learned not to blame the parents of grievously damaged children. She has learned not to blame her ex, though she's not yet sure if she wants to see him again.

She has learned not to blame.

She has learned the hardest lesson, which is not to blame herself.

Fran finds this mindset fascinating, and wonders what it may have to do with religion and faith in God.

Nobody is to blame, but God.

~

On the Tube home, Fran ponders the riddles of cause and effect and blame and the drawing pin, and manages to remember a vaguely pertinent case history which had been floating at the back of her mind for some days. She would have related it to Teresa this afternoon, had she managed to capture it in time, and its connection is so tenuous she fears she will forget it again before their next appointment.

It's not her own story, it's a story Jo had told her, about a persistent member of one of her adult education classes, an elderly man who had become fixated upon Jo, his somewhat younger teacher. He had been inappropriately and tediously infatuated by her, writing to her, waylaying her in corridors, hanging around after class, sending her newspaper cuttings. (Luckily he never managed to get hold of her phone number.) He was too old and slow-footed to stalk, and Josephine, although much more agile and more mobile, was too old to be stalked, but in other respects he was a stalker. And he, like Teresa Quinn, had been obsessed by questions of agency and blame. In his case, unhealthily obsessed. He specialised in newspaper cuttings about accidents and crimes and misdemeanours with unintended consequences, interests which Jo found at once tedious and upsetting and yet curiously compelling. Some of his disquisitions were, unfortunately, prompted by the books they were reading in class: Thomas Hardy and, in particular, *Tess of the d'Urbervilles* had provided him with rich material, but he could also find strange readings in Tolstoy and Chekhov and Conrad.

The cuttings, culled largely from the popular press, had headlines like FATHER KILLS OWN CHILD WHILE REVERSING OUT OF GARAGE or WOMAN STABBED TO DEATH BY FALLING ON KNIFE IN DISHWASHER or BUTCHER LOSES ARM IN MINCING MACHINE or DRIVER KILLED WHILE ADJUSTING SAFETY BELT or MAN STABBED OVER DISPUTE OVER HEDGE. Old Mr Winters had been gripped by the subtext of such incidents. Why, he wanted to know, was it worse to kill your own child than anyone else's? Was it worse or better to die after a quarrel? Was it worse to die while trying to do the right thing?

It was curiously difficult to explain to him why it was so much worse to kill your own child than somebody else's, Jo said.

When he talked about his own life, Jo told Fran, he seemed to have a sense missing, a screw loose. He hadn't attended his own wife's funeral, which occurred during the middle of Jo's course on Darwin and the Novel, and he had boasted about this omission to Jo. Why should he have gone to the funeral? She was dead, she wouldn't know if he was there or not, would she? He'd preferred to come and offer up his ideas on *Eyeless in Gaza*. Many years ago, he told Jo, he had destroyed his father's latest will; he'd torn it up and thrown it in the river. It was only paper, just a piece of paper, and he hadn't liked its terms. His father was senile when he made it, he'd never know what had happened, and what difference would it make? He'd never have known which will had come into effect, would he?

The circumstantial detail about the river was unsettling. It was the River Ouse, in York, and he had thrown the bits of paper off Lendal Bridge. His father had lived and died in York; he had spent his last years in The Retreat.

There was no arguing with this kind of stuff, Jo said to Fran. There was some horrible logic at work in him, some strange insistent raw intelligence. He didn't seem to have read any books of philosophy or logic or ethics, his ideas were all his own, but you couldn't completely disregard them.

You should kick him out of the class, Fran had said.

And, the next year, Jo had done exactly that. With the connivance of her Principal, she had invented a ruling that prevented students from attending her class for more than two consecutive years. Mr Winters disappeared. The messages stopped. He had probably attached himself to some other love object.

Yes, thinks Fran, Teresa would be interested in the story of Mr Winters, if she can remember to bring it up next time.

The train comes to a halt outside a busy intersection, and Fran, momentarily intensely bored, plays with her mobile and picks up a text from Poppet, in response to a motherly or (*faux* motherly, interfering, intrusive?) text of hers sent earlier in the day. Poppet replies, indicating that the levels are rising, but it's nowhere near the danger zone yet and she's got sandbags.

Fran has an embarrassment about Poppet, connected with her forthcoming Westmore Marsh project. She doesn't like to articulate it, even to herself.

~

Poppet, in her ceaseless monitoring of the planet's activities, has noted with interest that there's just been a violent submarine eruption in the Atlantic off the coast of El Hierro, the most remote, rocky and westerly of the Canary Islands, but she doesn't think it will be threatening her brother Christopher, who is on the flatter easterly and more African camel-farming isle of Lanzarote. He's been there for a week or two now, what can he be doing out there?

Poppet doesn't tell her mother about the eruption.

She never knows whether her mother worries too much about her children, or not enough. She's never known.

~

When Fran gets out of the Tube at King's Cross, to catch her bus home to the Towers, the London weather has worsened. Torrents of white slanting rain are pouring down from the blue-black neon-lit winter sky, and high-speed gusts are tormenting the garbage on the Euston Road. Umbrellas are being blown inside out, their broken ribs like the wings of dead crows. A large branch has blown off a plane tree and is obstructing the pavement. Pedestrians cluster at bus stops, stoically, with their backs to the wind. Those who have hooded garments pull their hoods miserably over their heads. Fran does not have a hood or a rain bonnet, but she has a beret, which is better than nothing. She squeezes herself under the roof of the bus shelter, and tries to think of higher things.

It would be bad to envy Teresa Quinn, who does not have to go out in this stuff, who will never again have to go out in this stuff, who has only the dark storms of the spirit and of the morphine-moderated pangs of the dying body to torment her. But sometimes, even though fit and well, Fran does feel like throwing in the sponge and going to bed for ever.

It would be bad to envy Claude (who will get his portion of the chicken soup tomorrow), although it has to be said that Claude, who is as far as Fran knows devoid of religious faith, of uplift, or of higher thoughts, does seem to have made a pact with mortality, and to be as happy in his confinement as a man may be. She would be bored out of her mind if she had to stay in bed.

Though maybe, if it goes on raining until the end of time, one could stop struggling and go to bed with honour.

It will be really annoying to Fran if she cannot get to inspect the housing development on Westmore Marsh as planned. Trivially annoying, not life-and-death annoying, but annoying. Westmore Marsh, as its name indicates, has been built on a West Country flood plain, but it incorporates various interesting and experimental anti-flood features in the form of ponds and hollows to hold run-off water. It would be ironic if flooding prevented her from getting over there to inspect these features. There is also, at Westmore Marsh, a unit of sheltered housing that has been of interest to the planning and architectural journals. Fran is hoping to get to chat to some of its residents, to see if they admire it, and if they have any view on the ponds and the hollows.

She has had an interesting talk over the phone with the warden of the sheltered housing unit, followed by various email exchanges. The warden is called Valerie Heritage. Fran thinks this is a splendid name. She wonders if she is robust and highly coloured, like Suzette Myers at Chestnut Court, or thin and iron-grey like the warden of Athene Grange, or black and generous, like Persephone Saint Just, whose name is almost too splendid to be true. You can't tell from Valerie's voice what colour she is. She has an ambiguous accent, something overlaid by something else. Fran's not very good at placing accents. And so many people are keen on concealing themselves these days.

∿

Claude sits in his large armchair with his feet up and his cat asleep on his lap, waiting for his ex-wife to arrive with his supplies. He is, as usual, watching daytime TV with half an eye and with the sound off, and simultaneously reading *The Times* on his Kindle. Cyrus so much prefers the Kindle to the print version of *The Times*, because it doesn't rustle and disturb his nap. On TV there is coverage of the deteriorating weather, and shots of railway track in the West Country under water. Claude has only the vaguest notion of where his daughter Poppet lives, but he thinks it's somewhere near these brown flooded fields and drowning cattle and weeping willows.

In *The Times*, he reads that his old colleague Andrew Wetherill has died. Andrew had been a madman, a joker, with a braying neighing laugh which had frequently resounded distinctively and often inappropriately around the auditoria of theatres and opera houses, a laugh that would wake the dead.

He'd had a colourful career, some of it literally on the battle-field, and had led a colourful private and semi-public life of considerable eccentricity. Married and the father of now grown sons and daughters, and (to Claude's certain knowledge) bisexual, he had in his later years usually been accompanied by a much younger woman, whom he would introduce at social gatherings as 'my fiancée'. There had been a succession of fiancées, whose function had never been wholly clear.

Claude hasn't seen Andrew for some years, though they once used to belong to the same dining club and to meet there almost regularly. The last time he saw him in person was at Glyndebourne, at a performance of one of Mozart's more frequently presented operas, and in the interval Claude had been introduced to Camellia (that can't have been her real name, surely, but that's the name that Claude thought he had heard), a tall thirty-year-old with a very long neck and very bare shoulders which rose upwards inexorably from a shimmering strapless short crimson ball gown. Camellia was a flamboyant accessory, and Claude can see her clearly, her gleaming ash-white marble flesh, her white teeth, her red lips, her flashing smile. He can see Andrew's curious expression, of mingled pride and bravado and collusion. Where is Camellia now?

Andrew had never divorced, despite the string of fiancées, and his obituary states, sedately and no doubt correctly, that his wife Marion and his two daughters survive him. How many scandals subsumed in that prim sentence. Claude, like most of his contemporaries, finds himself fascinated by the language of these brief retrospective résumés, by these truncated lives, with their ellipses and their hints and their double entendres.

Jax Conan had been bloody lucky to have predeceased Jimmy Savile.

Claude had divorced Fran because he had got himself into a position where he had to marry Jean, though his obituary won't divulge that. But it's Fran that looks after him now. It's Fran that comes with her hessian bag full of plates in cling film and filled plastic boxes. She'll be here soon, she'll let herself in, she's the chatelaine, she's got the bunch of keys.

Jean's still alive, and she's still costing him money, but he hasn't seen her in years and doesn't wish to.

He switches off the television, which, as the light fades and the early night thickens, is moving from daytime TV to early evening TV. He switches on Classic FM: a Dvořák piano trio, melancholy, reassuring and not too long. He is grateful to Classic FM. He is impressed by the trouble they take, whoever they are, to entertain him, him personally, in a manner that he finds acceptable. He's not a grateful or humble kind of person, but he is becoming more appreciative of small things than he ever thought he would be.

Will Fran stay for a drink and a chat? He rather hopes she will.

~

Poppet has been watching the waters rise with interest and with a slightly diminishing degree of bravado. The swelling brown water has covered the towpath and submerged all but the tops of the gateposts, and is lapping at her steps. On the local radio, there is a programme about the Great Flood of Lynton and Lynmouth of 1952 and an angry interview with the Minister about dredging. The canal is breached upstream, and the tides are high at this time of the month, though not quite as high as they had been in January. Rain pours down from the Welsh hills and engorges the Severn, the flat salt sea floods up from Bridgwater Bay and the Bristol Channel, the River Parrett over-flows its embankments. Many acres are submerged, and in the murky afternoon light she has seen the water level slowly approaching the lower boughs of the pollarded willows, the waving tips and fronds of the sedge and of the rushes and the reeds. Some villages have been marooned for many days.

The water fowl enjoy the transformation of the landscape. It suits them well, it enlarges their territory. The birds of the air also seem happy. The small ones twitter and flock and dart, exploring new perches, new perspectives, new nesting sites. Mating time is upon them, despite the downpours. Valentine's Day, the time of the Parliament of Fowls. Larger gatherings of ducks and moorhens and seagulls and Canada geese sail and swoop by and noisily crash into the water and soar up again, and her familiar pair of mating swans is liberated into a greater space. Graciously her swans float upon the fields, reclaiming the land as their own. She has seen the swans by moonlight, when the sky was clear. She sees them from her bedroom window, serenely adrift upon the flood.

There is one odd bird she knows well, a clumsy goose-like creature, neither goose nor duck nor swan, a loner, awkward, a grubby scruffy white-feathered thing with pink feet, which sometimes comes to her to be fed. She has not seen it for some days. It has abandoned her. It has found, perhaps, new protectors.

She thinks of Noah and his ark. She does not know many Bible stories, but this is one that everybody knows. They had had a Noah's Ark, given to them by Granny Stubbs, a Galt wooden Ark with stubby archetypal brightly painted animals.

She has a large egg, two years old, in a flowerpot on her soft damp flaking windowsill. It will never hatch now. She found it, abandoned, two springs ago, amongst her carrots and courgettes. A goose egg, she thinks, laid and abandoned by a foolish mother. She sometimes wonders what is in it now. It still weighs heavy in the hand. Will it burst, like the great ribbed dark-striped weighty orange gourd that her mother had used as a doorstop in the back porch of the Highgate garden flat, the flat where she had lived with Hamish? It had suddenly exploded one day and splattered into a fine dry vegetable dust. Hamish and Fran had laughed and laughed.

Her mother can still laugh. She finds pleasure in life, her mother, even though Hamish is dead and she is old. Poppet admires this gift, this blessing.

Poppet had shown the egg last summer to some children on a passing narrow boat. The holiday family was lingering by her waterside landing stage, their hired boat idling, the father taking a cigarette break, the mother pegging out multicoloured underwear on an improvised washing line. The children had a rabbit with them, a large blue-grey velvety thick-furred rabbit, sitting with them on the deck. She had waved at them, uncharacteristically sociable in the July sun, and asked them about the travelling rabbit, and in no time they were ashore, the three eager red-haired children, and she was proudly offering them lemonade (she made her own, from Taunton Co-op lemons) and showing them her egg. They enjoyed her lemonade and admired her egg. Might it hatch one day, they wondered? Might it release a tiny dragon?

Poppet had not found this playful childhood fantasy annoying, although she did not, as a rule, much care for children. For in truth she had sometimes wondered herself if a little dragon, a baby dinosaur, a featherless dark-pink and yellow embryo, lay coiled in there, biding its time.

The three red-haired children were special. She has forgotten their names, but she remembers that the travelling rabbit was called Mr Rex.

It did not dawn on her at the time that he was called Mr Rex because he was a Rex rabbit, *Oryctolagus cuniculus*, a popular and hardy breed.

One day she will break the egg to see what is waiting for her in there. One terminal day. But that day is a long and weary way ahead.

In the dying glimmer of a fitfully sunlit half-hour towards the early dusk, she notes the names of the colours of the floods and of the trees: brown, umber, sallow, gold, bronze, rust. A pink-tinged silver, a pale silvery grey-green, a tarnished copper. The subtle woody brushy winter shades of the wetlands, a spectrum of suspended but approaching growth. She has a good eye, and she likes the names of colours. This land has often flooded: whatever the locals say in protest, this inundation is nothing new. The water bides its time. Over hundreds and thousands of years the rivers have burst their banks, and then retreated. Her friend who built the Stone Age house knew all about the ancient ways, the wooden paths over the marshes, the timber causeways, the peat, the Sweet Tracks, the islanded knolls, the sacred eminences.

The locals complain that there has not been enough dredging and pumping, but this flood is beyond dredging. The upper reaches of the rivers to the east should never have been deforested, the fields should never have been scarified, the tributaries should never have been straightened. The oxbows should have been allowed to form their slow and simple circles, the streams to meander at their own sweet will. It is too late in history to plant now, too late to halt the process now. The debate rages, in the press, in the pubs, in Parliament. Poppet, once so sure of her ideologies, does not know what will happen, what should happen. The landscape educates, but it does not bring full enlightenment.

She knows that her mother has a date in the neighbourhood with the estate built on Westmore Marsh, on the flood plain. She is off to visit some exemplary housing. Poppet wonders how well it is withstanding what we call the extreme weather events. Her mother's pertinacity and stamina are remarkable.

She has not invited her mother to call in, and her mother has not suggested a visit. They respect boundaries. That's what they say to themselves. But they do text each other nearly every day.

Near Ouseby, five miles upstream, there is a house on stilts, like Baba Yaga's. An expensive experimental ecohouse. It's the spiritual twin of the Willow Cabin, at the other end of the spectrum. She wonders how it fares. In Holland, they are experimenting with floatable housing.

This morning she saw the cranes, a majestic visitation. They sailed in, the great birds of the east, and settled half a mile up the canal, as though they owned the landscape, as though they have been here forever. But they have not. They are new. They have been reintroduced. They are at once strange and familiar, and from another era. They are partly funded by a landfill operator, as well as by various conservation trusts. The landfill operator is the company that, from time to time, empties Poppet's septic tank. She finds this strangely pleasing. It's quite an imaginative sponsorship.

She hopes her septic tank won't be breached by floodwater.

When the light fails truly and thickens into darkness, Poppet thinks she should take her treasures upstairs. She has few treasures: she lives lightly. But in the little low many drawered mahogany Victorian cabinet that she and Jim had rescued from the unofficial rural dump behind the Little Chef on the A303 there are some objects that she would not like to lose.

She opens the drawers. She hasn't looked in here for a long time. In the top drawer there are shells and stones, collected long ago by the ancestors of the callous fly-tipping Little Chef depositor, but in the lower layers there are potent bits and pieces of her life that she has assembled over the decades. Photographs, letters, bits of jewellery, an anachronistic silver napkin ring with her initials engraved upon it, given to her when she was a baby by Granny Robinson. A photograph, taken by her mother, of the primary school play in which she had appeared as a fisher-woman, or was she a fishwife. There she is, a dumpy little shapeless old-young bundle in her plaid shawl and long skirts. It had been some kind of children's opera, set in the Scottish Isles: they sang laments about herring. Why on earth had they been doing that, in inland Essex, in Romley? And there is her brother Chris, a buccaneer, with a silver dagger in his belt.

Her mother had made the costumes. Her mother enjoys sewing and stitching and mending, she's one of the few women left in Britain who likes to mend. She isn't very good at it, but she still likes doing it. Poppet, who in principle should be good at this kind of thing, can hardly thread a needle.

Poppet had a good voice, she could sing well and in tune, but she didn't really enjoy singing. Her father had teased her once, very heavily, when he'd heard her singing hymns to herself in her bedroom. It had put her off. She hadn't been singing hymns because she was religious, but because, when she was six years old, they were the tunes and the words that she knew best. She hadn't wanted to explain that to him, she wouldn't have been able to find the words. The primary school in Romley had been a Church of England school, where assembly was still held, where morning hymns were still sung.

> All things bright and beautiful . . .
> We plough the fields and scatter . . .
> All creatures of our God and King . . .
> Morning has broken like the first morning . . .

There she is again, older, college-age, sitting on a bench with Annie in a formal summer garden.

And there is the little Baby Jesus that she'd made in her first year at Rowbridge. It is a miracle, the little Baby Jesus. She'd never thought she was any good at art or crafts, she'd been hopeless at St Jude's Infants, but at Rowbridge she had made, as it were by mistake, this wonderful thing. She had made the reverse journey from the norm – usually children who are good at art in Infants forget how to do it in Junior and Secondary, but Poppet, briefly, had travelled the other way. He had just made himself, the Baby Jesus, out of clay and bark and bits of cloth and wicker and nutshells and stitching. He was a wonder. Miss Sullivan, sprightly butch big-chested Miss Sullivan, with her tufted skull-sprouting boot-black hair and her glitter-spattered cardigans, had been amazed by him. Why, Poppy, how wonderful! she had exclaimed. And so He was. Poppet could see He was a serious success. But she also knew that she would never be able to repeat this miracle.

She turned her back on art, as she had turned her back on singing. As she had turned her back on dark-browed Annie, deep-voiced, ambiguously seductive Annie Stokes.

As Annie had turned her back on Poppy Stubbs.

Baby Jesus, she now thinks, contemplating Him, resembles a piece of Aboriginal Australian art. Or, as she would now say, First Nation art. He had welled up from the earth below. Somehow she had tapped her way down and back into the roots of time, but had never been able to return again. It was not permitted to her to go down there again.

She had been to Australia, a few years ago, just before air travel became a recognised eco-crime. To a conference on climate change. And in Adelaide, she had visited the museum and made her way up to the long gallery of Aboriginal art, and gazed, surprised to be so affected. It wasn't the (to her) incomprehensible dotted dreamtime paintings that struck her; it was the artefacts and the wide-eyed ghostly faces on the artefacts. The shields, the posts, the cylindrical bark coffins.

Big Sister. Young Child. Old Man.

They had a look of her Baby Jesus. He had a look of them.

Baby Jesus had made himself.

She touches him, gently. He has wide eyes and an ashen face.

He watched over her and her ashen dreams.

In the cabinet, her favourite *objet trouvé* is a little polished wooden box with a brass monogram, 'JSS', which contains geological specimens from Tenerife. They rest on a crumpled crimson velvet cushioned bed, a collection of fifteen neatly labelled lava stones garnered from Mount Teide. The ink of the handwritten labels is fading but she can still read the words *azufre, pozzolana, basalt, phonolite* and *obsidian*, and the information that the first eruption on Tenerife was 'recorded by Genoese sailors' in 1393. The stones that had spewed up from the depths are enchanting. Some are minutely or coarsely pitted, like pumice; some are more rough and rugged in texture; some have smooth shining planes of cleavage like jet or coal. One is an astounding pale yellow, like a pale stick of Edinburgh Rock, one is sage green, one is as white as snow, one is black flecked with white, and three are of a mottled dried-blood clay-red.

The brown water laps, the muddy brown water of the Levels rises, and beneath the Atlantic Ocean to the west of the island of El Hierro, as yet but not for ever the most westerly of the Canaries, the crack in the earth widens.

~

The chicken soup that Fran presents to Claude is of the same stock as the soup she gave to Teresa, gently rendered from the same plump allegedly free-range fowl, but it is thicker, and reinforced with vegetables and macaroni. It has got more bits in it. Claude is a man, and he has more of an appetite than Teresa. He needs bits. Claude looks polite and appreciative as she puts the plastic box in the microwave and tells him he can warm it up later when she has gone. She stacks other labelled items into the freezer. She has come on the Tube, with her burlap bag. There's nowhere to park in Kensington. Her car is safe at home, home and dry, resting underground amongst the Kentucky Fried Chicken cartons and the fox-chewed carcasses of less fortunate birds. In a couple of days it will be allowed an outing to the west, for a good long battery-charging drive to Westmore Marsh.

Claude asks her if she has time to stay for a glass of wine and, if so, would she like to pour one for him too. She hesitates, selfishly, because she'd really rather go back to her flat and cross the strange high perilous thin bridge into the evening with a stiff stunner of a killer whisky, before embarking on the milder palliative glass of the corner shop Sauvignon that awaits her with her supper. Before settling down to her planned viewing of the borrowed DVD about *The Tibetan Book of the Dead*. But she is feeling indulgent towards Claude and pleased with the look of her chicken soup, so she agrees to stay for a chat. She pours the Chablis, sinks down into the dark-red well-worn Parker Knoll armchair, kicks off her boots, and puts her feet up on the old oak javelin box that for some reason lies at the end of Claude's bed. It hasn't got any javelins in it. It's full of old copies of *The Lancet* and the *New Scientist* and *The Spectator* and *Private Eye*, of old programmes from Glyndebourne and Covent Garden and ENO.

The oak could do with a polish. The carved and knotted wood looks dry and thirsty and in places it is patchy pale. But she's not going to start feeding Claude's furniture for him.

She longs to nourish the famished wood.

Fran has been known to water drooping pot plants in airport lounges and in the Ladies' toilets in motorway service stations.

Claude asks after Josephine, as he often does. The Romley days had been intense although disastrous, and they speak to him still. Like his son Christopher, he had fancied Jo, though he had not gone further than a squeezed hand and a fulsome compliment. He had been slightly frightened of Jo.

Fran hasn't really got much to say about Jo, so she contents herself with telling him that they are booked to go together to see *Happy Days* at the Young Vic, God knows why. Perhaps because Jo thinks it might illuminate the Adult Education course she is teaching? She immediately regrets mentioning this outing, even in a suitably deprecating tone, for in her view the semi-bed-ridden predicament of Claude is not unlike that of the half-buried Winnie in Beckett's play. But Claude doesn't seem to register this, for, rather like Winnie, he tends to ignore or deny the most inauspicious aspects of his condition.

So that's all right then, Fran says to herself, as Claude maintains that wild horses wouldn't drag him to see a Beckett play, or indeed any play, on any stage, ever again.

You always preferred the opera, says Fran, diplomatically or provocatively: at this stage in the game, who could say? I didn't really enjoy opera, or not enough to justify the cost.

One of our differences, says Claude, amicably. One of our many differences.

If Fran remembers rightly, Winnie quite often remarks, during the course of her monologue, on her gratitude for being free from pain.

At least. Free from pain. At least.

Great mercies. Great mercies.

She must look out for the lines, when she goes to the theatre with Jo.

Claude tells her about the obituary of Glyndebourne-frequenting Andrew Wetherill. It has been puzzling him, its tone had been a bit odd, and he didn't know the chap who wrote it, though he feels he should have done. Fran doesn't recognise the obituarist's name either. There's a new generation of potentially vindictive and almost certainly ignorant obituarists taking to the page these days, suggests Claude.

Fran doesn't expect an obituary, although Claude can't avoid one.

She had known Andrew, very slightly, but hadn't really moved in the circles where she might be likely to bump into him. She was aware, however, of his eccentricities. She listens to Claude's reminiscences about Andrew's selfish and piggish behaviour at the Marsden, his gross eating habits, his penchant for the double entendre, his abuse of his patients' vulnerability and confidentiality, his deafening bray of a laugh. His laugh frightened his assistants out of their skins and made them drop his instruments on the sterile floors.

She retaliates with her recollections of the elegantly raddled Stella Hartleap, and her irritation with the *Schadenfreude* of the press coverage of her death. Stella had been a star, in her way, an avant-garde sculptor of the old school whose Modernist works adorn many a public building.

Stella's London pad was in Highgate, and Fran had known her through Hamish.

Stella's flat had overlooked that deep leafy urban gulch that runs under the Archway, beneath the Bridge of the Suicides. Hamish and Fran had been there once or twice for drinks. Fran had liked the plunging view. She had always liked a view from a height. (*Why?* Will she work out the answer one day? Love of heights, love of movement, eating problems, cooking problems, sex problems, not much time left to work all that out now, and not much point in doing so, even if one could. But she must keep trying, she notes to herself.)

Stella Hartleap had also known Christopher, he had done a programme about her work, but Fran hadn't bothered to watch it. She'd pretended that she had, but she hadn't. She finds arts programmes boring, even when they feature her own son featuring a woman she likes, a woman whose work she admires. She can do without that kind of stuff.

Christopher had filmed Stella in the Black Mountains, not in her Highgate pad, because he thought it was more scenic there and he fancied a trip to Wales. Fran thought the mysterious layers and levels of Highgate were more scenic than Wales, although she had abandoned them when Hamish died. She had sold their flat and moved to the east. She hadn't wanted to live in Highgate on her own. She'd wanted a new place, a new life, for what was left of life.

She doesn't think very often of her happiness with Hamish, or of her sadness at losing him. It's as though her twenty years with him had been an interlude in the struggle of her life, an unmerited interlude. She had been fortunate to have them, but they had been irrelevant.

Now she has returned to the fray.

These thoughts flit through her busy mind, as she watches Claude frowning at *The Times* within his Kindle, and listens to him complaining about the upstart unknown obituarist.

Claude and Fran live in the world of obituaries now, in the malicious crepuscular light of memorial services. Claude is more embedded in it than Fran, but she takes, as we have seen, an interest.

Christopher is still out there in the Canaries. He is basking idly in the sun, but the rain pours down on his sister Poppet. Fran thinks of them, her children, as she places her wine glass in Claude's dishwasher, zips up her boots, and leaves Claude to his chicken soup as she goes out once more to face the weather.

~

Suzette is worried about Dorothy. Year upon year there has been little change in the uncanny sweetness of her charge Dorothy.

Suzette has been running the care home for nearly fifteen years now and in all that time Dorothy, who has been there much longer, has been peaceable, grateful, amenable, easy to tidy and handle, a good advertisement for Chestnut Court. She has been no trouble at all. Sometimes Suzette gives her an impulsive hug, and says, Dorothy, you're no trouble at all! But now Dorothy seems to be fretting, there is something caught in her drifting mind, some snag or tangle. Suzette sits by Dorothy in her room, patiently and gently massaging her thin shoulders for a couple of minutes, then brushing the silvery waves of her neat well-trimmed hair.

Dorothy is looking anxious, and she keeps repeating that she has 'lost' it. She doesn't know where she has put 'it'. It has gone.

Suzette can't work out what 'it' is. Dorothy has accumulated few possessions over her lifetime, though those that she has are precious to her. In the little space of her neat well-ordered room there is nowhere to lose anything.

Her brush and comb, her necklaces, her rings. On her dressing table stands an old-fashioned toiletry set with a soap dish and a pale blue and white Wedgwood china ring tree and a Wedgwood thimble upon it, relics from her early married days. From padded coat hangers in her wardrobe depend her skirts and blouses and frocks, her summer coat and her winter coat. Dorothy had made the coat hanger covers herself, from pretty floral fabric remnants that Suzette's predecessor Linda had picked up for a song in Beatties department store in Wolverhampton. Dorothy had been good with her needle, but her fingers are too stiff for sewing now. They can hold a pen but they can't thread a needle. Her gilt-edged pocket Bible is on the little table by her bed. Her magazines are stacked in a cane magazine rack, and her pens and pencils stand in stencil-decorated jam jars on what she calls her work desk. She is kept well supplied with drawing materials, and has a bright variety of acrylic pens, crayons, glitter brushes and stick-on-stars, as well as colouring-in books. On the mantelpiece above the boxed-in 1930s fireplace are photographs in silver frames, of long dead family members, and of her late husband who had disappeared when she was in her twenties, and of Ralph, her son in Australia.

There is no photograph of her sister Emily, or of her nephew Paul, although Paul is the only person who keeps in touch with her and sees to her finances and paper work.

Suzette likes Paul: he is reliable, he is a professional. He knows the field, and she knows that he, in turn, relies on her.

But since Paul's last visit, a few days ago, Dorothy has been unsettled. She'd seemed fine at the time, she'd seemed to enjoy chatting to Paul's friend, that chirpy woman in the stripy jersey, and has mentioned her with approval several times. She's even, so far, remembered her name. *Fran. I liked Fran.* But since then she has been fretful, worrying about whatever it is that she has lost.

Suzette doesn't like the suggestion that something has gone missing from Chestnut Court. She prides herself on running a secure outfit, a safe retreat, where everything is accounted for, even to those who can't count and don't notice. When she was younger, she'd worked in a care home where a lot of things went missing, as a matter of course, where clothes ended up in the wrong wardrobes, where the residents were dressed in whatever came to hand. It's true that some of them didn't care what they wore, but some of them did. And anyway, Suzette thought it was wrong, wrong in principle.

And worse things than missing clothes had happened. You couldn't call it abuse, or even neglect. It was more like indifference.

It's a mystery to Suzette, that Dorothy's personality is so distinct, even though she is so confused. She's a bit of a prima donna, in her own modest way. No, Suzette reconsiders, prima donna isn't the right word, it's too vain, too self-important. But Dorothy is special. She's a character. She's herself. She insists on being herself. Some of her guests (Suzette likes to think of them as guests) have lost themselves, have thinned out into speechlessness, forgetfulness, dormancy, a poorly remembered past. They're hardly there, inside themselves, there's not much of them left, they're half asleep, waiting to wake up somewhere else or not at all.

Suzette thinks from time to time about where they might wake up, and as what.

Suzette was brought up as a Christian, as a sort of Christian, sort of as a Christian. Her parents didn't go to church, except for weddings and christenings and funerals, but they paid lip service, and encouraged her to go to the Brownies and to promise to do her duty to God. She'd loved the Brownies. Their Tawny Owl had been her school dinner lady Mrs Rose, and she was a hoot, full of fun ideas, some of them quite risky, like that day at Dudley Castle with the treasure hunt. She'd put a lot of work into them, had Mrs Rose.

Suzette teases a few of Dorothy's silver hairs out of the brush, drops them into the plastic-bag-lined wicker waste-paper basket.

Who could believe in heaven? It's just too silly. Yet the church says it believes in heaven, the minister who comes regularly to visit has to say he believes in heaven, it's part of his job. She's seen too many people die to believe in heaven.

But if anyone is in heaven, Mrs Rose the Tawny Owl will be. They might make an exception for her.

Perhaps Dorothy is on the way out. Perhaps she's had a premonition. Suzette believes in premonitions.

Suzette has known so many final rooms, so many relicts, so many family photographs, so many lives shrunk into a little space. Will they ever burst out again into where they were before they were so diminished? Will they ever again walk free and unencumbered, in a different, perhaps even a better, element? How good it would be to think so.

She remembers a coach outing from West Bromwich they'd been on, a long day trip a few years ago now, when, after a stately home and a bit of shopping, they'd all been taken to see a chapel, or was it a war memorial, or a little gallery, she can't remember now, but she can still see those paintings. Of churchyards, with leaning tombstones and graves, and solid stout cheery ordinary men and women in ordinary old-fashioned clothes like her Nana wore, clambering up out of the earth, greeting one another, all happy, reunited, ready for eternity. The tour guide said it was the Resurrection. They had stared at it, subdued.

There was another painting, by the same artist, of black and white cows. He was famous, or they wouldn't have been taken to see his work. She can't remember his name.

It was all too silly, to think we'd clamber up out of the clay. But some people are very fussy about wanting or not wanting to be cremated. They have views on what happens or should happen or will happen to the body.

Suzette knows how to cater for all these options, in a practical manner. She'd failed with the old boy who wanted to be buried at sea, but she'd arranged it so that his family could scatter his ashes, discreetly, off the pier at Penarth. He'd been a captain, he'd been skipper of the old pleasure steamer that went up and down the Bristol Channel. He used to like to talk about his seafaring days. You'd have thought he'd sailed the China seas, the way he went on. But he'd been a game old chap, for all that.

Her own view, despite the possible exception she makes for Mrs Rose, is that when you die, that's it. That's the end. This prospect doesn't alarm her at all. You're here for your lifetime, and then you're gone.

But it's odd that Dorothy has been here-and-not-here for so long. It's puzzling.

Her guests had enjoyed the outings, and so had she. It's harder to organise them now, there are so many regulations and so much worry about health and safety, and there have been one or two spectacular coach disasters, it's fair to say. But the family firm of Judges Coaches had kept going. She thinks they won't last long when Bill Judge gives up, but she's booked those who are fit to go onto the Easter outing to Chillington Hall. Dorothy will go. She loves an outing.

Dorothy will go, if she lasts that long.

~

Christopher Stubbs, Simon Aguilera and the sure-footed Ishmael climb the shallow steps of the winding stair of stone inside the famine tower. Ivor has stayed at the foot of the tower, sitting on a warm stone slab in the late afternoon sun. He'd been up there once, a couple of years ago, to please Simon, but never again. Bennett had stayed behind on Simon's terrace, dozing and reading and dozing again, but Christopher had agreed to go to look at the murals in progress that Simon had commissioned, although he is almost sure that he will not like them, and that his lack of enthusiasm might be embarrassing.

La Fortaleza del Hambre. The Famine Tower, the Tower of Hunger. It's old, it's ageless, it's probably medieval. It's undocumented. It may have been built at the time of de Béthencourt, the Norman knight, the first invader. It was mentioned by the explorers von Humboldt and Richard Burton, both of whom had called by: one on his way to the West, the other on his way to the East. The tower had stored grain, it had kept watch for pirates, it had kept watch for sardines and whales, and now it keeps watch for the *immigrantes*.

Christopher thinks there may be more in Bennett's notion of writing a little history of the Canaries than the weary and protective Ivor can allow himself to hope. He has picked up Ivor's guarded scepticism about the project, and also his need to humour Bennett, but he has also been much affected by what little he has so far seen of these islands. It is not Sara's angry political vision that has held him captive here. It is the place itself. Its topography, its geography, its geology, its strange palette of dark sand, pale earth, red iron. Its palette of the grey-blue-green of cactus and aloe and lichen and euphorbia. Its calm beyond all anger, all desire.

The soft dry light is of uncanny beauty and clarity and purity, it has an unearthly radiance. No wonder astronomers make this their home, for they are nearer here to the unveiled heavens than in most places on earth. The air meets the skin gently here, it lingers with a soft beneficence, it breathes into the body calmly and sweetly, it is temperate and benign.

The Isles of the Blessed. Circe's Island.

A painter's light, a painter's landscape. But the Canaries do not seem, as Simon has acknowledged, to have produced much of significance in the way of art, apart from the ubiquitous and highly visible works of César Manrique, and the collectable burlap works of Millares, which may or may not have been inspired by the Guanche mummies. De Chirico had never been here, as far as Christopher knows, although one of his paintings hangs in Simon's gallery, although the little white towns and chapels and beaches and colonnades of the islands seem to have been created with his approval and in his style.

Back at La Suerte, Christopher has had time for a late-night laptop search (quite a strong signal) for visual arts links with the islands, but has not as yet found anything of interest. He cannot get beyond César Manrique, who crowds the screen. He has only just heard of Millares and his stitchings, and will look them up when he gets back. He has a nagging recollection that somebody once told him (a Welsh chap called Gareth Morgan with BBC Wales?) that the Welsh artist James Dickson Innes, dying of tuberculosis, had visited the Canaries for the sake of his health: could Innes, in his last days, have painted these scrub-spotted, dotted grey-green volcanic landscapes, these large skies, these turquoise lagoons, these scrawls of tufa? They do have a look of his work. They imitate his style. He made Wales look like the Canaries. And if he had painted here, does any memory of him remain, hovering, embedded, or wandering the foothills? Christopher had thought of asking Bennett about him, for Bennett is knowledgeable about the visual arts, and seems to know or have known quite a few artists, although none of them go as far back as Innes, who had died, if he remembers rightly, during the First World War. Before Bennett's time, before Chopping and Wirth-Miller's time, before Francis Bacon's time, before Stanley Spencer's time.

But he'd felt uneasy about asking Bennett. It's not a good idea to ask old people questions they may not know how to answer. He'll bide his time, see if the right moment for reminiscence comes.

A colouring of Ivor's solicitude for Bennett has reached him. There is something affecting and poignant in Bennett's game sprightliness, in his eagerness to entertain, to make the best of his last years for himself and for others.

The murals are, as he had feared, distressing, and not likely to enhance the painterly profile of Fuerteventura. They are bold, blue, expressionist, exploitative, melodramatic, public, ghastly, and appear to have been crudely slapped onto clumsily erected panels of a kind of rough plaster hardboard. They are supposed to begin with the story, Simon explains, of the original conquest in the Middle Ages: that unfinished scene shows the arrival of three ships from Lisbon in the quattrocento, with their mixed crew of Florentines, Genoese, Castilian and Portuguese adventurers, with their warhorses.

The islanders, says Simon, had never seen either horses or ships.

The next panel sketches the welcome and the feast, and the next shows the four innocent and guileless Canary islanders embarking – not as captives, not slaves, but as honoured guests – for their voyage to Lisbon. Handsome, free, elegantly clothed in embroidered goat skins. The history of enslavement has not begun. Slavery was yet to come, centuries later.

The painter had become bored by all this history, and had leaped ahead to splash away at his final and more topical panel, of a twenty-first-century shipwreck, of a sinking patera and drowning immigrants.

It is clear that Simon's protégé is familiar with the works of Delacroix and Géricault. *The Raft of the Medusa* and the Senegalese patera spring from the same source, welter in the same waves. It is also clear that Ishmael has been used as a model, for there he is, recognisably himself, standing at the helm (if that's the word) of the sinking vessel. Not a bad likeness, it must be admitted. A heroic figure, signalling hopelessly to shore, to the beach and the lighthouse and the walled cemetery of Gran Tarajal. There are bodies in the water, faces of men, women and children looking up through the water. The piece is declamatory and lacking in finesse.

Christopher, Simon and Ishmael stare silently at the image of the wreck. Ishmael shrugs, in a faint disclaimer, as though the whole thing has nothing to do with him. Although it has. 'It had a Yamaha motor,' he offers, as some kind of apology, some kind of explanation. Christopher can't think of anything at all to say, in the face of this tragedy.

A brand from the burning, a soul rescued from the surges.

It is Simon who speaks. 'Good Time and Bad Time,' he says, enigmatically. Christopher nods, knowingly, but at a loss.

As they trudge silently down again, Christopher works out that Simon's words remind him of Ghalia Namarome, sitting colourfully on her carpet at the airport, on hunger strike amidst the ignorant, indifferent and incurious tourist tribes. And he thinks also of some extraordinary YouTube footage he and Sara had watched together, in Queen's Park, W10, not long before they'd come out here. YouTube had delivered to them an immigrant who had struggled ashore onto a holiday beach in Fuerteventura from a sinking vessel, as Ishmael had done: he can be seen sitting, slumped, exhausted, expressionless, amidst the parasols, and a holiday-maker had calmly filmed him as he sat there, breathless, staring at nothing. Some person had seen fit to film this moment, and then had posted it, as far as Christopher and Sara could see, without comment, for all to see.

You can see it now, unless it's lapsed.

Holiday footage. Good Time, Bad Time.

Malta. Lampedusa. Mare Nostrum. Fuerteventura, Lanzarote, El Hierro. The Mediterranean and the Atlantic. The Pillars of Hercules. Frontex of the Frontiers. The Great Berm. The Wall of Shame.

Christopher's daughter Amy, at the University of Sussex, is writing a 10,000-word dissertation on walls, partitions, frontiers. A big subject, for an English girl, an island girl.

Christopher has tried not to build a high wall between himself and his daughter Amy and his ex-wife Ellie. There is no wall of shame dividing them.

Sara and Christopher, late at night, safe in bed together in Queen's Park under their duvet in a miserable and increasingly wet January, comfortable and warm, had watched the miseries of others on their little screen, not knowing that they too, or one of them, was in the firing line, on the last stretch.

It's a pity that Sara's months of research on devolution and repatriation had been wasted. It's a pity that she never got to meet Tomás at the Spanish Red Cross in Puerto del Rosario. He'd been waiting for her. He'd had much to tell her, about asylum conditions, about the deportation treaties with Morocco and Nigeria.

It's a pity she never got to meet Ishmael and hear him speak in French, English, Arabic, Wolof.

Senegal has no repatriation treaties with Spain.

The sun is warm on Bennett Carpenter's papery creased eyelids and white eyelashes, on his tanned and freckled forehead and his bushy brows. His weathered straw hat rests idly on the table. He doesn't worry about melanoma. He likes the warmth. He is dreaming, pleasantly, one of those strange levitating dreams of the late afternoon. At night, in deeper sleep, he dreams unpleasant, panicky but trivial dreams, of airports and lectures, of missed appointments and the malice of his enemies, dreams which reflect badly, as he sadly knows, on his lack of spiritual composure and magnanimity. But in the afternoons he some-times wanders into better realms. Gardens, riverbanks, woodland, churches. He and Ivor, in England, in their middle period, had enjoyed visiting churches, sometimes deeply obscure and unim-portant churches, humble churches hardly noticed by the county guides and Pevsner, a relief after the Moorish splendours and tragic baroque aspirations and grandiose Fascist war memorials of Spain. They did cathedrals too, but they preferred the out-of-the-way. Bennett was not religious, he was a free-thinking agnostic, and living so much with the Spanish Civil War had not inclined him towards a favourable view of the Roman Catholic or indeed of any Christian faith. He wouldn't have said he was anti-clerical, but he was.

His parents had also been agnostics, although, when questioned or required to fill in a form, they meekly said they were Church of England. It was easier that way.

Ivor, ever faithful to Bennett's beliefs, had, as it seemed, shared his conventional scepticism. But Bennett had once seen him crossing himself and mildly and reverently inclining his head, in an unassuming little Norman church on a dry knoll in the spreading flatness of the pylon-bestridden Midlands. Dry Doddington, that had been the name of the village. Ivor didn't know Bennett had seen him, but he had.

Had he been saying a covert prayer for Bennett, whose health was limping unevenly downhill? Or praying for action, for release?

Not very long after this moment, they had moved to the dry Canaries, to a new life and to new townscapes for which Pevsner offered no guide. For which, in Bennett's view, a guide would be very beneficial.

He doesn't yet know he has a possible convert in the entertaining and lively young Christopher Stubbs.

Bennett, dozing on Simon's terrace, dreams he is sitting on a riverbank by the derelict little flour mill near his grandparents' home in Leicestershire. He had played and fished there as a little boy, with his big brothers, and sometimes returns there in his dreams, peaceably but with a sense of longing, always hoping that the great fish he once glimpsed there will swim up into the sunny shallows from the flowing sunlit electric-green weed-fronded depths of the slowly flowing water. The fish never comes, and his brothers had never believed him when he told them what he had seen. A great broad-headed fish, as large as a baby. It had risen up, basked a little, then descended into the depths. A tench, a dace, a pike?

His brothers had teased him for years, for decades, about the large fish he said he had seen.

'The fish that got away,' they tediously teased him.

They had envied his professional success, his worldly acclaim, his honour. Sir Bennett Carpenter. They hadn't liked that, though they had to pretend they did. They had fared well enough, but not as well as he.

They are both dead now.

These recurring dreams of a smugly archetypal fish are pastoral and full of yearning, but they are also light in spirit. They belong to a time before his life had been contaminated by ambition, competition, academe, success and sex. To the time when he first met young Owen English.

Owen is a romantic. His life has been lonely. It had begun well, but it had ended in a chilly loneliness. Owen, Bennett believes, lives in some sort of retirement home in damp and foggy Cambridge, at the mercy of the winds from the east, writing a monograph about clouds. It had been good to lure him over to the sun for a week or two at Christmas. He'd been an easy and appreciative guest.

Bennett has been blessed in the company and dedication of Ivor Walters. On some levels of his waking and dreaming, he knows this, and on other levels he resists the knowledge and feels he has been confined by Ivor's fidelity.

Ivor had been the most beautiful young man anyone could ever have desired to see. He was a pure calm blond Aryan beauty from Staines. Whereas Bennett had been squat and comic and verbose, clever and impetuous and colourful, witty and adored. Highly coloured, highly charged, high blood pressure, bad lungs.

Beauty and the Beast.

~

In his later years, the mildly demented poet Alphonse de Lamartine often escaped after dinner and they would find him wandering in the fields. Bennett sometimes thinks of this, as he thinks of Unamuno. They were both, in their way, casualties of revolutionary politics.

∽

Bennett occasionally puzzles Ivor with a phrase which he cannot decode. 'I apprehend caducity,' says Bennett. He says it in the same mournful but dignified tone in which he announces, 'I've lost my alacrity'.

Ivor doesn't understand the word 'caducity'. He can't even find it in his dictionary. Maybe that's because he doesn't know how to spell it. And he doesn't like to ask.

∽

Fran, sitting in her stationary little Peugeot, unable to advance or retreat, says to herself: you're a fucking idiot, you're a fucking stubborn old fool, what the fuck do you think you're doing? Are you *mad*?

Valerie Heritage had emailed the night before to tell her that the road was risky and the forecast bad. But that hadn't put her off, oh no, not at all. It had egged her on. She'd set off, well before dawn, to drive westward to the marshes, and here she is, where satnav has brought her: to a standstill on a country road that isn't even a B road.

She reflects, angrily, that she is here because of that fucking awful depressingly stupid and yet mesmerising production of *Happy Days*, which she and Jo had clocked up three nights ago. Jo had doubled it with an appointment with a foot surgeon, to see if anything could be done about her hammer toe.

It couldn't.

Fran can't understand why Jo couldn't have seen a foot

surgeon in Cambridge, which must have both demand and supply for this specialty, but apparently the best man for the job is Mr Sillitoe at St Luke's in Chelsea. The choice of Sillitoe, she gathers, also had something to do with Jo's late husband's medical insurance.

Claude had approved the name of surgeon Sillitoe, when Fran had mentioned it. He's a good man, Claude said.

The name is bizarre. Had the name affected his career choice?

Samuel Beckett had a hammer toe. He also had an obsession with the slow processes of dying. Fran had really really disliked this. He'd lived to a good old age, hadn't he, so what had he been on about?

His mother, the Second World War – she knew the theories.

Sitting grimly upright on a small hard insecure seat through the mercifully short *Happy Days*, watching Maroussia Darling playing Winnie buried up to her neck in sand, Fran had been through torments of resistance and denial, on her own behalf, on behalf of all the ageing women in the land. Boredom and rage had combined and accumulated in her, minute after minute, as Maroussia sat there, trapped beneath the pitiless lights of the stage sun. It didn't help to know that Maroussia Darling was herself in poor health, and that this would probably be her last bravura stage performance. This was not general knowledge: she had had it from Jo, who had it from Jo's friend Eleanor, who had been Maroussia Darling's friend and neighbour in Highbury for forty years. Why Maroussia would agree to play such a death-confronting role at her time of life and in her state of health was another mystery. It could hardly be an accidental or arbitrary choice. It couldn't be very cheery, going through that stuff night after night, knowing you weren't going to leap up rejuvenated when the curtain fell.

Of course, at the end, there was the applause, indeed a standing ovation. Maybe, at the end, what we need most, in order to make a good exit, is applause. Applause, in a showy part. Going out bravely. And, for Maroussia, this grim evening was also work, paid work. Work is a saviour, of sorts. Fran had thought several times, during the short but interminable stage performance, of her Ashley Combe contract, of the smallish but honourable sums of money that would slide silently into her bank account. She always checked online to see if they were there. They always were. They were a lifeline, in more ways than one.

'The theatre is so *uncomfortable*,' Jo had conceded to Fran over their post-show plate of pasta. 'I'm glad we went, but it really is an endurance test.'

'It's our age,' said Fran, who didn't want to be too negative, as Jo had bought the tickets. 'The young people didn't seem to care about comfort at all. There were a lot of young people there, I thought. Is Beckett in fashion?'

'I suppose he is,' said Jo, poking suspiciously at a foreign body in her linguine.

'I used to be able to stand, at the back of the cinema,' said Fran. 'I couldn't do that now.'

'You don't have to,' said Jo.

Yes, that's how much of their conversation had gone, reflected Fran. There'd been some asides about Jo's discovery of some Spanish Civil War diaries, but she had not quite got to grips with why Jo found them so interesting. She couldn't really follow the meanderings of Jo's research project, which seemed of late to have changed direction. She'd been more absorbed with the Beckett theme. And here she is now, stuck on a flooded road, with a useless satnav, wondering what on earth she was supposed to do next. She'd been so angry with Samuel Beckett and Winnie that she'd ignored all the weather warnings and set off defiantly. She'd rather die fighting, like Siward the Dane, than lying in a ditch, like a cow, or buried up to her neck with a handbag, like

Winnie. But now she is in a predicament. It's a narrow road, and she can see three stationary vehicles ahead of her, before a curving corner around which she can't see, and behind her there are a couple of cars. Everything, over time, has come to a halt. There is standing water on the road, inches of it. If she could get moving, she could drive through it, at whatever risk to her gear box or exhaust or whatever parts of the car are most vulnerable to water, but she can't move. She has switched her engine off, and looks down at the pedals. It's hard to see, in modern cars, what connects with what, or where the water would rise, if it were to start to rise. Everything is concealed, sealed off, hidden away. Where's the air intake, which presumably will turn into a water intake if this goes on? She's no idea.

Is it called the footwell, this place where her feet and the pedals are? What an odd word, one she's never had cause to use. It won't be good if it starts to fill up with water, as wells do.

It's still raining, no longer heavily, but persistently. She's always thought of herself as a competent driver, but she knows she's not a mechanic. She wouldn't know what to do with a submerging car. Will her engine and her electrical system be ruined? She seems to remember reading that one should never drive into water that is more than four inches deep, or flowing, or more than half way up the wheels. She opens her window and stares down. Is it already halfway up the wheels? Is it rising? She can't see. She's in no danger, no danger at all, she could easily (well, quite easily) get out and wade through that brown weed-filled ditch of reeds and teasels and clamber up that muddy willow bank and make an AA rescue call, but she doesn't want to abandon her poor vehicle. If she gets out, she'll be really and truly stranded, in the February countryside, with her handbag. Stranded, stupid, feckless.

Bloody old fool.

There hadn't been any 'Road Closed' notices. These other fools, young and old, had gone ahead as well as her, and followed her from behind. Why the fuck hadn't they kept moving? What's stopping them? Is there some disaster around that corner, stopping them all in their tracks? If you keep moving, you don't get stuck. Should she get out and ask the driver in the car in front what's going on? Should she make contact with the chap in the car behind? She doesn't like the look of him in her mirror. He's youngish, red-faced, with ginger sideburns, and is wearing a grey and white striped woolly hat. He looks cross (she can't blame him for that) and is talking angrily into his mobile phone. His car (she peers) is, she thinks, a Toyota. A metal grey not-so-new country-style Toyota.

French cars are better made than Japanese cars. Or they used to be.

She doesn't really fancy getting her feet wet. She'd rather *drown* than get her feet wet. Her comfortable smart fawn red-laced suede shoes are far from watertight. She's got wellies in the boot, but she can't get at them without wading. Should she ring Valerie Heritage? She's only been here five minutes, nothing by London traffic-jam standards, but it seems like hours. It won't matter if she's late, it won't matter if she doesn't get there at all, but she doesn't want Valerie Heritage to be cross with her. This delay is constructing in Valerie Heritage's name a figure of authority and disapproval, a superior being who will look down on Fran as an incompetent idiot.

Fran hates reversing. She's bad at reversing. She really really doesn't want to have to reverse out of this impasse, back down this narrow road. She wants to go on.

At the moment she has no choice. She can't move.

She'd switched off her engine, but now she turns it back on to make contact with her radio. So far so good, everything still working. *Woman's Hour!* Wonderful! Jenni Murray! Wonderful!

They are talking about assisted suicide, which isn't quite so wonderful. She's all in favour of it, of course. But not yet. As St Augustine said, not yet. Not now, not yet.

She switches it off.

She thinks of her new-old friend Teresa, who probably doesn't approve of assisted suicide, because she is a believer, of a sort, although she would be far too polite and considerate to argue unpleasantly about it with Fran.

Irritation and frustration are building up in Fran, along with the increasingly large and portentous figure of the judgmental Warden of Westmore Marsh Sheltered Housing. She can hear a bit of hooting and engine revving ahead, as though some movement were about to start to happen, but it dies down again. She thinks there's probably a little bridge a bit further on, one of the many little low bridges in this watery flatland of the Levels, and maybe that's what's stopping them.

Gripped by boredom, depressed by the brown, bare and hardly budding twigs of the hedgerow and by the dead wood of yester-year, she starts to text everybody she knows, or everyone with whom she is on texting terms. She doesn't want to ring them, she doesn't want to speak to anybody, she just wants to make some kind of contact.

She texts Josephine Drummond, Teresa Quinn, Paul Scobey, Peter Boddicote of Ashley Combe, her daughter Poppet, and her ex-daughter-in-law Ella, with whom she tried to maintain a friendship, for the sake of the grandchildren.

She doesn't text Claude, he doesn't do texts.

NOT WAVING MAYBE DROWNING, she idly texts Christopher, then notices that her battery has lost one of its little segment things, and switches her mobile off. She'd better conserve what's left of it. It doesn't occur to her that her message might be enigmatic.

~

Christopher, in the warm dry south but in the same time zone as his mother, receives this message as he sits on Bennett's terrace with a mid-morning high-caffeine solo coffee in an eloquently foreign little glass cup, a vessel which reminds him of youth, of other lives, of paths not taken. What is his stupid mother up to now? It's not like her not to sign off properly. She invariably signs herself off as Fx.

He texts her back. WHERE R U? CX

He is beginning to worry, at times, about Fran. There is something slightly manic about her restlessness. She buzzes about too much. What is she after? She's not ill, like Claude: if anything, she's a bit too well. She should slow down.

He knows he ought to be moving on from this warm plateau, getting back to London to organise some work, to confront the next problematically open phase of his career, but La Suerte is seductive. The weather in England has been dreadful, dark and unprecedentedly wet and gloomy, global-warming-gloomy, drown-in-a ditch gloomy, and he knows he would have to get to grips with the meaning of the absence of Sara were he to go home to their empty London flat in expensive but joyless Queen's Park. He enjoys the undemanding and appreciative company of Ivor and Bennett. There is something restful about their intercourse, with its practised repartee, its occasional flashes of mild outgoing malice or of comic inward mutual reproach. They have weathered it out together, these two: their non-marriage has in years outlasted most of the marriages he has known, and without legal or any other discernible compulsion. It is good being with a couple so calm, so un-needy. They don't need him, but they like him to be there. He feels liberated into an un-usually comfortable sense of inertia.

The temperature is benign. Blood, air, water, and a light and favourable breeze.

The Simon Aguilera outing had added colour and drama to

the sense of a prevailing washed-up peace. The story of Ishmael is too strange. How could one ever know what was going on, in that handsome head of his? Sara would have been able to make contact with him, on a more serious political level, on an ethnic and linguistic level, but Christopher knows he cannot. He is too English. However cosmopolitan a life he leads, however international the so-called 'arts scene' which brings him his livelihood, he is English. It's out-of-date, being English, in the modern world. His quasi-professional alliance with Sara (for they were of the media, had met through the media) had seemed to lead him onwards, but it has been killed off in its infancy. He has no idea where to go next. Sara's death had been so sudden, so utterly unexpected and unprogrammed. So meaningless. Cut off in the prime of life.

He thinks, suddenly, of the painter Pauline Boty, the beautiful blonde, the Wimbledon Bardot, who had died even younger than Sara. She'd died in the mid-1960s, if he remembers rightly, at the age of twenty-eight, of malignant thymoma, a rare kind of cancer, as rare as the pheochromocytoma that had killed Sara. Some ten years ago he'd made a programme about Boty's work as a pop artist, when there'd been a revival of interest in her, marked by a scattering of exhibitions, at home and abroad. He'd interviewed some of those who had known her in the 1960s, and had got into a memorable spat with a feminist about Boty's agenda on sexism. The feminist had insisted on portraying Boty as embattled and ill-treated, the victim of discrimination. Christopher hadn't been able to read her in that way at all. To him, she had seemed powerful, free-spirited, experimental, erotic and happy in her body. Of course, he'd never met her, but neither had the feminist. They'd both been infants when she died.

The feminist person had made much of the fact that Boty had told the novelist Nell Dunn, in an interview the year before she died, that she thought she had 'an ugly cunt', because she'd played with it as a child, trying to make herself look more like her brothers. Trying, presumably, to grow a penis. The feminist person had interpreted this as an illustration of Boty's subjection to a male stereotype, but to Christopher it had seemed to be something quite different – an example of extraordinary self-confidence and outspokenness, a certainty of her own strength. A woman who could say to an interviewer, 'I used to think I had an ugly cunt', and be prepared to look at the words in print, was afraid of nothing. The feminist person, thought Christopher, had imposed her own reading on Boty's life, had retrospectively attempted to deny her beauty, her womanhood, her lifeblood.

He'd been very rude to that woman, but she had been provocative. It had made good TV, but it had handed ammunition to the enemy. Christopher, for a while, had been reviled in the press as a sexist swine, or hailed as an Iron Man. He hadn't liked either role.

Sara is newly dead, Pauline Boty is long dead, Simon Aguilera's wife is long dead, and Ishmael is improbably very much alive.

He ought to be heading home, away from the Fortunate Isles, but he can't make himself get round to booking a flight, and he knows Ivor doesn't want him to leave just yet. He feels for Ivor. Ivor has been almost uncannily helpful about Sara's Transaerovac insurance invoices, and tactful with it. He'd instantly got on good terms with the lawyers for Sara's production company, Falling Water, back home, and with the insurance company's representatives on the island. What could have been a prolonged and expensive legal tussle has been smoothed out for him. Ivor is good at managing. He's negotiated the hotel bills, some of them left unpaid during the outgoing flurry. (The bar bills would have been, potentially, revealing.) He has decades of expertise, from managing the erratic and temperamental Bennett and his many medical mini-crises around the globe.

Ivor has revealed to Christopher that he has learned the phrase 'The professor has lost his glasses' in several different languages, including Japanese. He's not a linguist, but, like Bennett, he's a mimic, and can sound misleadingly convincing in foreign tongues. *Der Professor hat seine Brille verloren. Le Professeur a perdu ses lunettes. Il Professore ha perso gli occhiali. El Profesor ha perdido sus gafas.* He has even learned the difference between glasses mislaid in Spanish territories (*gafas*) and glasses mislaid in Mexico (*lentes*), and the polite non-judgmental way of saying that the professor's glasses have gone and lost themselves. 'I have lost my glasses' becomes '*Se me olvido mis anteojos*'.

The title of Professor goes down well, around the globe. It's multilingual, and it commands just the right degree of respect. Respect without sycophancy.

Ivor has promised to display his linguistic expertise on the topic of mislaid glasses this very afternoon, on a post-siesta visit with Christopher to the Grand Hotel to see if by any chance Christopher's expensive tinted varifocals have turned up. They are highly desirable, but not much use to anyone else, as Christopher has one long eye, one short eye, and his prescription is highly personalised. (Christopher is ashamed of how much he'd paid for these specs, but he is a public person and he needs to look good. They are – or were? – by way of being his trademark.) The management has promised to keep looking for them, and there is no harm in going round there to nudge them.

Bennett has declined the outing, he says he's tired, he'll stay at La Suerte and re-read Saramago's *Stone Raft*. He's now remembered the name of the apocalyptic book that had eluded him over the sea bass in the restaurant at Nazaret. Renewed reports this morning of yet more tremors off westerly El Hierro have combined to summon up the title of this entertaining novel, in which his late friend Saramago imagines that the whole of the Iberian peninsula has broken free from the continental land mass along the ridge of the Pyrenees and drifted out into the Atlantic. Excellent. He enjoys alternative, what-if histories, though some of them can be rather silly. What if the Germans had won the First World War, what if Hitler had been assassinated, what if Kennedy hadn't been assassinated. There's quite a vogue for them these days, he gathers. Although of course Saramago is in a class of his own.

Winston Churchill had planned to invade the Canaries, if the Germans had seized Gibraltar. He had 24,000 men on standby, in Operation Pilgrim, but he had never had to do it.

There are far more than 24,000 Brits in the Canaries now.

Simon Aguilera had been the victim of revisionism, on his father's behalf. Inevitable, really. We do so like to unpick heroism. Revisionists have gone over George Orwell's record in the Spanish Civil War with what we used to call a toothcomb, whatever a toothcomb may be. Orwell revisionists have revised Orwell revisionists. POUM, the NKVD, Harry Pollitt, Arthur Koestler, Victor Gollancz. *We petty men do find ourselves dishonourable graves . . .* Of course Carlos Aguilera couldn't have escaped that posthumous process. Too much ideology, too many careers invested in the arguments.

Owen England had liked Simon's Augustus John drawing of Valentine Studdert Meade, commissioned by Valentine's Cambridge-based parents in support of Artists International. Simon's uncles, martyrs of the Civil War, had known Valentine. Valentine had died young. Valentine had been a beautiful young man. Owen had been beautiful once, in his Downing days. Hard for Bennett to remember that now. Unlike Ivor, he hasn't kept even a shadow of his youthful beauty. He's just a fidgety dried-up rather yellow old man. But at least he's still alive.

Of course, he's a lot older than Ivor.

Studdert Meade's father Hubert had translated most of Aeschylus and Euripides. Bad Edwardian verse translations, not even useful as a crib.

Bennett thinks he'll settle in the shade, and browse through Saramago's whimsical Quixotic apocalypse. He's got a bit of a headache, and fancies he can feel a slight pulmonary flutter in his upper left chest. He's been a little unsteady on his feet today. He doesn't need a trip to the Grand Hotel in Costa Teguise. And the young men will enjoy an outing on their own, without the old boy holding forth and holding them up. He'd be happy for Ivor to strike up a friendship with Christopher. It would be good for both of them.

He's amused by the thought of himself 'holding forth'. Ivor's been very good at keeping him under control.

But he knows he holds Ivor up. He can't walk very fast these days. And he'd nearly slipped on the stairs down to the car deck on the ferry back to Playa Blanca. He apprehends caducity. Best to take it easy, at his age.

~

Fran has been extricated from the impasse and the mud and the ditch. It hadn't been easy, and it hadn't been very dignified, though all the drivers had been, as it were, in the same boat, and none of them was able to blame the others. There had been no opportunity for abuse of women drivers. She had been sand-wiched in the middle, and they were all bloody fools. The operation had involved the police, a tractor and some tricky reversing, and the ginger sideburns in the Toyota behind had been quite helpful. (Well, he had to be, didn't he?) Fran's car is now safely but inaccessibly parked in a sloping field, up on some higher ground, and Fran, insisting on progress rather than retreat, has been delivered to Westmore Marsh by tractor and is now drying her feet in Valerie Heritage's office. Valerie has given her a very nice small red and yellow checked fluffy hand towel for this purpose. Fran's old bare feet create an intimacy between them. Fran hasn't got a hammer toe, though she has got bunions. But Valerie Heritage is familiar with bunions, and worse.

It is an adventure. That's the best way of looking at it.

Valerie is not censorious. She doesn't suggest that Fran's stubbornness is highly inconvenient, and that stranded Fran is a bloody nuisance. Instead, she offers a towel and a cup of coffee, and says she'll see about sandwiches. Fran had been careful, in her emails, to say that she wouldn't be needing lunch, but in the circumstances, she might as well accept. Now that she's getting less cross and less anxious, she is beginning to feel hungry.

It's a fairly remote spot for a retirement home. Most of the Athene Group's properties are in the suburbs of small towns or just off ring roads, in quiet seaside resorts or in new-build precincts, in cathedral cities or university towns. Valerie explains Westmore Marsh. It's expensive. It has an experimental design, innovative features and an upmarket clientele, consisting of clients who would hitherto have been housed in converted country homes and historic decommissioned mental institutions with Grade Two listings. Fran understands the background? Yes, Fran does. Those who still have family have relatives with good access to transport, with cars or drivers or accounts with the local taxi company. And the amenities here really are very very pleasant. It looks better in better weather, of course, but it's always pleasant.

Yes, Fran would like a ham and cheese toastie.

Poor Peugeot, perched alone on a sloping furrow.

Most of them really like it here, continues Valerie.

Of course, the boot is on the other foot. It is Valerie Heritage who has to prove herself to Fran, for Fran is in the position of the inspector, Valerie the inspected. Ashley Combe's endorsement and investment are important to Westmore Marsh. Hence the towel and the toastie. Fran is so deeply incapable of seeing herself in a powerful position that, when she is involved in a tricky situation such as this, she is not good at discerning obsequious mannerisms or the gradations of subservience. She is always ready to put herself in the wrong, and in this instance has succeeded very thoroughly in so doing.

Valerie is a competent woman. Her accent Fran had been unable to place, during their only phone conversation, but she now begins to understand that she is from Bristol, and that her speech aspires to merge with that of her superior county clientele. As does her outfit. Her shoes are classic expensive brown leather lace-up (Fran tries but fails to remember the footwear of Suzette in West Brom, which certainly wasn't at all like this) and she is wearing a suit of a heathery tweed, enlivened and lightened by a lilac-pink silky polo neck. Quite a cunning combo.

Fran had managed under stress to remember to extract her flower-patterned wellies from the car boot when the car came to rest in its field, along with her hessian bag, and now she puts them on. They feel scratchy and uncomfortable, on her bare feet, but her shoes and socks were soaked and are now drying out on a radiator. She is recovering enough to want to explore the eco-village, but the weather has not recovered. It is still raining. She can tell that Valerie is not at all eager to venture outdoors, into the wet. Fran will have to content herself with being shown around the Retirement Living part of the complex.

Yet more unwelcome aspects of her predicament are beginning to make themselves apparent, but she pushes them to the back of her mind and sips her hot coffee, and distracts herself by volunteering the information that she has a friend who lives very comfortably in an Athene retirement home in Cambridge. Does Valerie know Athene Grange? Yes, she does, it was one of the company's earliest ventures, and very successful and well established, always fully occupied and much in demand. They discuss, in a low-key mode, the changing vocabulary of care homes and accommodation for the elderly: Retirement Living, Later Living, Assisted Living . . . There is no full-time assistance available here at Westmore Marsh, and Valerie herself is present only from ten o'clock to four in the afternoon on weekdays. They discuss fees, rentals, maintenance and extras, and Fran makes notes and stuffs a lot of smiling brochures into her hessian bag.

It's expensive, getting old. This place makes Dorothy's £390 a week seem like a bargain. And God knows what Persephone is costing Claude.

Valerie walks her round, introducing her to one or two residents. The accommodation is good, well planned and thoughtful. The architect had not been forbiddingly ambitious, although he is, in ecological terms, avant-garde. The guest suite, not unlike the one she had stayed in at Cambridge for Jo's birthday party, is very pleasant and, like the Cambridge suites, costs only twenty pounds a night to guests of residents. The show flat, also furnished by the Trust, is soothing, with its turquoise-and-ivory framed prints of birds and butterflies, its cool beige incident-free furniture, its deep-pile old rose rugs, its handy fitted modern kitchen where no appliances are plugged in on skirting boards at ground level. Fran has a sudden urge to give up the struggle and move in to Westmore Marsh at once and begin to lead a restful orderly stationary life.

She makes notes on her notepad.

She loves going round other people's homes, imagining herself becoming another person, born again. She'd be quite different, surely, if she lived in a model apartment like this. Maybe it's not too late to try?

In the communal lounge, two men and two women are grouped around a coffee table, the men reading newspapers, one of the women busy with a colourful iPad, the other woman doing a crossword in a puzzle book. They greet Valerie with what seems like a mixture of friendly respect and social condescension, register Fran's visiting card with the name of Ashley Combe, comment in jocular manner to Fran that she's chosen a bad day for sightseeing. Fran explains her wellies and the state of the rural approach road. Yes, she'd been brought here on a tractor, quite an adventure! They talk about the weather, about what a long winter it's been, about climate change and dredging and the River Parrett, about the local flooding. Westmore Marsh has been standing up well, they tell her. They don't seem deeply interested in its novel architecture.

The crossword puzzler pays no attention to the weather talk, but chips in to read out one of her clues to Fran and Valerie: I'm really stuck on this one, she says, and this lot can't help, they're useless, what do you think? I'm hopeless too, says Fran, but miraculously she gets the answer in a trice. Big yellow bird is the clue, 4 and 7, ends with an A, first letter G. Gran Canaria, says Fran, without even thinking. Spot on! says the puzzler, joyfully, gratefully, humbly, and fills it in.

And so the hours pass, and so the days pass, and so the years pass.

Fran explains that although she's not very good at crosswords, the Canaries are on her mind because her son is in Lanzarote, and that must be why the words had come to mind so quickly. (She doesn't describe the circumstances of his visit: they will assume he is on holiday.) Three of the quartet have been to the Canaries, and proceed competitively to compare the attractions of Tenerife and Lanzarote. Grotty Lanzarote, says the Tenerife champion. Not at all, says the iPad woman, it's Tenerife that's grotty, all that high-rise; Lanzarote is very well cared for, it's really *manicured*, or it was when I was there. Immaculate. Not a plastic bag in sight.

Fran isn't really listening. She wants to get out into the rain to see how the landscaped ponds and hollows are coping with the run-off. She doesn't think this cosily marooned indoor quartet would be very interested in that. She had thought they might have been, but, now she sees them, looking at them, she can see they would not. They don't go out much, she can tell.

She is also worrying about how she is going to get back to London without causing too much trouble to herself or anyone else. Valerie Heritage says the minor B road towards the West and the A303 is still open, but that's not much use to her, as her car is stuck in a field to the east. She'll have to order a taxi from Taunton or Bridgwater, it will cost a fortune. She really doesn't want to have to spend a night here, even though the guest suite is such good value and looks so temptingly comfortable. How on earth would she fill in the rest of the day? It's only midday. She supposes the Trust would pay, for a taxi or for the suite, but she feels guilty, she should have heeded the weather warnings, she knows already that she'll never be bold enough to put in a bill for her own folly.

She would die of boredom if she had to spend much more time with the crossword and iPad quartet.

On the other hand, there is something to be said for inspecting the rest of the development in these challenging conditions. Valerie gives her a site map, but, with a glance at her own well-polished shoes, sensibly declines to accompany her, so off Fran goes on her own, under her umbrella, to splash around exploring the layout of detention ponds and balancing ponds, admiring the green roofs of the new building units, looking out for the green swale. It's a new word to her, 'swale', and she likes it. The terrain seems to be coping well with the groundwater, better than the country lane with its reeds and its teasels and its traffic jam. There is some standing water in the main car park, but nothing too serious. Westmore Marsh is a new village, of some affordable but mostly unaffordable housing, built on what was once a small and secret Second World War airfield. Who can be choosing to live in this flat out-of-the-way place? Is there some kind of Intelligence Unit nearby, providing discreet employment for the sons and daughters of those who once serviced the air field? A kind of offshoot of Porton Down or GCHQ?

She's visited care homes and sheltered housing built in some strange spots in her time. There was one in a little market town near Oxford called The Old Gaol. She hadn't thought that a very suitable name for a care home. Better than the Old Abattoir, which had once been tactlessly proposed for a development in Sunderland. But not that good, as she had pointed out. At least Westmore Marsh is innocuously, if too appropriately, named.

She finds what she thinks may be the swale. It's a sort of ditch, between two muddy grassy banks, and its purpose seems to be to absorb and carry groundwater and rainwater away from the clusters of new buildings, towards the river, towards the estuary. Is it the same sort of thing as a rhyne? Is swale a fancy new name for a rhyne? A word fished out of the dictionary? She likes it, anyway. She likes this ditch.

Rhynes and reans. According to Paul, who should know, one of the most notorious and impoverished Black Country estates is called Whitmore Reans. Whitmore Reans, formerly known as Hungry Leas. It is still hungry but it has food banks now.

She thinks again of Suzette and Aunt Dorothy, the Sleeping Beauty. She is glad she met them. She should send Dorothy a card.

She stands, under her Liquorice Allsorts striped umbrella, and gazes at the brown water. She knows what she ought to do, if she had any sense. She knows someone who would know all about rhynes and swales and culverts and run-off and the Michael Pitt Flood Review, and she also knows she's only fifteen miles away.

I'm a coward, says Fran to herself, glumly, in the dripping rain. I'm reluctant to go to impose myself upon my own daughter.

~

Christopher and Ivor have reached the bar in the atrium of the ziggurat hotel and are sitting in an indoor grove amidst small palms and cacti, beneath a high dome of tropical lianas and vines and blossoming bougainvillea. Bloated languid pink and silver and golden fishes swim lazily in shallow water around their feet. They are sipping a glass of Prosecco. They are celebrating the finding of Christopher's glasses. His glasses had lost themselves, and, with a little encouragement from Ivor, had found themselves. They had been sitting in a safe in the manager's office, along with, the suave young gentleman confided, some pieces of quite serious jewellery that have been unclaimed for months. Not jewellery *de voyage*, but real stones. He had managed to look simultaneously disapproving of this negligence and proud of the careless *richesses* of his clientele. He had also informed them that there had been that afternoon another large tremor off El Hierro, and joked that maybe a new westerly isle would arise from the ocean bed. There have been many sightings over the centuries of the phantom isle of San Borondon, the eighth Canary, but maybe this time it will at last manifest itself! Bets are already being taken on how soon after it emerges the San Borondon airport will open.

San Borondon, St Brendan's Isle. Lucky Bennett isn't here to tell them more about it than they need to know. Bennett is interested in the fact that Oscar Wilde's surgeon father, visiting the Canaries as a young man in the 1830s, had claimed that the mummified Guanche remains he saw there had reminded him of Celtic heads found in Irish tumuli. 'The sculls I was shown of those aborigines were decidedly of a well-formed Caucasian race; the forehead low, but not retreating like the negro.' And no less an authority than Sabin Berthelot had suggested a Celtic connection on the basis of megalithic structures on El Hierro (also known as l'Isle de Fer, Ferro, the Iron Island). Berthelot came to believe that the Canarians had crossed the Atlantic and reached America. Oscar Wilde's father speculated that the Guanches were of 'a branch of the great Libyan or Atlantic stock', whose history was, he conceded, 'wrapped in obscurity'.

Bennett finds all this speculation fascinating, and some of it has settled in Ivor's memory, whether he wants it there or not. Owen English had been a better listener than Ivor, but then he hadn't had to listen to so much of it. Owen had particularly liked the Celtic possibilities.

Christopher and Ivor sit comfortably with one another, free of responsibility for Sir Bennett and his needs and his whims. Christopher is airing his problems with the television company which has recently dispensed with his services, and wondering, as Ivor had hoped that he might, if he could find a project that would bring him back to the Canaries. It's so scenic, it's so theatrical, it's so *painterly*, it so asks to be painted and to be filmed, says Christopher, but all you get back home are tourist movies and bodies on beaches.

With the exception, of course, of that footage of the immigrant sitting on the sand at Gran Tarajal which he and Sara had gazed at it in their bed. A different kind of body on a beach. He describes it to Ivor, who makes a gesture as though to cross himself.

It's obvious to Ivor that Christopher hasn't got the wish or doesn't feel he has the right to encroach on Sara's human rights territory, but there are many other areas to explore. It is while they are discussing the case of Simon Aguilera and Ishmael and the ghastly murals in the tower that Ivor's mobile starts to bleep at him, and he apologetically responds to it, in case it is Bennett.

It is Bennett. He has had a fall, he's not well, he sounds confused and faint, his voice is breaking up and soon vanishes completely. Shit, says Ivor, snapping his phone off and then on again.

Shit, repeats Ivor.

So it's happened.

He tries to ring back, updates Christopher on what he's heard, and they decide, before hitting the road to La Suerte, that Ivor should ring for an ambulance to meet them there. While he's ringing, Christopher throws a large pile of euros on the table (the last thing he wants is another pursuant bar bill from Las Salinas) and off they go.

They get to La Suerte before the ambulance, to find Bennett on the terrace, lying awkwardly with a crumpled leg, and semi-propped-up against an unsupportive frail cane table. He seems conscious, but he is groaning. He must have managed to trip on one of the only steps on the premises, a shallow step leading from the open glass doors from the living room down onto the stone terrace. Or perhaps he has had a stroke, a heart attack? He is beyond cogent speech. Ivor kneels by him, Christopher goes to the kitchen to find a glass of water, in case a glass of water might be of use. (He later learns that it would have been not useful but dangerous, but how was he to have known that?)

'What happened, what happened?' Ivor is repeating, uselessly, when they hear the welcome sound of the approaching ambulance, on its way from not-very-distant Arrecife. Christopher has a strong sense of déjà vu as the paramedics check Bennett's pulse, heart rate, or whatever it is that they are checking. They seem to think he has broken his leg, or his hip. Is it safe to move him? He's not as heavy as some old men Christopher knows, not nearly as heavy as Claude, who is still corpulent, sustained by his ex-wife's plated meals and by Persephone and by inertia. But he's no lightweight either, and not very pliable. Christopher can hardly bear to watch as they ease him onto a stretcher and into the back of the startlingly yellow vehicle.

Ivor clambers in with the recumbent Bennett. He gestures to Christopher to come too. Christopher is not sure what his role should be.

But he thinks he'd better stick with Ivor.

He doesn't want to be left alone at La Suerte.

Maybe he can make himself useful at the hospital.

He recues the book that had been wedged under Bennett's knee by his fall. *Stone Raft*. He puts it into his shoulder bag. Maybe Bennett will come round shortly and want to pick up Saramago's novel where he left off. One always needs a good book to read, in the tedium of a hospital.

When Sara was dying, he'd been kept company somewhat inappropriately by a colourful new book about a 1990s forgery/ attribution scandal, involving impeccably trustworthy art historian Esther Breuer, who is a friend of his equally impeccable Auntie Jo, and some of his more foolish, gullibly greedy and unlikeable colleagues in the world of media and the visual arts. He'd also summoned up for company a cloud of titles – thrillers, books about the 2008 financial crash, biographies, misery memoirs – purchased somewhat randomly on his e-reader.

He's not a very persistent reader; he reads very fast and very badly.

Stone Raft is the first edition of an English translation from the Portuguese (Bennett can't easily read Portuguese) and it is a signed copy, dedicated to '*My good friend Bennett, Comrade in Arms, La Suerte, August* 2004'. But Christopher doesn't know that yet. When he does discover it, in the small hours, at a time when he has nothing better to do, he still won't know that Saramago remained a Communist until his dying day. He'll have more than enough time to puzzle inconclusively about whether 'comrade in arms' has anything to do with Bennett's political history, or whether it's simply a jocular reference to their joint membership of the literary profession.

But he does now remember, disconcertingly, as the ambulance speeds along, a prissy and entertaining old-style gallery owner, an old queen with a proud white crest of hair, who had broken his femur. He'd broken that big bone badly. He'd broken it in St John's Wood, in his home – home, that most dangerous of places – by slipping as he trod on a pretentious glossy arts magazine that he'd left at the top of his stairs. (He'd left it there deliberately, he later explained at pedantic length, because at night he always left things he wanted to take down in the morning at the *top* of the stairs, so he could retrieve them from the fourth step down without bending down too far as he went *down* to his breakfast. He'd got it all worked out, but his cunning had undone him.)

Very *very* slippery, he had delighted to repeat, as he blamed his downfall on the highly laminated texture of the *Renaissance Review*, a *very* suspect publication.

His leg had taken a long time to mend. And he'd died within a year or two. He hadn't really recovered.

Death by glossy magazine.

Christopher climbs into the back of the ambulance. It's a steep hike up, only a very fit person could make it. Christopher is quite fit, and comparatively young, but it's a heave.

The material world seems suddenly steeper, more intransigent.

He and Ivor and Bennett make their noisy way towards the hospital.

The great calm light fades towards the west.

~

As Sir Bennett Carpenter is being submitted to scans and exam-
inations and as Ivor and Christopher are sitting together
anxiously in a waiting room, Fran is sitting with her daughter
Poppet in the little low dark house by the green-brown canal,
nursing a glass of lightly watered peat-brown whisky. She has
faced the fear/sorrow/anxiety that had occupied her at the
thought of ringing Poppet, and here she is, uninvited, marooned.
Jim had been to get her, and here she is, though her car is still
some twenty miles away, in a field two miles up the sunken road
from Westmore Marsh. She'll deal with that in the morning,
with Jim's help. But she'll spend the night upstairs in Poppet's
bed. Probably with Poppet's cat, but she won't mind that.

Poppet has volunteered to sleep downstairs on the cane couch,
and her offer has been accepted.

Fran had been worried that Poppet would have neither food
nor drink in the cottage, and Jim had made a request stop at
the village mini-market for her to stock up with toothbrush,
toothpaste, moisturiser, whisky, eggs, tomatoes, broccoli and
one red chilli.

She hasn't got her medication on her, but she'll survive a
night without it. She knows she ought to keep a supply in her
handbag, she's always advising other old people to do that. But
she doesn't.

She's filled in her report on Westmore Marsh's Retirement
Living facilities, ticking boxes and adding brief descriptive para-
graphs of amenities and decor. The Ashley Combe Trust, she
explains to her daughter, appreciates her prose. Unlike the local
authorities, it doesn't just go by ticking the boxes. It welcomes
a bit of personal evaluation.

Teresa Quinn had been impressed by the quality of Fran's
reflections when she'd read her housing review on the internet,
the review that had reintroduced them to one another. She'd
told Fran how much she'd enjoyed them. And Fran is proud of

them. Fran is proud of her perceptions. She still enjoys perceiving. When she ceases to enjoy perceiving, she'll know she is about to be dead.

Not many people enjoy reading housing reports. Fran knows she is lucky to have rediscovered Teresa.

Fran has developed, during the past decade, her own idiosyncratic views on architecture. As she sips her whisky and thinks of low-build low-carbon retirement homes, little flashes or illuminations of anger and indignation flicker through her consciousness, accompanied by images of the populist pomposity of the Pompidou, and the grandiosity of some of the new billionaire apartment blocks in central London, in Kensington and Mayfair, built for foreigners, bought by foreigners, let out by foreigners, but designed by British architects who voted for New Labour and who still call themselves socialists. A plague on their new luxury apartments, which, during their years of construction, had created traffic jams and diversions and paralysed bus routes, preventing ordinary Londoners from going about their daily lives. Her own block, the block where she now lives, is brutal. But it isn't hypocritical.

Fran has made an omelette and a tomato and broccoli side salad, dressed with sesame oil and some dubiously aged sunflower seeds. She needn't have done that bit of shopping with Jim, as Poppet is well provided with tinned goods and dried pulses and unusual condiments: one of her many useful professional deformities is a siege mentality, unusual in her age group, though common in her mother's. But Fran is pleased to have contributed to a meal. It makes her feel less of an intruder, more of a provider.

Fran is feeling fairly relaxed and fairly companionable. The house is dark and intimate, and the water level doesn't seem to be rising. It's stopped raining at last. The wood and wicker decor is pleasing: it's primitive, without being punitive. Poppet's little home sits lightly on the earth. They will see the night through. Poppet needn't have bothered to move her treasures upstairs. They talk about floods, and about Christopher and Sara, and about the tremor off El Hierro. Fran describes the TV news coverage of the small earthquake in Dudley, and the small wave that had poured through the limestone caverns.

Poppet, somewhat to her mother's surprise, has accepted a beaker of Scotch, and has made good progress with it. Will there be confidences to come? Is now the time?

It's only nine, but Fran is dozy. It's been a long and stressful, though in its way triumphant day, and she was up very early. But she can't go to bed yet.

She's noticed that one of the subjects that old people love to discuss, when gathered freshly together, is the time that they go to bed. The topic is at once indescribably boring and not without some interest.

Poppet isn't ready for bed. She wants to switch on her Climate Crisis programme and demonstrate its capacities. Up it comes, with its multiple options, on her clever screen. They note a meteorite in Managua, forest fires in Sumatra, a tornado in Texas. They browse the Levels and Westmore Marsh (it's no worse than it was there, yet, though the Thames Valley isn't doing well, and Abingdon is now cut off from Oxford). 'Put in El Hierro,' suggests Fran, getting into the spirit of the thing. So Poppet punches in El Hierro, and is confronted by interesting headlines in English and in Spanish. An earthquake swarm of dozens of small eruptions indicates a new magmatic intrusion, according to the tracking agencies Involcan and Pelvolca. There has been much activity during the day. A 5.1 magnitude quake has been recorded. The level of alert has been raised to orange. That's *high*, says Poppet, impressed.

Poppet searches on her screen for graphs, sketches and photographs of the rocky iron island and its boiling watery skirts.

There are images of a great seething mass of white and turquoise bubbles, like a gigantic jellyfish, rising monstrously up through the azure ocean. It is very dramatic. Fran waits for Poppet to apportion blame, but she doesn't. It is just happening, from the ocean bed, from deep deep within the core of the planet. It happens.

It is beautiful, the gravity-defying watery monster.

'Do you think Christopher knows about this?' asks Fran. 'Will he be able to feel the tremors, in Lanzarote?'

(Christopher, even as she speaks, is wondering whether some almost imperceptible quiver of the earth had tripped the unsteady Bennett on the threshold of the terrace and laid him low. It's beginning to look as though he's fractured his hip, and they may have to operate. If they need to, will Bennett be in a position to give consent? Christopher's dubious legal status with regard to Sara's treatment and evacuation had added to the trauma of her last days, and Ivor's status with regard to Bennett is equally uncertain. They'd talked of Lasting Power of Attorney and a Living Will, but, like most people, they'd never got round to it.)

'I imagine it's big news, in the islands,' says Poppet. 'But Lanzarote's a long way from El Hierro.'

'I think I'll text him,' says Fran. She texts Christopher: STRANDED AT POPPETS CAN U FEEL QUAKE WE BOTH SEND LOVE FX.

'He'll be surprised I'm here,' says Fran.

'*I'm* surprised you are here,' says Poppet, after a short pause. 'You should have planned to stay the night anyway, it's so near.'

'I don't like to be a nuisance,' says Fran.

There is a silence, as each of them ponders the reasons why it wouldn't have been easy for Fran to invite herself for the night. Their interchange, brief though it was, is portentous.

Fran, heavily, sadly, finds herself saying, 'I do worry about you sometimes, darling.'

'And I worry about you too,' retaliates Poppet, quickly. 'Since Hamish died, I've worried about you a lot.'

'Oh, I'm all right,' says Fran. 'Really, darling, I'm fine. I keep going fine.'

The light is very low, the shadows are profound. The two women can hardly see each other. Poppet has lighted a little brass-based Kelly oil lamp on the mantelpiece and it glows steadily with the smallest of yellowy blue flames. Poppet likes it because it is alive. It keeps her company.

Sometimes Poppet thinks she will die of loneliness. She knows that loneliness can kill.

The silence continues. Fran reaches for the whisky, tops up her glass, offers the bottle to Poppet, who shakes her head.

Fran is just about to dare to ask about Jim (who *is* Jim?) who is coming to collect her in the morning, when her phone buzzes.

It is Christopher, with a not very reassuring message: IN HOSPITAL ARRECIFE BENNETT HAD FALL MIGHT NEED SURGERY HELP CX.

Fran shows it to Poppet. They agree he doesn't really mean he wants help or thinks they could offer any; it's an exclamation, a plea for sympathy and solidarity.

'Old age,' says Fran, 'it's a fucking disaster. And Christopher thought those two old boys had got it all sorted.'

She is, at least temporarily, downcast.

'I don't think Ivor is all that old,' says Poppet.

Poppet seems to know more about the inhabitants of La Suerte than Fran does. Fran is jealous.

'What shall I reply?' she asks.

'God knows,' says Poppet.

Fran, inadequately, tried out the words VERY SORRY. They don't seem appropriate. She alters them to a noncommittal LOVE FROM US BOTH SPEAK SOON FX and sends.

It's so easy to Send.

She suddenly feels overwhelmingly tired and old and helpless. She needs to go to bed. She needs to ask Poppet if she can borrow a pair of clean pants and socks for the morning. She knows Poppet's pants. They are over-washed and over-worn and skimpily cut, with frayed gussets and perishing elastic. Poppet is skinny. Fran isn't fat, but her bum is bigger than Poppet's.

But she can't bear to think of putting her own once-worn underwear back on in the morning. She really doesn't like to do that. She'd say she was almost phobic about it. She can wear the same bra for a fortnight, but bras are different.

When she was a child, she'd worn her knickers for days on end without changing them. People did in those days. The avant-garde post-war housewives of Broughborough had heavy early-model top-loading washing machines with huge heavy aluminium paddles, gun-metal wartime grey paddles like the propellers of aircraft, but they were used sparingly.

She could have a washing-machine wash-day conversation with Teresa, on her next visit. The Quinns and the Robinsons had held strong and differing views on the subject of wash day. The Robinsons thought the Quinns washed too often, and the Quinns noted that the Robinsons did not always wipe their plastic-coated washing line free of smuts when they hung out their garments and their sheets. These wash days preceded the Clean Air Act, and clean clothes were often retrieved from the line flecked and peg-pinched with soot. Both Teresa and Fran had been too defensive to discuss these differences openly in their cellar, but each was aware of the positions taken. Now, in their seventies, they could come out on the topic, and laugh.

'Twas on a Monday morning when I beheld my darling . . .

Ah, how we love to differentiate ourselves from our neighbours. Religion, washing machines, washing lines, vegetables, the potato man, the bold Breton onion-seller, religion.

Who would have thought that Jacopo da Pontormo could have attracted the attention of David Quinn?

Fran is beginning to pass out, although her brain is still quite active, as she tries to knit it all together.

'I'll find you a nightie, Mum,' says Poppet, who has noticed her mother's yawns and her flagging spirits.

It's only nine thirty. It feels like midnight.

Fran wonders if those nice well-presented old folk at Westmore Marsh are tucked up properly in their beds by now. Or maybe they are playing Scrabble, or bridge, or whist. Not, she thinks, chess.

Jo plays bridge. Fran hasn't got time to learn how to play bridge. It's too late.

She had been unsettled by the two faces of Valerie Heritage.

She thinks, fleetingly, admiringly, of the vigorous Suzette of West Bromwich.

In a care home in Sandford, a young woman carer has just been taken into custody for allegedly attempting to poison some of the residents.

Fran could have been anonymously, comfortably, installed in the £20-a-night guest suite, with bedtime TV and shampoo sachets. Just like the Premier Inn.

She's taken a risk, coming to stay with Poppet. She's such a coward. But, on balance, she's glad to be here.

~

In the hospital at Lanzarote, Ivor has been told that the *ilustrísimo* Señor Bennett has, as suspected, fractured his hip, and that it should be operated on as soon as possible, probably first thing in the morning. He will have to sign a consent form, but as, calmed by morphine, he has now emerged from his wordless groaning and is looking very alert, this won't be a problem. He

is chattering away volubly to all around him, so there should
be no difficulty with a signature, say the hospital staff to Ivor.
Only Ivor, by the bedside, can tell Bennett is talking nonsense.
Many of the members of staff speak English, but they aren't
up to this baroque monologue. Bennett is free-associating in an
impressively high-grade range of gibberish, thinking he is back
in England and about to give a lecture on Unamuno and the
Falange in Oxford: 'I've got my notes ready, they're all ready,
but I won't be needing my notes, I speak *much* better without
notes,' he says happily, even euphorically.

Bennett has been worrying about Unamuno and the Falange
for decades. He'll be worrying about it on his deathbed. Maybe
this is his deathbed, and that's why he's worrying.

'Is the car on its way, Ivor? We must not be late,' he repeats
from time to time, rather formally and emphatically, and then
starts quoting, in Spanish, some words which Ivor assumes come
from that incomprehensible work, the *Tragic Sense of Life*.
They could have alerted his white-coated entourage to his state
of mind, but they don't.

'*Si muero*,' declaims Bennett, '*dejad el balcón abierto . . .
dejad el balcón abierto . . .*'

Ivor is in a dilemma. Bennett would probably sign any bit of
paper with which he was presented. Ivor could tell him it was
a BBC release form or a contract for £500 from the University
of Oxford or another appeal for support from the Terrence
Higgins Trust, and he wouldn't query it, he would sign. He
always leaves that kind of stuff to Ivor. But Ivor is a man of
scruples, and exceptionally law-abiding. Because his earlier years
of sexual activity had been ineluctably illegal, he has been careful
in other matters not to cross any lines. He parks their little car
with scrupulous care, pays Bennett's bills instantly, counts small
change in shops and hands back any over-payment, observes
dress codes respectfully. He doesn't like to ask a delirious Bennett

to sign what might well, at his age (Ivor does not fool himself), prove to be his own death warrant.

Ivor has by now calmed down enough to notice that the *ilustrísimo* Señor isn't wearing part of his dental plate. The upper left is missing. He wonders where it's got to. Had he taken it out himself, for an hour or two of solitary comfort, while reading and snoozing over his novel? Had it fallen out when he fell, is it still lying on the terrace, or is it safe in its little ceramic tooth mug in the bedroom?

Bennett sometimes takes the pink and white dental plate out and puts it on his blue and white majolica side plate during a meal. He's only done this once or twice when guests were at table, but Ivor fears he may soon start to do it more frequently. Ivor doesn't know whether he will mind this or not.

He does mind it when their old friend Gustavo hikes up his trouser leg and displays a twining catheter, which he then empties, at table, in company, into a plastic bottle. Ivor wishes Gustavo wouldn't do that.

Ivor fortunately fails to recapture the vanishing just-beyond-reach shade of a memory of a horror story of an acquaintance who, during the snoring of the night, had inhaled a detached crown. He had known it was coming loose, but had neglected to get it stuck back on properly, as with good reason he dreaded visiting his dentist. Swallowing crowns or bridgework is OK, they pass through the body and must be retrieved from the lavatory bowl, as they are so expensive. Inhaling is not OK. Rescuing an inhaled crown involves hacking into the left bronchiole, through the back, or into the larynx, from the front, or something like that. Or that's what Ivor has understood. But he's forgotten it. It doesn't bear thinking about. So Ivor doesn't think about it. He denies the memory.

Ivor decides to go back to the waiting room for Christopher's company, to consult Christopher. Christopher had spent transit time in this very hospital, with Sara, and had then, back in England, endured a worse hospitalisation than this, with the worst of all outcomes, but he may nevertheless or therefore have words of comfort or advice.

The two men sit together on the yellow plastic bench. Christopher has prepared himself for the long wait with a slug of vodka from the small bottle he always carries with him in his inner jacket pocket, just in case. This had seemed to be the case. A sociable glass of Prosecco wouldn't see him through. Nor will Saramago's *Stone Raft*, with which he is finding it hard to engage. It's a heavy book and its sentences are far, far too long. He is wishing he had brought his iPad. He hadn't taken it to the Grand Hotel, he hadn't thought he'd need it over an early evening drink, and he hadn't thought, in the flurry, to pick it up at La Suerte. If he'd had it with him, he could be trying to look up hip fractures right now.

Ivor hasn't yet reached the ever-changing ever-self-updating sophistication of the iPad.

Christopher acknowledges Ivor's ethical dilemma. They agree that the real problem is that they don't know how urgent the operation really is. Maybe it would be fine to wait until the morning for a signature, or the next day, by which time Bennett might have emerged from his delirium and gathered his wits together and be in a position to take responsibility for his own surgery.

Or maybe that would be very unwise. They don't know the risks, either way. And what would Bennett know about it, anyway?

In a moment of vodka-driven inspiration, Christopher decides to ring his father. He's the expert. He doesn't ring Claude very often, but he knows he'll be there at this time, he's almost always there, listening to music, watching TV, having a glass or two. If he has friends round for a drink, they've gone by eight, but it's still not too late, by Claude's standards. Unlike his mother, Claude always picks up. His mother, in the evenings, goes to bed early and takes refuge in the silent peace of text-land and refuses to answer her phone, but Claude always picks up.

Claude doesn't seem put out by an unexpected call from his son. He listens, gets to grips with the situation almost instantly, and says, 'Better get on with it. Get him to sign, or tell your friend to forge his signature, but get on with it. Don't hang about. They're right, the sooner it's done the better. At his age, you have to get on with it.'

'Are you sure?'

'Yes,' says Claude, authoritatively, irresponsibly, from far away. 'But remember to ask them what they're using. Be sure to get the name of the alloy. Titanium's better than cobalt chromium, if they've got it.'

He speaks a little longer about metals and plastics and ceramics, their merits and demerits, but Christopher knows he isn't up to retaining and relaying any of the technical information. He's got the message: *Go for it*. He thanks his father, and rings off.

'He says go for it,' he tells Ivor.

So they go for it. Ivor doesn't have to forge Bennett's signature: Bennett scribbles his own name willingly if illegibly at the bottom of the bilingual form, by the pencilled cross. Ivor has already filled in his dates and his medical history and the details of their insurance company, which he knows all too well. And Bennett seems unperturbed, as he is wheeled off to a private ward to be made comfortable for the night. Indeed, he starts singing to himself, one of his old favourites, Fats Waller's 'My Very Good Friend the Milkman', which he had chosen, decades ago, as one of his *Desert Island Discs*. He disappears, on his trolley, towards his bed. They will operate in the morning. The surgeon's name is Manolo Zerolo Herrara.

Ivor and Christopher are free. Bennett is in safe hands. Ivor will be back first thing in the morning, to see that Bennett is behaving himself and hasn't revoked his consent. Meanwhile, the night is still young, and the young men need something to eat.

~

Claude, in Kensington, curious, looks up the Canarian hospital at Arrecife on his iPad. It looks satisfactory. The healthcare in resorts like that is usually good. Then he looks up Bennett Carpenter. He'd managed to retain the name from Christopher's call, as he knows he's heard it before. He thinks he might even have met him. At a party? At a degree ceremony? At the Royal College of Surgeons? In the Inner Temple? At Buckingham Palace? He flicks around, with interest, for an hour. He finds a host of citations and cross references, including Bennett's choices for *Desert Island Discs*, which had included Fats Waller, de Falla's 'Nights in the Gardens of Spain', and Maria Callas singing *Medea*. Cross-checking on the website, he finds it very odd that only three other castaways seem to have chosen Callas. Compared with Brahms and the Beatles, Callas hardly scores at all. He can't quite believe it. Had he been asked, he would have chosen nothing but Callas. The website must be defective, the data inadequately cross-referenced.

This idle research prompts him to see how many surgeons and medical men have been invited to participate in this enviable exercise, but he finds very few, and those that are categorised and listed were, in his view, oddly selected. There aren't many historians either, come to that. But Bennett Carpenter had always been known to be an entertaining speaker and a fluent broadcaster. He'd have been an obvious choice.

He purchases and downloads Carpenter's seminal work on

the Spanish Civil War, *The Reaper and the Wheat*. The epigraph is a short poem in Spanish, by Lorca, entitled *Despedida*. '*Si muero, dejad el balcón abierto*'.

When I die, leave the balcony window open . . .

Claude reads some of the Introduction to the revised edition and tries to look at the photographs and illustrations, but they haven't come out very well on his e-reader. He nods off.

~

In Poppet's tiny bedroom, robed in Poppet's surprisingly pleasing pale-blue jersey nightdress and wrapped against the damp in a small tartan blanket, Fran finds, arrayed on the deep wooden ledge under the low window, her daughter's treasures. She is not to know that they are not always there, that they have been brought out, unusually, and as yet unnecessarily, for salvation from the flood, as Poppet had had no cause to mention this.

They go back a long time, these little objects, and the pathos of them catches at Fran's old heart. Tears come to her eyes. She's very tired, that's why. Her heart is tired. *The heart's only a muscle*, she's been told. Who said that? Samuel Beckett? She thinks not. But it was a playwright. It was definitely a playwright. She'll remember, if she tries not to think about it too much. It will come back to her.

She looks sadly at the brown envelopes full of old photographs, which she does not open, and at the solid silver napkin ring, an anachronism even when it had been engraved and presented as a non-christening present to baby Poppy. Her poor mother, Granny May Robinson, so long dead. She wonders if Poppet has kept it from sentiment, or from inertia. She opens the little monogrammed mahogany box of miniature minerals from the Canaries and gazes at their powdery bright and spangled colours, their rugged tiny mountain shapes. And there is Baby Jesus, from the days of Rowbridge School. So Poppet had kept Baby Jesus. She had realised what a miracle he was.

Fran feels a great tearfulness rising up in her, a grief for all things, a grief for her daughter and thence, from that grief, a grief for all things. She had feared that she would outlive such grief, that her heart would grow thin and cold, that grief would ebb from her as sexual hope and desire and much (though not yet all) of her social optimism had ebbed from her. She had thought, when Hamish died, that she would dry and harden, as she kept herself busy, as she prepared plated meals, as she climbed the winding stair, as she drove restlessly around the land. She had thought that ageing would bring calm and indifference and impersonality. She knew it was unlikely to bring her peace of mind, as perhaps it had brought Teresa Quinn, who was practised in an expectation of peace, but it might have brought her, at least, a dull amnesia. But no, she is, it would seem, condemned to grief, to an ever-replenishing well of grief, rising up from the centre of the earth of her body.

It's good to be able to weep, she tells herself, as she leans on the low sill and gazes out of the window. That's what she's always said to others, when called on to comfort them. To Christopher, when he broke his arm, aged eight. To Poppet, aged ten. To Poppet, aged twenty-two.

Her body has dried up, but not yet her tears. She lets them flow.

It has stopped raining, it is a clear night.

She thinks fondly of Christopher, keeping guard by an old man in a hospital. On death-watch again, in the Canaries. He's a good boy, although he doesn't look like a good boy.

Christopher had admired Poppet's Baby Jesus, he will be pleased to hear (if she dare tell him) that it has been preserved.

Christopher has always had a good eye, but he couldn't paint, although he'd tried. He wasn't a maker.

Neither is Poppet, now.

She has a random, friendly thought of Christopher, prompted by the speculative image of the morning's crossword-and-newspaper quartet playing evening whist in Westmore Marsh. She remembers him, suddenly, as a fifteen-year-old, as a disorderly scruffy experimental schoolboy at the hard-boiled London comprehensive where he had learned to put on the style. He and his three mates had gone through a year-long phase of playing cards, seriously, obsessively, for small stakes. They played whist and poker, they took on rival groups, they sweated at it. They fancied themselves as hard players. Fran had found this amusing, she was glad he had such friends, she didn't think for a moment that he'd grow up into a gambler. And she had been right. He doesn't play now. His friend Brodie still plays, but Christopher doesn't. He'd been put off by a group of old ladies who held a weekly whist drive down the road in the Crossroads Café. The boys had impudently, jokily, teasingly, challenged them on their own turf, and the old ladies had taken them on and cleaned them out.

Christopher, to his credit, had told his mother this story, and he'd told it well. They were a lot of old grannies, he said, they looked so harmless, they tricked us into putting our money down and then they wiped us out, and then they laughed and laughed.

They could play, said fifteen-year-old Christopher, admiringly. You should have seen them, Mum. They were brillo.

She smiles to herself, pleased with this flashback to the triumphant crones of Romley. He had been a sweet-natured boy, even while he was trying so hard to be hip. He'd gone in for a vainglorious career, but he is still in his own way tender-hearted.

Old grannies. Old crones. She is one of them now, she has

joined their haggard company, those Grimm words are her indicators.

But Christopher is a sweet boy, and kind to his old mother.

She gazes out, at the wide flood waters. A drunken, sloping, three-quarters moon, a waning gibbous moon is shining upon them. The higher branches of the half-submerged willows are a trembling ghostly silver in the moonlight. And floating in the drowned fields is a swan, a white heraldic swan, proud in its effortless, meaningless, soulless beauty. Its neck curves, its head turns slowly from side to side, it floats arrogantly, disdainfully, emblematically, surveying the glittering realm of night.

~

Owen England is not gazing at the staggering moon, though he has, earlier in the evening, looked briefly upwards and noted its cloud-streaked rising over the Backs as he returned from a prosy collegiate dinner. He is now reading Wordsworth and simultaneously watching a news programme about the Lebanon on TV. Like many older people of all sexes, he is good at multi-tasks and multi-diversions. He's not so good these days at productive concentration, but he can still take in several messages at once.

He hasn't yet had his second cigarette of the day. He's still got something to look forward to.

He is somewhat shocked by the clouds-as-heavenly-city Wordsworth passages he has so recently discovered. An ex-colleague at Jesus had tipped him off to look them up, and there they are, in all their tumultuous glory. Line after line, mounting, accumulating, overwhelming, like a Sibelius symphony of ever-rising mountains, horizon beyond horizon. An enormous, panoramic crescendo. He should have taken them into consideration long ago. They appear in the Second Book of

The Excursion, the book entitled 'The Solitary'. Nobody ever reads *The Excursion* now, apart from a few specialists. He doesn't think he can use these lines, but he would feel foolish if anyone discovered that he didn't even know they were there.

> Fabric it seemed of diamond and of gold,
> With alabaster domes, and silver spires,
> And blazing terrace upon terrace, high
> Uplifted; here, serene pavilions bright,
> In avenues disposed; there, towers begirt
> With battlements that on their restless fronts
> Bore stars – illumination of all gems!
> . . .
> Clouds of all tincture, rocks and sapphire sky,
> Confused, commingled, mutually inflamed,
> Molten together, and composing thus,
> Each lost in each, that marvellous array
> Of temple, palace, citadel, and huge
> Fantastic pomp of structure without name . . .

He reads on, dutifully, transported, with an admiration so painful that he can't work out what it signifies. What can it mean, to experience such awe? There is even a small element of irritation in his awe, an irritation that such genius could exist so freely, so effortlessly, and sustain itself upon such heights. What does it mean, this awe, this love, this irritation? Can he ask Josephine Drummond about it? She, too, relies on poetry. He suspects that she once tried to write poetry, although she has never said this to him.

Goethe once said that the only response to greater genius is love. Or something along those lines.

He wonders, not for the first time, what on earth literature is *for*, and why he has devoted his life to teaching it and thinking about it. None of the conventional answers to these questions are in any degree satisfactory. One might as well ask, what is one's life, why was one born, what is the meaning of a life.

He had seen Dr Leavis, small and dry and brown as an autumn leaf, speaking well of Wordsworth in the old brown wooden lecture room in Mill Lane. Leavis had been confident that he knew the uses of literature and literacy.

Owen had been young and green then, and so had Bennett Carpenter.

Jo hasn't returned Carpenter's first edition of *The Reaper and the Wheat* to him yet. He wonders if she has even opened it.

He thinks of Ivor, loyal Ivor, who has done such a good job with Bennett.

Nobody has done a good job for him, and he has not done a good job for anybody.

The Solitary.

But Wordsworth, as age came on, had surrounded himself with acolytes, with sycophants.

He thinks of the Castle of Zonzamas, so *suggestivo*, so implacable, so enduringly unknowable. So massive, so forgotten, so humbled.

The Castle of Zonzamas is the *arrière-pays*, the timeless hinterland that beckons us.

~

Teresa knows she is taking a turn for the worse. She feels worse. The pain is bad. One would not want to live with this degree of pain for very long. Pain may drive her into what she sometimes thinks of as the arms of God, although her faith does not allow her to make haste. She finds that phrase, 'the arms of God', a comfort. Phrases and biblical texts come to her aid, along with her childhood prayers.

She is good at reading her interchanges with her GP and her oncologist and the district nurse and the palliative care nurse and the merrily morose young bald black chap who had come a couple of days ago to adjust her NHS-provided day bed.

It's not going well. There had been a muddle about the adjustments to the day bed technology which had resulted in Teresa saying to the young man, tartly, 'Don't worry, you can take it back and collect all those spare spanners and struts and things when I'm dead. Just shove them under the bed for now, don't worry about itemising them, they won't go anywhere.'

The chap hadn't seemed to take note of these unkind remarks, but he had been very young.

Teresa had regretted her sharpness. But was relieved to think he hadn't noticed.

Father Goodall had been more attentive.

Fran had been wrong about Teresa's attitude to Father Goodall and his clumsy dripping black umbrella. Teresa finds Father Goodall's ineptitudes endearing, they do not annoy her at all. She is used to priests. He is not, it is true, a very clever man, in an academic sense; he is not very quick-witted, but he is a man of conventional wisdoms, and his fidelity to her and to their God is a comfort to her. He too knows about the welcoming arms of God. Now death is coming upon her, he will not prevaricate. He will do his job. He will know what to do. He may even enjoy doing it. And she has always been pleased to give joy to others.

She has taught herself to aspire to a humble and a contrite heart.

Those words of the psalmist also comfort her.

A *humble and a contrite heart*.

Her old friend and colleague Birdie Bardwell is to move into the spare room. She and Birdie go back a long way. Birdie had been a member of her staff for twenty odd years, her second

in command. Birdie is a professional. Teresa is comfortable with
Birdie, although she knows that not all her friends will be.
Teresa would prefer to be on her own, with her accustomed
privacy, for she likes her own company, but she needs somebody
in the house, and Birdie could do with the small addition to
her income and will make no bones about accepting it. Birdie
is large and loud-mouthed and outgoing, and some find her
overwhelming, but Teresa had always been grateful to her for
her brutal buoyancy. She is the sort of woman that people call
a tower of strength. A pig farmer's daughter from Suffolk, once
broad and blonde, she is now a solid matriarchal white-haired
figure, although her only child is long dead, of the terminal
spinal condition that had first introduced Birdie to Teresa
Quinn's establishment. She is a good cook and very fond of her
food; indeed, much of her conversation is about food, and as
Teresa is now ethereally thin and picks at her meals like a small
but polite and willing bird, this might seem inappropriate. But
Teresa, who has always considered herself inadequate in the
kitchen, enjoys listening to Birdie's riffs about celebrity chefs,
about fast food and slow food, about tripe and pigs' trotters.
And she is grateful for the cauliflower cheese, for the oxtail
soup, for the chicken and ham pie, for the clove-flavoured ham
knuckle, for the delicious apple strudel with crème fraîche, for
the astonishingly light and perfectly shaped profiteroles.

Birdie is good at pastry, and although Teresa can't eat much
pastry now, she applauds and enjoys Birdie's expertise.

She looks forward (almost, in a way, perhaps?) to watching
TV food programmes with Birdie. There are so many of them,
and she would never dream of watching them by herself, but
Birdie loves them, although they annoy her. This will be Birdie's
evening treat, and Teresa will go along with her yelps of
contempt, her occasional plaudits, her reaching for the Rioja
and the charcoal biscuits and the thin slices of Emmental. (Birdie

believes that charcoal is good for Teresa's condition, and who is to contradict her?) And then Birdie will help her to her bed, and listen for her in the night watch, and come to her if she calls out in pain or in need. Her mottled matronly arms will willingly enfold her, more present and more fleshly than the arms of God.

And she'll be getting more than the minimum wage.

Teresa does not often invoke the arms of Liam, or those of her subsequent lovers. But sometimes she thinks of them. She occasionally has a sexual dream, but she wakes to find that she is happier where she is now. Sex had been a hassle, no doubt about it.

Teresa has sent for her son Luke. She has texted him, and emailed him, and requested his presence. She tells him she would like to see him very soon. He must know what that means. Surely he must. He has been following her accounts of her condition, and he will know how to interpret them.

He is in Mozambique, working for Médecins Sans Frontières. He says he's trying to book a flight.

She'd like to see her grandson Xavier too, but she's not sure she's a fit sight for a healthy teenage boy. She knows that she looks wasted. Xavier is at the International School in Maputo, where he is doing well. He is bilingual. His mother works at the eye clinic. Teresa and Xavier have occasionally communicated by Skype, and Luke sends photos of him. Teresa doesn't like Skype very much: it's frustrating, it's distorting, it's a step too far.

She doesn't know what to do about Liam O'Connor, her ex in Canada, the father of Luke. He won't want to be excluded. Perhaps, together with Luke, she should see him. They could appear together at her deathbed. She is still married to him in the eyes of God, or so Father Goodall would quite correctly tell her.

Luke and Liam get on tolerably well, as she understands it, though they do not see much of one another, divided as they are by land and sea.

Teresa had lost her hair, through chemo, but it has grown back again, with a richer and wirier texture than before. Now it curls bravely upwards in its crisp short white bob, in a sprightly halo. It has more strength in it than the rest of her wasting body. She suspects that it will go on growing in her coffin. She does not wish to be cremated. She has chosen her plot of land, at St Mary's in Kensal Green Cemetery, near the canal. She has walked the towpath many times, in her good walking days, and heard the birdsong in the trees, and seen the foxes sauntering brazenly along, and studied the inscriptions on the tombstones.

Liam, too, has as much hair as he ever had and shows no sign of an ageing manly baldness. He has so much hair that, as some men of his advanced age do, he has boastfully let it grow thick and long and magisterially grey, well down below his shoulders, like a dorsal penis, and he ties it back with a coloured ribbon. He dresses formally, in suits and ties, but he wears his hair long. She knows this because she can see him on the internet, if she bothers to look, and Luke and her grandson Xavier sometimes send her what she still calls 'snaps'. She receives them in her ever-ready little mobile phone.

She is told that Liam's silver ponytail is an alternative modern academic look. She quite likes it.

Liam lost his faith, long ago. She doesn't know what Luke believes.

Teresa does not believe very firmly in a personal afterlife, although she sometimes has to pretend that she does, because that makes it so much easier for everyone else. Father Goodall is certainly comforted by her profession of faith in arriving in a heavenly Jerusalem, and she does not want to upset or alienate

Father Goodall in her hours of dependence and need. And who knows, there may well be a better place.

Her friend Fran is not a believer. She sometimes says she is a pantheist, but she isn't very consistent about that. On a good day, with good weather, she's a pantheist. A fair-weather pantheist. She's pointed out to Teresa that February isn't a good month for pantheists. Fran, Teresa knows, is longing for the spring. The snowdrops in Teresa's own garden and in her ugly North London churchyard are already displaying an ivory white and a streaked green, and the aconites will be a joyous buttery yellow around the gravestones, although Teresa cannot go to see them, and Fran would not even know where they are.

Fran is somewhere in the sodden West Country, stranded with her fierce daughter Poppet. She'll be back soon, they have fixed a date. Maybe she will have to introduce Fran to Birdie. She wonders how they will get on.

Her son Luke and Birdie get on fine. They've known each other forever. They tease one another a lot. That won't be a problem, when Luke comes.

Teresa has enjoyed discussing the last things with Fran, who, although an expert in trivia, is more than willing to apply her mind to eschatology. Teresa lies on her day bed, under a cheerful tartan once-much-travelled car blanket, with a new book about the Etruscans open upon her knee, contemplating the new (to her) discovery that both pain and trivia can be a welcome distraction from the ultimately serious business of dying. Pain alters perceptions of time, and makes one wish to be elsewhere, to be speeding on one's journey, whereas trivia comfortably and companionably block the forefront of the mind, occupying the space that might otherwise be devoted to prayer or thought or meditation or despair.

Trivia: a comfortable blanket, a mug of soup, a text message or two, a radio quiz, a book upon one's lap.

Trivia: the meeting of the three ways, the lower arts.

The book on the Etruscans had been sent to her by her brother David. It is a lavish but scholarly new work by his long-term partner, Massimo Vignoli, with whom he shares an apartment in Orvieto. As David had said, in the covering email heralding its arrival, the illustrations are wonderful. Teresa does not object to the implication that she may not be up to reading any heavy stuff about the Etruscans, because it's almost but not quite true. She is happy to read a paragraph here and there, but happier to browse through the photographs of sarcophagi, of reclining matrons with their stout and gentle husbands, of details of delicately coloured tomb wall paintings of ducks and deer and vines and suntanned dancing men and pale women. The Etruscan deities have such strange names. Vanth, Fufluns, Uni, Turan, Turms. What kind of a language is that? Names from an *arrière-pays*. She particularly likes the ancient little Villanovan hut-houses of the dead. She had read, long ago, D. H. Lawrence's *Etruscan Places*, and is inclined to share his view that the Etruscans were a happy breed, happy in life as in death, a view not upheld by Massimo Vignoli, who dismisses Lawrence, not with contempt but with a scholarly compassion. Lawrence's views are out of date, but he couldn't, at that period, have known any better.

Lawrence had been dying when he visited Tarquinia and Cerveteri and Volterra. He had died so young, and he had so much hated to be dying. He'd been bravely building his ship of death for the dark flood, and fitting it out with food and little cakes and wine and cooking pans, but he hadn't wanted to die. She is too old to die young, and that's a comfort. She often counts, on her fingers, her remaining comforts.

The little terracotta red-brown cinerary huts of the dead are small and homely. Like doll's houses. She thinks Fran would like to see them. They do not quite come into the Ashley Combe category of accommodation for the elderly, but they have a metaphysical connection with it. She must remember to show them to Fran.

The book is heavy on her lap. She can hardly lift it to move it safely to one side of her day bed. Never again will she be able to climb up her library steps, to reach the art books on the top shelf. She had not thought to note the last time when she felt able to ascend. It hadn't seemed a marker, a milestone, though it had been one. Even Fran, who is fit, strong and wiry, had found David's *Pontormo* weighty and unwieldy and had complained, as she clambered carefully down, that her wrists were not what they were.

Teresa gazes at her bookcases, at the collection of novels and poems from the 1960s and 70s, some still with their original dust jackets, at her more recent work-related medical case histories, at the top shelves with their dust-collecting, rarely visited volumes of Constable and Matisse, of Artemisia Gentileschi and El Greco, of Rembrandt and Rubens, of Hockney and Hogarth. She wonders at the thick catalogues of exhibitions visited over the years. How had she ever had the energy to go so often to the Tate and the National Gallery, to the Courtauld and the Ashmolean and Kenwood? When she was working, and working more than full-time? And how had she had the strength to carry such doorstep tomes home with her on the Tube, on the bus? It amazes her now, to think of how much she has seen and done.

And now, lifting a single book, even a book of average weight, exhausts her. It is sad, not to be able to lift up a book. Sometimes she feels terminally weary, and wishes, in a cowardly manner, that she might die in her sleep, without having to look her God or her faith or her oncologist in the eye.

She sees Fran standing at the top of the library steps, *Pontormo* clutched to her thin but still shapely chest, arrested as she carefully tests her balance, preparing for the descent.

When she had got safely down, Fran had told her about a friend of her friend Jo, who had been seized by a severe panic attack on top of a rolling ten-foot-high grasshopper-green library ladder in one of the lofty vaulted Reading Rooms in the Bodleian in Oxford. She had had to call for assistance, for a helping hand to steady her on her way down. Those ladders are like *siege engines*, Jo had told Fran. They are *perilous*. They are not safe for older folk. They have rolling-ball feet like *Daleks*.

When Teresa and Fran were young in Broughborough, they hadn't spent all their time crouching conspiratorially in the cellar, aspiring to higher things. They had played giddy games, spun themselves around on the grass like whirling dervishes until they fell over with ecstatic dizziness, performed handstands and backwards somersaults, unsuccessfully attempted cart-wheels, jumped over and off walls, climbed trees. The sap had risen in them each year in the spring, for those few years of mutual girlhood, and they had explored the semi-rural corners of suburbia, where an occasional pony stood patiently in a neglected field. They had sucked the sweet juice of the red flowers of the horse chestnut and eaten the delicate stripped white pithy stems of grasses, and once, daringly, laid the dry, black and deadly poisonous seeds of the laburnum pod and the glowing sticky translucent pink berries of the yew upon their tongues, to see if they would die.

They hadn't swallowed them, the black seeds and the lethal reddish pink globe berries, they had spat them out. Of course. And they hadn't died. They hadn't wanted to die. There had been moments since then when Teresa had wished to die, but not when she was a schoolgirl in Broughborough.

She's feeling low. She's disappointed in herself. She's tired of being ill. She doesn't think that she's afraid of dying, and she isn't, for the moment, in much pain, restored by her latest chemical fix. She leans back on her high pillow, closes her eyes.

It's not clear to her what she's supposed to do, on a spiritual level, with the rest of the time she has left. She's never much liked the language of struggle and battle, and anyway, she knows the battle is already lost. She hasn't thought of her relationship with her cancer in terms of fighting the good fight, as some do. But the lines from Timothy come back to her, nevertheless: *Fight the good fight of faith, lay hold on eternal life, whereunto thou art also called . . .*

Lay hold on eternal life. Fight the good fight of faith.

She can't do it.

Whereunto thou art also called.

She has known some who have lost their faith late in life, in their sixties, in their seventies, even in their eighties. Because the human story is so very disappointing, because the cruelty of it is so very great, and God's care of his creation so hard to interpret.

The saddest case she had ever known had been that of an old woman of the parish, a sinless friendly kind old woman, a neighbour, a practising but not particularly devout Catholic who had, in her last years, been plunged into a state of appalling panic and depression and guilt. It had seemed causeless, to Teresa and to the professionals. The old woman thought she had committed the Sin against the Holy Ghost, whatever that might be. Perhaps she simply meant that she had lost her faith. She had been hospitalised, and then transferred to an expensive psychiatric home in North London, her stay there funded, Teresa gathered, by the son who had done well in the City. Teresa had been to visit her once or twice and had been deeply affected by her condition. Mrs Taylor (they were not on first-name terms, and Teresa was always Mrs Quinn to Mrs Taylor) had been in a state of abject terror. Each day had been an insurmountable and seemingly unendurable ordeal. Her refuge was in playing games of Solitaire – always the same game of Patience, never venturing on any other – again and again, again and again, on a little digital games device. Teresa had not thought much of the staff at the home, who could not work up any interest in so old and so dull a patient.

Once, exasperated, she had told Birdie that some of the staff couldn't have run a Pets' Parlour, let alone a psychiatric unit for the deeply disturbed.

Mrs Taylor had one friend there, an inmate in her forties, herself in the throes of a clinical depression, who would listen and attempt to engage Mrs Taylor in games of Scrabble. Teresa could tell that this good-natured person would emerge before too long into the light of day.

She had an interesting conversation with the good-natured person, on her way down a corridor. The good-natured person, who said her name was Ginnie, had said to Teresa, 'You look just like my psychotherapist.' Teresa could tell that this was a compliment. This was one of the reasons why she knew Ginnie would come through.

The very name of Ginnie seemed to be cause for hope.

But now, thinking of Mrs Taylor arouses a wave of panic, which rises helplessly up in her like an acid reflux. It rises up through her gorge and sours her throat. She needs to be rescued.

It is a terrible thing, when God, who should comfort us, who should give us wings, becomes our jailer and our persecutor. It is terrible when His eye stares at us in anger.

Her right hand cradles her mobile phone. She waits for it to bleep or buzz or flash or ring. If only somebody would ring or text, someone, anyone, someone from out there, from the world of the living. Even that false and endlessly repeating recorded message purporting to be from her bank would do. She wills her little gadget to speak to her. It remains silent.

Any sound would rescue her.

Her hands are withered and wrinkled, as well as enfeebled,

and their backs have for some years now been manifesting the pale-brown liver spots of age. She stares at them, attempting to distract herself. She doesn't dislike these spots. They have a certain charm, even an elegance. She'll miss them when she's dead. If she remembers rightly, the Catholic novelist Graham Greene was teased for the high incidence of liver spots in his later novels.

He didn't like being called a Catholic novelist. He said he was a novelist who happened to be a Catholic. Teresa thinks that was casuistry.

When she was young, the ball of the palm of her right hand had been distinguished by an attractive fairly large golden brown birthmark, shaped a little like a heart. She had been very fond of this distinctive stigma, and had gazed at it for hours when nothing much else was going on – in class, in church, at tram stops, in bed, while listening to the news with her family on the radio. It would bring her, as she thought, good luck. As her life got busier, she forgot to stare at it so attentively, and, neglected it had begun to fade, and (she inspects its site) it has now vanished altogether. Now she has time to look at it again, it's gone. As in the fable about the ass's skin. If she'd stared at it harder, she might have lived longer.

She clutches her mobile, beseeches it. And it obliges. She hears and feels its friendly burr.

It is better than a message from the bank. It is a text from her son Luke. He has booked his flight. He'll be with her in a couple of days. Hang on there, Mum, he adjures her. See you soon.

He'll be with her for his birthday. He doesn't say this in his message, but he is probably as aware of it as she is. It seems like some kind of good luck.

Yes, that's all she has to do. Hang on.

Her spirits soar. She can wait two days, for she will see him soon. She has been rescued from the deep and from spiritual disgrace, and she can hang on.

He was born in a February blizzard, snowed in, in Canada.

Her fretfulness and self-pity fade, and she feels herself rising up, into a higher and better place. She closes her eyes again, and is borne upwards, as she begins to doze and dream and sleep. She is released upwards into dreaming, as the nagging little thorns of memory and anxiety and fear and rationality unhook themselves from the old heavy matted stuff of her consciousness, and allow her to rise from her body. She is released into the presence of a dream landscape: she is observing (but is not quite inhabiting) a scene with a foreground of a grassy hollow with olive trees and great tawny slabs of broken, antique stone. In the centre of the scene, the huge deep-rooted trunk of an ancient tree bears upwards in its forked branches a slab of stone like a sarcophagus. Far away, in the background, upon the distant hillside, far beyond and behind, in a higher country, stands a little white chapel. The place is known and unknown, familiar and unfamiliar.

When she wakes, she will recognise in this dream landscape an allusion to the Etruscan tombs, and to the saving of the virtuous heathen from antiquity, and to a hand-coloured print given to her one year for Christmas by grateful parents. The print had shown just such a scene, but without the Christian chapel. The parents had purchased it, as they said, 'for a song', in Athens, in a stall in a street overlooking the Agora. They had thought she would like it, and she did. She had had it framed, and it hangs on her bedroom wall.

A heavy stone coffin, a flesh-eating sarcophagus, borne upwards in the living growing branches of a tree.

Her dream had married Jerusalem and Athens. She is pleased with the inventiveness of her dream life.

~

Christopher and Ivor have been keeping vigil in the Bar Volcan. They have been back to La Suerte and have retrieved Bennett's dental plate, which they discovered sitting agape in its tooth mug on the kitchen table. This had been a small but significant relief. He won't be needing it yet, but it's good to know where it is. And it has now been safely deposited with the very soothing, very-dark-skinned, dark-green-coated, deeply indigenous orderly who tells them that his name is Bencomo, and that they can rely on him. If the Señor wakes up and wants his teeth, if he seems distressed that he has lost them, Bencomo will reassure him that he can have them back soon. Everything had seemed in hand. Bennett, sedated, was snoring comfortably.

Christopher has also retrieved his iPad, and discreetly looked up surgeon Manolo Zerolo Herrara. He looks fine, but how can one tell? They all look fine, on their websites, with their white shirts and their excellent teeth and their confident smiles.

Ivor knows a lot of bars in Arrecife – the Picasso, the Astorias, the Terrazza, the Timanfaya, the Salinas. He likes the Volcan: they know him there. Ivor and Christopher have been talking about Morocco, so near to them over the waters of the Atlantic Ocean. Christopher has spoken a little of Sara's doomed project and of the wrecked vessels in Port-Étienne, which he now finds himself unaccountably longing to see, as Sara had longed to see them. Ivor has been describing Bennett's interest in General Lyautey and telling indiscreet but not very improper stories about Bennett's erotic adventures in Morocco in the 1970s.

As Western Europe has become less homophobic, North Africa has become more homophobic. It's as though the blot and stain of it moves around the map, settling here, settling there. You can get yourself slammed into a Moroccan jail these days for the things Bennett and Ivor had got up to in Essaouira in the 1970s, whereas in England now, anything goes.

Christopher is drinking but Ivor is not. Christopher no longer minds that Ivor knows he is a drinker. They have reached that stage in their acquaintance.

In the corner over the bar, suspended from high brackets at a precarious and uneasy angle, a television set is playing footage of the recent oceanic eruption off El Hierro. It is strangely beautiful, and they glance towards it from time to time. The programme morphs into other sequences showing other eruptions and volcanic flows, some Canarian, some not. They can't hear the commentary. Vesuvius, Etna, Stromboli, the eponymous island of Vulcano. Christopher still hasn't been to the fragile landscape of Timanfaya.

Ivor tells Christopher of an entertaining Spanish television programme, of which Bennett had been fond, about car crashes, aeroplane crashes and other disasters. It was called *Impacto*, and it was, as its title proclaimed, about impacts, in a fairly wide interpretation of the word. Stones on windscreens, gunshots, motorway pile-ups, trees struck by lightning, aeroplanes imploding on runways, cruise ships run aground. Its naive enjoyment of these moments had charmed Bennett. Ivor had liked it too, though he couldn't follow the commentary. Bennett had said he wasn't missing much.

There are worse ways to die than by *impacto*, Christopher says to himself as he makes his way to the Servicion.

He feels a little unsteady on his feet as he returns to the table where Ivor is sitting, and is surprised to find that he is stumbling slightly. He certainly hasn't drunk nearly enough to justify staggering. He hasn't staggered in years. He can take far more than a Prosecco and a closet vodka and a brandy and a couple of glasses of El Grifo. Maybe he's in shock. They'd better go to find something to eat. The Canarians don't eat as late as the Spanish, but Arrecife is more Spanish than most of the tourist island, and here the night is yet young.

As he and Ivor are discussing where to go to find a meal, they both fall silent as they notice, mesmerised, that Ivor's empty beer glass is travelling slowly across the glass of the table top, as though the table were beginning to tilt, as though they were sitting at a séance. At the other side of the bar, they hear a plate crash to the floor. The customers are looking around at one another, curiously, and the barman laughs. Is this the promised end?

The barman's bottles rattle.

The television set wobbles, the picture streaks and flashes, and then settles again.

It's all OK. Bennett will be safely sedated and strapped into his hospital bed when the earth splits open, when the wind turbines crumple and tangle and the chalky caverns implode, when the tidal wave bears the glittering ziggurat of the anchored Norwegian cruise ship over the concrete moles from Puerto Naos to crash into the still and green inland heart of the lagoon. For Bennett, all shall be well.

~

Fran has not slept much at Poppet's, although she has not been uncomfortable. She has been too anxious about rescuing her poor car from the ploughed field. It had begun to rain again during the night, so the water level will be rising. She's not really in a hurry to get home, but she has no wish to hang around with her daughter, getting in her daughter's way. Jim will come to get her, which is embarrassing, but not disastrous. If she manages to get safely back onto the A303, she'll be fine. She has promised Poppet that she will look out for the cranes.

~

Josephine Drummond has taken an impromptu day off (off from what, she asks herself) to go to London to pursue the

Studdert Meades in the British Library, so easy to access from Cambridge and King's Cross. She has finished reading Bennett Carpenter's *The Reaper and the Wheat* and is now becoming obsessed by the Spanish Civil War, a more mainstream topic than that of the Deceased Wife's Sister. She knows more about the young man who died at Jamara, and is making her way through his unpublished diaries and letters in the Cambridge University Library. They have led her to items in the Manuscripts and Rare Books departments of the British Library, which will be waiting in their boxes for her when she arrives, if the *Explore the British Library* login page has worked as well as it says it has. She is pleased with herself for having remembered her password, as she hasn't logged in for a while.

In finding out about Valentine, she will also discover more about his mother Alice.

The Fatal Kinship had provided a surprising and intriguing denouement. The young couple, Olive and Vesey, had not taken the route to legal matrimony in Jersey, or Paris, or Normandy, or Neuchâtel, as others in their predicament, in fact and in fiction, had done: they had parted, but they hoped only for a year, while they awaited the outcome of the debating of the Deceased Wife's Sister Bill in Parliament. In order not to suffer temptation, they had gone their separate ways. Vesey had sailed to New York, to work for a year and a day in Wall Street, whereas Olive had set off for Cape Town on the steamship *Ariadne*, to engage with her Quaker banking family connections and their post-Boer War programme of land redistribution. When we last see Olive, she is on deck, as a great storm begins to bluster off the coast of Tenerife. *Thou God of this great vast, rebuke these surges*, implores the well-read Olive, as she gazes at the violent Atlantic. Will she drown? Who knows? The *Waratah* went down without trace on this route in 1909, and not a stick or a stone or a bone from it has ever been found, one of the great ocean mysteries: but we are only in 1907, the year of the novel's publication, when, Jo has realised, Alice Studdert Meade probably did not know the outcome of the Bill, let alone the fate of the *Waratah*. She must certainly have written the novel in a state of uncertainty. She was writing a modernist open-ended novel. She was on the edge of history. The fate of Vesey and Olive depended on a vote.

Jo has grown to admire Alice, and is happy to think that she has seen an interesting possibility of a link with her own family history. One of Jo's Cambridge-based aunts, her favourite aunt, had been a successful illustrator of children's books, and had also designed some once-famous and not-yet-forgotten posters for progressive political causes: in these days of instant access to images, it is easy to find Marian Heber's designs for the Children's Circle (a short-lived offshoot of the Left Book Club) and her posters for Medical Aid for Spain and for a play about Goya and the atrocities of war at the Unity Theatre. Aunt Marian had always been, unsurprisingly, a source of well-chosen and much-appreciated Christmas and birthday present books, including Munro Leaf's 1936 classic about a reluctant bull, *The Story of Ferdinand,* Kathleen Hale's colourful *Orlando the Marmalade Cat* of 1938, and J. B. S. Haldane's *My Friend Mr Leakey*, all stalwart favourites which Jo and her sister Susie had read again and again. But Marian had rarely mentioned her adult work to her nieces, and the only tribute to the Spanish Civil War and the Second World War with which they had been familiar had been a children's book about evacuees, with a sound left-wing slant and an introduction by a social historian connected with the Mass Observation project. Printed on cheap paper with narrow margins, and with a restricted palette, it had portrayed the adventures of Walter and Katie Ward who had been evacuated from the East End of Sheffield to a sheep farm in the Peak District. Jo had loved this book, with its contrasting landscapes of factory chimneys and pit heads and flaring furnaces and sheep and meadows and windswept moorland and dry stone walls. She liked the words 'Peak District' too, though she wasn't quite sure where or what the Peak District was.

Aunt Marian, whose Quaker husband came from Hathersage, had been particularly good at sheep. The sweet-faced lambs bounded on their stiff sprigged legs, their rounded woolly mothers grazed and gravely chewed. Jo was particularly fond of one large full-page ewe that stared out of the picture at the reader with a quizzical expression, a divine silliness. They were very comforting animals, accepting of the city strangers who had come to join them. The storyline included a little Spanish boy, José, who had also been taken in by the kindly farmers. Josephine, as a child, had had no idea what he was doing there, amidst the alien bog cotton, and it was only many years later, indeed only yesterday, as she was reading a footnote in *The Reaper and the Wheat*, that she had realised that José was standing in for a generation of Basque refugees who had been exported to Britain from Bilbao on the *Habana* in May 1937, shortly after the bombing of Guernica. The disobliging British government, according to Bennett Carpenter, had been reluctant to accept the children and argued that taking in these 'useless mouths' would contravene the treaty of non intervention.

Young José had at first been sorry that there were no cattle at Long Stone Farm, coming as he did from the land of the bull, but he too had come to love the sheep.

The three children all wore very pleasing woollen jerseys, and in the Christmas chapter they wore jumpers with reindeer patterns, a very avant-garde motif for those days.

This story had been popular in its day, though it had not gone through many editions, as had the tales of Ferdinand the Bull and Orlando, which are still in print.

Jo Drummond thinks it more than likely that Marian Heber

had known the Studdert Meades. They had all lived much of their lives in Cambridge and had similar intellectual, religious and political affiliations. She can't quite work out how the generations would have connected: Aunt Marian, she thinks, would have been younger than Alice, but older than Valentine who died in his twenties at Jarama. Marian had died not long ago, in her nineties.

It had not occurred to Jo until very recently that Ferdinand had been a pacifist anti-Franco bull, but it was obvious once one knew. She now knows that he had been banned in Spain and Nazi Germany, although Stalin, apparently, had liked him.

Nobody would have thought to ban Aunt Marian's sheep. Her sheep did not have names: they were just sheep. Maybe Aunt Marian had missed a trick there. Only the children had names. Walt and Katie and the generic José.

She'd been able to find out about Ferdinand's political history from the internet. It was all there, accessible in seconds. Some of the fun has gone out of scholarship, it's become too easy. She's had to work hard to find an excuse to come to the British Library for the day, where she will be happy and at peace for a few hours in the silent company of scholars. But she has found herself a pretext. Maybe in the boxes of uncatalogued and unpublished letters of Hubert Studdert Meade, and in the papers of his old college, and in the manuscript drafts of his translations, she will find something new, something unre-marked – about his wife Alice, the forgotten novelist with her uncut pages.

And louder sang that ghost, what then?

Valentine, although quoted by Carpenter, and still often cited by other Hispanists with reference to Carpenter, has not been the subject yet of any major independent study. She is slightly surprised that he has not been taken up. The diaries are just as interesting as much that is available in print. He makes a tragic story, with a good image readymade for the jacket. He was as handsome as Rupert Brooke.

The weather on this February Wednesday is not wild, but it is steadily damp and bitterly cold. The pavements are greasy with a thin slick of dirty brown mud, dotted with pale scabs of trodden chewing gum and the skeletons of leaves. Luckily it is only a short walk from King's Cross to the British Library, some of it under cover, and she hurries along, past the restored red-brick façade of St Pancras and the cowed and cowled sellers of the *Big Issue*, thinking of the wisdom of those who migrate to warmer climes and counting up the weeks that must be endured before one could reasonably expect the discernible coming of spring. Winter in the Midwest had been unpleasant, and she and Alec had usually flown south for the winter vacation, to Florida, to Mexico, and once to St Lucia.

Now she does not even think of escaping England. It seems to be her duty to ride this rough weather out. She and Fran are in agreement about this. They do not plan to set off together on a widows' cruise to the sun, although they could. They remember the bitter years in Romley, when the children were small and had chicken pox and the plumbing froze and they could not afford to heat their homes properly and had to collect water in plastic buckets from a standpipe. Athene Grange is warm, and so is Fran's flat. They will stick it out.

Owen England had liked the Canaries, he had sung their praises, but then he had been invited to visit them. It wouldn't be the same, going without a purpose, for pleasure. Owen had been welcomed by old friends.

The library welcomes her. Her items are waiting for her. She installs herself at her desk, plugs in her lightweight mini-laptop, and begins to browse through the contents of the slim old-fashioned dark-red string-tied cardboard folder and the larger and smarter pale green canvas box.

The box reminds her of bookbinding lessons at school, in a Wednesday afternoon slot called Craft Work. She can still smell the fabric and the glue.

She knows that others before her have read Hubert's letters. A few quotations from them have surfaced in print in biographies and cultural studies, establishing dates and connections, charting changing attitudes to the Cambridge Classical Tripos and to Greats in Oxford, to Greek tragedy, to fashions in translation. Hubert had been acquainted with A. E. Housman and Gilbert Murray and with A. W. Verrall, all famous in their day. Hubert seems to have been a kindly and well-principled man, although his versions of Aeschylus and Euripides are, in Jo's view, as texts, both dated and deplorable. She had managed to acquire some of them on her Kindle, and has been puzzled and amused by some of the typographical errors that have crept in, which would certainly have startled Professor Studdert Meade. The word 'fanes', for example, appears throughout as 'fannies', and 'corselets' as 'corsets'. How can this be? What human error or fallible technological process has introduced these louche innuendoes? Had non-English speaking technicians on the far side of the world seen fit to interpret the text of Euripides in this ingenious way? Or had some scanner automatically readjusted to the more familiar?

Hubert wouldn't have known the word 'fanny', and neither would his son Valentine, but he'd have known about corsets. Alice would undoubtedly have worn corsets. Everybody did. Just as she and Fran when they were young had worn what were then called girdles, Alice and Aunt Marian had worn corsets.

As she begins to think it's nearly time to allow herself to go to find some lunch, she discovers she's on the track of something she may have been searching for. It looks like a reference to the Basque refugees.

Dear Hubert [writes somebody called Jack, from Grindleford, in December 1938]

You will be pleased to hear that Eduardo and Manolita are settling in. The camp does its best but some of the children are very disturbed and it is good to be able to offer a temporary refuge in a proper home. Our thanks to Alice for suggesting us. The children are company for Elizabeth who has been in very low spirits. Marian has been to visit, and has made some beautiful sketches of the children walking on Stanage Edge. Did you see her poster for the A.I.A.? She is now a member of the Basque Children's Committee.

I know Alice is very busy with the Dependents Aid Committee and Medical Aid. I am sure that she is finding such work a lifeline. This is such a hard time for you both and we send you our deepest and continuing sympathy.

Yours ever,

Jack

This has to be a reference to Aunt Marian. It had not occurred to Josephine that José had been standing in not only for a generation of Basque refugees, but also for a real child, or perhaps two real children. Now it seems that this must have been so, and why not?

Marian herself had briefly taken in a family of Hungarian refugees in the crisis of 1956. She had invited them into her large under-occupied Edwardian Cambridge home in Grange Road. They'd been billeted on her by the Quaker Meeting. Jo can remember them well, though she has no idea what had happened to them subsequently. They'd been around over Christmas and everyone had had to improvise little presents for them, and watch the little girl dance a sugary show-off ballet routine beneath Aunt Marian's annually resurrected silver-tinsel

Christmas tree. Jo hadn't taken to these particular Hungarians at all, although she'd been of an age to take an intellectual interest in the uprising. She'd wanted to like them, but she didn't. They had seemed too pleased with themselves, too certain of deserving attention. Her unpleasant teenage self would have preferred them to be more humble. They had nearly spoiled the annual visit to Aunt Marian.

This is all a very long way from Jo's dilettante interest in the plot of Alice's novel, *The Fatal Kinship*. She feels she has strayed far from her subject. As she descends the luminous white staircase of Portland stone, past the portholes, past the classical seats of travertine, past the varicoloured busts of literati, past the disturbing Kitaj tapestry, she tries in vain to remember why she became arbitrarily interested in the Deceased Wives' Sisters in the first place. The link has gone.

As she ladles out her orange-red roast pepper soup, she is not very pleased to hear her name being called. She'd been looking forward to a quiet, anonymous lunch keeping up to date by reading a new American novel on her Kindle, and it is hard to adjust from this comfortable prospect to conviviality. It is her old friend Geraldine, calling at her from over by the salad bar where she is piling her little glass bowl high with leaves and lentils and other more new-fangled pulses. There is Geraldine, with her startling orange hair, her scarlet sweater, her spangled scarf. There is no way of avoiding her. You can't miss Geraldine, or pretend you haven't seen her. Jo adjusts her soup bowl on her tray, changes mode, smiles and decides to go for it: it's always fun with Geraldine, if you surrender.

They find a table by the window, in the glass-covered extension, and exchange news as they tuck into their healthy soup and salad combo. Geraldine, as usual, is highly excited. '*Darling*,' she exclaims from time to time, as she reports in her loud, highly inflected and resounding voice on the various activities and dramas that have occupied her since they last met ('*yonks* ago'): more grandchildren, a lecture recently delivered at the Italian Institute, an invitation to a festival in Mantua in the spring, a foot operation (of which she displays, beneath the table, the aesthetically pleasing results), a few friends and relatives dismissed as dead or dying (Geraldine has no truck with illness, her own or anyone else's), a flirtation with a Venetian art historian, a row with her publisher over e-books and royalties on reprints. Geraldine has always been volatile and combative, and Jo has learned that the enemy of today may well be the hero of tomorrow, so she listens and exclaims and sympathises and lets the flow wash over her. Unlike many big talkers, Geraldine is also insatiably interested in the lives of others (all fodder for future gossip of her own) and she plies Josephine with a series of questions: how is Cambridge, how is Athene Grange working out, is she still playing bridge, did she see the new *Tosca* at Covent Garden, what is she writing, how is the disruptive and demanding Sally Lyttelton, why is Jo in the British Library, how are Jo's children, how is that friend of hers, what's her name, Fran, who used to live next door to Stella Hartleap in Highgate? *Poor* Stella, *what* a ghastly death, and did Jo hear about what happened to Martin Stuart? *Too* terrible.

Jo fields all these questions expertly and doesn't think she's given away too many secrets. Geraldine shows a mild interest in Jo's new preoccupation with Basque refugees, says she can speak a word or two of Basque, and that she is in the middle of reading a new Italian novel set in the Second World War with some stuff about Franco and Mussolini. Mussolini, she says, is popping up a lot in fiction these days, it's his turn, but she doesn't think she's going to recommend this one to her publishers.

Geraldine is so well if sporadically connected that Jo is half expecting her to say that she knows the Studdert Meade family. She doesn't, but she does declare, having finished her résumé of the past few months and leapt forward to the immediate future, that she is off with the other Geraldine to the Canary Isles in a couple of days, to Lanzarote, for a week or two of winter sunshine. Has Jo ever been to the Canaries?

It is very Geraldine to have a best friend called Geraldine. Jo thinks she knows all about her, as, no doubt, the other Geraldine will think she knows all about Josephine Drummond.

Jo says no, she has never been to the Canaries, and had been of the impression, rather snobbishly, that they are full of high-rise hotels and English pubs and hooligans. But, she cautiously volunteers, her Thursday evening fiancé (she has allowed Geraldine to label him thus) had been there for Christmas, staying with ex-pat friends, and had given a very good report of the climate and scenery of Lanzarote. Even as she is speaking, she slightly regrets this potential contribution to Geraldine's store of tittle-tattle, and the more so when her friend seems keen to find out the identity of the ex-pats and, possibly, to call on them. Jo hesitates, wondering whether to pretend she's forgotten their names and rapidly assessing the chances of Geraldine knowing Bennett Carpenter already. She does know a hell of a lot of people, and her field of scholarship (Italian twentieth- and twenty-first-century fiction and cinematography) is not a million miles removed from Bennett Carpenter's own. And Geraldine is no fool, although she tried very hard to look and sound like one.

Maybe Bennett would be delighted to welcome the Geraldines? He seems to be a sociable and hospitable chap: she's heard all about his kindness to the wayward Christopher Stubbs. She tries to create a diversion by asking Geraldine whether she'd like a coffee or a tea (interesting but well-recognised use of the indefinite article), but Geraldine isn't going to let go. So Jo, who is not very good at subterfuge, finds herself offering up the name of Bennett Carpenter, the author of *The Reaper and the Wheat* and, latterly, *The Shadows in the Square*. She makes it plain that she herself has never met him, and doesn't know his address, so is hardly in the position of effecting an introduction, but she need not have worried about that particular delicacy, for, as soon as his name is released, Geraldine lets out a cry of delight and recognition.

'Bennett Carpenter!' she shouts, causing several more heads to turn in their direction. 'I *know* Bennett! So that's where he's got to! Does he *live* there now? I used to go to their parties when they lived in South Ken! I haven't seen them for *yonks*!'

She rambles playfully on, over a double espresso. It is clear that she will get in touch with him and Ivor as soon as she arrives, if not before. Jo, by now thoroughly distracted from her pursuit of Alice, wonders if she'll have to confess all this to Owen over cloudscapes and Bourbon tomorrow evening.

It's well known that Bennett Carpenter lives in Lanzarote. It's in the public domain. It's not a secret. He's not in hiding, or a recluse. None of this is Jo's fault.

Geraldine is even more animated than usual, and as they part, she to Humanities One where she is doing a bit of background reading on the Italian debacle at Guadalajara under General Roatta, and Jo to her handwritten letters in Manuscripts, she throws her arms around Jo and cries, 'Why don't you come too! There's plenty of room in our apartment! And a lovely swimming pool! Think what fun we could have! You could bring your fiancé!'

'I think *not*,' says Jo, with reproving gravitas. Though a lovely swimming pool does sound attractive.

Despite all, she does rather love Geraldine. And she can see that her style of academic camp could go down very well at La Suerte. Perhaps it's all for the best.

~

Fran is looking out for the cranes, as she had said she would, but she is also concentrating harder than usual on her driving, as she doesn't want any more adventures. Killed while craning her neck to look at a crane, not a good epitaph. The car seems none the worse for its night out and Jim had managed to rescue it without much difficulty. He had also given her helpful instructions about where best to get back onto the A303, and warned her to avoid the service station just beyond Stonehenge, where, he claims, the concrete forecourt is always awash with water in this kind of weather. Built below the flood plain – big mistake, according to Jim.

Jim is a puzzle to Fran, and this recent encounter has done nothing to clarify him or his role in her daughter's life. He's a farmer, but he seems to have a preoccupying and contradictory sideline in antiques and second-hand books. Unlike Poppet, he's deeply local. He knows the vicinity, it's in his bones, born and bred. He's married, with a wife and grown children, one of them in catering, one a long-distance trucker, but his attitude to Poppet is not simply that of a helpful neighbour. They seem to have some kind of collaborative relationship, but Fran has no idea what it is. It doesn't feel sexual, though they are physically at ease with one another, almost intimate. Brotherly? No, not quite. Something else, something other.

Poppet's brother Christopher has never met Jim. But Christopher remains brotherly towards Poppet.

She wonders how poor old Bennett Carpenter is getting on.

Jim, though short of stature, is a heavy, powerful man, with a blunt nose and a fine head of tightly curled reddish-grey hair, like a bull. He'd heaved her poor car's nose up and attached it to his tow rope with no trouble at all.

Fran doesn't see much of her two brothers, but she's not on bad terms with them, it's just a cool English-style fraternal relationship, with joshing and reminiscing and meetings once or twice a year. Her older brother's very deaf now, and lame too. He has a bad hip which he refuses to have fixed, so he doesn't get out much and therefore hasn't got much to say. He and his loyal wife have closed in upon themselves, as ageing couples sometimes do, and do not seem as unhappy as Fran would be if she were they. Her younger brother is sprightlier and more outgoing, although (she doesn't like to admit this, even to herself) rather dull. He talks a lot, but he talks about cars and golf and keeping fit. Fran likes trivia, but she's more interested in female trivia than male.

Teresa's brothers, the boys next door, aren't very close to Teresa either, though she frequently mentions David and his partner in Orvieto, as though they are often on her mind. David, of the six Broughborough neighbours, the two cellar girls and the four bicycling boys, has had the most distinguished career. He's made a name for himself in art history. It's a small world, but he's made a name in it.

She hasn't yet got round to asking Christopher if he knows anything of David Quinn. She keeps meaning to, but then she keeps forgetting. It's of no importance. It's idle curiosity.

The weather has changed; the large sky is now blue, bright and cloudless, a thin high clear wintery azure. A copse of pink and silver trees and copper bracken by the roadside gives way to a rising open field of a tender washed green, to a field of a ploughed and rusty red. Springtime is lying down there in the earth, in Wiltshire, waiting. The birds will be building their nests.

Teresa would have liked to have seen the snowdrops of her last winter. Fran had wondered whether to pick her a few from St Helen's churchyard, and she'd even located the church, down the hill from Teresa's, and around the corner. But she hadn't got round to it. No, it wasn't that she hadn't got round to it, she had thought better of it. It would have been too pointed, too poignant an act. And anyway, it would have been theft. Father Goodall might have caught her at it, and that would have been very embarrassing.

The traffic slows to a halt for a while as the road narrows near Stonehenge.

The standstill gives her time to admire the ancient Wiltshire landscape and, when she's done enough of that, to check her mobile. There are messages: from Christopher, from Teresa, from Jo, from Paul Scobey, and from various companies she wishes she had never patronised. Omega Hotel Rooms, who needs them? They will not let her go, and all because she once had to book herself in somewhere at the last moment in Berwick-upon-Tweed. And there are more messages from various theatre companies promoting shows that she would pay not to see. That Beckett play had nearly finished her off.

She's not sure if she wants to see what Teresa and Christopher have to say. Their lives are tinged by death. An aura of death and of deadly misfortune glows cold and luminous from their virtual and unopened envelopes. There might be bad news in either of those packages, a convergence of ill messaging.

She decides to try Jo, as more likely to be on good form, though she will have to get to grips with Christopher soon, in the next traffic jam.

After all, his last word to her had been 'HELP'.

~

Jo is relaying the latest news of Bennett Carpenter to her friend Owen. She has heard it from Fran Stubbs, who has brought her up to date with Bennett's condition and Christopher's extended sojourn. Bennett has undergone hip surgery, a major event for a man of his age and in his state of health, and is now, unaccountably, saying that he wants to come back to

England. So Christopher has reported. He and Ivor don't know what to do.

They really don't know what to do.

Jo and Owen sip their Bourbon, meditatively, and count their blessings. They are alive, and not in pain, and not, as far as they can tell, deranged. Nor are they homeless. They are far from homeless. They are embedded.

Jo is much more interested in Bennett Carpenter than she had been in previous discussions of him, because now she has read his book. His fate is a concern for her. His name is now surrounded by a thick cluster of thoughts and associations, crowding around him, from the Studdert Meades to her Aunt Marian, to the battle of Jarama and the Basque refugees and Winston Churchill's plan to invade the Canary Islands. Hovering around him are also the contemporary figures of the two Geraldines, who won't find it so easy to invite themselves for cocktails now the old man is in hospital, badly surviving a hip operation.

'He says he wants to come back, but you say he hasn't anywhere to come back *to*,' says Jo.

'That's right,' says Owen.

They are both selfishly thinking how lucky they are, safe here in Athene Grange. The price of these units has gone up steadily, since they bought their way in. So has the cost of the maintenance, but they can keep pace with it. They are sitting pretty.

'And I know they'd told Christopher how good the healthcare is on Lanzarote,' says Jo.

'Maybe he had a stroke, when he fell,' says Owen. 'Maybe his mind isn't quite clear. He seemed well enough at Christmas, but he may have had a stroke.'

'Poor Ivor,' says Jo, feelingly. She is concerned for this man whom she has never met.

'And poor Christopher,' says Owen, who has never met

Christopher, although he has seen him (though he would not readily admit this) on TV. 'He's had what I think we call a double whammy.'

The phrase sounds so quaint coming from Owen's pale nicotine-dry lips that Jo gives a short laugh, although there is nothing much to laugh about.

'I wonder whether Bennett's health insurance would cover repatriation,' speculates Owen.

Jo takes another sip, and looks around her comfortably standardised but pleasantly personalised living room with a complacent sorrow. She is surrounded by the best of the remnants salvaged from several moves over her long life, and this is her last home. Her charming rust-red velvet Edwardian Bergère chair and ottoman, inherited from her parents-in-law, many times reupholstered and heaped high with the tapestry cushions she has worked over the years; Aunt Marian's small eighteenth-century marquetry table, with its beautiful fan inlay; her oval gilt-framed chipped and never-restored French mirror, purchased for a song in Romley market; her elegant ruby-red Bristol glass vase, given to her by Alec for their ruby wedding, and holding some dried grasses and a peacock feather; her library of books, the early poetry first editions still in their dust jackets, and probably worth a pretty penny now; her mantelpiece full of photographs and knick-knacks and objects given to her over the years by children and grandchildren and grateful students. Her little William Nicholson still life, her Picasso print, her delicate hand-coloured Edward Lear land-scapes of Petra and Smyrna and Nicopolis, her pencilled Jack Yeats horse and foal standing in a quiet field by a dry stone wall, her Marian Heber sheep on Stanage Edge. These things have made their home here, and she intends to die with them around her.

'Maybe he just wants to die in England,' she ventures.

'Maybe,' says Owen, glumly.

They decide to break protocol and have another snifter.

'But it was such a *convenient* house to die in,' says Owen, after a long pause. 'I was quite envious. Athene Grange is all very well, it's very good here, but La Suerte was amazing. It might have been made for them. And Bennett's Spanish was excellent.'

'Who *did* design it?' asks Jo, at a tangent.

Owen doesn't know.

'Poor Ivor,' repeats Jo.

'Yes, poor Ivor,' says Owen. 'He really wouldn't like it here at all. In England. Not his scene, at all. I think he'd got a scene, out there. I hope he had. Poor Ivor.'

~

In bed, meditating on Bennett Carpenter's homing instincts as she tries to fall asleep, Jo remembers a story told to her by a friend who had recently visited the Living Museum in Dudley, in the Black Country, where streets and shops and houses from the time of the Industrial Revolution to the 1930s had been painstakingly recreated, brick by brick. So realistic were the replications that one confused old woman, visiting in her wheelchair on an outing with fellow inmates from her care home in West Bromwich, had thought that she was home again at last. She wanted to stay, to settle back in. When she was told the little artisan's house was only a show, despite its kitchen range and its dresser and its peg rug and its carefully selected period branded products, she had cried, and refused to accept this information. She had not wanted to leave. She had not wanted to go back on the coach to her care home.

Or so the woman got up in fancy dress had told Jo's friend, who had told Jo.

This was a distressing story.

Jo wonders what Bennett wants to come home for.

~

Ivor is nearer to panic than he has been for years. Decades of calm solicitude, carefully banked up in him against such emergencies, begin to collapse, and he doesn't know what he should do for the best, or where to find his footing. Bennett has clearly lost his wits, possibly temporarily, possibly permanently, and his insistence that he wants to return to England is vehement and irrational. He seems to have turned against the Spanish-speaking hospital staff; he has even turned against the impeccably polite, patient and helpful Bencomo. And he has been making slightly racist remarks, which make Ivor feel hot and cold all over. He has mentioned Franco, as though he were still alive. What on earth has happened to him? The tremor that rattled the bottles in the volcano bar has dislodged some particle in Bennett's brain.

Maybe something's gone wrong with the magnetic pull of the earth, thinks Ivor.

Surgically, the hip operation is said to be a success, and Bennett is recovering from it in his private ward. The care is good, and he won't be getting bed sores while he is safe in here. Ivor seems to be the only person who can detect that he is not making much sense. He relays his anxieties to Christopher, and together the two of them go over possible courses of action: to wait and see what happens; to seek further medical and psychiatric advice; to fly somebody reassuring out from England (James Robbins might come, he'd dealt capably with some of Bennett's earlier medical crises, and Bennett likes him); to fly back to England anyway and try to find a hospital bed there, as Christopher had done for Sara.

Christopher now can't remember how he'd wangled the bed, even though it all happened so recently: maybe it was the TV crew that had fixed it? That young man Jonathan had been a brilliant fixer. When he looks back at those days, which now seem months ago, it's a blur of panic, the panic that Ivor must be feeling now.

Most of Bennett's friends on the island are as old and shaky as he is, and not likely to be much use, though good will messages from them come through as news of his misadventure gets about. Simon Aguilera rings and says Pilar is willing to come over and housekeep for a while at La Suerte, when Bennett is allowed to go home. This surprisingly practical offer cheers Ivor, momentarily, but it's hardly a long-term solution.

Christopher doesn't like to ask about Bennett's and Ivor's finances, though he does grasp without being told that selling La Suerte wouldn't be easy, if it should come to that, and that most of their capital will be tied up in the property. They had, as Ivor has said several times, well and truly burned their boats when they had sold the lease on their London flat. They'll find it very hard to get off the island.

It is Ivor who, on the third night of Bennett's hospitalisation, raises the subject. After dinner, he suddenly gets to his feet, crosses the room and opens Bennett's old roll-top desk. He extracts the will from its pigeonhole. It's obvious, at a glance, that it is a will. Wills still preserve their archaic form: their long brown envelopes, their old-fashioned Gothic script.

Ivor sits down and breathes rather heavily. He has a good idea what's in there, but he can't be sure.

'The income hasn't been too good, of late,' he says, apologetically, as he slowly makes his way through the legal prose. 'The royalties are right down. We never got to grips with the contracts for the e-books, I think the publishers took him for a ride. He never really understood about e-books. And because we moved around so much, he didn't really build up a proper pension. He wasn't very careful about money matters. And the health insurance has been costing us a fortune.'

Christopher can tell that Ivor isn't very clued up about money either. For all their worldly charm and suavity, these had been two innocents, washed up on their island in the sun. Almost as unable to sail or swim away as the original inhabitants had been, all those centuries ago.

Ivor reads, frowning as he reads. He seems, as far as Christopher can tell, relieved rather than disturbed by what he finds, and he suddenly lets out a laugh and shakes his head, but more in amusement than in sorrow or in anger.

'He's left a choice of books from his library to Owen England, and £5,000 to maintain the goldfish pond at Haycombe House, more than he's left to the Terrence Higgins Trust. And he wants Owen to have his Picasso dinner plates.'

'But he's left you all right?' Christopher feels compelled to ask. He doesn't really want to know about the goldfish. It's too late to go back that far.

He has a sudden image of his father, corpulent in his bed. He had been a top-rate earner. How much will go to his second wife's family? In Christopher's view, he owes the lot to Fran, to whom he is now doubly indebted. And he and Poppet haven't wholly neglected him.

Or have they? Perhaps they have.

Fran is a proud woman and will probably say she doesn't want or need anything. And that will be true.

'Yes,' says Ivor, 'he's left me the house, and his royalties, and his investments, and his PLR.'

'Investments' is a grand word, thinks Ivor, for those little deposits here and there in building societies and ISAs and National Savings Certificates and Premium Bonds. A grand and misleading word for Bennett's shares in Eurotunnel, which had been bringing him in regularly about 18p a year. Bennett hadn't been shrewd about stocks and shares, but he had liked the idea of a tunnel under the Channel. Their friend Jack Stringer, former Master of Gladwyn College and now Lord Stringer of Medmenham, had been smarter at finance than he had been at his subject of eighteenth-century history, and would die a rich man, without heirs. In his old age Jack was forever at his computer, buying and selling, trading online. He'd given Bennett a tip or two, but the only one he'd taken up had been a disaster, and he'd often wondered, aloud, if Jack had given it to him out of spite.

If Jack loses his wits, how long will he go on trading before anyone notices? He lives, deservedly, a very solitary life.

Bennett had, against the odds, made a little money out of the £500 he'd put into the new swimming pool at the club, which had done all too well with the wrong kind of members: Bennett loved to swim, but he'd staidly disapproved of the new pool clientele, and had sold his shares for a surprisingly large profit. Ivor had quite liked the new members, although he was too old and set in his ways to take advantage of them. That was another reason why Bennett had taken against the pool.

Bennett wants to be cremated, and he had asked, when this will was made and witnessed by an English lawyer in Arrecife and by non-beneficiary Simon Aguilera, that Ivor should scatter his ashes into the crater of Monte Corona. If Bennett doesn't die soon, Ivor won't be able to get up there to do it, and will have to delegate the duty. And maybe, now that Bennett is disenchanted by the island, he won't want to be scattered into a Spanish-territory Canarian crater; he may wish to be dispersed in English woodland. How can one guess what he wants, in this rambling unbalanced frame of mind?

Ivor reads out to Christopher the sentences about the cremation and the ashes, and the secular service which Bennett had envisaged being held in the euphorbia garden, with readings from W. H. Auden and Cecil Day-Lewis and Lorca. Lorca had given Bennett the title for his best-known book, taken from a poem the title of which, Ivor knows, means 'Farewell', and this is the poem he wishes to be read. The Day-Lewis is a heroic extract from 'The Nabarra', and the Auden poem was to be 'Thanksgiving for a Habitat':

Territory, status,

and love, sing all the birds, are what matter:
what I dared not hope or fight for
is, in my fifties, mine . . .

Ivor doesn't like 'The Nabarra', but he knows the Auden lines by heart, and they always bring tears to his eyes.

Bennett had also, long ago, received a pledge from their friend Piers Carline, to sing Britten's setting of 'Down by the Salley Gardens', but Piers had predeceased him, so he won't be able to do that.

Ivor describes the volcano of Monte Corona and the purple flowers that blossomed on its lower slopes in spring. In their first year here, he and Bennett had been fit enough to scramble up the slippery slopes of scree to reach the crater, and to gaze down into its mineral lichen-encrusted mouth. Ivor had liked the idea of the volcano ascent enough to overcome his tendency to vertigo, which afflicted him more in cityscapes with tall buildings than outdoors, and he'd enjoyed hearing Bennett ranting about Empedocles on the summit.

Their spirits are rising, now that Ivor has braved his fate and discovered that he has not been disinherited. He doesn't tell Christopher, but he has also found some affectionate phrasing, carefully inserted into the codicils and clauses, which has warmed his loyal heart. *Territory, status and love* . . .The panic of fear of the immediate future, of displacement and estate agents and furniture removals, is tempered by a sense that his life has, after all, been worthwhile, and that Bennett has, however erratically and at times imperiously and selfishly, loved him. The end may be upon them, and it may in its details be horrifying, but the journey towards it has been worthwhile.

When they talk about the immediate future, into the small hours, they both assume that Christopher will be staying on to see it through. He hasn't got anything better to do, has he? A kind of gallows hilarity overcomes them as they discuss the macabre possibilities ahead. And as they talk, Christopher is in the process of realising more fully that his affair with Sara had been going nowhere: she had been beautiful, gifted, powerful, serious, too serious for him, on another plane of engagement with her career. Her subjects had been too big for him. Saharan politics, Ghalia Namarome, the Wall of Shame, Port-Étienne, the frontiers drawn in the sand, the rusting ships, the sinking pateras, the *immigrantes* wrapped in gold foil, the Red Cross in Puerto del Rosaria. She had been one too many for him, as Bennett had always been one too many for Ivor. He wasn't up to her level. But unlike Ivor, he had not been able to espouse a role of submission. She had been an alpha female, and she had outclassed him. In time, he would have come to resent this. But time had not been given to them.

Bennett and Ivor have had a lifetime together. Nearly fifty years, says Ivor, as he recalls their first meeting. They'd met in a tea shop in Oxford, where Ivor had been waiting at table as a favour to his Auntie Rosie who was short of staff. He had just left school, just turned seventeen, and was about to take up a lowly job with Reading Council. Bennett had been sitting at a little table in the window with an important-looking Oxford type, gowned, deep in conversation, and they had ordered what Ivor had heard as buttered scones. But when he arrived back with the requested tray of Darjeeling and china cups and napkins and buttered scones, Bennett's guest had vehemently and petulantly protested that he had asked not for scones, but for buttered *toast*. Bennett, faced with this petty explosion, had winked imperceptibly at Ivor and declared, 'But my dear Frazier, I distinctly heard you ask for scones!'

Ivor had soothingly scuttled away to replace the scones with toast, and had found himself, on their departure, in receipt of a handsome tip.

Bennett, calling back for his tea on several subsequent occasions, had failed to find the temporary waiter in attendance, but, undeterred, had tracked him down by brazenly asking Auntie Rosie how to contact him. She had obliged, and Ivor's informal lifelong education had begun.

Auntie Rosie had taken a pride in her part in this story, and had thoroughly enjoyed Bennett's famous New Year parties.

Nearly fifty years, repeats Ivor.

If Bennett is really out of his mind, he won't know whether he's back in England or not, will he?

England is so uncomfortable, so damp, so cramped. Ivor can't face it, ever again. He's got accustomed to warmth, and space, and a wide clear sky. He likes the little white chapel where nobody knows him but God.

~

Teresa Quinn is elated. She had hung on, as commanded by her son Luke, and here he is, at her bedside. He hasn't managed to bring grandson Xavier, but Teresa doesn't mind about that at all, in fact she'd rather Xavier didn't see her in this state. Seeing Luke is enough. The newly installed Birdie has tactfully reintroduced herself, and tactfully disappeared, leaving them with tea and toast.

'My handsome, handsome boy,' says Teresa, admiringly.

'My beautiful, beautiful mother,' says Luke.

And she is beautiful: wasted, but elevated, ethereal.

He is robust, and very brown of skin. He brings with him the vigour of the open air, of the outdoors. His dark hair, like his father's, shows no signs of thinning and, unlike his father's, has not a streak of grey. He is in the prime of life. His bodily solidity is a comfort to her. It will carry her along.

They hold hands and talk about Africa, and Ebola, and Luke's work, and his wife Monica, and the clinic, and Xavier, and Xavier's schooling. They talk about pain levels and medication. Luke is a professional, it is easy to talk to him about pain, the subject does not embarrass him. Pain is his familiar. He looks through her rattling plastic boxes and her partitioned containers of pills and her bottles of syrup, examines the labels, cross-questions her about what she takes when, decides she is being quite competent about the regime, and notes that there are so many different kinds of medications that she hasn't really grasped which are analgesics, which are sedatives, and which are mood stabilisers. That's probably just as well, provided she sticks to the timings and the dosage. He'll have a word with Birdie about it later, and with the district nurse in the morning.

The nurse's name is Connie, and Birdie says she is OK and fairly reliable. Connie likes Teresa, which is fortunate.

But who wouldn't, says Birdie, who is in love with Teresa, and has been for years.

'So you're back for your birthday,' says Teresa to Luke, brightly, into a small sad pause that falls between them. He smiles. He is pleased she has remembered, that she hasn't sunk deep into her own condition, as some old people do.

'You're so grown up!' says Teresa, as she tells him once more the old familiar story of his birth, of the snow storm, the four-foot-long icicles, the Canadian winter, his father's well-controlled panic, the midwife and the pudding bowl for the afterbirth and the bony Irish stew. She remembers, as she tells it for the last time, a detail she'd almost forgotten – that little white satin-beribboned light wool bed-jacket, given to her and knitted by Granny O'Connor as though it were an item of a trousseau. A lying-in jacket, would that have been what it was called? The shiny white ribbons had been threaded through the curving neckline of the wool so charmingly. Liam's mother had been very fond of Teresa. It had been a hard parting, on both sides.

Women don't wear bed-jackets these days. Young people wouldn't even know what they were. Mothers don't lie-in, they get straight out of bed with their newborn babies and go shopping the next day in Sainsbury's, like kangaroos, and quite right too.

She isn't quite sure how old Luke is, though she knows his birth date, it is fixed in her memory, because she uses it as part of her login banking security. He was born in 1962. How old does that make him now? In his fifties, surely. Sometimes she forgets how old she is herself.

Old enough. She has outlived her span of three score years and ten.

Enough.

They hold hands. You're allowed to do that when you are dying.

~

Maroussia Darling, in the North London house which she has owned for nearly fifty years and lived in for many of them, looks at herself in her bathroom mirror. She is yet and always has been a beautiful woman. She has borne this burden well.

She is thinking that at the end of the run, which is imminent, she will give her last performance as Winnie, hear one more round of applause, and then she will come back to her home and take her dose of Nembutal. That's what she defiantly tells herself that she will do. She will send an email or two, with delayed transmission, and then she will take her exit. She smiles as she thinks of the headlines which she will never read. It will serve Beckett right. She has served him well and loyally, and she deserves a grand finale, at his expense. He has set it up for her.

Poor old Winnie. Oh Happy Days.

~

It's getting very near the end, but we are not yet at the end. Ivor, Christopher, Geraldine and Geraldine are sitting at a café table on the corner in the little inland palm-tree oasis of Haría. They wait with the crowds of locals, and with a few discerning tourists, for the carnival procession to pass. These days, the towns and the islands stagger the celebrations over weeks, getting the best of a prolonged period of Mardi Gras. The street is decked with bunting, the café is gay with paper flowers and lanterns, and false canaries sing in winking cages. The quartet of spectators is well placed to view the pageantry. The theme this year is 'Pirates of the Pacific', which Ivor predicts will be a bizarre mixture of Johnny Depp, Christopher Columbus and local legend. Sir Lancelot, who some think gave his name to Lanzarote, may ride forth in knitted chain-mail and cardboard armour, and so may the medieval mistress of Zonzamas in spectacular drag. Ivor describes the parades of recent years and the unfortunate laughter at the tragic moment when the young man fell off the platform at the festivities at Las Palmas in Gran Canaria. Bennett had hoped his mother wasn't watching, he tells them.

Ivor has risen to the sense of occasion by adding a little sapphire-blue frosted glitter to his gold-white hair, and a heart-shaped jet-black patch to his brow, which covers the slightly ominous blot that nature has recently bestowed upon him. Geraldine the First does not need to advance far beyond her usual flamboyance, although she has done her best to add extra gaiety with a twinkling and flashing tiara of electric violet stars. The other Geraldine, who is a few years younger and much larger than her friend, is comfortably clothed in a vast black tent, and Christopher is wearing his best pink-and-yellow striped Jermyn Street shirt.

There has been much talk this evening of Christopher's Auntie Josephine and the chance encounter in the British Library that has indirectly introduced the Geraldines to Ivor Walters. Bennett, of course, they have not met, though he has rallied and is in better shape, or Ivor would not be sitting here at the street corner pretending to enjoy himself. Bennett is still in hospital and he is still confused, but his hip is mending well and the fever of his desire to get back to England appears to have abated. It may return, Ivor fears, but for the time being, he seems happy to contemplate being restored shortly to the comforts of La Suerte. He has shed his truculence and become his more customary well-mannered self. He has been characteristically grateful and gracious to the helpful Bencomo, and has even taken in Bencomo's name and asked him if he was named after a Guanche chieftain.

He was.

Bennett and Bencomo now address each other by their first names. Bennett doesn't seem to mind this at all.

Bencomo, Acaymo, Pelicar, Tegueste, Pelinor, mutters Bennett mysteriously to himself, from time to time, like a mantra. He may have lost some of his wits, but he hasn't (alas, thinks Ivor) forgotten his Canarian history.

Christopher Stubbs had almost decided that he couldn't hang around lotus-eating any longer, and had made several abortive attempts to book a flight home when the Geraldines arrived on Ivor's doorstep, unannounced, with a great clumsy sheaf of gawky parrot and dragon flowers encased in cellophane and prickly silver foil. They had been only slightly appalled to find that their host was in hospital. A little problem like that would not deter them from seeking society. Quickly they changed their demeanour from gregarious lightweight fun-loving party-goers to supportive handmaidens: it was done in a trice, done as they stood on the threshold of La Suerte, holding their awkward bouquet. They were invited in, put in the picture, given space to exclaim and sympathise, given time to identify themselves (Ivor dimly remembered Geraldine the First, from the days when even university press publishing parties aspired to glamour), and they were welcomed as accomplices into the unfolding situation. Geraldine the Second has been full of good advice about hip replacements, having had one herself a couple of years ago. Geraldine the First, in contrast, is very keen to talk to Bennett about Franco and Mussolini and Gabriele D'Annunzio. Ivor has explained that now may not be the moment, but Geraldine has not abandoned hope of a serious discussion with the maestro. They've got another three days on the island, plenty of time for him to pull himself together. She would love to hear his views on what really happened to the Italians at Guadalajara.

And here come the floats, with their motley and colourful array of pirates and pirate queens and conquistadores and Norman invaders and Guanche princesses in goatskins. There is even what looks like a tribute to the *immigrantes*, in the form of a fishing boat perilously perched on a tractor, containing a few dark gesticulating figures wrapped in gold foil, bearing huge gilded boughs and palm fronds – is this a sign of acceptance, of integration, or a political protest? It's hard to tell, but the gold stuff glitters, the dark eyes behind the huge masks flash, and the clumsy Ship of Death lurches on. The makeshift painted vehicles rumble and teeter along the streets, the young men drunkenly dance and hurl golden leaves and twigs into the crowd like confetti. It is just as well that the island has ceased to tremble, or they would all be falling over and falling off their floats.

A gilded spray lands on the café table, right in front of Christopher Stubbs, aimed at Christopher Stubbs. He picks it up and sticks it in the third buttonhole of his striped shirt.

None of them are to know that the story of the *immigrantes* is far from over; indeed, it is only at its beginning. Over the coming years, fewer will risk the Atlantic passage from North Africa, but more and more will be crowding onto ill-equipped vessels in the Eastern Mediterranean, as violence in the Middle East and Libya drives them to further desperation. They will aim for Greece and Malta and Sicily and Italy and thousands upon thousands will drown, as Europe fortifies itself, ceases to send rescue missions, leaves the boats to sink in sight of shore. The more people drown, hopes Europe, the more immigrants will be discouraged, and the fewer mouths to feed in Europe.

But it won't work out like that. The tidal wave will not be stopped.

Some will still reach the Canaries, bringing with them scares of Ebola as they land on tourist beaches, but fewer and fewer will embark from the Western Sahara and Port-Étienne. The cemetery of Gran Tarajal will not be overcrowded. The tragedy shifts to the east. And Sara will not be there to follow it. No one knows how it will end. Sara's unfinished project will haunt Christopher. He won't be able to forget it. It will grow and swell in his mind.

Ivor watches the parade. His mind is restless with torment. He doesn't feel up to making any of the ineluctable big decisions that lie ahead. It's not as though he hadn't seen this coming, he'd been dreading it ever since they arrived on this beautiful and arid island. But he'd been in denial of his own future for years. He doesn't even know what to do, right now, this day, tomorrow, with these two extremely silly women who have arrived unannounced in his territory. He and Bennett had always been vulnerable and exposed to random visitors, some of whom had been unwelcome, but this invasion seems like a parody of all previous visitations.

The girls clearly consider they are providing a welcome distraction, and in a way they are. They have even made him laugh a couple of times, and Christopher seems to find them amusing. They are full of stories. Geraldine Two tells them that as an underemployed actress, she had once worked as a home help, and has many indiscretions to impart about old folk she had looked after, one of whom had actually died on her watch, died in his bed while she was in the kitchen getting the reheated 'meal on wheels' out of the oven. What a shock, what a surprise! Not a sound came out of him, she says, not a murmur. When she'd gone back into his bedsitting room with the shepherd's pie, he'd gone. As easy as going to sleep: a comfort really, to know you can pass the barrier so easily. Painless, silent, peaceful. A very easy death.

She does not notice Ivor crossing himself as she tells this story. But Christopher notices.

Christopher admires Ivor. He has found somewhere to be, thinks Christopher.

It had been a shock to her, all the same, Geraldine Two said, and it had driven her into accepting a part in a panto in Sheffield, at the Lyceum. In *Cinderella*, if you want to know, she says, and laughs heartily, quakingly. I was a little maid waiting on the Ugly Sisters, I danced in the chorus and I flew in the flying ballet! Our star was Jax Conan, do you remember Jax? He was our Buttons. Bit of a groper, our Jax, but he was very funny. We didn't mind a bit of groping in those days. In fact we quite liked it, but you aren't allowed to say so now.

Dead now, of course. Poor old Jax.

Too much talk of death, thinks Christopher. He doesn't mention that his father had successfully operated on Jax's oesophagus, but seizes on the theatrical diversion and initiates a more high-flown discussion of the ancient traditions of cross-dressing and drag, of pantomime and carnival, and of Danny La Rue, whom he'd once seen on stage in all his feathers at the Golders Green Hippodrome. But he notices that Ivor doesn't seem very happy with this line of talk either.

Ivor is looking distracted, abstracted.

He is back in his parents' bedroom in Oxford Road in Staines, in their terraced house two doors up from the newsagent's, trying on his mother's shimmering peacock-blue cocktail dress. She hardly ever went out, hardly ever wore it. It hung there in the wardrobe, on its padded hanger, year after year. Such a pretty dress, he had thought it. She had been so pretty, his mother, but she hadn't had much of a life.

Whereas he and Bennett had seen the world.

~

Fran is worried about almost everybody and almost everything. She's worried about Poppet and Jim and the flood waters and Baby Jesus, she's worried about Christopher dawdling out there in the Canaries, she's worried about climate change and the lateness of the spring, she's worried about Paul Scobey, she's worried about Teresa.

She's had a text from Paul telling her that his Auntie Dorothy has died, which shouldn't be upsetting to her as she'd only met the woman once, and she had been ill in a care home for years, burdened by some form of dementia and a colostomy bag, but nevertheless it is a disconcerting message. She's glad he bothered to tell her, and she's also glad to learn that Dorothy had received her card thanking her for her coloured-in pictures. She nearly hadn't bothered to send it, wondering if Dorothy would remember who she was, but now she's very pleased she did. But the apparent meaningless of Dorothy's later life is worryingly incomprehensible to Fran, and the force of it revisits her. It begs some big metaphysical questions that she cannot even formulate, let alone answer. Dorothy had been so outgoing, so engaging, so beautifully turned out, and yet so disconnected.

She'd have liked to have discussed these aspects of Dorothy's life and death with Teresa, who had taken a keen interest in the story of Fran's encounter with Dorothy and the energetic and vibrantly coloured Suzette, but Teresa has abruptly and in few words cancelled or postponed their next meeting. That's not very surprising, but it's not good, and it makes Fran feel rejected. Teresa hasn't even suggested looking for another date. Fran knows that Teresa's son Luke was about to come to England, so that's probably the cause. Unreasonably, she feels excluded, and is ashamed of feeling excluded.

She's worried about Bennett Carpenter and Ivor Walters, although she's never met them.

She's worried about her car's brakes. She should get them checked, after all that standing in water, after the car's damp night in a ploughed field, but she hasn't got round to it and she knows she's probably not going to bother. The deep inertia of not-bothering has settled into her mindset.

She hadn't seen the cranes. It would have been cheering to see the cranes.

She's worried about her eyesight, which is scratchy. Her cataract must be nearly operable by now and she's not looking forward to that at all. She's worried about the free-range chicken which has been defrosting overnight on the breadboard. She's worried about poisoning her ex-husband Claude with campylo-bacter. She's decided to make lemon chicken for her next visit, but she hasn't got any lemons. She knows she should change her planned menu, in view of this deficiency, but she can't think of anything else to cook. The notion of lemon chicken has occupied all the space in her plated-meal brain. She'll have to go out soon to get some lemons.

The long drive back from the West Country had taken it out of her, and now, two days later, she's still not feeling back up to strength. She lies an extra hour in bed, feeling guilty and exhausted. *Going downhill. Losing her grip.* She reads her daily newspaper online, she's too tired to go down and buy one from the grilled and barricaded newsagent on the street corner.

The twenty-four-year-old care home worker who had purpose-ly poisoned her patients with bleach products has been convicted and remanded in custody, awaiting sentencing. Planning permission has been granted for a controversial green-field site in Warwickshire. A poet much admired by Jo Drummond has died. The Middle East is murderous. There is a fine double-spread photograph of a leafless tree in Yorkshire, with some brave and defiant words by the ageless David Hockney about the beauty of trees in winter.

But Fran needs the leaves.

She wishes she were back in the Premier Inn, in easy reach of the comfort of a perfect soft-boiled egg.

The egg yolk on the dressing-gown lapel.

Jo has got it all sorted. She is comfortable in her Grange, with its sundial and its little clipped box hedges. She can even get her paper delivered to the quasi porter's lodge.

In the Romley days, Christopher Stubbs and Nat Drummond

had shared a paper round. The streets in Romley had been safe then, even though it wasn't a very good neighbourhood. No knives, no guns, not many drugs.

Nat writes about cricket and talks about it on the radio. Fran isn't very interested in cricket, but she's always pleased to hear his voice, for old times' sake.

As she lies there, with her mug of coffee and her online newspaper, conscientiously flexing her ankles and exercising her finger joints with a special gadget she'd bought online, her mobile buzzes. It's an incoming text. Superstitiously, she doesn't want to look at it. There's so much bad news around.

But of course she does.

It's a message from an unknown number, and it's from Birdie Bardwell, the woman who has moved in to help look after Teresa. It's bad, but not as bad as she had feared. It reads: TERESA HAD A FALL, ASKING AFTER YOU, CAN YOU GIVE ME A RING? BEST, BIRDIE.

It's bad, but Fran momentarily, selfishly, cheers up a little. She has been asked for.

She envisages Teresa falling or tripping as she tries to struggle out of her day bed, or to make her painful way along the corridor. But that's not the way it was.

Birdie sounds distressed and flustered. We don't know how it happened, says Birdie. She must have tried to get up the library steps, God knows what for. And you know how she is, she's so frail. We can't think what possessed her. She had a fall. I was in the kitchen, I'd have heard her if she'd called.

Fran hears that Birdie feels guilty, responsible.

Anyway, says Birdie, she's all right, she's still in hospital under observation and having her wrist fixed. But she can't text, and she was worried that she'd sent you an incomplete message. She'd meant to explain about Luke's visit, but the palliative care nurse had just turned up and she'd pressed SEND without quite intending to. But she's all right, repeats Birdie, she's all right, and Luke's still here.

Teresa doesn't sound very all right to Fran, who hasn't listened very carefully to this muddled and self-exculpatory explanation. Fran understands that she is being told that she's not to visit the hospital. She doesn't mind that, she's not keen on hospital-visiting, but it's too sad.

Clambering up the library steps? Whatever for?

A dying fall.

I summon to the winding ancient stair . . .

I'd better get up, says Fran to herself, aloud. But she does not move. She can feel that the bit of the brain that instructs her body to move is not yet functioning properly. It's trying to get her up, but it can't. It jerks towards action, then it stalls, then tries again and stalls again. She's not as stuck as Winnie in her pile of sand, but she's getting on that way. You have to hand it to Beckett, it's a bloody good image, a bloody good metaphor, that pile of sand. She ought to have been more appreciative when thanking Jo for the hard-to-get tickets; she'd probably sounded a bit grumpy and reluctant about the outing. She's had some more thoughts about Beckett since that evening, she must try to remember them for the next time she sees Jo.

Shall she move now? She had heard on the radio recently a discussion about how all our actions, however trivial, are preordained, and you can read them on a scan of the about-to-be and of readiness-potential well before they occur. The lifting of a hand, the opening of an eye, the getting out of bed. Neuroscientists argue that this does away with the notion of free will, but that's rubbish. It simply means that we can learn to read the pre-sequences of action more clearly. She's quite good at tracing the locations in her brain that impel decision and action, though she doesn't know the names for them. As she gets older, she can feel the processes of tracking and stalling and failing and re-engaging very clearly. As though the lobes and zones were separating off, one from another, as though the pathways were connecting less rapidly.

Interesting.

She's still lying there, gazing out of her high window at her lowering cityscape and wondering whether she ought to try to read a long article on wind farms, when her landline calls her. This does get her out of her bed, as she can't reach it from her bedside.

Not many people ring on her landline. Tarrant Towers' reception is excellent, it is one of the building's few virtues, on a par with and in accord with its view, and she relies on her mobile.

It's Claude. She can tell he's just rung up for a chat. He sounds absolutely fine. She's relieved to hear him. They have an animated conversation about Poppet, the possibility of lemon chicken, Bennett Carpenter's new hip, and Bennett's choice of Desert Island Discs. Claude says he'd have chosen Callas singing 'Vissi d'arte, vissi d'amore', if anybody had ever asked him, which they hadn't, though he can't think why not. He says that as a joke, so he's in a good mood, something has pleased him. Fran makes a date and a time to go round with the as-yet-uncooked chicken. She's cheered up.

She gets moving.

If she'd been asked to do Desert Island Discs, would they have let her choose 'I Can't Get No Satisfaction'? It's not as elevated as Tosca, it's not on the plane of living for art and living for love, but it's pretty damn satisfactory, all the same.

Jo says that her friend Eleanor says that Maroussia Darling, when a rising star in the old Roy Plomley days of Desert Island Discs, wasn't allowed to choose Billie Holiday singing 'Gloomy Sunday', because it was on the BBC's suicide watch list. She wonders if that can possibly be true.

She's feeling a lot better.

The zones have reconnected; her sense of purpose is restored.

Down she goes to buy the arbitrary lemons.

~

The Geraldines have flown home on their package tourist flight, having had an unexpectedly entertaining break, full of drama; and Christopher Stubbs has at last booked his flight to Gatwick. Bennett Carpenter continues, physically at least, to make a reasonable recovery, and it looks as though Ivor isn't going to have to up sticks and pack their bags and their furniture and find a new home, or not just yet. He's been worrying inordinately about that incongruous mahogany roll-top desk, by which Bennett sets such store. But a reprieve has been granted, on this mild island of remission. Where better to convalesce than at La Suerte?

While Ivor is driving Christopher to the airport, Ishmael is pushing Bennett's wheelchair along the modest pier at the little fishing port of Arrieta. He wheels him along, towards Africa House with its low white walls and its pretty finials and its small stone lions. The beacon of its cupola gazes east, towards Morocco and Mauritania and the unacknowledged territory of the Western Sahara, where Ghalia Namarome maintains her defiant political stance. She's recovered from her hunger strike, but she hasn't given up the cause, although we no longer read about it in the Western press.

The beacon lures seafarers to their death or to their deliverance.

The giant bones of Antaeus are buried somewhere over there, over the waters. According to Pliny, or was it Plutarch, the noble Roman general Sertorius had seen them with his own eyes. Giant bones, elephant bones, whale bones.

Bencomo, Acaymo, Pelicar, Tegueste, Pelinor, mutters Bennett.

Bennett loves this stretch of seafront, even though its rolling surf had once assaulted him and knocked him over. Bennett and Ishmael make a striking couple, the one so old-world and so distinguished and so rubicund, with his mane of white hair and his bushy eyebrows and his old panama hat and his pale blue shirt; the other so handsome and dark and elegant in his designer jeans and his matelot jersey. Bennett has a friendly old navy-blue rug with a border of comforting red blanket stitching tucked over his knees. A hot dry Saharan wind is blowing from Africa, from Port-Étienne, from Ishmael's homeland, and both men wear dark glasses against the grit and the sand. Bennett's teeth are safely back in place, and he smiles with a kind of rapture as he is bowled along.

Bennett is in a good place. He has passed beyond the panic longing for repatriation and the xenophobic spasms and hallucinations of morphine into timelessness. (Xenophobia is one of the under-recorded side effects of morphine.) Ishmael pushes him towards the brink of eternity, to the lip of the great crater. And Bennett sees, rising hugely, rising soundlessly, far out to sea, the great wave that will greet him soon and carry him to the eighth island. He is happy with this vision. He has always longed for this wave, be it of the sea or of the land. He has passed through a dark confined space, an uncomfortable, indoor, medical space, but now he surges forward, into the light, with Ishmael as his guide. He is happy. Ah, so be it. Ah, his heart rises. He smiles into the sun and the salt wind.

Ishmael is on his mobile phone, speaking to his mother in Wolof. Bennett listens, benignly, to this animated chatter in an unknown tongue. These isles are full of marvels.

Bennett is not quite sure where he is, or who Ishmael is. But it doesn't seem to matter anymore. He knows that he likes it

here. Ishmael is a pleasant change from Ivor. New blood. Ivor
has been looking rather tired of late.

~

Liam O'Neill kneels by Teresa's bedside. He lays his grizzled
head upon the slight blanketed hillock of her wasted knees. His
thick grey plait reaches almost to his waist, a grey rope against
the dark green of his corduroy jacket. His hands are clasped
and he is muttering words to himself, so maybe he is praying.
He is a penitential, old-fashioned, medieval figure, a figure from
a dark painting of grief, of remorse or perhaps of reconciliation.
He has placed a little bunch of snowdrops, gathered from her
own garden, on her dark-blue pillowslip.

His son, Luke O'Neill, sitting very upright on a bentwood
chair by the window, gazes in dulled amazement at this strange
tableau. He cannot hear his father's words, but he can hear
their mumbled rhythm.

Liam has come too late. Teresa died while he was still miles
high over the mid-Atlantic, and he will maintain for years to
come, to the end of his long life, that he heard a chord break,
felt a twang, as she departed. It is easy enough, with hindsight,
to fancy that one senses such moments of passing, but Liam
will continue to insist that in mid-air, in his own flesh, he felt
and heard her spirit leave her body.

Teresa had never really recovered from her fall, though she
had been released from hospital to die at home, as she would
have wished. Both Birdie Bardwell and Luke had been with her
at the end. Birdie had been more distressed than Luke at the
time, for she felt she had failed in her duty, and had been greedily
looking forward to having her beloved Teresa all to herself for
at least a few evenings, for however long it would take, to make
things good between them, to share their last secrets.

Luke is relieved that his mother has died. Not pleased, but relieved. He's not thinking of the airfare, though that consideration comes into it, and not wholly of her increasing pain and her dwindling tolerance of medication, though they come into it too. He is glad to have seen her out. He had recognised that she did not have long, and he is pleased he timed his visit wisely. She had sent the correct signals, and he had responded correctly. She had always had a great deal of common sense.

So he doesn't know why she had tried to clamber up the fragile little wooden spiral of the library stairs. He can't think that she had intended to hasten her end, though she had in effect done so. He'd only been out for an hour, he'd popped out rather shamefully to buy some cigarettes and have a nose around the old neighbourhood, but Birdie had been in charge, so how can it have happened? He has tried to work out which book she was reaching for, and why. His Uncle David's partner's tome of Etruscan tombs had been (and still is) lying on her bedside table, along with her Bible, her leather-bound gilt-edged biblical concordance, her e-reader and, incongruously, a new and notoriously violent Scandinavian paperback thriller. She'd never have tried to get up to the top shelf of exhibition catalogues and the heavy volumes of Matisse and Constable: was she trying to reach for the lower shelves, for her novels of the 1960s and 70s, for Saul Bellow or Updike or Angus Wilson or Iris Murdoch? Or for Winnicott and Freud and Jung and R. D. Laing and her small collection of recent disability study theorists on the shelves above? Or for the comfort of Elizabeth Bennet or Dorothea Brooke? Nobody will ever know. She has taken this small secret with her, and will shortly take it to her grave in St Mary's churchyard, Kensal Green.

Teresa lies calmly now, very slight under her blanket, her eyes closed, her hair a silver halo, teased out by Birdie upon her blue

pillow. She had told him that her hair had grown back luxuri-
antly, but he had not expected this curled abundance.

The undertakers will come for her in the morning. The young
chap will be back for the NHS day bed and the struts and
spanners as soon as is decent, and possibly sooner.

Luke has seen a lot of dead people, but few as composed as
his mother. He doesn't believe in heaven, or in an afterlife, nor
does he know if she does or did, but such considerations seem
of no moment. More pressing are the funeral arrangements,
the notices, the network, the getting through the next few days.
Now he will leave the room, and leave his mother and his father
alone together for a while. Later, he and his father will go out
for a meal at his father's Charlotte Street hotel, and Liam will
get very drunk and maudlin and apologise endlessly for having
forgotten his son's birthday, for having forgotten it year after
year after year. He will start to tell Luke about the other women
in his life, and Luke will not know whether to try to stop him
or not.

In the end he lets him ramble and lets him order another
bottle. What is there to lose, at this stage in the game? He
explains to his father about mesothelioma, and how it had
nothing to do with smoking. He listens, as his father describes
the snowy night of his son's birth. That at least he has not
forgotten, and his account tallies with Teresa's. The midwife,
the pudding bowl, the afterbirth thrown out for the dogs, the
Irish stew. Teresa has told him this story many times, a ritual
narration, but he thinks it's the first time he's heard it from
Liam, and Teresa hadn't been as brutal about the fate of the
afterbirth.

Neither Liam nor Teresa had other children. He is their sole
heir, Xavier their only grandson. The burden is on him.

Luke doesn't smoke very heavily, but as the meal and the
confidences drag on, he finds himself longing for a cigarette.

He has the packet in his pocket, the packet he was buying when Teresa fell. He's only smoked twelve of the twenty and he is longing for the thirteenth. He has vowed to make them last until the day of the funeral. He fingers the packet, for comfort.

Birdie has already started going through Teresa's old address book, trying to work out who must be asked to St Helen's, her parish church, to St Mary's at Kensal Green, to the reception in Teresa's home, but she and Liam both know that address books are more or less obsolete, that all her more recent contacts will be in her email account and her mobile phone. Liam and Luke begin to make a list, over their second double espresso. Her brothers, David and Peter Quinn, and David's partner Massimo Vignoli. Peter's wife and children and grandchildren. Cousins on the Quinn side. Liam's sister, who had remained in touch with Teresa, should be invited, but probably won't come over. Who else from Canada and the US? Liam will get to work on this. North London colleagues, parents, surviving alumni from Teresa's school, neighbourhood friends – there's someone called Ginnie that she mentioned, says Luke, can't remember where she comes in but if I trawl back I may find her. I know Teresa liked her a lot. And there was a Mrs Taylor? And then there's Fran Stubbs, who knew Mum way back in Broughborough days. Mum saw a lot of Fran in the last few months.

Fine, fine, says Liam, who is staring suddenly but not painfully at the lively mural on the wall of the Charlotte Street hotel restaurant.

The mural is the reason why he booked into this hotel. Liam knows somebody who knows somebody who knows somebody who painted it. And it's just as good as he'd been told. He's glad he's staying here. England, London, Fitzrovia: something is still happening here.

He says to Luke, impulsively, why don't you stay here for the night? I've got a vast double bed. Super king-size. The pillows are heaven. You don't want to spend the night in that morgue, do you?

Luke doesn't know whether to be touched or not. He has no intention of spending the night in bed with his father, but he honours the invitation. It's original and in its way it's inspired. He admires it.

No, Dad, he says: thanks, though. Good to see you. I'll be OK in the morgue. She's not very morgue-like, Mum, is she? I'm in my old bedroom. I'm fine there. I think I need to be there.

This pretentious phrasing is incontrovertible.

Luke is being very polite, and at least half-sincere.

Kiss her goodnight for me, says Liam.

A profound banality, a banal profundity unites them, as they awkwardly embrace to say goodbye on the pavement of Charlotte Street.

Liam staggers up to bed and, jet-lagged, passes out in the super king-size bed.

~

Luke stands in the cold garden of his mother's home at midnight, amidst the cold closed snowdrops, smoking his thirteenth cigarette. The air is damp and chill and smells intensely, sweetly, of honey, a thin but strong wintery scent reaching him in wafts from some unseen early-flowering shrub. The hellebores are full of dark purple bud. The garden looks neat and cherished, so somebody must have been looking after it.

There is a view, eastwards, over the city. Its myriad lights glitter below him.

He has decided not to send for Monica and Xavier. The cross-currents would be too disturbing, too uncontrollable. Liam is enough of a handful. He wouldn't want Monica to have to come to terms with Liam. His mother, of course, had been 'wonderful' with Monica, but Liam had never met her. It wouldn't be good to meet for the first and last time in a cemetery.

He can't get the image of the kneeling Liam out of his head.

Birdie is already planning the funeral baked meats. She's good at that kind of thing. She'd probably been thinking about it for weeks, if not for months. She will get some pleasure out of doing it all well.

He has yet to meet Father Goodall, who will want to know about Mozambique and the church and the missions and Luke's views on the Pope.

He is thinking back over the many texts and emails he's had from his mother in the past few months and of his conversation with her new-old friend Fran, with whom he had spoken briefly that morning. Fran's voice had sounded eerily like his mother's, and he wonders if she had some lingering overlaid trace of a Broughborough accent, or perhaps the two women had caught one another's inflections in these last few intense months of rapprochement. Or maybe it was an age thing: their voices had aged together, in parallel, and had converged into the same tone, the same register.

They had talked about Teresa, and about the timing of the funeral. yes, Fran can make Saturday, and of course she would be there. I look forward to meeting you, Fran had said, encouragingly, cheerfully, tearfully.

'She spoke so much about you.'

'I hope not *too* much,' Luke had said.

No, no, said Fran. I could never hear enough of whatever it was she wanted to talk about. You know what I think when I think of your mother? That she never said a dull word! Never! In all the years I've known her, and I've known her all my life! There's an epitaph! Never a dull word!

Luke inhales the honey, the tobacco, the chill air. The piercingly tender sweetness of a well-tended London garden assails him. Maybe he should come home soon, while he is in his prime. He believes he will inherit this house, though of course she may have left it to one of her good causes. And so be it if she has.

He'd better get on to the solicitors tomorrow.

He should stake his claim in this shifting monstrous beautiful city, the swelling hub of everything that is about to be. Each time he comes back from Africa, he finds it has transformed itself once more, into more glass and shard and glitter, into more terror and glory. Africa still breathes warmly, expansively, with its smell of vegetation, with its red roads, its red earth, its huge horizons, its blue distances. Here, the horizons are precipitous and sheer and near. They are the cliffs of fall.

~

Claude and Fran are sharing the campylobacter-free lemon chicken. Fran doesn't often eat with him, but she has decided that the meal smells so delicious and there is so much of it that she'll stay and have a comfortable supper and a glass of good wine with the old beastie, instead of trudging back on the Tube to a killer drink and a cold meal in the Tower. She is in need of comfort. The chicken had, when defrosted, turned out to be an excellent fowl – plump, its flesh a healthy succulent pale yellow, its skin now crisp and honeyed and lemon-encrusted. It would have been a shame to freeze it, argues Fran.

Claude discloses that he is pleased with himself because he has won a prize in a Classic FM quiz, consisting of a three-day trip to Verona. He won't be able to go on it, of course, he'll have to turn it in and send it back to the kitty, but he's pleased with himself just the same. He's never bothered to phone in before, often they ask you to text and he doesn't do texts, but this time they'd given a phone number as well, and as he knew all the answers, he thought, why not. He's not sure if the prize is transferable. Would Fran like to go to Verona? No, he thought not.

He knows they won't allow you to ring in on phone lines for much longer.

Fran offers to buy him a cheap mobile and to teach him how to text, but he doesn't seem at all keen on the idea. You can't teach an old dog new tricks, he says. He looks very pleased with himself as he says this.

They talk about Poppet, and the cranes, and Fran promises to have her brakes checked. Claude had no interest in the cranes, but he had enjoyed the tale of the car in the ploughed field.

She tells him about Teresa's death and they talk about meso-thelioma and the drawing pin and the horseshoe nail. Fran complains that she had still had so many questions to ask Teresa, some of the greatest profundity (life after death, coma and the deep sleep) and some of the greatest triviality (washing machines of the 1950s).

Fran is simultaneously slightly embarrassed and slightly proud that she has remembered to bring, secreted in her handbag, some beeswax-reinforced furniture oil to anoint the javelin box. Why should she care about dead wood? But she does. She'll try to leave the bottle in the kitchen, where she can find it next time, and have a rub of the pale dried oak while Claude isn't looking. She thinks he might be cross with her for trying to nourish his neglected javelin box.

Why the fuck should she care whether Claude is cross with her or not?

When she was pregnant with Christopher, her first-born, she had rubbed her swelling belly with industrial lanolin, from a large brown glass jar. A recipe to prevent scarring, and also something of a prophylactic. They hadn't been able to afford fancy body lotions in those days, or maybe they hadn't yet been invented. The lanolin had smelled disgusting, of sheep and meat, and it was a horrible dark fatty yellow. She can smell it now. Was it Jo who'd recommended it to her? They'd been pregnant at the same time, with Nat and Christopher.

The beeswax polish, in contrast, smells delightful.

In Teresa's garden, in Kensal Green cemetery, in the trim little parterres of Athene Grange, the bees scent the spring.

~

Fran had said, politely, that she was looking forward to meeting Luke from Mozambique, but on reflection she's not really all that sure that she is. He's a grown man, a broad-shouldered suntanned tennis-playing full-bodied male adult, in the prime of his important life, and he's an expert at putting people under and out. She's seen photos of him, looking powerful. She recognises that maybe she's becoming more at home these days with the incapacitated and the enfeebled, which is a shaming, maybe humiliating, notion. She's had a pleasant telephone conversation with Luke, but she will never get to know him, and it will be an effort to smile and say the right things when they meet.

The energising effect of the transfusion from Paul, Julia and Graham is beginning to wear off, although she had it only a couple of weeks ago. Maybe she needs another trip to the Premier Inn, another glass of black Merlot and some bright Agent Orange scampi.

She hopes her Christopher will come home soon. He's an adult male, but she can cope with him, he's her flesh and blood. She'd like to see him, to hear him teasing her, calling her by his silly pet names for her – Maman, Frankie, Frangipani, Granny Franny.

She knows she is obliged, for Teresa's sake, to go to Teresa's funeral, but there won't be many people there that she knows, and she will probably feel awkward and unwelcome. She's never met Birdie, who has taken over on the domestic front, or Father Goodall, who will officiate at the funeral mass before the cortège leaves for the cemetery. She's never set foot in St Helen's, Teresa's parish church, and she's never been to any kind of Roman Catholic service. She won't know where to sit or what to wear or what to do. She rightly suspects that Birdie is bossily possessive about Teresa and will see herself as custodian of the flame as well as carer and caterer. Fran has only a slight curiosity about meeting David Quinn and Massimo Vignoli, and an even slighter curiosity about Teresa's younger brother, of whom she has hardly any recollection. Sixty years is a very long time, and their acquaintance had been tenuous in the first place. The very thought of those next-door boys of the 1940s makes her sad, as does the thought of her own brothers, with their deafness and their bad hips and their golf and their BMWs.

Fran, in her tower, succumbs at last to the temptation of looking up images of Maybrook Park and the street where they had lived. And there it is, little changed except for a few added conservatories and the house prices. The prices, some veering towards half a million, keep popping up in the sidebar however hard she tries to get rid of them. But there is the very building where she and Teresa had played. The cellars of both of the semi-detached residences have been turned into garages, facing frontwards onto the road, but otherwise everything looks much the same. Somebody has planted what is now a very tall conifer in the front garden of Number 26, surely a mistake, but otherwise a deep suburban stagnation appears to prevail. Fran is quite glad that she doesn't live anywhere near there these days. Even Romley had been better, and Clapham and Highgate had been heaven. And Tarrant Towers

– well, it is Tarrant Towers, defiant and rude, making its own abrasive statement.

Luke will never have been to Broughborough. Nor have her own children, come to think of it. Whatever would take them there?

Teresa hadn't lived long enough to show Fran the book about Etruscan tombs and the little terracotta hut urns of the Villanovan dead. She will never see them now.

Fran will have a conversation with David Quinn at the funeral, but it won't be about the Etruscans, or about Jacopo da Pontormo, or about the afterlife. It will be about the old tram routes to the town centre, and what colour the trams had been. Neither of them will be able to remember. David thinks they were dark green, but Fran thinks they were a kind of dirty cream with blue trim. They can't ask Teresa to adjudicate, as she's already under the cold ground.

And Christopher does come back to England, and like a good son he lets his mother know almost as soon as he's back. He'd been informed by several texts of the bad news about Teresa, and although he knows it was in no way unexpected, he also knows his mother can't choose but be downcast, so he arranges to take her out to dinner. He tries to think of somewhere cheering and fun, but it's so hard to know what she'd like. She has this weird affection for Wetherspoons and Premier Inns, and he can't face any of that. So he settles for the expensive fish restaurant off Piccadilly, where he'd had that lunch with Simon Aguilera: it's still there, still smart, but traditional, not too outré, and it's easy for both of them to get to. And she likes fish.

He'd thought there wouldn't be limpets on the menu, but

there are. They must be the new thing. As they go in, they pass vast platters of *fruits de mer*, heaped high on a fishmonger's marble slab – mountains of limpets, razor shells, clams, crabs, mussels, sea urchins, oysters, the lot, all draped with bladder-wrack and kelp, and tastefully bordered with a fringe of emerald-green samphire.

Fran is looking good, he can see she's made an effort. She's wearing what he can tell is an expensive grey and beige and black striped jacket made of a heavy ribbed silk, but when he compliments her on it, she somewhat spoils the effect by telling him how cheaply she'd bought it in the Harvey Nichols sale. Still, it does look good, and she is pleased that he likes it.

Over the bisque, he tells her about Lanzarote, and about Bennett Carpenter's strange journey through xenophobia towards calm and peace and affability. Fran is gripped but not astonished by this tale. She's professionally acquainted with many forms of geriatric aberration, and retaliates with the story of the woman in St Frideswide's Hospice who kept crying out that she could see a black man's face in her bathroom mirror, and could only be cured of this illusion when told that it wasn't a black man's face, it was a Jungian archetype. An Oxford academic by trade, she had been satisfied by this explanation.

Christopher describes Ishmael, and Simon Aguilera, and the famine tower. You have been jaunting amongst the archetypes, says Fran, and instantly regrets the word 'jaunting', but he doesn't seem to have taken it amiss.

The Dover sole is very good. It's a long time since either of them has had Dover sole. Fran is slightly surprised that it still exists. It's a restaurant fish, they agree. Fran's few attempts to cook it had been extravagantly and destructively disastrous. It needs to arrive, whole, on a plate, before the calmly seated diner, like a godly gift.

A description of the lively incursion of the Geraldines leads to talk of Jo Drummond and Owen England and Jo's new interest in the Studdert Meades and the Spanish Civil War. Jo is always finding herself new projects, says Fran, a little forlornly. But you've got a proper job, says her son. Yes, says Fran, but it's sometimes a bit of a downer, my job. It's a losing battle, you know, the fight against the ageing process. You see and hear some terrible things.

Jo calls old age '*La Vieillesse*', adds Fran, and explains why.

I always admired Auntie Josephine, says Christopher, sentimentally.

And now Fran, emboldened by half a bottle of Sauvignon, says what she's several times over the past weeks prevented herself from saying: There are worse things than dying young and beautiful and beloved and in the middle of a great project.

Christopher is touched.

I know, Maman, I know, he says, and pats the back of her pale wintery sun-starved blue-veined hand.

But you're looking fine, he continues. You keep going wonderfully.

And so, against the odds, does your *father*, comes back Fran: and over coffee and white chocolate truffles they gossip about Claude and Persephone and Maria Callas. They remind themselves of the Jax Conan medical drama and the gift hamper, and Christopher tells Fran about Jax playing Buttons in panto in *Cinderella* with the other Geraldine. They move on, treacherously, collusively, to the subject of Claude's second marriage, and say indiscreetly bad things about the unacceptably Sloaney Jean, with her cashmere and her shiny boots and her strange whining nasal upper-crust accent. They laugh a lot, and both feel better. Fran perks up as she recalls and describes her forthcoming Ashley Combe assignment, which involves visiting a sheltered housing development now under construction near Blackpool, and attending meetings with social workers, GPs and trustees. It will be fun, says Fran. I don't know that part of the world, it will be an adventure.

'Will you drive?' asks Christopher. 'It's a long way; you do a hell of a lot of driving.'

'I *like* driving,' says Fran, but even as she asserts this, she remembers that she still hasn't checked her brakes. She really ought to get the car serviced before she sets off on the 200- or 300-mile journey. She promises herself that she will, as Christopher ushers her out and hails a taxi for his mother and gives the driver her unfashionable postcode.

She's fine, thinks Christopher, as he returns on the rattling Bakerloo line to his empty and stupidly expensive flat in Queen's Park.

He's fine, thinks Fran, as she presses the button for the lift and, happily, finds her call grudgingly, noisily accepted. She'd have taken the stairs in her stride tonight, thanks to Christopher and the Dover sole, but she's glad she doesn't need to.

~

Slowly comes the late spring. It has never been so late, people in England say to one another, as the bare black twigs of the hedges at last begin to bud, as the waters sink in the levels, exposing mud and scrubby couch grass, as dangling catkins and plush pussy willows take on their yellowy silvery March plumage and celandines open their shining petals. The Met Office says the lateness is nothing exceptional; the *Daily Express* says it's unprecedented. Some say the weather pattern confirms global warming; others claim it's evidence of a new ice age. The English have always talked about the weather, but now they talk about it more obsessively, divisively, aggressively than ever. Although it's a hot topic, paradoxically, it simultaneously lacks urgency. People can't get their minds around the time spans involved.

Further south, above the deep Atlantic Mountains, the surges of time's troubled fountains have abated, and the Canary Islands have been restored to their seemingly ageless dormancy. Atlantis slumbers, and Bennett Carpenter sits in the afternoon sun in his wheelchair, dozing and dreaming from time to time of large freshwater fish. He can take a few steps now, with an arm to lean upon. The little yellow canary birds in their cages no longer prophesy disaster in their anxious songs and twitterings. The bottles in El Volcan no longer rattle, and the TV set in the bar has not fallen off its perch. *Impacto* continues its run, adding to its violent repertoire more sensational and inexplicable air disasters, but on Lanzarote, at the spreading foothills of the volcanoes, and in the seas off El Hierro, all is calm.

Ivor offers up his cautious thanks in the unfrequented little chapel on the hill.

At Athene Grange, the ragged damp purple and yellow of the crocus brighten the borders and straggle untidily from the grass beneath the willow trees. Jo Drummond bicycles to the University Library to read more of Valentine's diaries, and wonders whether she should suggest editing them to one of her contacts in the academic publishing world. Who would own the copyright? Or will it have expired? She reads a Hardy poem with her class, the one that begins 'I look into my glass, /And view my wasted skin', and is impressed when Mr Pennington is willing to interpret Hardy's phrase about 'throbbings of noontide' as evidence of the ageing Hardy's pre-Viagran potency. Some of the women look embarrassed, but most of them are amused. It's a good class, she's proud of them, and she's already planning next autumn's course: it would be good to do prose or drama next time, would any of them be up for Samuel Beckett? Or she could suggest that they do prose and poetry of the Spanish Civil War – Orwell, Hemingway, Lorca, Auden and Day-Lewis?

Men, men, too many men. She must try to think of some women whose work she wants to teach. Caryl Churchill? Margaret Atwood? Toni Morrison? Doris Lessing? She's done Lessing, but not for years, and not with any of this group.

She's sometimes thought of proposing a course of French poetry with bilingual texts – Baudelaire, Verlaine, Rimbaud, *les poètes symbolistes*. But they probably wouldn't let her do that, it would be transgressive. And she's not really qualified. And they are all men too.

Owen, on Thursday, suggests she could construct a course themed around *Beowulf*, *Sir Gawaine*, John Cowper Powys and Kazuo Ishiguro. When she points out that this too is an all-male cast list, he suggests adding Angela Carter. She says she'll think about it. She can't quite see the links, but knowing Owen, there are bound to be some.

She enjoys planning courses. She's pleased that the Institute gives her a free hand. It values her. She always gets a full class.

Poppet Stubbs goes to an auction in Tiverton with Jim and buys a strange ceramic colander for fifty pence. It has an interesting muddy green and cream-coloured glaze. He thinks it could be Saintonge ware, and at that price, it's a bargain whatever it is. He can't think how it can have got to Devon. It may or may not be functional. Poppet will test it when she gets it home.

Jim buys a pair of Sheffield plate candlesticks and an escritoire and an almost complete run of *Horizon*. He's got barns full of junk, full of treasures.

They both enjoy these outings, as you never know what will turn up. Stuff from clearance sales, from ploughed fields, from pre-history.

Fran is writing up her report on the Westmore Marsh project, and planning her next trip to the North-west. Ashley Combe doesn't mind when she goes, within the next two or three months, provided she gives them a week or two to set up a meeting, and something in her tells her that she ought to wait for better weather, for spring, for Easter time. But she does like to get on with things. There's a gap in her life, now that Teresa has gone. She hadn't seen her very often, but she'd been a part of the fabric, part of the pattern, part of the routine. It's such a dull and empty time of year. She might as well put her foot down and hit the M40 and the M6 sooner rather than later. She thinks she might spend a night in Blackpool. She's never been to Blackpool. It has the lure of the truly desperate and dreadful. The black pool. It has a bad name, but it may be very nice when you get there.

Yes, she thinks she might pop in on Blackpool. That's what she tells herself, as she falls asleep. The prospect is alluring. Yes, that's what she'll do.

~

Fran wakes in good spirits and rises easily and this morning painlessly, skipping the tedious dialogue with the neurones of the decision-making processes, and goes comfortably back to bed with her mug of coffee and her guidebook to Lancashire. Blackpool, it tells her, has no architectural merits whatsoever. She looks forward to what her snobbish book describes as its 'supreme ugliness'.

The sky is still dark, but each day it is and will be lightening. The year has turned, and at last we can begin to feel its turning. She is warm in her bed with her book.

She wonders if she's getting into the habit of getting up later and, if so, whether this would be a bad thing or whether it wouldn't be of any significance at all.

She is a little surprised when the mobile phone on her bedside table disturbs her browsing. Nobody rings her so early, it isn't yet nine. She reaches for it, amidst the clutter of medications and pencils and notepads and Post-it notes and paperclips and rings and bracelets, and accepts the call. It's probably a scam, she thinks, though she hardly ever gets scams these days. She's managed to screen them out, with the help of one of the young Ashley Combe techno-wizards.

But it isn't a scam. It's Nat Drummond.

He doesn't need to say anything. As soon as she hears his voice saying 'Fran?' she knows. What she feels is the thud of knowledge. That's not a very nice word, *thud*, but it is what it is. A thud.

She'll never be able to think of a better word.

Fran, he says, this man she's known since before he was born, Fran, I have to tell you, I'm so sorry, I'm so sorry, I can't believe it.

He tells her that Josephine Drummond had died in the night.

There was nothing wrong with her, he says, more than once.

Where are you, asks Fran, when she thinks of something to say.

He is at King's Cross. That accounts for the background noise. He is on his way to Cambridge.

I had to tell you, he says.

Of course, she says. Shall I come, she asks.

He says he'll ring her when he gets to Athene Grange.

I'm so sorry, I'm so sorry, he repeats. They think it was a cardiac arrest. She died in her bed, they think in the late evening.

I could come, she repeats.

I needed to tell you, he repeats.

Keep in touch, Nat, she says, and anything I can do . . .

Her voice trails away. What is there to do? That's the end. This is the end. It wasn't what she'd expected, as an ending.

Thanks, Fran, he says. You could let Chris know. And Poppet.

I will, she says.

He rings off. They have put his platform number up. He needs to hurry along to board his train. They don't give you long these days.

~

During the day, Fran comes to terms with what seems to have happened at Athene Grange. Cardiac arrhythmia, reports Nat. He rings her from Jo's own landline, at some point during the long drag of the afternoon. But she cannot come to terms with its meaning – for her, for Jo's children, for her worldview, for the yet more lonely future. Of course, we can all expect to die at any moment, as she and Jo had many times comfortably told one another. But it's different when it happens, without warning.

Claude gives her his views on cardiac arrests. Inevitably he says it was a good way to go, as everyone will say. Yes, Fran agrees, meekly. It doesn't feel very good, yet.

He has the grace to sound shaken. She was quite a woman, says Claude.

He had fancied Josephine Drummond. She'd been handsome, in her youth, and into her old age. He doesn't mention this to Fran, but she appreciates his appreciative tone.

~

Ô toi que j'eusse aimée, ô toi qui le savais . . .

A perfect example of the pluperfect subjunctive, as Josephine Drummond would have said.

~

They'd found her because her lights were on and her radio was playing music all night and on into the darkness of the morning.

A neighbour from across the courtyard, alerted by this unusual pattern and leaving to catch an early train, had knocked as she passed, received no answer, cautiously entered (Jo never locked her door at night) and discovered Josephine Drummond dead in her bed. You wouldn't lie long unnoticed in Athene Grange, as you could in some London housing estates. As you could in Tarrant Towers.

Fran doesn't seem to be able to cry. She cries easily, with mini-rage, when she is tired and late and has just missed a bus, when she can't find her keys and is in a hurry, when she gets a speeding ticket and more fixed points on her licence. She can cry when she reads a sad poem or hears an everyday human tragedy rehearsed on the radio. She had wept, deeply, sadly, happily, over Poppet's relics, as the moon shone on the waters. But now her eyes are dry. She hadn't been able to weep much for Hamish either, until long after his death, and then she had wept through the selfishness of loneliness. This, like Hamish's illness and death, is too serious for tears.

She awaits instructions about the funeral. Her consolation is that Nat, and now Andrew, seem to wish to keep in constant touch with her. At Jo's funeral, she will not be an extra, an outsider; she will not have to talk about tram routes in the 1950s. They need her to be there.

She postpones her trip to Blackpool and rearranges her dates.

She refuses to deliver an eulogium. She refuses to read a poem. But she tells the boys that somebody should read some Yeats. Jo had been very fond of Yeats.

~

Sally Lyttelton had offered to host what would have been a grand reception at Charteris Hall after the cremation, but this hadn't seemed a good idea to anybody except Sally. She'd have taken over, bossed people about, set too high a standard, made Jo's other old students feel uncomfortable. Athene Grange had facilities for events of this nature, but it was agreed that this would have been too institutional, too gloomy. So Nat and Andrew had settled for neutral ground and booked an expensive, efficient, modern, anonymous, slightly out-of-town hotel. There they would gather, and eat canapés and drink themselves stupid, if they wanted to, and as some of them will.

Christopher Stubbs, sitting with his mother in the second row of the crematorium chapel, feels there have been too many funerals recently, and hopes this is the last of the run. Fran, thank God, is not frail or ailing, but she does suddenly look very small. He'd noticed how small she was when he'd met her at Cambridge station. She'd seemed dwarfed by the crowds of healthy young people pouring off the platforms and milling about the concourse and queuing up for cabs. And now she is sitting here beside him neatly, tidily, in a black winter coat that seems to swallow her up. She looks diminished.

Sitting so far forward in the hall, he can't inconspicuously make a check of who else is there, though he's already spoken to Nat and Andrew, in the front row, and Poppet, who is sitting on the other side of Fran. But it's a good turnout, the chapel is full. He sees Cambridge and Norwich friends and colleagues, students and family, most of them individually unrecognisable to Christopher, but generically easy to place, though there are one or two younger guests that he seems to know by sight but finds hard to identify. He thinks he may have glimpsed his acquaintance, art historian Esther Breuer. He admires her and he is hoping she is here.

He doesn't like to think that this is Auntie Josephine's actual coffin, covered in floral tributes, and that she is about to go up in flames. His mind goes back to Romley days, and school, and playing with the Drummond boys on the marshes, and smoking and drinking in bus shelters, and freewheeling down the hill, and games of whist in the Crossroads Café.

There are speeches, but not too many: a professor from Norwich, a Cambridge Quaker cousin, Nat himself. An aged woman poet with wire hair and a gravel voice reads a short poem called 'The Wheel' by Yeats, which makes Fran get out a wad of tissue and blow her nose several times, though Christopher can't concentrate on the words and can't work out what it's about. He is thinking now of Ivor and Bennett, and of Bennett's careful plans for his own send-off, which it seems Ivor won't be needing to organise for some time. Bennett has settled well, he is on a peaceful plateau, he could go on for years. All is calm at La Suerte.

But Josephine had been taken by surprise and hadn't had time to plan anything.

Bennett's old friend Owen English must be here somewhere, but Christopher wouldn't know him if he saw him. He'll catch up with him later. And he hasn't yet seen either of the Geraldines, who had erupted so strangely into his Lanzarote dream-life, though they surely must be here. They wouldn't miss a party.

His father Claude had expressed a desire to attend, for old times' sake, but Christopher doesn't think he can have been serious about this.

And yet, when they get to The Willows, there is Claude in his wheelchair, the first of the guests, attended by Persephone St Just, with a glass of wine already in his hand. He'd skipped the service and the speeches and the sermons and come straight to the reception in a chauffeur-driven Mercedes, now parked in the hotel's spacious car park. Christopher, Fran and Poppet don't know whether to be pleased or annoyed to see him. He's not quite as intrusive as Sally Lyttelton, in her charcoal suit, who is already not very successfully attempting to dominate a group of dowdy Cambridge dons, but he does fill up a lot of space.

There is space. It's a large reception room, with vast well-draped windows looking down over some well-kept greensward towards a willow-fringed brook, some tributary of the Cam or the Ouse or the Granta. The champagne flows. (Claude doesn't like champagne.) Fran knocks back a glass or two. She doesn't have to worry about drinking and driving as she's staying the night in the guest suite at Athene Grange; she's already dropped off her overnight bag there. In the morning she and the boys are going to have a sort through of Jo's things.

There are a lot of people here that she ought to talk to. Owen England introduces himself and reminds her politely that they'd met before at Jo's birthday party. They speak about what a good friend Jo had been to both of them, and how much they will miss her. He's a very *small* man, thinks Fran, he's almost on her own eye level; he seems even smaller than when she saw him last. But that's good, as it means she can hear him more easily as they chat about the Thursday evenings and the excursions to Samuel Beckett and Deceased Wife's Sisters and Bennett Carpenter. She can't hear very tall people any more when she's in a crowd, but she can log in with Owen well, intimately, almost conspiratorially, on this lower plane.

'I shall miss our Thursdays,' repeats Owen sadly. 'I'd planned a gimlet for next week.'

Fran can believe that he will miss her. He has all the outward characteristics of a lonely man. She says she'll go and find Christopher to introduce to him, and leaves him standing to stare over the lawns with his glass of Laurent-Perrier. But she is intercepted on her way to look for her son by Eleanor Masters. Eleanor is a friend of Maroussia Darling, so they speak about her performance as Winnie in *Happy Days*, and of Maroussia's long illness, and of Jo's robust health. She forgets about Owen.

Owen is left staring at the lawns. He has noticed in the mid-distance, in the gathering dusk, a delicate little muntjac deer, browsing daintily amidst the crocuses and the scillas and the grape hyacinths of spring. It is a charming little beige creature, a faunlike apparition. It would be tempting to think it were a spirit, a soul, a messenger from the other world, from the *arrière-pays*. Perhaps that innocuous well-tended lawn *is* the *arrière-pays*. Maybe there is no further to go. If that's so, it's a bit disappointing.

Christopher finds Esther Breuer and they exchange notes about scandals in the auction rooms and the Turner Prize and the recent debate about Delacroix's oil painting of an unmade bed, the painting which hangs in the little house museum in Paris. Esther expands her praise of Delacroix with disparaging remarks about Tracey Emin, but Christopher is too canny to be caught by that line. It's all right for Esther, at her age and with her reputation, to be rude about fashionable art, but it would be dangerous for him to enter into the argument, especially when he's temporarily unemployed. He wouldn't trust Esther not to pass his remarks on to the wrong people. She has a sharp tongue and could do damage: he hasn't forgotten that sorry business with feminists and Pauline Boty. He diverts her by asking what she thinks of the work of Canarian artist Manolo Millares, and is pleased when she says she's never heard of him. But she does, he discovers, know Simon Aguilera, who turns out to be an old friend of her husband Robert Oxenholme, and she is very interested to hear about his sardine-factory gallery on Fuerteventura, and the stately sixteenth-century depiction of St Helena which had reminded Christopher of Josephine Drummond. She says she'd like to go and have a look at it, and Christopher tells her that he's sure she would be welcome, as Simon is in fine form and seems pleased to have guests and visitors.

Yes, agrees Esther, Josephine did have an imposing presence. Esther had known Jo since the 1980s, when she'd met her and her husband in Boston at a conference. They'd kept in touch and become friends. They'd all enjoyed a trip to a Crivelli exhibition at the gallery at Fort Worth together, in the Drummonds' Midwest days. Esther had been giving the keynote address, and had invited Jo and Alec to a very grand reception, which had featured edible garlands and elaborate Crivelli swags made of real fruit and flowers and nuts and vegetables.

She's never heard of any painting featuring a Madonna del Nido. She tells Christopher she'll look into it.

Claude, meanwhile, has identified two of the more unlikely looking mourners as ex-test cricketers. One of them is brown and bearded, the other is clean-shaven and white. They are talking about matches that they have played and he has watched. They turn out to be old friends of Nat's. They had hoped to engage the beautiful Persephone in conversation, but she has no interest in cricket whatsoever. Nor, she declares haughtily and provocatively, has anyone in Zimbabwe. They all laugh a lot.

Unlike Claude, Persephone likes champagne and is enjoying herself.

Claude is wearing a white rose in his buttonhole.

The muntjac feeds amongst the hyacinths.

Eventually and inevitably, Fran finds herself with her back to the wall, deep in a semi-serious conversation with Sally Lyttelton: they speak of Thomas Hardy, of late Shakespeare, of the lamentable state of the funding of adult and continuing education, of the value of the humanities, and of Jo's deft handling of her class. It's quite hard work, but it's a lot better than a conversation about tram routes in Broughborough. Sally reveals that Jo's friend Geraldine, whom she also knows quite well, has failed the feast, as she's better fish to fry: she is in Venice, carrying on with an American Professor Emeritus called Gerry in a grand apartment overlooking the Grand Canal.

Fran supposes it's a good thing that life goes on, and she supposes she admires this person called Geraldine for having the energy to carry on, at her age, and she supposes Jo wouldn't have cared a tuppenny fuck about Geraldine's presence or absence at her wake. But Sally is tiring, and so is Jo's sister Susie, who now appears, elbows out Sally, and makes herself known. Fran feels she must have met Susie, over the years, but she has no meaningful recollection of her (she certainly hadn't been present at Jo's big birthday party) and she finds she can't strike a good note with her. Susie is all elbows. She is like a parody of Jo. She is pedantic to a fault, whereas Jo had only been amused by and interested in unorthodox demotic or grammatical usages, and she is judgmental (as Jo had been), but surely now was not the moment to be caustic about the ageing poet who had read the Yeats poem with, in Fran's view, proper feeling.

> Through winter-time we call on spring,
> And through the spring on summer call . . .

Fran can't cope with Susie's aggression. She is feeling faint. She has quickly come to the view that Susie hadn't been at Jo's birthday because she hadn't, for good reason, been invited. She is not an uplifting or engaging person.

You can fail to invite people to your birthday party, but you can't ban family members from funerals. Funerals are public events, and people just turn up at them. They just turn up, though they may not always know their way to the champagne.

These are mean thoughts.

Fran excuses herself, says she needs to go to the powder room, and plunges off into the hotel hinterland, with its disconcertingly flexible spatial arrangements and temporary demarcations and screens and antechambers. In an antechamber off a corridor, she is surprised to glimpse Poppet and Andrew Drummond, sitting with their arms around one another on a pale green banquette. Poppet's face is buried in Andrew's shoulder, and she seems to be sobbing. What can be going on there? Some terrible Romley memory, some primal Romley scene is being re-enacted. Fran hurries past, having no wish to interrupt or to be seen to observe, and takes refuge in the glittering black and white marbled hall of the Ladies room.

Emerging from the super-modern stall, having made sure her underwear is all correctly aligned, she advances towards the row of gleaming white wash-basins, but is there defeated by the turning on of the water to wash her hands. It's a simple-looking stream-lined but incomprehensible mechanism she's never seen before: does one twist something, depress something, or wave one's hands at a certain distance beneath the orifice? There's nothing as obvious as a tap, and she is about to give up hope when another older woman arrives by her side to share, momentarily, her bewilderment, and then to solve the problem by a deft turn of a discreet lower spigot. Fran smiles, gratefully, and successfully copies the action, and their eyes meet in the mirror.

'Thanks,' says Fran, to the mirror image.

It is a strange and intense moment, a strange angle of oblique communion. They smile at one another, two old women triumphing over the mystery of the flowing of the water of life, flowing towards them from some invisible aqueduct, from some snowy mountain. The other woman says, tentatively, as she combs her white hair, 'I think we met at Jo's birthday? You won't remember me, I'm Betty Figueroa.'

Of course, says Fran, you're Betty. Jo used to speak of you: and I'm Fran Stubbs.

Together they slowly make their way back to the throng.

There is something extraordinarily gallant and moving about Betty, the survivor, the noble atheist of the left. She is nearing ninety, and yet she shines with an undiminished, with an increasing radiance. Like Teresa, but having travelled further onwards along the way than Teresa, with no hope or expectation of a resurrection, she shines. She and Fran find a couple of chairs by the window and sit together for a while, talking quietly of little things that they remember. Fran could not have said, will not be able to say, what it is that speaks to her through Betty Figueroa, who has travelled the oceans of the wide world and come home to Cambridge to rest. It is a light from another world, from another shore, from a distant mountain. A great and sad calmness descends on Fran. It will not last, she knows she will soon be reclaimed by grief and anger and restlessness, but for a while, sitting amidst the chatter and the crumbs and the growing debris with Betty, in the same haven, she is almost at peace.

~

By the time Fran drives north to the reconvened meeting, the cowslips are out on the motorway verges, and the hedges are in bloom. Her calm has turned into a kind of low-grade settled desperation, a more normal condition for Fran. She is trying not to exceed the speed limit.

She is driving towards the site of the new housing project, on the edge of a small country town in the Fylde. Its postcode has not yet been allocated. Her destination has no postcode. Her destination does not as yet exist.

But on the way towards it, the sloping verges are burgeoning with cowslips, and even from the M6 at seventy-two miles an hour, one can see the scattered clumps of pale yellow flowers with their tender nodding heads. And, in the central reservation between the carriageways, there is a carpet of white and grey-green, a low growing mat of tiny dense white flowers, maritime salt-loving flowers which have in recent years taken over the motorways of Britain. They thrive on the salted grit of winter and blossom bravely in the spring. They come from the east, and have settled here.

This is a better time of year for pantheists, as she had told Teresa, in expectation, months ago. But Teresa had not waited to see the better weather. She had not waited for Easter and the springtime.

Neither had Josephine. She hadn't even had time to say goodbye. Fran has tried to get her mind around the abruptness of Jo's leaving, but it's hard. She tells herself that Jo had died the perfect death, but that puts the burden of living squarely back on her. She's got to keep going. There's nothing else to do. You keep going until you can't go any further. And you can't count on the perfect death, at the end of the run.

She'd been taken aback by Maroussia Darling's dramatic suicide. The papers had been full of it, and the columnists had gone to town on the ethics of celebrity self-slaughter. Mind your own fucking business, you fucking vultures, Fran had yelled at them, as she saw the headlines, and turned the pages. It was even worse than all that crap about Stella Hartleap. She'd have liked to have discussed it with Jo, but of course she can't do that. She even thinks of writing a note of condolence to Maroussia's friend Eleanor Masters, but of course she won't. She doesn't know her well enough. She won't interfere. It's none of her business either.

Although each death, each survival, seems to be her business.

~

She has taken on Jo's unfinished needlework. It's in her overnight bag now. It's a conventional pink and gold and green floral piece, probably given to Jo for Christmas by a grandchild.

Tapestry is easy, any fool can do gross point and petit point and bargello.

And, at Nat's urging, she'd also taken a couple of the finished cushions home to her tower. A very early one, worn a little thin, from Romley days, and a later, plumper one, from Illinois.

She'd spent an hour at Athene Grange with Owen, talking about Christopher and Bennett and Ivor and Lanzarote. Ivor certainly isn't in a position to finish Jo's monograph on Deceased Wife's Sisters. Nobody will ever know now which way her mind was wandering, to what small revelations her enquiries were leading her. It's of no importance whatsoever, as Jo would have been the first to say, but it's sad. Owen has said he will take up the possibility and desirability of publishing Valentine's letters and diaries with Bennett, though he doubts if Bennett will be up to making any serious moves on this front. But perhaps Ivor will put in a word to Bennett's agent. And Owen will have done his duty to Jo by mentioning it.

Owen doesn't tell Fran that he is losing his interest in clouds. They have begun to seem a pointless preoccupation. His smoking count has gone up, and he's wondering whether to explore the world of e-cigarettes. He is as indistinct as water is in water. He keeps thinking about that little muntjac feeding at the water's edge.

Fran is to spend the night in the Premier Inn in Blackpool, before clocking on in the morning at the meeting with the social services and the NHS representatives and another Ashley Combe trustee in the allegedly 'charming' small country town where the new housing is to be built. She is hoping that Paul Scobey might get there, but he hasn't confirmed. The town lies in the Fylde, a plain not unlike Poppet's West Country Levels, and in some of its web images it looks charming enough, though she suspects it may not be. They are meeting in the offices of a surveyor who had been involved in the land purchase. She'll look at the site this afternoon, though at this stage there won't be much to see. Some demolition, a hole in the ground.

Poppet says the Fylde is a flood plain. They are yet again, despite all they know, planning to build in a flood plain. Fran should ask them about this, at the meeting.

She'll have a look down the hole. She'll see if she can smell the rising water. Then she'll head for the Premier Inn.

When she leaves the motorways, her satnav route takes her past a kitsch and over-restored but presumably historic windmill, along some narrow lanes, and slowly through flat terrain that is partly agricultural, partly post-industrial, partly wasteland. It's no man's land. She is guided onto a one-way system right through the centre of the charming country town, and notes that it is the usual mess of tattoo parlours, pet clinics, nail bars, charity shops, curry takeaways, fish and chips, Thai restaurants, shabby old pubs and chemists. The site is on the other side of town, and she drives through some standardised 1920s and 1930s suburban housing that could be anywhere in England, and comes to a halt by a crater next to a tennis court, marked by some diggers and skips and cement-mixers and bales of orange mesh netting. There doesn't seem to be much point in parking to look at a hole in the ground surrounded by wire fencing, but she does.

It gapes, not very dramatically. She gazes at slices of yellowish earth, at heaps of rubble, and at the exposed foundations and severed drains and sewers of the buildings that have been demolished to make way for the new wave of old residents. By the end of next year there will be apartments with Alzheimer's-proof locks and pretty pale carpets and button-operated blinds and curtains and fitted kitchens. There will be modest landscaped gardens, featuring, if Fran's suggestions are adopted, raised beds where residents can do a little planting and weeding. There will be show flats and a guest suite. And access by public transport, in due course, to the pubs and tattoo parlours. Pets will be permitted, so the pet clinics may come in handy. And it will have a new postcode, the last postcode of old age.

Fran leans on a wall and stares into the raw earth. She sighs. Then she gets back into her car and resets her satnav for Blackpool. There may be a bit more life in Blackpool than here in the flatness of the Fylde.

~

Fran walks along the front, but the wind is icy. The cowslips are out on the verges, and Easter and the anniversary of Hamish's death are over, but it's not warm yet. She's left her car in a worryingly cheap vacant-plot parking lot near the unfashionable South Beach, but is determined to explore for an hour or two before she turns in to the comfort and safety of the Premier Inn. But it's cold, cold, and the sea is the colour of cement. She can't face much of this. There are a lot of care homes in the side streets, and some crumbling guest houses as well as a lot of chip shops on the front. There's an ageing population here. The ageing Blackpool Tower ahead of her is encased in scaffolding. She's tired; it's been a long drive. She can't walk much further, though she would like to get to the Tower, to be able to say she'd reached the Tower.

See Blackpool and die.

I'm a stubborn old fool, she tells herself.

She notices that she's walking along a tramline and spots an approaching tram, going north to Fleetwood: she hops on it, finds her London Freedom Pass isn't valid, but is more than happy to pay £1.50 to the friendly conductor in order to get out of the wind. It's her duty to investigate the 'supreme ugliness' of this famous town of illuminations, and she perseveres.

There are sculptures, of sorts, and ghost trains, and restaurants shaped like skulls and pirate hulks, and street decorations featuring mermaids. A sad little skewbald pony trots beside the tram, pulling a tacky little pink Cinderella pumpkin coach with a transparent plastic dome, in which a parent and a small child huddle. Fran is sad. It's not meant to be like this, it's meant to be fun. Her eyes are watering, but she's not weeping for Hamish's death or for Teresa's death or for Josephine's death. Her eyes are watering because of the brutal English wind.

She gets off at the Tower, gazes bleakly at its shrouded lower levels, and heads off inland, out of the blast, towards the pedestrianised town centre. She plods dutifully on, past posters advertising tours and pantomimes and concerts long gone and yet to come, and identifies one or two architectural features she'd told herself to look out for – the Opera House (closed), the Winter Gardens of white faience, some Deco office blocks, and the imposing post office of Portland stone, where two crouched and kneeling Atlas figures wearily support its heavy canopy.

Surprisingly, the post office still seems to be functioning as a post office. It must be one of the few grand purpose-built post offices left in the land. She wonders how long it will survive.

Outside the post office, an elderly couple asks her the way. They want to find W. H. Smith's. I can't help you, she says, I'm a stranger here myself. They nod and smile at one another, politely, all of them lost, all of them at sea.

She doesn't find the old Miners' Convalescent Home, said by her guidebook to be the best building in town. It must be further along the North Beach. She's not going to get that far.

She's had enough. She heads back towards the tram, hoping she'll remember where to get off, hoping she'll remember where she left her car. It's nearly suppertime. She's tired and hungry. She hadn't really enjoyed the Kentucky Fried Chicken at the motorway service station, but there hadn't been much of a choice. She'd lost a bit of one of her fillings on a wing bone, but even in her brief perambulation of Blackpool she's had time to notice that being toothless is quite the fashion here.

~

The Premier Inn is safe and familiar. The Inn of Happy Days. The plump ginger-haired young man at Reception welcomes her warmly, as an old friend, or at least as an old customer, and assures her that if all she wants for her cooked breakfast is a boiled egg, it's fine if she just pays for a continental. So she trundles her wheelie bag through a security door and along the corridor and up a short flight of stairs. There is the familiar and unfailing space, the room with its dotted carpet and its spotted decor and its white pillows and its purple messaging. Can it be only a couple of months since she and Paul and Julia and Graham had been eating scampi and barbecued ribs and drinking Merlot in the Premier Inn in the Black Country? She checks out the bathroom, and congratulates herself on having remembered to bring some proper soap, a leftover from a Christmas present gift box from Ellie. She's not wholly keen on the hospital-style liquid stuff they supply here, though that's her only criticism.

It's been a very long two months. She'd been a lot younger, two months ago. She'd been walking steadily on a plateau, for years, through her sixties into her seventies, but now she's suddenly taken a step down. That's what happens. She knows all about it. She's been warned many times about this downwards step, this lower shelf. It's not a cliff of fall, but it's a descent to a new kind of plateau, to a lower level. You hope to stay there on the flat for a few more years, but you may not be so lucky.

In your middle decades, you're on a roller coaster. Up and down, sometimes without warning. That's not really true when you're in your seventies.

She pours herself a whisky from her little travel bottle, tops it up with tap water, kicks off her shoes, climbs up onto her bed, puts her feet up, switches on her TV, and finds the regional news. These beds do seem higher than they used to be, but that's because she is getting smaller.

She is warming up nicely, after the chill of her sightseeing. And here, before her, on the screen, is 'Life in the North-west'. It will keep her company in her terminal loneliness, in her sense of rapidly encroaching despair. She may be near the end of the road, but *they* are not – no, there they all are, as busy as ever, the poisoner care worker who contaminated the saline solution with insulin, the plane spotters arrested in the United Arab Emirates, the politician delivering his lines on the set of *Coronation Street*, the young man who ran away to Syria and was hauled back again, the parents petitioning to fill in the quarry where their child had drowned, the daughters fundraising for their mother with a rare cancer of the gall bladder, the football manager apologising for his team, the dog that didn't die in the fire. There are the academics from Lancaster University, proudly showing off their new inventions, and the woman who keeps bees.

There is no item quite as curious and cheering as that interview with the woman on the narrow boat who had survived the small earthquake and the tidal wave of Dudley, but it's good stuff, just the same.

She's in despair, but she can't help but be a little interested in what is going on out there, and the manner in which it's being relayed to her. It's part of her and she's part of it. Her life has been full of failure and defeat and triviality and small concerns, and at times she fears it is ending sadly. Her courage is running out, her energy is running out. She has lived vicariously, in the small concerns of others. The larger themes are leaving her.

She stares at the screen. Her eyes are dry.

But they keep on, out there, the unknown people of the North-west.

She'll have her supper in the restaurant. There must be some meals on the menu without chips. The KFC chips had been like cold dry matchsticks, she'd eaten a few but wished she hadn't. She can't face another chip. The wings had been fine, surprisingly nice, but they'd broken her tooth.

It's curry night at the Inn, curry night at the long buffet bar, so it's easy to avoid chips. The large room is full, but not many of these diners are business people. It's a different demographic from West Brom. There are a lot of family groups with children, a hangover from the Easter holidays. At the next table, there is a young middle-aged couple with a little fair-haired girl and a pale teenage boy in a table-adapted wheelchair, to whom the mother pays the most delicate attention. The boy is handsome, in a pallid, dark-haired, Byronic way, despite his hunched shoulder and his paralysed hand and his awkward slouched position. His mother bends towards him, helps him to spoon his rice and dhal, wipes his chin with her paper napkin, gazes intently and lovingly upon his every move. The father appears more detached: he is drinking his beer, joshing with his daughter, crinkling and cracking his poppadoms. But he is attuned to his boy and to his wife's intense devotion. Nothing escapes him. And the little girl glances from time to time, approvingly, at her brother, and seems pleased that he is enjoying his supper.

From time to time the boy lets out a strange high-pitched moan, but it seems to signify pleasure rather than distress.

Fran does not stare at the family group, as she was brought up not to stare, but as she forks down her saag paneer and rice and chicken and sips her Merlot, she takes in and honours the energy and care and love that have gone into this holiday meal, into creating and maintaining the fragile balance of this quartet. Years and years have been poured into these moments. The family of four is self-contained, triumphant in its overcoming of difficulties, enjoying a night out.

On the other side of her table, almost too close to her and impossible to ignore, indeed soliciting her attention, sits a duo at a table for two. At first she thinks it's a mother with her little boy, but then she thinks no, this is granny and grandson. The women have their babies young around here, as they do in the Black Country, and they are still young, still in their forties, when they become grandmothers. The grandmother is as solicitous as the mother at the table for four, but much more vocal, as is the child. He is of mixed race, about four years old, with curly hair and a wide smile. He is as lively as a cricket. He finds it hard to sit still. He restlessly wriggles and bounces and rocks his chair and plays with his cutlery, and chatters and asks question after question. He is an enchanting infant, extrovert, showing off in the most endearing manner, utterly confident that he is adorable. He is immensely pleased with himself and everything around him. He is even pleased with Fran. His good will overflows and crosses the small gap between their separate tables. He catches her eye, plays to her as his audience, engages her attention. She cannot help but smile at him.

It's impossible not to overhear their conversation, as he questions his nan about the rides they can go on tomorrow, the games they can play, the chips they can eat, and the Blackpool Rock they can buy for his mum. He longs to see the sharks and stingrays in the aquarium, and he knows the names of the dolphins. He is mad keen on the aquarium, and it is clear that his grandmother has primed him with curiosity and enthusiasm. And he is passionately eager to get his nan to commit to letting him go on the Big Dipper. She demurs, she doesn't know if they let little tiddlers like him on it, it's really enormous, she'd be scared to go on it herself, it reaches right up into the sky, it goes up into the clouds, it goes at fifty miles an hour! Oh come on, Nan, we've got to do it, he urges. You *said* we could. You *promised*.

Fran can tell he will get his way.

He's seen it on telly, on that popular roller-coaster advert for Specsavers, an ad about old folk with a plot so complicated that Fran's never been able to follow it. But he has.

Brum brum, he says, racing his little plastic car noisily along the table and up the side of the laminated menu, and over his side plate, and over the silver dishes of chutneys, and over the remains of a chapatti, and off the edge of the table, where it crash-lands under Fran's chair. There is a lot of proud apologetic smiling as Fran retrieves it and restores it. Fran feels she should express her appreciation of this small child's fine qualities, but can't think of anything to say except, 'You're the best!' as she hands him back his yellow vehicle. He laughs, because he knows he is, but he manages to look a little bashful at the same time.

'He's the king!' says his grandmother.

It's a small moment, but it will see her more cheerfully on her way, in the morning, to the unknown destination. Seeing it through, that's the best she can do.

ENVOI

Fran finished Jo's tapestry in a matter of weeks, much more quickly than Jo would have done. She enjoyed working on it, in a melancholy way, and even wondered whether to buy herself a needlework pack of her own. She didn't, but she sometimes thought about it.

Owen English never wrote his paper on dragon clouds, but he did strike up a friendship with another inmate of Athene Grange, who was pleased to share his Thursday evenings and to talk about poetry. He was entrusted by Nat Drummond with Jo's computer, and located her work on *The Fatal Kinship* and the Studdert Meades, but decided that nothing could be made of it. He printed it out and put it in a drawer, and forgot about it. He flew out once more to the Canaries, where Ivor seemed happy to see him, and Bennett seemed to recognise him, but he knew that would be the last time.

Ivor Walter's future seemed a little bleak, to Owen.

When Bennett died, Ivor sold up, at a considerable loss, and came back to England, where he is now living peacefully and uneventfully in a monastic care home in the shadow of a West Country cathedral. The home was found for him by a friendly Spanish priest in Las Palmas. Uncle Ivor's wheelchair is being pushed around the close and the green by a succession of lay brothers. What he thinks of this we do not know. But things could be much worse, for Ivor.

Owen England outlived Bennett Carpenter and Fran Stubbs and Claude Stubbs and Simon Aguilera. They are all dead now. We won't stand upon the order or the manner of their going. Owen was to be puzzled by the way in which he had quietly outlived so many.

Poppet Stubbs is still alive and well. She does not change much. When Fran died, Poppet took her addled and abandoned egg from its flowerpot on her windowsill, and released it, one summer evening, very gently, into the canal. She slid it into the green water, wondering if it would sink or float. It floated, a little lopsidedly, and then, very slowly, drifted away with the current and out of sight.

Christopher Stubbs and Ishmael Diatta, still in the prime of life, have sailed on. They lashed themselves to the mast, and crossed the narrow Atlantic straits from Africa House, and they have arrived here, in the dry and blistering sun, at Nouadhibou, formerly Port-Étienne. It is a scene as astonishing, as terminal, as apocalyptic as Sara had imagined. Here they are at the last stockade, with a crew that is setting up its cameras in the last redoubt. Before them lie the rusting graveyard and the ships of death. Behind them lie the many miles of desert sands.

These ignoble comrades will tell this story or die in the attempt. They will finish Sara's project, and they will finish Bennett Carpenter's project. They already have an update of Ghalia Namarome in the can. They will tell the history of the last journeys, of the gold foil and the golden bough, of the brands that were saved from the burning and the sailors who were saved from the sea.

They will tell the last chapter of the history of the Isles of the Blessed, before they are engulfed beneath the rising waves.

Acknowledgements

I would like to thank Robert Nye for permission to cite his poem, 'Going On'. I also thank Sowon Park for introducing me to a domestic robot, and to Leonard Cohen's DVD about *The Tibetan Book of the Dead*.

I owe a considerable debt to Helen Small's *The Long Life* (2007), which gave me much food for thought, and provided me with a useful reading list. Her book is a fitting successor to Simone de Beauvoir's classic work on the subject of age, *La Vieillesse*.

My thanks also to all at Canongate, and to my agent, James Gill.